A BILLION
Little Lies

WICKED *Hot* BILLIONAIRES

JANE McBAY

cat whisker press
Boston

First Paperback Edition
ISBN: 978-1-957421-48-3

Published by Cat Whisker Press
Cover: Philip Ré, Rex Video Productions
Book Design: Cat Whisker Studio
Editor: Chloe Bearuski

For you, Mr. Phil
Because here we are
Still ♥
Squeeeee!

WICKED HOT BILLIONAIRES

ACKNOWLEDGMENTS

I want to offer my heartfelt gratitude to my daughter, Pandora, and her significant other, Jacob, *a.k.a.* the Cider Miser, for letting me ask them questions regarding all manner of twenty- and thirty-something language. Not that I dove so deep into Gen-Z or Millennial lingo that readers will need a slang dictionary. In fact, much of it was left on the cutting room floor.

Nevertheless, I was using a few words that sounded too old-fashioned, and I needed some frank honesty from a pair of huntys. You two are totally bae and never act salty or give me clap back. In fact, you're dank, and that's the high-key, trill, hundo P!! *Yeet!!*

I also want to give a big *thank you* to the following beta readers who took a chance on me as I ventured into a new romance genre. They gave me the gift of their most precious asset, time: Toni Young, Philip Ré, Kyrstin Poyson, Lynsey Drury, Miroslava Kral, April Frisch, and Nicole McCurdy. As always, thank you to my long-time editor, Chloe Bearuski, and to my new proofreader, Julie Evans.

Quite simply, your combined efforts made this a better book. I am exceedingly grateful. All mistakes, of course, are my own.

PROLOGUE

Clover

Adam Bonvier knows how to push my buttons and not in a good way. Not in a *yes, right there! Do that again* way. Although I have a feeling that could be true, too. At this moment, however, he is button-pushing in a *that freaks me out and makes me want to get in my car and drive fast and far* type of way.

Because I want him too much.

That's the problem with billionaire playboys. They are button-pushers because they can be. Handsome, sexy, button-pushers!

So when the elevator doors open and I realize my new boss, Mr. Bonvier, is the only occupant, I freeze like my favorite raspberry-chocolate-chip ice cream. He's supposed to be in his private lift that travels up and down the other end of the building. *His* building in Boston's financial district, near the harbor.

Adam Bonvier definitely shouldn't be making us minions nervous by riding in one of our worker-bee elevators.

I glance behind me, hoping for a buffer. But it's already a quarter after six and my team of designers have long-since vacated the building.

Stunned into silence, I stare at the boss, and he stares back at me before flashing his impressively lopsided grin— Pushing. All. My. Buttons. He is too good looking, too smart, too much in control of *my* financial existence, and I am far too affected by him.

None of this is good for my continued employment, nor is the fact that we recently kissed.

An impossibly stupid, mutually desired, incredible, sparks-flying kiss!

The elevator doors start to close. Adam reaches out and blocks it. I've never liked doing that, irrationally believing my arm will be crushed. But the doors just bounce back, sliding open again.

"Are you coming?" he asks, his tone utterly neutral, the opposite of the clanging sirens and fizzing fireworks going on inside me.

Stiffly, I nod and step into the suddenly too-small space before turning to face the closing doors.

Coincidentally, we had a conversation a week earlier about elevator etiquette. I said some weird and paranoid stuff simply to fill the empty air because we had just shared that ill-advised, unexpected, and crazy-awesome kiss, reducing me to a babbling twit.

However, having already turned my life into a dumpster fire once before by falling in love with my previous boss, I will never get close to doing that again. Not with this boss. Not with any man who has the power to kick my ass to the curb and take away my job.

Tonight, I keep my eyes forward, counting the seconds until I can escape.

Then he touches me. More than touches. Through the fabric of my blouse, it feels like he runs the pad of his thumb down my shoulder blade.

I swear he did, although when I jump and look around, he's scrolling on his cell phone, leaning against the corner, seemingly oblivious to my presence. *Had I imagined it?*

Was he toying with me, making my nerve endings jangle, or had my bra strap simply shifted? All I know is that his close presence is messing with my sanity.

And why is that? Because of the prior encounter in which our hands had been all over one another and our lips had been crushed together like pages of a book. Adam Bonvier is fully aware of what I'm feeling tonight as I stand primly with my back to him. He knows I am perfectly ready to let him take me up against the elevator wall.

Just hit the big red stop button and go for it!

1

One month before

Clover

Early on a Monday, fresh off Boston's T, what locals call their ancient subway system, I enter the lobby of Bonvier, Inc. through the Pearl Street entrance, and see one of the friendliest faces in the company.

"Hey, Sean." I give the daytime security officer a wave with my free hand while my other holds a travel mug of coffee, and I receive a smile in return.

"Good morning, Miss Mitchell." He's got a burly vibe going on, perfect for his job. I wouldn't mess with him or this luxurious lobby he guards.

We've spoken a few words every day since I was hired at the advertising firm nearly three weeks ago. For instance, Sean has given me advice on the best coffee and lunch places nearby.

"Nothing's too woop from here," which I found out meant *not too far away*. His local accent, like he's straight out of central casting, comes from being born and bred in South Boston, as I've since discovered.

"It's brick out there, kid," he said when I came in for my interview.

"*Um*, is it?"

"Cold as a witch's fridge," he added, cleaning up the term somewhat. "For November."

But as I nodded and walked by toward the elevators, he said, "Bang a U-ey, kid. I've got to sign you in and take a photo of your license."

So, bang a U-ey, I did and returned to his desk.

Today, I'm about to keep moving when I remember our conversation from Friday.

"Did your son's team win?" I've already learned that this city is enthusiastic to the point of obsessed with their sports teams, whether hockey, football, or baseball. And Sean's boy plays high school hockey.

He seems pleased I thought to ask. "Damn straight, kid. Same as the B's this weekend, three to zip."

I know nothing about hockey, but I give a thumb's up. "That's great! Tell him I said congrats."

Then I feel a little weird because I don't even know his son. And why would congratulations from a stranger at work mean anything?

But Sean doesn't miss a beat. "I will," he says. "Conor will be wicked thrilled that I'm making him famous."

Speaking of famous, as I make my way across the ivory marble floor, so polished I can see my reflection, I glance to my right as I always do to get a glimpse of the three 6-foot-tall paintings.

The first time I saw them when I came in for my interview with Bonvier, Inc.'s accounts VP, I stopped, totally transfixed. I'd bet no straight girl can pass them by without appreciating Adam Bonvier's fabulous face, framed by coal-black hair, and his broad shoulders in the sexiest flint-gray suitcoat.

He isn't yet thirty-two. Single, smart, sexy, running the family business for half a decade to massive financial gain. It was big before he took over from his father. Now it's international.

I didn't have to snoop to learn any of that. His life as one of the most desirable bachelors in the entire world is front page news. Every time Adam Bonvier goes out to dinner or donates to charity, we all get a front row seat. If he buys a new brand of toothpaste, someone tweets about it, and it's immediately sold out.

Maybe that was a bit of an exaggeration, but I'm not far off. He told a reporter he enjoyed a certain wine and . . . *Whamo!* You couldn't buy it for weeks and when you could, it had tripled in price. That is the power of a rich man's taste.

From his oil-on-canvas portrait, he stares out, a little severely if one were to describe the look, with eyes as smoky slate as his coat, seemingly examining each and every person who enters his company's headquarters.

Next to Adam's painting is his father's equally large and handsome portrait, and next to his is, I assume, his striking grandfather's likeness from when the patriarch was about sixty.

What a family!

Despite having previously learned a painful lesson about dating one's boss, there's nothing wrong with some healthy fantasizing about a sexy, single billionaire.

Although I haven't met Adam Bonvier yet, that's fine by me. I am happy to be just the new hire, still finding my sea legs, not making waves, not even drawing attention for any reason other than my consistently good design work.

One thing I am trying *not* to do here is stand out to the point where someone thinks my face looks familiar and realizes my true identity. It may be inevitable, but for now, I am simply Clover Mitchell, the new art director for this upscale advertising agency.

The other thing I'm trying not to do is repeat the disaster of my last job. Fully educated and trained, I worked my way up until I landed the perfect position in New York City. And then I made the biggest mistake of my life. I dated my boss. Even worse, I fell in love. My first *big* love to be honest.

When my boss, Mr. Decker, who by then was Jason to me, turned out to be a scumbag, I lost everything. Not only my job but where I was living—mostly with him at that time—and all but two of my work friends.

Starting over became a necessity, and I decided to do it in a new place and with a new last name, legally changed, because my old one is *that* recognizable, especially with the unusual first name my parents gave me. *Clover!*

I don't want to be known as the candy heiress who fled a bad relationship with her CEO boss only to go play at being a designer somewhere else. I simply want to be a great designer.

I take the elevator up to the design floor and weave my way through the desks and workspaces of my team of designers, many of whom think I'm too young and cocky.

And maybe I am, a little.

I hope to become work friends with a few of the people whom I now guide and assist—occasional lunches together, after work drinks on a Friday, maybe get invited to a wedding or a baby shower.

Two of them especially have been super supportive, despite my being a newcomer who took the helm from someone they respected, the previous art director.

As for the rest of my design team, many if not all are trying to knock me down a peg. But I'll win them over.

Have I mentioned my corner office? I love it! This floor, like all of them apart from the top one, has maintained the exterior appearance from when the brick building was built, about a hundred and fifty years ago. I have windows, but not floor-to-ceiling modern ones. Those are reserved for Adam Bonvier's ninth-floor office suite. I've never been up there, but I can see the different design from the street.

The interior of the building, however, is totally twenty-first century, with glass-walled offices like mine, interior lighting throughout that senses an occupant and turns on automatically, creating instant daylight, and comfortable, stylish ergonomic furniture.

A lot of what I might unkindly call Scandinavian chic. Pale palette, minimalist, airy. Oh, and water filling stations with six-stage water filters. The boss has to keep me hydrated.

Well, not *me* exactly. Adam Bonvier wasn't involved in hiring me or is even aware of my existence, as far as I know. That suits me perfectly.

Cara, the head designer under me, follows me into my office. She is multi-racial, with wild dark hair curling around the striking, creamy mocha skin of her face and highlighting her pale blue eyes. No one else has come in to work yet. That's how I want it for a while, until I have a handle on the projects and understand what's going on with every member of my team.

"Good weekend?" she asks as she has done the past two Mondays.

"Yep. You?" I always turn it around quickly because I am not about seeming pathetic. I've lived in Boston for about two months, the first spent frantically looking for an affordable place to live and a job that wasn't a step down from my last one. I only know the people at work and my almost-always-absent apartment mate. I'll make friends in time, but my focus right now is on this job.

After Cara tells me about a movie she saw with her girlfriend, I open my laptop and show her the ideas I kicked around for most of the past forty-eight hours. I respect her opinion. Turns out she's also a fellow Parsons School of Design alum.

"Ooohh!" she says, leaning closer to the screen, looking at a label I tweaked for a beeswax-based face cream. "Love the new color. It's happier."

I swipe the screen aside to the next image. Her eyes open wide, then she frowns.

"I thought this one was a done deal." She's looking at the latest iteration of a graphic for an expensive, small-batch candy company. "Didn't you sign off on what Kim and I did?"

"Yeah, but I had some free time." Not to mention the fact that I know candy like the back of my hand. And the front of it. And in my mouth. And on my tongue. And in dishes all around our home growing up, and in bins at my father's factories. That's my family's business, after all. "My brain was whirling," I add with a shrug.

"And your creative juices were flowing. I like it," she says, but not as enthusiastically as I had hoped.

Just like that, I feel like I messed up. "Maybe we'll leave it as it was." Suddenly, I'm not sure mine is better, only different. I could make "different" all day long.

Graphic design, which I'd merely played around with in high school, became my sole focus during my first year in college. So much so that I transferred from a liberal arts school to the Parsons School of Design in Greenwich Village. Unlike some students, I think it was worth every single one of the quarter of a million dollars my parents spent.

When I discovered I was really talented at it—"you have a good eye" said every one of my teachers—then I was on my way.

I've never floundered or been unsure in that area of my life. In need of the perfect packaging design for potato chips, eye makeup, or the hottest electronic device? I'm your girl. Create a logo that makes you want to own whatever is under it, that's my forte.

I take a long sip of coffee from the stainless-steel travel mug. I hate feeling doubtful.

"No, it's really good," she adds, and I hope Cara isn't saying that because I'm her boss.

"We'll see. I'll give Mr. Arruda both."

"You know we just call him Chris," Cara reminds me.

Chris Arruda, the olive-skinned Bonvier VP who hired me, is the head of accounts, and I still feel weird calling everyone by their first names.

"Right," I agree. "I'll make sure he gets a chance to review both designs."

Cara nods and goes back to her desk, so I can do triage on my emails and then plan the week. But I'm also still thinking how I changed her finished work and keep both versions open side-by-side on my spare flatscreen. I need to remind myself that I don't have to prove anything here as a designer. I was hired because I'm good. Better than good. And I certainly don't have to work weekends like a freelancer.

Eventually, I let it go and do the part of my job that is new to me, assign my team members to various projects, as well as send them quick messages of when I need them to come in and show me how their concepts are coming along.

A couple hours later, when all the chairs have been filled by designers, I hear *his* approach even before I see it. There's a low rumble floating through my open doorway. Alert: *Bossman on the design floor!*

I look up, glad the dove-gray curtains that line my office's glass walls are open. I can watch Adam Bonvier strolling through my department. Half my female designers start staring and posing, and easily, half my male designers, too.

And me? I admit to getting hot and bothered at the sight of this man. I've seen him on TV, online, and in magazines, as well as the oil portrait—and I can tell you that nothing except hot, hard physical reality does him justice.

After working there for three weeks and never laying eyes on him, I'd started to assume he was never in the building, or I was super unlucky at getting a glimpse. Apparently, my luck had changed. For good or bad, I didn't yet know.

Having woven his way through the state-of-the-art work stations, past the cubicle areas where some of my designers can have a little privacy while brainstorming, he comes all the way to my corner office.

I realize he's already looking at me like I am looking at him. For a moment, I think I should put my collared cardigan back on to look more professional. But he would see me, so I don't fuss.

It's a good thing my door is open because I have a feeling he wouldn't have knocked anyway. Adam Bonvier might, at the most, rap the light wood-grain while pushing it open.

As if he owns the place.

Which he does. Lock, stock, and freakin' barrel. I guess I was wrong. He is aware of my existence.

Rising to my feet, I fight the urge to look down and make sure my blouse buttons are done up and my fitted, butter-soft, black suede skirt is as smooth as possible.

Instead, I keep my eyes straight ahead, hopefully not disclosing even a hint of nervousness—despite how seeing my new boss in the flesh for the first time has my heart racing.

And what flesh! Shoulders as developed as if he rowed a Viking long boat are sat atop his torso, which is clothed in a perfectly fitted, tapered silk suit.

Managing to keep my tongue from lolling out like one of my father's dogs, I can't help my gaze swiftly skimming down his long muscular thighs—still bringing Vikings to mind except for his thick, dark hair.

Raven black, in person, it's a little longer than in the oil painting, combed back but natural like he just toweled it dry. Curling slightly at the ends resting on his pure-white collar, his hair looks absurdly soft, rather than coarse.

I would love to find out precisely how soft.

Down, girl! I'm not trying to repeat the mistake—some would say the career ender, of sleeping with the boss. Been there, done that! But if you saw Adam Bonvier, he's in a league of his own.

He must know it. He's probably arrogant as hell. Even if I can't stand that type of conceit, he's so hot that, when his gorgeous gaze flickers over me, I imagine giving in to the inferno. But I won't. Never again. Not with this boss. Not with any boss.

"Ms. Mitchell," he says by way of greeting.

"Mr. Vonbier," I say, totally flubbing it. "I mean, Bonvier. Whoops!" I add and stick out my hand even though he is too far away for a handshake.

Real smooth, Clover!

By the satisfied smirk, he knows what he's doing to me. He probably thinks I'm already damp for him, and he would be right. Not just because of his perfect face, interesting eyes, and killer bod. But because of the unbelievable magnetism he radiates, kind of like I'm oozing anxiety.

Closing the distance between us while my arm is extended for an embarrassingly long time, finally, he takes hold of my hand.

I will swear to my dying day that an electric shock jumped from his large hand to mine and right up my forearm to my shoulder. Maybe, if I think about it, I would say it goes right to my nipples. In any case, I have to fight to stop myself from yanking my fingers away.

His smirk slips, which makes me believe he feels it, too, and then the moment is over.

"I've heard good things," he says, releasing my hand. "But I wanted to come see for myself."

2

Adam

From the instant I get off the elevator on the fourth floor, with a single purpose in mind, every head in the art department swivels in my direction. Occasionally, it would be a relief if I was no one of import at work. A day without the responsibility of all my employees' livelihoods resting in my hands, here and abroad.

"Don't fuck up the business," my father said, giving me the same advice his father gave him.

Not that he expected I would. I've put my time in since before I graduated from Harvard and have run the company single-handedly since Dad retired early, six years ago. If there's one thing I know and love and care for, it's Bonvier, Inc.

About a dozen pairs of eyes track my movements. Better even than a day without responsibility would be a day without every female, single or married, on all nine floors looking at me like I'm more chocolate bonbon than human Bonvier.

But I don't know anyone who would pity me, including myself.

I nod to everyone and wear my congenial smile, while making a casual beeline for the corner office. Already, I can see the new hire looking at me. Clover Mitchell, my new art director.

The company dogs—assorted account men, some guys in the data and media departments, especially the seventh-floor IT geeks—have been talking about her since the day she was hired. Man-gossip is all bravado and bullshit. They've found out what they can, which is next to nothing, and rated her on their juvenile scale.

Sriracha-level hotness! They are not wrong.

But they know they can only look. We have a zero-tolerance policy for intra-company dating. The rule is intended to protect those on the lower rungs from those in higher positions. Although Ms. Mitchell can't be fired by any of those guys, an ugly breakup could disrupt two departments.

Besides, I saw her first. How's that for juvenile?

About three weeks ago, give or take, from the fifth floor, I noticed her crossing the street toward my building, wearing a black-and-white check skirt that ended mid-thigh and high-heeled black boots that made her legs appear endless. If I had been in my office on the ninth floor with my back to the window instead of dealing with a European client in the account team's conference room, Ms. Mitchell would have entered Bonvier, Inc. unnoticed. But notice her, I did.

That afternoon, I asked Sean at the security desk, betting he would remember a leggy brunette in a checkerboard skirt. Sure enough, he recalled giving her a badge.

"You bet, kid. I sent her to HR."

Except for my father, Sean calls everyone kid. It's a local thing. My dentist calls me kid, too.

Feeling like a detective, CSI Boston, as casually as possible, I learned her name from Tina in HR and that Clover Mitchell worked for me.

Not what I wanted to hear. While it makes it easy to get her phone number if I choose, the whole boss-employee affair is not happening. Never again.

On the other hand, I can look and admire. I'd intended to come introduce myself prior to this, but I've been obscenely busy with virtual meetings to set up our new Bonvier Paris office. Besides, I didn't want to appear as eager as I felt.

Now that I'm finally in the same room with her, I'm glad I came to see who was filling out that skirt. All curves and a goddamn perfect mouth and interesting, tawny, tiger eyes when I was expecting ordinary blue.

I've already heard good things from my head of accounts, who spearheaded hiring our new art director, and even from Sean, who said he talks to her most every morning.

"She's wicked sweet," he said, "like a fluffernutter sandwich."

Ms. Mitchell's height, maybe five foot seven, is not conclusive. She could be wearing high heels or flats, and suddenly, I'm curious to find out. Either way, I'm sure her legs are sexy and would wrap around me perfectly.

I am a leg man!

I'm aware how sexualizing I sound. And I'm not a fan of that kind of talk among the guys on the seventh floor, which is why such thoughts stay in my head. That's where they belong. Although once a woman has expressed mutual interest, I've found she kind of likes those words said out loud or whispered in her ear while I'm undressing her.

On the other hand, if Ms. Mitchell opened her mouth and couldn't string words together into a sentence or was mean-spirited or rude—all of which I know isn't the case after talking to Chris and to Sean—then her hotness level would take a nosedive.

I wouldn't be in her office, appreciating the way the buttons of her silky, charcoal-colored blouse seem a little strained, as if it wouldn't take much for one to pop. If she takes a really deep breath, for instance, while I nibble my way down her neck. Like I said, she's someone a man can't help fantasizing about. And I know she has brains and talent, too.

But no matter how strongly my libido is locked on this honey-brunette like a heat-seeking missile, the answer in my head is *no*. Never again. No fraternizing of any kind. That includes no sex—not with her, not with any employee.

From executive to cleaning lady to the weekend-shift security guard who currently happens to be female, any woman who works for me is firmly off limits.

That doesn't mean I can't fantasize a little. And the new hire is worth more than a little imagining. For some reason beyond her pretty heart-shaped face and curvy body, I find her mesmerizing.

If I had raced downstairs onto Pearl Street three weeks ago and asked her out while blocking her from coming in for an interview, then we would have hooked up by now. From the way we're looking at one another right now, we would've already had sex on every surface and level of my townhouse.

Damn if she's not the first employee in years to make me want to break the unbreakable company rule!

Clover Mitchell has no clue what she's doing to me. I've never traipsed down to the design floor specifically to meet anyone else, but she doesn't know that. I realize someone will probably tell her.

Adorably, she lets slip that she's equally affected. *Vonbier!* I nearly snort with laughter.

I also discover that her voice is practically accentless, impossible to tell precisely where she grew up. Not a little girl's voice, nor whiny or nasally. Better than pleasant, it's as sexy as the rest of her.

I know my face wears a stupid smile, trying to be extra welcoming and nonchalant, because Ms. Mitchell seems unnerved. My walking into someone's office can do that. Normally, I don't care, but I want to get off on the right foot and put her at ease if possible.

So I close the gap to take hold of her prematurely outstretched hand as quickly as I can without jogging across the floor like a maniac.

Then, once I grasp it, I don't want to let go. I feel my smile slip. It's not just the way I fall into her caramel-colored eyes or the way her soft hand with its firm grip sends a message through my body straight to my groin.

It's the unexpected jolt, like when scuffing your feet before being zapped by the next thing you touch. It's my first hint we could sizzle together if I let anything happen, which I won't.

"Why don't you sit so I can too?" I suggest because, despite feeling like a horn dog, my mother raised me right.

Her golden-brown eyes widen, but she complies. Soon, I'm relaxed, leaning back in one of the two chairs in front of her desk, while she's sitting up straight, shoulders back.

"How is work going?" I ask. It's a lame but passable question.

"*Gooood,*" she says, drawing the word out.

Clearly, she's stymied over why I'm here. I am too, to be honest. I can hardly tell her I was compelled to come check her out after spying her through a window.

"Glad to hear it." My banal response does nothing to further our conversation, but I'm content to finally be close and enjoying the view.

While I'm happily taking in Ms. Mitchell like she's a work of art at a museum, her cheeks turn ruddy. The deep blush is hot as hell to witness. *What is she thinking?*

I see the instant she gets her nervousness under control, tucks a strand of light-brown hair behind her ear, and then she's all business. I like that. I need to get my thoughts off her body and back to work. As I said, I'm not here to initiate a fling. I wanted to look and listen, but I won't touch.

I'll try one more benign question before I leave her in peace.

"Everything up to your standards, Ms. Mitchell?"

She tilts her head slightly, and her neck looks ideal for kissing. "Isn't that what I should be asking you?" she retorts. "Whether everything *I'm* doing is up to *your* standards?"

I have a feeling I will like anything she does.

"I doubt you've had the time to produce something so great or so terrible," I point out.

Her perfectly pink, glossed lips curve into a killer smile that ought to be illegal. Like she's radiating sexy sweetness. Before I know it, she remembers who I am and reins in her smile. A damn shame.

"I'm not so sure about that," she says.

Watching her mouth forming the words, I have to remind myself to pay attention to what we're discussing.

"Not to disagree with *the boss* at our first meeting," she adds, "but I could have screwed up a few things if I were utterly incompetent."

I would like to screw you, is my only thought. Not chill at all and not very professional. Again, it's the only time in years this attraction has happened at work. *The only time.* And it's high-caliber, maximum strength, which throws me.

Basically, Clover Mitchell brings me back to how I behaved when I first began working for my father, the summer after I started college. The place seemed like a small pond full of squirmy, pretty fish, all opening their mouths for me to reel them in.

And there I was, nineteen years old, with my giant, untamable pole, causing mayhem. My past behavior triggered some firings that I'm not proud of. Let's face it, whenever the situation got awkward, someone had to go. And if it was them or me, it was them. Each one was let go with a massive amount of money, making them thrilled to have literally been screwed out of a job. Frankly, I'm surprised my dad gave me a second and a third chance.

But they're not the only reason for the company's golden rule or why I won't consider dating anyone at work ever again. The actual reason is Rachel.

She *happened* with all the unforeseen consequences of a few weeks of pleasure that shockingly turned deadly. Rachel had serious issues before I came along, but I didn't know that.

Still, I was the catalyst. We had a few after-work drinks, and, of course, a few hookups at her place. For me, it was never going any farther, and that's why I hold myself entirely responsible. I knew early on it would never be anything more than fucking for fun.

She couldn't accept when it was over. And I should've seen how fragile she was.

Of those employees who know what happened, how she left the building, got herself shit-faced, and crashed her car, they didn't talk. As far as I know, no one blamed me then or now, except myself. That doesn't matter. If I hadn't played around with an employee who wanted more than I could give, she would still be alive.

Yet I stare at Miss Checkerboard Skirt, today wearing a black one that hugs her curves, wishing I could say, "You interest me like no one has in a long time. I know it's shallow and visceral, but I would love to see you panting with desire." It simply cannot happen.

Rachel had been more than a lesson in not dating those over whom you have authority. She had been a goddamned master class, leaving me gutted at the time. Unable to do anything but think about the pain I'd caused her, I couldn't focus at work or at school. Useless for anything and anyone except wallowing in my own guilt, I'm beholden to my parents who finally *loved* me out of my despair. That's how I think of what they did for me to bring me back to a fully functioning, contributing member of humanity. I can never repay them.

So why am I still sitting here?

Because something inside of me is roaring to life like it never has before. I'm merely sitting in this woman's presence, knowing she's a stranger yet craving her. Quite separate from the other part of my anatomy, my brain is saying, *She's mine.* If I believed in such bullshit, I'd say my sixth sense knows Clover Mitchell is meant for me. And I wonder how long I can ignore it.

"Will you tell me what you're working on?"

She looks surprised. In her place, I probably would, too. If I wandered into one of my VPs' offices and asked the same question, those who are relaxed enough would laugh or tell me to fuck off. Those who aren't might ask for twenty-four hours to prepare a presentation. Clover Mitchell does neither.

"I'm showing these to Mr. Arruda this afternoon." And she swivels the massive display on her desk so I can see two similar graphics. It only takes a second to see they're for a new, local client who makes delicious, wildly expensive candy.

I like them both, but one is over-the-top good, making me want a bite of something decadent, creamy, and chocolate that very instant.

"I think Chris will be pleased," I tell her, giving my honest response.

While I'm no ad man myself in terms of creating the design or even writing clever ad copy, when it comes to a striking graphic, I'm usually on target with what works. "But I don't think you need to show him both. The one on the right is better."

She tries to hide her reaction, but I see it in her eyes. Ms. Mitchell is pleased I chose that one. It's classy and sensual, rather like her. And suddenly, I'm certain she designed it.

"Thanks for the input," she says with a cute, casual shrug, straining those buttons a little.

We share another moment of silence, and I know I should get out of here and let her get on with her day. It would be inappropriate to ask more questions just to keep her talking no matter how much I've enjoyed meeting her and making her smile.

Still, I want to ask her how long she's lived in Boston and where she's from, weird-ass questions from a man she's never met before, even weirder from her boss.

I'd hoped satisfying my curiosity about her would put her out of my mind. But I don't feel satisfied in the least.

3

Clover

Mr. Bonvier looks as though he has no plans to leave anytime soon. He also looks absolutely scrumptious. Kissable, touchable, bangable, and much more. *Why did a man with a shit-ton of money also get to be drop-dead gorgeous, tall, and hot AF?*

I stare for way too long. Or maybe it's only a couple seconds.

Focus, Clover.

"As to your first question, everything and everyone are up to my standards. I think your Bonvier design team is great."

"*Your* design team," he reminds me.

He's right. "Mine with which to succeed or fail," I say, half to myself. Then I add, "We have everything we need to do excellent work. The graphic software is all up-to-date, and everyone's well-trained on it. And so far, communication with the accounts department as to what they need has been clear. The first big presentation under my watch happens next week." I will have been here for a month by then, and I'm itching to prove myself.

"Excited?" he asks. "Or scared?"

Those words should not be sexual, but when Mr. Bonvier says them, my mind swoops to the image of him raised over me, anchoring my wrists over my head with one of his hands, and beginning to skim my naked body with the other. My mouth goes dry, but I answer.

"I'll be waiting on pins and needles to know whether the design is well-received."

He cocks his head. "Don't wait for an invitation. This department is yours to run, and if you think it best for the art director to go to the launch meeting, then you should go."

I nod. It sounds as though he means I can do what I want instead of whatever the previous person who sat in my chair did. No one told me I could make my own rules. Certainly not Chris Arruda, the VP who hired me.

"I'll be there, too," Mr. Bonvier adds.

What?!

"Will you?" I ask before wondering aloud, "Do you go to all the presentations?" I glance again at the monitor, which has gone to sleep. He chose my version of the candy graphic, making me internally high-five myself.

At the same time, I know I ought to have brought out the best in my designers rather than redoing their work. What's more, having him go to a presentation of my first project makes my stomach twinge.

What if the client hates it?

"I go wherever I want to go," he says softly.

Rightfully so, and I shouldn't have asked.

"Has Chris been easy to work with?" Mr. Bonvier looks like he really wants to know how I'm getting on with the head of accounts.

I would never say that the only dull spot on this bright shiny job has been the VP's hot and cold manner. Eager to hire me after our interview, he's been a little less enthusiastic since I arrived. On the other hand, there's no problem I can put my finger on.

Eager to be a team player, I reply, "Chris has been super helpful. It's going to be a pleasure working with him."

Adam Bonvier's eyebrows raise before his gray eyes narrow, and I suddenly wonder if I sounded too familiar. The culture here isn't any more reserved than my previous place of employment, at least what I've experienced of the company's ethos so far. And most everyone has been introduced to me by their first name.

The boss nods his handsome head. "I'm glad. You'll be working closely with a number of departments, not just accounts, and workflow is more expedient when there's not only respect for one's colleagues but a genuine liking."

I'm watching him speak, thinking his is the most perfect male mouth I've ever seen, and I'd be content to sit here all day staring at it. More than content if he wasn't my boss. Ecstatic if I could try to tempt him into showing me what those lips can do. I'm guessing, from the women he's been associated with in the press, he's an all-around capable guy.

As if Mr. Bonvier knows the thoughts swirling in my brain, he says, "About dating fellow employees, I came down here to ask you—"

"Please!" I blurt as heat rushes to my cheeks and not for the first time since this man entered my office.

Damn! I so do not want to leave this ideal new position. Not till I have saved a few months' rent at the very least!

"I'm *not* interested," I tell him, which is the first lie I ever tell Adam Bonvier. "I do *not* want to go out with you." I know his world—the realm of the super-rich. I grew up in it. I have dated boys who thought they were men because of the cost and size of their toys. I left it behind, and doing so was easier than one might imagine.

For so many reasons, I can't go there again.

His expression can only be described as shocked, before becoming placidly disinterested. Perhaps that's a mask to cover his irritation. I bet no one ever says no to him, not in business nor in his personal life. And I haven't even said it nicely.

"I apologize for how rude that sounded." I rush my words as I lean forward. His glance darts to my cleavage, and I sit up straight again. My skin prickles, thinking of him looking at more of my bare skin. It isn't like me, either. I can usually ignore a handsome man. Or at least be around one without coming unglued.

"Miss Mitchell," he begins, but I interrupt.

"Look, I don't want this to be weird. But I don't want people talking about me. If we went out and then broke up, I would have to quit."

He closes his eyes a second and lets out a puff of air, like a sigh. Then he actually grins. It's crooked and sets off butterflies inside me.

"Normally, a woman waits until I ask her out before she answers, and then, it's usually with a resounding *yes*. So, I'm a bit caught off guard by you jumping the gun by a mile."

Shit! My cheeks are flaming. "Weren't you asking me out?"

"No. The opposite. I was about to ask you *not* to date any of the company employees. That would include me. We're a close-knit group despite our size, and as you suggested, if you date someone on staff and it crashes and burns, usually someone has to go. As the new hire, that would be you, and I'd hate to lose your reputed talent before I've even seen what you can do."

He stands, and I jump to my feet.

"Let my assistant, Janet, know if you need help with anything," he adds. "Although it seems like you've got everything under control."

If he means being a presumptive idiot, then I guess I do have it under control.

"Mr. Bonvier." I need to stop him from leaving before I have the chance to bring things back to normal—whatever that would be between a boss and an employee who has foot-in-mouth disease. He halts, and I come out from behind the safety of my desk to within three feet of this GQ man.

Even in my comfy but gorgeous three-inch heels, I have to look up at him. And with the awkwardness of what just happened, I calm my fidgeting hands by clasping them in front of me.

"I apologize for assuming you would be interested in going out with me," I confess. "That was stupid and awfully vain."

He frowns slightly. His gaze flickers downward, stopping short of explicitly looking me over, although he definitely checks out my legs. He's a man after all.

"I don't think you're stupid or vain," he says when he's looking me in the eyes again. "Nor was your assumption incorrect. Only your timing."

With that, Adam Bonvier raises a dark eyebrow and walks out without a backward glance.

Huh! While I watch him walk through my department, I replay what I'd said and what he'd said to get to the meat of the meaning. It seems the bossman *does* want to go out with me. But obviously not while I work for him.

That gives me a multitude of sensations. On the one hand, dear God, a night with the sexiest man I've ever met! My sex-deprived body is already heating up at the thought. On the other, I think of what happened at my last job. If Decker Financial had such a great rule, then I wouldn't be here now. I wouldn't have been fired and had to leave everything behind.

After the unnerving conversation with Adam Bonvier, is it any wonder I say yes to lunch with Cara at a small Thai bistro down the street? And with the smallest of prompts, I begin to spill my guts. It feels so good to tell her something personal and make some small connection.

"At Decker Financial," I tell Cara, as our plates of mango curry and panang curry are put before us, "I worked in happy obscurity in their small marketing department."

Because of my famously "good eye" and my talent, I'd moved up quickly in our industry, from grunt position to junior designer to creative director at Decker Financial, which is when I blew it so badly by letting a relationship cloud my judgment.

"There were three of us," I tell her around forkfuls of aromatic and savory deliciousness. "I was the lead designer, and I had a total of two people, who to be honest, weren't actually trained graphic designers. One was a fine arts student at NYU, and the other was more of a wordsmith."

I can't help smiling wryly at my change in status, and she laughs. "Quite a step up in prestige at Bonvier," Cara says. "Also, more headaches if you ask me."

I nod because I'm already seeing the vast difference between doing all the design work myself and designating, scheduling, and interacting with other departments.

"I was totally content at the time. We created for B to B, interoffice print work, and investor pamphlets. Occasionally, we were asked to dream up a special 'gift' idea for the company's clients. Everything was great until Jason Decker spotted me quite by chance in the lobby and decided to pursue."

Her eyes widen with interest. Who doesn't love office gossip? Me, that's who! Not anymore.

"It ended abruptly a few months later"—five months and sixteen days to be exact—"and he fired me."

"Prick!" she says, already on my side, and I haven't even mentioned seeing him screwing his executive assistant. Instead, I take a sip of the traditional Thai orangey-red, spicey tea before adding, "No paycheck, no job, and no boyfriend, in one fell swoop."

"One swell foop," she says, making me smile.

I think of Adam Bonvier's awesome smile. If he weren't my boss, I totally would jump into something with him without thinking twice. Because, man oh man, is he ever attractive. If I didn't work for him and on my way home tonight, he boarded the Green Line, for instance . . . because you encounter so many billionaires on the subway. *Not!*

Now that I've finally met him, I'll stop imagining scenarios that put us together. He should be easy to avoid. At work, normally, the CEO and I will rarely interact. Above all, I'm determined to do well here and to succeed—without any help from my parents. Again! Because Mom and Dad would happily drench me in money if I asked, with the minor condition that I immediately change my name back to theirs.

"Before I landed this position, I was this close"—I hold my thumb and pointer finger about a quarter inch apart—"to packing up and going home to New York." Home means retreating to New York. My parents' home, the place I hadn't let myself run to after the really bad mistake with Jason Decker, no matter how much I wanted to hide.

Then I confess, "I moved here specifically for this job. I rolled the dice with no backup plan. Isn't that idiotic?"

"Rolled the dice and won," she reminds me.

"Thank God," I say. "Because my coffers were empty."

Currently, I live in a ridiculously expensive, shared apartment in the Allston suburb of Boston. I was lucky enough to land the second bedroom in a third-floor walk-up. My share of first and last month's rent and security, buying food and my half of the utilities—all that has left me without much cushion. More like a deflated balloon.

"I've been barely making it," I confess, "after burning through my savings while moving and out of work."

"I get that," she says. "If Jenny and I didn't both have good jobs, we would not be living in Boston. We thought for half a second last year about going to London, also super expensive, but super fun if we could find work. But we never considered New York City. After attending Parsons, I know that place takes every penny."

I nod and take another bite of chicken curry. It's nice to have a gal-pal again. I want to put down roots and succeed.

Like at Decker Financial but without crashing and burning, which means no bossman boyfriend.

As we head back to the office, I try not to look forward to the presentation in a week when Adam Bonvier said he would attend. But I can't help planning what I'll wear and feeling a little shiver go down my spine.

So maybe he'll be in my head if not my bed.

4

Clover

The presentation is not the worst one in the history of presentations. That's the best I can say. But it obviously misses the mark. Nowhere near the bullseye. Perhaps it hits a tree in another forest. A humbling experience—more like humiliating, since Adam Bonvier is quietly watching the proceedings from a chair at the end of the conference table.

Humiliating and entirely unexpected. I would swear my designers delivered on all the parameters that Chris requested, and yet the client, Mr. Monroe, seems perplexed by our angle, by the artwork's color scheme and style. You can see it in his expression and that of his assistant, who keeps looking at him with concern. They don't like what we're serving up.

Looking at the graphics on the screen, I know what Chris told me, and I feel sure he'll explain to the client that he got what he asked for.

Glancing at Mr. Bonvier, I nod at him, and he returns a small, impartial smile. It distracts me for a moment—because *he* distracts me, with his ultra-masculine presence that makes the other men in the room seem diminished.

But I don't miss the client's audible groan when the next slide shows a close up. It's the graphic for the product label. An illustrated, friendly looking apple seems to be giving a cheeky and cheerful wink. Yes, the apple has eyes.

Hey, we made it as classy as such a thing can be, given the parameters. By the final shot, for a full-page magazine ad, the tension has grown thick with disapproval, and I wish to hell I was back in my corner office.

Chris begins smoothing things over with talk of "first draft" and "idea stage," which I know is bullshit. This is the finished design. Then Leslie, an account exec whom I've met a few times and who's in charge of this particular account, starts to explain how the art department—read *Clover Mitchell*—hasn't precisely grasped the concept of what the client is looking for.

Hello! I'm sitting right here. I open my mouth, but Mr. Bonvier stands up, which silences everyone. To my mortification, speaking only to Mr. Monroe, he tells him we'll get it right next time. Our boss seems totally unruffled, not to mention certain there will be another opportunity.

The client hesitates, but when faced with our confident CEO, what can Mr. Monroe do but agree to another pitch in a few days? The man's blue gaze turns to me.

"I have a copy of our specs." He barely raises a hand before his assistant puts a couple sheets of paper into it. "These are on a thumb drive, too," Mr. Monroe adds, "which I believe you already have a copy of."

He says it as though I am an imbecile. And of course I don't have the thumb drive because I was never given one. I glance down at the page with a bullet-point list of wants and needs while my eyebrows go up. No wonder he doesn't like what we showed him.

"We'll get it wrapped up before the office closes for the holidays," Mr. Bonvier promises. "No pun intended."

Again, I wish I had been safely downstairs on the design floor when this presentation went south. Instead, I wait until Mr. Monroe and his assistant leave for Leslie to turn on me. Despite her platinum blonde hair cut in a modern, jagged, layered pixie cut, there's nothing fairy-friendly about her. Instead, she's like a hawk swooping down onto a mouse in one of those nature programs.

"What the hell were you thinking?" she demands, and I can practically feel her talons.

"Well," I begin, "what I understood—"

"Your misunderstanding nearly lost us that client. If Adam hadn't been here, with his usual serenity and assurance, Mr. Monroe might have walked and not given us another shot. Hours of acquiring the client in the first place, wooing and dining, and then to lose him over some piss-poor graphics like that! Do you, in fact, appreciate the nuances of his brand?"

My cheeks are burning. Nerves jangling like sleigh bells on my parents' estate, I dare to look at Mr. Bonvier. I don't see condemnation or judgment, simply curiosity to hear my response.

What can I say? Before I respond, I also look at Chris. Isn't he going to explain how my team and I delivered exactly what his department asked for?

His face is as neutral as vanilla ice cream, my least favorite kind. *Shit!*

I guess I have to stick up for myself. "With all due respect, Leslie, I can show you from my project notes what I believed the client wanted." I depress the power button on my tablet.

"What you believed!" she repeats, throwing her hands in the air.

"You weren't in the meeting I had with Mr. Arruda," I remind her. It seems a good time to gesture in his direction

32

and to respectfully use his last name. If he's going to jump in, now would be the time.

"Don't blame Chris for this," she shoots back. Leslie is fuming. "He's guided the accounts team to great success for *years*."

She's reminding me that, in comparison, I've only been here a month and done nothing to prove myself.

"Agreed," Adam Bonvier says. "Chris is usually on the money."

His words are crushing. In any case, I'm starting to feel like a sacrificial lamb. *Someone* mistook what the client wanted. Maybe Chris. Maybe Leslie, who I think initially met with the client. She couldn't brief me because she was out sick two weeks ago, causing the VP to do it. Since neither have a reason to sabotage my first major contribution to the company, I have to conclude unintentional mistakes were made.

I try to catch Chris's eye, but he's looking through his own notes. Only he knows the truth. Then I realize how bad this could be for him. For me, it can be seen as beginner's failure. If not exactly expected of a new employee, then at least tolerated. However, if the blame falls on the experienced head of accounts, the ramifications might be a lot worse.

That's why I suck it up and say, "I must have misunderstood Mr. Arruda. I'll go back to my department now and make this right. With what the client has just given me, I think it's only a matter of a few tweaks to satisfy him."

Basically, redoing the entire design!

Leslie is still seething, but she turns to Mr. Bonvier. "It's your call. And Chris's, of course."

At that moment, I realize she means it's their prerogative to fire me on the spot. This is a bigger deal than I first thought. This is a job-losing offense.

Taking in a breath, I hold it until my fate is decided.

$♥$♥$♥$

Adam

That was not the presentation I expected. Normally, I wouldn't even be in attendance, and I noticed Chris and Leslie's stunned expressions when I entered and took a seat. But I was curious to see what Ms. Mitchell delivered. Even more curious to see if she took my advice and showed up to an account meeting with a client.

My father would've done the same thing back in the day. He loved showing up and scaring the shit out of people, making them nervous just by his presence. That's not really my style. Not intentionally, although it still happens by default. Which is why I usually stay away. For key positions, like Chris's, I like to think I've hired great people who will keep the company not only functioning smoothly, but thriving. And I let them do their job without interference from me.

Frankly, I thought the new hire would hit it out of the park. My mistake! Chris looks like he doesn't want to criticize Ms. Mitchell since he's the one who decided she was the best candidate and hired her. But Leslie is like a bleach-blonde tiger.

I don't rein her in because I want to see how Clover Mitchell handles herself. Seeing her perplexed expression, not intimidated or guilty, I decide to give her another chance. Besides, it's nearly Christmas. What kind of Scrooge would I be to fire her right before the holidays?

Also, she could have thrown Chris under the bus and said he'd been unclear. Instead, she accepts the blame.

When all gazes snap to me, including Ms. Mitchell's amazing copper-colored eyes, more defiant that they ought to be at that precarious moment, I say, "Everyone deserves a second chance. Let's see if our new head art director can tweak this to perfection."

"I'll help," Chris immediately volunteers, which rubs me the wrong way. For reasons I can't explain, I don't want him working too closely with her.

"No," I say, perhaps a bit abruptly. "She needs to do this with her team."

Chris frowns. "If she didn't correctly understand the assignment the first time, then I should go over it with her and offer some direction."

First off, I don't think he's right. Head of accounts has never looked over the shoulder of the art department. That's a sloppy, ineffective way to work. Secondly, Ms. Mitchell is simmering with annoyance at how we're discussing her. If she were a cat, she'd be hissing and spitting. Besides, I would want to solve this myself if I was in her shoes, which I notice are deep-blue suede with a strap around her slender heel. Too easy to imagine her wearing *only* those sexy shoes.

"Clover, are you able to make the necessary changes?"

I watch her face—a determined set to her mouth and annoyance shining out of her eyes—and I know she has this.

"Of course." She swipes her tablet from the conference table. "I'll get right to work. If you'll all excuse me."

Our lithe, blue-clad designer strides out of the conference room, leaving me watching her perfect ass. I notice Chris staring after her in a way I recognize as interested, while Leslie keeps her arms crossed, plainly pissed off.

After Clover has gone, I round on my VP. I would never blame him in front of the new hire, but I am curious. "Didn't you look everything over *before* this meeting? You should have seen that it wasn't right."

Chris's mouth opens and closes, then he looks sheepish, and I know he didn't look at it ahead of the presentation.

"I ran out of time," he says, then he glances at Leslie, and I follow his gaze.

"Did *you* have the final signoff on this one?' I ask her. "I know I'm not usually in these meetings, but when you're going to present something to a client, I would expect one of you has vetted it first."

Her face reddens. She glances at Chris who returns her gaze with the same perplexed expression that Clover Mitchell had worn.

What was going on? More and more I'm thinking no one expected me to see this mess.

"I admit I assumed the design would match what Mr. Monroe wanted," Leslie finally says, chin lifted. "Since I didn't attend the meeting with Chris and Clover, you're right, I absolutely should have taken a look at what she created."

"But someone took a look," I insist, staring hard at my VP.

He shrugs. Not the response I'm looking for. I'm more than a little shocked at the lax attitude.

I dismiss Leslie, who lingers as if she doesn't want to abandon her colleague. But with a curt nod, she finally leaves. As soon as the door closes, I finally tell Chris what I'm thinking.

"I hate to say it, but it sounds like *you* got it wrong."

His face reddens with anger.

"You have the hots for our new designer, so you're blaming me?"

The best defense is a good offense, but I'm not letting him get away with it.

"Is that really how you're going to answer for this mess?"

We've known each other for a few years, at least five if memory serves as to when I hired him. Not exactly buddies, but we usually treat one another as professional equals. Still, I'm in charge. And if I do, in fact, have the hots for anyone, it's none of his business. He knows he's just crossed the line and visibly relaxes his posture.

"I don't know who dropped the ball," he finally confesses.

"Dropped the ball? Interesting," I muse. "That implies you do think someone screwed up. Since you hired our designer, since your department, whether you alone or in conjunction with Leslie, gave Clover direction on this campaign, it's your fault, don't you agree? Despite what our new art director said about misunderstanding, it sounds as though you and Leslie had the same confusion until about half an hour ago. A big, shiny, red goofy apple was not the logo the client wanted, was it?"

"Someone got it wrong," Chris finally allows, still not taking the blame but not placing it elsewhere, either. Maybe he's being a gentleman and covering for Leslie. Then he cracks a smile. "I have some private stuff going on right now. I guess it's possible I was only half listening when I met with the clients the first time."

That not only stuns me but really annoys me. As Leslie pointed out, we'd spent hours and money getting Mr. Monroe to the table.

"Fix your personal issues, and don't let it happen again. That's not fair to Leslie or Clover."

If he didn't look more and more regretful, I would be angrier. But we're not on the footing of "friends who share," so I don't ask and he doesn't tell whatever it was that distracted him from work. Not my business, not my concern.

"Do better next time," I say.

5

Clover

I'm shaking with anger by the time I return to the design floor. As I'd hoped, Cara and I have become friends in a short time.

"How'd it go?" she asks. An hour earlier, she'd admired my tailored, cobalt-blue dress and sent me to the presentation like a proud parent sending her daughter to the first day of kindergarten.

I hate to disappoint her, but I can't sugarcoat what happened. "Not good. I know this sounds paranoid, but I think I was set up."

She physically reels, then shakes her head. "Our work was spot on."

"Spot on for what the accounts department told me, but apparently *not* for what the client wanted. Are you ready to try again?"

"Sure. But first, we order lattes. Fuel for thought."

I nod. The entire design team drinks them constantly because of a café only steps away from the side door. Thanks to a subsidy from our generous boss, all Bonvier employees pay half price. Some departments run on Adderall or worse. Lattes were a delicious alternative.

"Lattes all around," I say. "Make mine a peppermint mocha for the holidays, please. Then gather up the same principals and meet me at *the table*."

That's what we call the meeting room on the design floor because its main feature is a long steel table that someone in HR must have thought was edgy and cool. It's uninspiring, cold, and ugly. On the other hand, the four state-of-the-art, large pedestal monitors around the room are amazing, allowing us to lay out our graphics in real time while we work together. The stupid table just holds our lattes and tablets.

I try not to think of Leslie's scowl or the verbal lashing she gave me. Chris's bland expression over his swarthy, attractive face also makes me cringe inside. But worse than either was needing Adam Bonvier to smooth the path with the client and then ask me in front of my colleagues if I thought I could do the work properly. *Ugh!*

A few hours later, I'm satisfied. More than that, I'm thrilled and relieved. The four of us haven't merely tweaked, we've redone the graphics from scratch. A sophisticated green glass apple with pale gold leaves encircles the client's company name, Monroe Home. No friendly faced apple with googly eyes like before.

After the others depart, for good measure, I make the same thing with a golden apple and shiny green leaves. It only takes a few clicks to alter it. In either case, both are classy, urbane, and understated, as the home fragrance company deserves. Mr. Monroe specializes in upscale scents made with essential oils. They're known for their sprays but are about to launch a line of candles.

Honestly, when I think about his brand, I should have known the specs were wrong. That's on me, and I won't make the mistake again of trusting without verifying. From this moment on, I'll make sure I know the client's vibe.

I waver with what to do. Send the new design to Chris and Leslie now? If they don't like it, will they think I rushed it? Should I send only to Chris? Should I let Adam know my team pulled it together within hours, not days?

Thinking about the optics and the chain of command, I email the files to Chris, while cc'ing the others. When I look up from my desk, I realize many of the designers have left and the rest are leaving now. It's after five on a Friday, and I have nowhere to be so I don't dash out after them.

When we were finishing the apple, I thought about asking Cara if she wanted to go for drinks tonight, but she suddenly jumped up from her seat and exclaimed about being late. I know she has a live-in girlfriend waiting for her at home, so I wasn't surprised when she grabbed her oversized purse and hurried out.

In my office, I wait a few minutes for a response to my emails, wondering if there is anyone still working. Circling the room, I look out the windows facing the harbor and then the other one facing Fort Point Channel and the Boston Tea Party Museum, not that I can see anything other than buildings from my floor even if it were daylight.

At this hour, by the lights on in offices nearby, I can tell whether people are still working. Some click off while I watch. A few short months ago, this would be when Jason and I headed out for a night at NYC's finest restaurants, followed by a play or a concert. At the very least, I would get together with my friends Julia and Sam from work or my Parsons' friends and hit the clubs.

Funny how I don't miss *him* any longer, only the good company of my friends.

Thinking about my journey home on the T tonight, maybe later is better. Some nights, with commuter crowds and delays, it takes an hour to get to the western suburb of Allston where I live. And I have yet to experience the train commute when it snows.

Although my savings are growing, and I'll be able to afford city parking soon, winter seems like the worst time to drive in, especially without all-wheel drive. And my current car, while not a shitbox, is no Range Rover, either.

When I changed my name and turned my back on some serious wealth, I never intended to go grungy poor. I'm not an idiot. What I am, in fact, is grateful, not only for what I grew up with, but for how I was raised. I sincerely want to be so much more than my rich parents' rich daughter. In fact, I plan on being successful.

Wildly successful, if possible. I've simply had a setback and a major life change, but now I'm starting over.

"Growing my wealth," I mutter, something my dad talks about, like money is a crop of corn. Mostly I want to be able to indulge again in my favorite pastime, buying expensive shoes, shallow and wasteful as that is.

My inbox notification dings, and I glance over at the open laptop to see something from *c_arruda*. Feeling apprehensive, I click open the email from Chris: **Good work. This should be satisfactory.**

No apology despite he and I both knowing it was his fault. Also "good" seems a little mild for the 3D glistening apple I'd created with my team in a short time.

I notice he cc'd the others. I suppose he has to play it cool, and it would have been impossible for him to thank me for taking the fall.

While I'm answering with a brief **Thank you, glad you like it**, my phone croaks with the dominant call of a male tree frog, indicating I've received a text. I know it's weird, but I adore frogs. However, it's not a number I recognize.

Frowning, I click on it. *Hi, it's Chris. I want to make it up to you. I've already left tonight, but we could meet up this weekend?*

Shit! What is he thinking? Maybe he didn't get the no-dating memo that I'd received loud and clear by way of in-person delivery from Mr. Bonvier the first time we met. This is whacky! I wouldn't respond favorably to such a text even if the bossman asked me. Especially *not* the bossman!

41

And then, right on cue, *a_bonvier* appears in my inbox. Apparently, the company culture does not respect late Friday afternoon as off-work time.

I can't believe those perfectly elegant apples came from the same design team. You killed it! Enjoy your weekend.

The boss has cc'd the others, too. I hit *reply all* to his email and thank him.

I don't hold my breath waiting for something from Leslie, nor do I expect anything personal from Mr. Bonvier solely to me. It would be thrilling, but I doubt I'll get two inappropriate messages in a row.

When nothing else appears, I turn back to Chris's text and consider my reply.

Thanks for offering the extra help with work.

I nearly all-cap the word "work" so he gets the *message*, no pun intended. Then I add an excuse.

Super busy this weekend, shopping for Christmas. A lie but I can't think of anything else. I also don't want to seem as though my job isn't important, so I continue.

I'm eager to learn what Mr. Monroe thinks of my team's new design at the next presentation. Because I will most certainly be there.

I hope we can schedule for early in the week before the office closes for the holidays.

That's clear enough. Send. Wait. Bite my lip. *Croak, croak!* Chris's next text is short: *OK. Enjoy your weekend.*

Nothing more than that. *Good!*

I put on my coat, grab my bag and scarf, and leave. I can't hide from my nothing of a life forever. Waiting by the elevator, alone on the design floor, I glance around and have a real sense of accomplishment. We pulled victory from the jaws of defeat, as they say. I am so impressed by the talent of those around me.

When the elevator opens to the lobby, I see only one figure in the center of the cool marble floor, facing the old-style double front door, head down, looking at his phone. Undeniably Adam Bonvier. Although he now looks full-on GQ in a duster-length, black coat, I guess from the end of his tie hanging out of one pocket that he's in after-work mode.

Damn! The male animal in perfect, virile form. The elevator closes behind me while I'm staring, or I might have retreated. Instead, I take a breath and walk past Jake, the nighttime security guard, at his desk, giving him a goodbye nod. My footsteps catch Adam's attention. He pockets his phone and delivers his sexy, lopsided grin. My insides flutter.

"There she is," he says. "Employee of the hour."

My cheeks burn.

"Whoa," he adds, as I draw closer. "I didn't mean anything by that remark."

I have to tilt my head to look up at him. "Really? You weren't mocking me for my massive screw up?" I know I sounded defensive, but I still feel testy about being set up to fail.

He shakes his head slowly. "I was not mocking. I was praising you for your incredible turnabout."

"That could have been today's original presentation if—" I cut myself off, determined not to ruin my short career by blaming the guy above me.

"If what?" he asks, and his stone-gray eyes demand I finish my sentence.

I choose my words carefully. "If only I hadn't got it wrong the first time." My jaw is clenched as I lie, and I try to relax my face into a normal smile.

He narrows his eyes. I have the feeling he knows what I'm determined not to say. But then he shrugs.

"Heading home?" he asks. "Or off for drinks?"

I nearly glance around to see whom I might be having drinks with.

"My team left already," I explain. "So, it's home for me." I hope I don't sound pitiful.

For a second, our eyes lock, and my breath catches in my throat. He looks as though he might be about to say something more, perhaps invite me for those drinks he mentioned, but then one of the front doors opens behind him.

"I'm sorry I'm late, Mr. Bonvier. Traffic was at a standstill on Storrow Drive."

"Not a problem," Adam says to the man who is obviously his driver. Then he looks back at me. "Heading for the Franklin Street garage?"

Not that it's his business, but I answer. "I'm taking the T."

His smooth forehead creases as though he's genuinely concerned. And I have a feeling he's going to offer me a ride.

"Don't worry," I add, walking past him straight for the exit, causing the driver to snap open the door for me. "I have mace in my purse." I do, somewhere in the bottom of the bag, covered in tissue lint, loose mints, and a comb.

"Better to have it clenched in your fingers," Adam says behind me.

I hold up a hand in farewell and dash out into an overcast, chilly evening only to realize it's drizzling. That would explain the dripping driver. I was so distracted by Adam, the other man's damp shoulders and hat hadn't registered.

Why wasn't rain in the forecast? My gorgeous, blue suede Marion Parke strappy pumps will be ruined! I try to hold my coat out as I walk to protect my feet.

A moment later, I hear Adam call after me, "Ms. Mitchell."

Now what?

6

Clover

Adam appears beside me on the sidewalk under the traditional awning with BONVIER stamped across the black-and-gray striped canvas in a cream-colored, uppercase font.

Currently, I am very much appreciating this touch of old-world style to the nineteenth-century façade, keeping me dry.

"You dropped your scarf."

The soft, winter-white scarf had been draped over my purse, and apparently my jaunty little escape sent it sliding to the floor. Adam holds it out to me.

For a second, I can't take my eyes off his large hand, clenching the fabric. Seeing my scarf tangled in his fingers looks so intimate, I swear I tingle all over.

"Thank you." I sound wooden, but the man unnerves me. Or rather, the attraction I feel leaves me utterly off-kilter. "I guess I would have noticed by the time I got to the station."

Wow. That is some scintillating conversation. I tug at the garment, but he holds onto it another second. I stare up at him.

"I was thinking," he stops himself, then starts again. "It seems fortuitous that we happened to meet in the lobby, what with David being unusually late." He gestures with his head toward his driver who's now standing on the sidewalk, too.

"Fortuitous," I echo. *What is he about to say?*

"Since I'm going home and so are you, and with the unexpected rain, I'd be happy to give you a lift."

My jaw must have dropped slightly because he releases my scarf and puts his hand up, like he's warding off my thoughts.

"I know that sounds like a come-on." He glances again at his driver who takes a few steps away, making it seem even more like a lure.

"We're going in the same direction," Adam adds, "me above ground and you below it."

I can't help cocking my head with curiosity. I have to accept that, for some inexplicable reason, Bonvier's CEO knows where I live. But I can't accept that he lives in *my* neighborhood, or even in the direction of it.

"You live in Allston?" I ask as I wrap the scarf over the top of my head and around my neck.

He grins. That sort of riles me. Like it's unbelievable, although it absolutely is. A billionaire does not live off Commonwealth Avenue that far up the Charles River. I'm fairly new, and I can testify to that. My neighborhood has turned out to be all college students and young professionals trying to make enough to move somewhere else.

"No," he says. "But it's on my way. Or rather, on David's way."

My expression shows my disbelief because he laughs. A sexy sound that makes me wish I had a reason to stand here longer. But it's going to get awkward really quick.

"Thanks," I say, gathering my wits despite thinking there would be nothing more exciting at that instant than traveling in the back of Adam Bonvier's limo with him. "But the station isn't far. Good night."

I resume my quick trot, making a mental note to carry a tote umbrella in the future, and I jog up Pearl Street before taking a left onto Franklin.

"Ugh!" I feel water seep through to my toes after stepping in a puddle. Glancing down, I wince at the ruin of my shoes, a former pricey indulgence from a time when I had saved some serious money in New York City.

Silently, I curse the useless weatherman. I guess I'm lucky it isn't snow, which there has been none of yet this winter. But I decide to bring in my thermal boots and keep them at the office.

"Clover," comes Adam's voice again, this time not from behind me. I glance over to my right to see him in the rear of his limo, window down a couple inches, as the car dogs my steps on the one-way street.

I take a second glance. Not normally a car person, even I know this is something special—a Maybach Landaulet. I'm staring. My brother would be drooling since he's a car person. Our father included us once in choosing his limo from stacks of glossy brochures, just for fun. My sister was too little at the time to care, but I know this superbly designed vehicle costs over a million.

I suppose it speaks volumes as to Adam Bonvier's personality. The white sedan is understatedly elegant with no need to scream *limousine* the way the long ones do.

Built for only two passengers, I can't help thinking Adam intended the white leather reclining seats for himself and whomever he is dating, rather than for clients or business associates.

Behind the Maybach, horns blare from jealous drivers as the car's slow pace holds up traffic. My boss puts the window down farther, rests his arm on the door frame, looking utterly unconcerned by what is behind him and by the rain spattering his suit.

"Yes, Mr. Bonvier," I respond, not slowing down even a little.

"Call me Adam. Everyone who works for me does."

"OK. Call me Clover."

"I already did," he reminds me.

"Can I help you, Adam?"

"First, I have to confess, I lied. Allston is not on my way at all, but I would willingly drive you there or at least let us take you to the station. You look ill-equipped for the deluge that's coming."

Deluge? The sound of thunder drowns out everything else for an instant, making me shiver. I glance up to see the winter sky isn't just darkening because the sun set already. It's dark from thick clouds overhead, and . . . *Shit!* Lightning flashes in the distance. The streets are clearing in front of me as people scramble for cover.

Ignoring him and the weather, I don't wait for the light to change but race across Devonshire Street.

As thunder rumbles again and the bone-chilling, icy rain comes down harder, I begin to walk closer to the car. I'm tempted.

"You're getting wet," I point out as rain hits his face. It might ruin the car's expensive interior.

"You're getting wetter," he says.

Sensual-sounding words from an impossibly sexy man.

My worsted wool coat, meant to keep out the cold not a sheeting downpour, looks more black than gray. And I'm soaked from collar to the knee-skimming hem. But his words remind me of the danger I'd be in if I got in his car. I cross Arch Street, hurrying the last block in silence. Adam and his limo still escort me.

"What about your company rule?" I ask him before taking a left onto Hawley Street and slowing to a walk. Hardly much point in running any longer since my shoes are squeaking and my hair is dripping around my face despite the Jackie-O style of my winter scarf. David has brought the car down the small street, too.

Adam knows immediately what I mean.

"Giving a fellow employee a lift is not a date. If you're squeamish I promise, I've never had sexual relations with anyone back here."

I gape at his words. He takes a moment to depress the button that lowers the glass divider between him and his driver. The front seats and dashboard are all black, making the car's two sections even more distinct.

"Have I ever had sex on these pristine leather seats, David?"

Sex! Why is my boss thinking about sex, and why is he bringing his driver into the conversation?

"Mr. Bonvier has never had sex in the back of this car," David yells to me over his shoulder to be heard despite traffic and thunder. "Not to my knowledge," he adds a second later, earning a scowl from Adam.

I laugh. Finally, I stop completely under a red awning.

"Are you getting in?" Adam asks, looking smug. Instantly, he's a billionaire bossman, determined to win and sure of getting his way.

I shake my head and point toward the pedestrian-only sign for the single block ahead of me on Summer Street. I can see the T station sign from here.

"Thanks for keeping me company on my walk," I say as his smile becomes a frown. "Have a great weekend."

Honestly, the whole thing has lifted my spirits. And they stay lifted through the crowded, soggy train journey, even though my wool coat smells like a wet dog. But when I arrive home to my empty apartment, I admit that it's time to make some friends or at least, call some old ones.

Pam, my roommate, has gone out for the night. She's a nurse, clean and tidy, and knows a million people, all of whom she's eager to spend time with whenever she doesn't have a late shift. I like her, what I've seen of her, but we rarely hang out. However, she has a major flaw. Never having lived in New York City, or apparently anywhere that she felt threatened, Pam has a nasty habit of carelessness. All of which means while the building's front entry is securely locked, our apartment door, three floors up, isn't.

I don't bother fishing in my purse. Instead, after grabbing the mace off the shelf by the coat closet, as I always do when this happens, I walk around our apartment, opening any closed doors, looking onto our fire escape, and finally, snatching open the shower curtain, ready to squirt any intruder in the eyes.

When I finish this routine, I put my sad-looking shoes near the trash bin and take a hot shower to chase away the freezing rain that chilled me to my bones. Changing into yoga pants and a comfy T-shirt, I add a knit hoodie and immediately think about Adam.

I mean, I think about what I'm going to eat. *Not* Adam! I decide on take-out delivered, and punch in my order. Opening a hard seltzer, I plop down on the sofa that isn't mine and lean my head back.

I am so predictable—a single woman on a Friday night, about to eat Chinese food, probably straight out of the box, and watch Netflix. Instantly feeling sorry for myself, I do a mental shake.

What if I had got into Adam Bonvier's limo? That single dangerous act might have opened up a new chapter in my life. One with excitement and passion, dining out and sex! And then, quite probably termination from my job. And I have an ideal job.

It has only been about four months since I last saw Jason Decker. That was also a Friday. I'd headed upstairs to his office suite a little early, stopped in the bathroom, and taken off all my clothes except for my boots. They were black, shiny leather, knee-highs, perfect for September in New York. As well as being super sexy for seduction. Then I'd wrapped myself in nothing but my thigh-skimming black coat and threw open his office door.

My boss—also my boyfriend of half a year—was having sex with his executive assistant. Another cliché as sad as my current Friday night solo Netflix and Chinese.

Not only was his assistant, Laura, married, she was well-aware Jason and I were a couple. At Decker Financial, there was no anti-dating policy in place, and I hadn't been asked to hide anything. Nevertheless, Jason and I were always discreet, both in and out of work. If it wasn't already six-thirty, I wouldn't have gone to his office dressed like an expensive whore!

Anyway, I don't blame Laura, although I still feel sorry for her husband. I never went back so I don't know what the recriminations were, if any. Seriously shocked, feeling my legs go all trembly, I wobbled my way back to the bathroom and, utterly humiliated, dressed as fast as I could.

Jason didn't come after me immediately, although I know he saw my shocked face. Maybe it turned him on and he finished what he'd started with Laura because they'd looked very into one another.

Hours later, he showed up in the Bronx at my door. I loved that Morris Park apartment, a cute little place I hardly ever stayed at after hooking up with Jason since it was more thrilling to play house in his condo in Tribeca. Of course, it was near the top of the Jenga Building with its multi-million-dollar views.

We talked. I was proud of how well I'd pulled myself together. No tears, no screaming, not to mention having calmly collected anything of his in my apartment. There wasn't much, but I'd put it into a plastic bag.

Jason said it didn't have to be over between us. But it so did.

And then while I was busy assuring him I wouldn't make a scene at work or even tell anyone why we weren't dating any longer, promising not to make it awkward if we passed in the lobby of Decker Financial, he fired me.

He said, "Clover, if we're not dating, you can't work for me. It would be too weird."

As I digested this startling news, he said his company also couldn't provide me with references. Not for Clover Henley, the candy heiress.

"You're too public. People will be mad at my company, like we kicked a puppy. And no one will believe a glowing reference anyway, since you were sleeping with me."

And then the asshole offered me only two weeks' pay. I am not even kidding. Momentarily speechless, I wondered if he knew anything about wrongful termination and how much of a stink I could make. But I wouldn't. The last thing I wanted was a whiff of scandal early in my career, or any hint that I was sleeping my way into jobs. In other words, Jason was damn fortunate.

After I wrangled a month's severance out of him, he left. I had just let him close the door on our relationship when I wrenched it open and hurled the bag of assorted socks, a belt, and two ties hitting him between the shoulder blades. I wished it had contained a few books, too.

I started packing before I even heard the roar of his stupid, flashy Aston Martin.

The intercom for the downstairs door buzzes, and I run down three flights of stairs to claim my dinner. Soon, I'm giving in to my hunger, practically inhaling ginger scallion chicken and spicy *mei fun,* as good as any I had in New York City.

But there is a lot about NYC I miss.

While downing another hard seltzer, I call Julia, one of my two closest friends at Decker Financial. She was half the reason I got the job with Bonvier, Inc. Sam was the other half. And I'm not proud of taking them up on this, but when they heard what a beast Jason had been, each offered to fake an internal Decker reference.

After all, they both had numbers with Decker extensions. It hadn't been that hard to provide Julia's name and number as the contact person supposedly in HR, even though she works in mutual funds. And Sam, bless his heart, despite being the nerdiest of all nerdy accountants, he played Jason Decker himself.

And it had worked beautifully. They followed up phone conversations with Chris Arruda and Bonvier's HR head by sending written recommendations about my work. All five star and glowing. They weren't lies, although technically no one named Clover *Mitchell* had ever worked at Decker Financial.

I reach Julia on the first ring, but she's out on a date and promises to give me the details later. Then I call Sam, who talks my ear off about Decker company gossip before asking questions. I nearly spill the beans and tell him the only guy since Jason who has tickled my fancy, who makes me want to climb into the relationship saddle again—or climb into his bed—is my new boss.

I would be an idiot to revisit such a mistake, even if Adam wanted to.

Despite knowing in my bones that he could make me melt.

Despite wanting to feel his strength as he rises over me.

Despite wanting to taste his mouth, as well as the rest of him.

I can't be with a man remotely similar to Jason. Powerful, able to run roughshod over anyone. I can't trust that type of man to keep my heart safe when he can have anyone or anything. I definitely can't trust him with my secrets.

So I tell Sam only about my new friendship with Cara and how talented the rest of my team are, about my apartment and my roommate. And I keep my love life, such as it isn't, to myself.

I sigh as I hang up. Thank God Bonvier, Inc. has its strict no-dating policy. What I need is a nice, regular boyfriend.

7

Adam

I go home and take a cold shower despite the seasonal temps. I can't believe I toyed with Clover. And that was exactly what I was doing. Because if she'd got into my car and let me take her home, I might've pressed to go upstairs. I like to think I wouldn't have.

At the very least, though, I would've felt sorry for the drowned rat that was my art director and asked her to have dinner with me.

Maybe she'd have to strip off those wet clothes to dry.

Obviously, *sorry for her* is not what I'm feeling.

I think of her smile and intelligent eyes, and of course, her luscious figure. If she'd accepted a ride and dinner, then where would we be? Practically dating. Or maybe just fucking.

Right then, while frigid water from the showerhead battles my cock and is slowly winning, I close my eyes and imagine her cute little ass as she ran along in the rain.

Besides a leg man, I guess I'm an ass-man, too.

I really wanted her to get in the back seat and let me make her evening a better one. It's obvious she's not having good sex by her skittish nature. All that adorable blushing and dropping things. I would place a bet she doesn't have a boyfriend, or if she does, he's an idiot.

I'm not such a jerk that I honestly believe I'd improve her life by hot sex, although it's easy to imagine Clover beneath me or taking her up against a wall, thrusting into her. No matter how satisfying it would be for both of us— and I guarantee a good time for all—then what? It would be bye-bye Clover.

After she turned around that apple graphic, I knew she was going to do a great job for my company. That's more important than getting my rocks off, so I'm going to do better to keep my thoughts, along with my hands, off the new designer.

A month or so ago, I was fooling around with Lydia, a Hollywood actor, *not* a Broadway one. Yes, there is a difference. We had a good time, some laughs, some OK sex.

I admit I like sex, even if it's only OK. But I'm not averse to something mind-blowing once in a while. Sex like that is scarce.

I have a sense that sex with Clover would be mind-blowing and then some.

My cock is ramrod hard once more despite the cold shower. It's pointless to fight the lust coursing through my veins, so I put the water temperature up until I can feel my toes again. And then I take matters into my own hand.

Resting one forearm and palm against the shower's stone enclosure, I close my eyes and grasp hold of my cock. Picturing Clover's heart-shaped face, I imagine her under the steamy spray, looking up at me, her luscious lips parted, her eyes lit with desire. I would map out her full breasts with my mouth and tongue, while she stroked me.

Before I could stop her, she'd slip from my grasp and sit on the corner marble seat, drawing me towards her mouth with her hands on my ass. When she has me where she wants me, she'd fist her fingers around my cock and take me between her lips, using her other soft hand to caress my balls. And then she'd suck me off.

When I get to that part of the fantasy, I'm so hard thinking about her, it hurts. Stroking myself fast and firm, I feel the pressure building. There's that momentary calm before the storm, and then I climax, with a long, shuddering orgasm.

It only makes me want the reality of Clover Mitchell in the flesh even more.

With a sharp twist, I shut off the water and run options through my mind as I towel dry. *Call a friend, go out, stay in?*

In the end, I change into basketball shorts and decide to shoot baskets in my own house. A room on the fourth level directly over the stairwell has a thick, clear plexiglass floor, a skylight overhead, and a regulation-height hoop. I keep some Boston Celtics' memorabilia on the walls and a flatscreen TV. It's my equivalent of a man-cave. In the daytime, the sunlight streams down through all the floors via the main staircase, to the foyer below.

Before playing, I give in to a craving and ask Ray, my weekday private chef who provides dinner any night I'm here, if he can switch up whatever he's making for a medium-rare steak and a baked potato.

Then I turn on the lights, switch on the TV to a sports channel, and warm up. There isn't space to do much more than dribble and shoot, but it's better than nothing. And I can do it twenty-four/seven.

By the time dinner is ready, I've worked up a sweat, showered again, and am seated in the theater in my cellar, wondering what movies Clover enjoys.

I can't help laughing at myself as I drink a spicy, fruity Belgian beer and eat in the darkness. All the money in the world, women throwing themselves at me, and I'm spending a Friday night alone, thinking of my company's new hire—the one pussy I can't touch.

I probably need to get a new girlfriend.

$♥$♥$$♥$

Monday morning, I'm determined to keep my distance. Give Clover Mitchell all the space in the world. It's only fair. She ought to go clubbing after work and find herself some nice guy. Lucky bastard!

I stay away from any account presentations. It's not where I belong, and my employees will start to wonder. I hear through the grapevine—actually, that's not true, I ask Chris outright and find out Clover's glass apple was a hole in one. Mr. Monroe is a happy man.

While I have Chris in my office, I remind him that his behavior was unacceptable, and I ask if he's going to tell Clover it wasn't her fault.

"I'll let her know it was my misunderstanding," Chris says coolly.

I can't force the man to apologize like we're in grade school, but I think he'll do the right thing.

"And Leslie?" I ask.

Chris frowns. "What about her?"

"Are you going to tell her, too?" Crossing my arms, I think of the account manager's hostility. "She laid into Clover pretty hard. Maybe Leslie needs to apologize, too."

"Maybe," he agrees. "But she didn't know, and Leslie was only being loyal. To me and to you, and to the company."

"True, but the company includes Clover now." I stare him down until Chris shrugs.

"I'll make sure Leslie understands the situation," he promises.

And then I dismiss him and get to work. It's a slow time of year actually for the art and accounts departments, with nearly every one of our clients having used up their fourth-quarter ad budgets. But it's when I do a lot of internal meetings with operations, media, and analytics, and catching up with clients, making sure they're happy.

When I'm not on the phone, I'm doing lunches and hosting dinners, with large and small accounts because I'm fully aware they could all go elsewhere.

I believe in the personal touch. My father did the same thing.

It's also strategic planning time. As a numbers guy, I don't mind the hours spent with the penny-pushers. Plus, there's the burgeoning Paris office to consider and their new accounts. A lot of European companies don't want to make the leap to the U.S., but find it perfectly acceptable to deal with us on their own turf.

After about a week, I'm itching to see Clover again. That's a bad sign. I'm not a randy dog. *Dammit*, I'm lying to myself. I am horny as hell whenever I think of her. Thankfully, testosterone flows high in my family. But it can also be a nuisance. And with her gorgeous eyes, shapely tits and ass, as well as her legs—basically she's taken up the real estate in my head and filling my free hours with salacious thoughts.

It's not sheer lust, either. I've dated women in the past few years merely because of an initial attraction. The wrong women, ones who didn't get under my skin after the sex cooled, like Lydia. That kind of woman leaves you lonely. I had a long-term with a college girlfriend that ended up in a huge, ugly break-up. Finding out how rich a man is can make even a nice girl a little nuts.

More recently, I dated a client. It had the same effect as dating an employee. Despite parting ways amicably, she took her account elsewhere. It's not like I can go clubbing anymore, nor do I want to relive my early twenties, even if I could trust that anyone I meet doesn't already know who I am and have her eyes on the Bonvier fortune.

Must be why my brain and body have zeroed in on Clover Mitchell. Not a celebrity or a high-flier, not an airhead, not pretentious. Smart and normal, as well as drop-dead gorgeous. And more than any of that. Something else. It has to be those invisible pheromones—something chemical she's sending my way—because I'm bordering on obsession.

Knowing she's under me all day, four floors below to be exact, when I want her under me, skin-to-skin, is making me a little crazy. I must be insane because I knee-jerk into ruining my evening by contacting a former hookup. What my dad would call *an old flame.*

I stamp the intercom with my thumb.

"Get me Chelsea Sweeney on the phone."

No response, although I can hear my assistant breathing.

"Janet?"

"Yes, *sir.*" My assistant is a redheaded force of nature, who keeps my work-life humming along, knows the ins and outs of Bonvier's Boston office better than anyone, and also handles her husband and children. Sometimes, she seems to think I belong in the latter category.

"Is there a problem?" I ask.

Her long hesitation irks me. I'm not asking permission to talk to Chelsea. A former girlfriend and local socialite, she's usually up for a dinner out and a fuck with no strings attached. I haven't seen her in over a year. I frown. *Has it been longer?* She might no longer be interested in a one-nighter, which is all Chelsea and I have done after a short trial of dating and a friendly parting.

"No, sir." I can practically see Janet pursing her lips. Plus, she never calls me "sir" unless annoyed.

I wait a minute, and then my desk phone rings.

Janet's tone is crisp. "I have Chelsea Swine on the line."

"That's *Sweeney* and you know it."

But I'm no longer speaking to my assistant, who drops off after letting her dislike be known. Having been with the company since the incident with Rachel, before I was the CEO, Janet has a bit of a maternal issue where I'm concerned, even though she's only about fifteen years older. What's more, she holds a grudge against people who don't meet her high standards. And Chelsea doesn't meet those standards.

Once, when attending a charitable banquet as my date, Chelsea dressed inappropriately enough that even the tabloids said she'd gone too far. Then she got ripped. It was a children's charity, so not a good image all around.

Come to think of it, that was the last time we went out.

"Adam, you magnificent man," Chelsea gushes. "Where have you been?" As if she's been sitting around waiting for my call rather than jet-setting with all the beautiful people and spending last winter in Dubai. "Never mind. I consider you fabulously *naughty* for not calling sooner, but you can make it up to me."

Just like that, I remember her overblown, put-on, ostentatious personality. A couple years ago, she was a good time, but my tastes have changed. Even my former Hollywood actress girlfriend is less showy.

Too late, though. She's on the phone. Besides it can't hurt to spend a few hours with her.

It's not as though I'm going to spend every moment comparing her to Clover Mitchell. Except I do. All evening. And Chelsea is woefully lacking.

We don't go to bed together, not even close. Nor do I need another cold shower when I drop her home. My biggest regret is how she invites herself to our Christmas party, which is going to royally piss off Janet.

8

Clover

I'm not usually distrustful, but as some wit once said, even the paranoid have enemies. After the first disastrous presentation, I decide to sit in on all pitches of my team's work.

"I wasn't expecting you," Chris says when I show up at the next one, latte in hand, wearing a coral-colored power dress. After a double-take, Leslie's lips tighten and she gives Chris the stink-eye before burying her head in her laptop.

"The last art director didn't sit in. It's unnecessary, a waste of manpower, pointless," Chris adds.

"Is it, though?" I shoot back. Actually, I don't know what's entirely regular at an ad agency, especially a big one like Bonvier with branding specialists, packaging design, and all that. Representatives from both are at the conference table as we await the client.

But just because I haven't been invited, that doesn't mean I shouldn't be here.

"Adam told me it was OK. If you have a problem with my being here, then you'll have to take it up with him." And I take a seat, resting my tablet on the table in front of me.

Leslie looks up again, locks gazes with Chris, and then raises a dyed blonde eyebrow. If one were to ask me, I'd say they were closer than VP and account exec, the no-dating rule notwithstanding. But that isn't any of my business. As long as I don't break any rules, I don't care what the others do.

I don't look for Adam to enter because I assume he has bigger fish to fry than this frozen dessert rebranding. Still, I can't help looking up with a sliver of hope each time the door opens. Someone from the digital division comes in, as well as the packaging prototype director. And everyone is in a good mood. It's the last presentation before the Christmas party. After that, the company closes for a full week until January 2nd. Kind of unheard of, but rather spectacular.

Kudos to Bonvier, Inc.

Eventually, one of the associate account managers, a young woman with large brown eyes and an even larger smile, comes through the door with the client she was sent downstairs to await. Introductions are made, and then Chris begins. He has a storyboard on the large screen with his team's words and my team's art, including labels for four new flavors.

"Love it," says the client every few minutes.

"The commercial is ready to view," Leslie said. "Our head designer," she gestures to me, "put some finishing touches on it yesterday."

I'd been given the file to add the last two frames with the approved mockups of the product before sending it back to Leslie's inbox. I'm surprised, however, that she even mentions me.

The lights dim, and Leslie inserts a flash drive into the projector.

Friendly summertime music plays while people splash in a pool. Those seated around it are eating the client's Italian ice from little paper cups. Suddenly, the music switches to a Christmas carol as the pool ices over. Everyone runs inside to collect around a cozy hearth with a lit fire. The kids are loud and obviously discontented. The frazzled hostess goes into the kitchen and opens her freezer to bring out the client's treats, gelato in the same ubiquitous cups.

In real life, our client claps her hands.

"Well done," she says.

The cups fly out of the freezer, each pausing mid-air so you can read the flavors on the new labels I designed— caramel chocolate, pumpkin pie, spiced apple-vanilla, and peppermint-chocolate gelato were showcased. This campaign would launch next summer to get a buzz, and then the products would be in the freezer section for early-autumn and run through the winter months.

The cups land on the platter the hostess is holding, and she closes the freezer. When she turns, I gasp as do a few others at the table. It is unmistakably Leslie's face crudely stuck onto the body of the female actor through photo manipulation. Without using her hands, because the hostess is holding the tray as she goes back into the living room, Leslie appears to give an enthusiastic blow job to a competitor's frozen treat on a stick.

"Dammit!" Chris exclaims into the shocked silence. With a click, he switches off the commercial before the final few frames.

"Oh my God!" Leslie says, and she covers her face with her hands.

"What's going on?" the client asks, not sounding as upset as our account department appears to be.

"Seems to be a prank," Chris says tightly. And for some reason, he glares at me. *What the hell!*

More silence ensues until finally, I turn to the client.

"I suppose you got the gist of the rebranding as an all-season dessert," I say despite knowing it isn't my job to pull this one out of the gutter. "I hope you could see the small details of autumn leaves and snowflakes on the new cups before—"

I stop short of saying *before our own Leslie appeared to perform fellatio on an icy pop.* But no one steps in to fill the gap. The younger account associate with the big eyes laughs nervously, then claps a hand over her mouth.

"I'm terribly sorry," Chris says. "Whoever is responsible will be fired."

Leslie pulls herself together and shakes it off like a prizefighter who's taken a blow to the chin. It's comical the way she adjusts her posture, lifts her chin, and even rolls her shoulders back dramatically a few times. Then she, too, gives me a long, hard look.

The client steps in. "Don't fire anyone over a joke." She rises to her feet. "What I saw, apart from the . . . *uh* . . . The part I watched that was intentional, I really liked. You all nailed it. Send me the fixed version, and I'll look it over. Do you have a copy of all the new elements to our brand?"

"Of course," Chris says. "We have a packet for you to take with all the art work on a flash drive."

Leslie produces a folder, with the Bonvier logo on the front above the dessert logo.

"Perfect," the client says, then adds, "The pool freezing over was so clever."

"That was Leslie's idea," Chris says.

I thought that was big of him. As VP, he could have simply accepted the praise on behalf of the team. Anyway, I'm the one who executed the animation.

"And I adore the new cup labels and the color scheme for the container." She picks up the packaging prototype that rests on the table.

I wait for Chris to say those are both my doing, but nothing comes. In fact, I have a feeling I'm about to take the fall. Again! So, I rise with the client and say, "I would be happy to walk you out."

The account associate seems pleased to have her menial task taken from her. Five minutes later, after all the handshakes, I'm in the elevator with the client. Suddenly, her body starts shaking.

I realize with a start that she's laughing. Relieved, I say, "I'm glad you're not upset."

"That poor woman. Leslie! Her face! It's wicked of me to laugh." She pauses before eyeing me. "Never mind. Bonvier, Inc. is obviously filled with creative, spirited types. I do really like what you've done."

I see her to the curb and her waiting car. The one thing I'm not going to do is return to the conference room. The prank, as Chris called it, has nothing to do with me. However, I've barely started telling Cara of our success— and haven't even mentioned the ice pop yet—when he steps off the elevator.

Taking one look at his face, I head for my office with him right behind me. When we're in it, I close the door.

"You're not going to try to pin Leslie's phallic feast on me, are you?"

"She just showed me the file that came directly from you."

I shake my head. "Ridiculous! What's my motive?"

He runs a hand through his brown hair, looking thoroughly annoyed. "You tell me."

I cross my arms and remain silent. I can't tell him since I don't have one.

"Payback for the dressing down she gave you in front of Adam," he suggests.

I gape. "What is this? High school?"

"OK, fine," he says. "If not you, then perhaps someone in your department? Leslie used to work down here for the previous art director. Maybe someone's jealous she landed a job upstairs."

"Upstairs?" I repeat. "You act as though being in the account department on the fifth floor is somehow better than being a designer on the fourth floor."

"Because it is," he says. "As the senior executive, as a VP of this company, I'm telling you to get to the bottom of this debacle. We're lucky the client has a sense of humor."

He's right about that. In front of the wrong person, the crude visual could have lost us an account.

"*If* it was one of my designers, I'll find out," I promise. "However, I can open the file from my send box and easily prove the fellatio footage wasn't there when I sent it."

"You can?" His surprise is priceless, and then I know that he knows that I didn't do it. Because he shrugs. "Not necessary. I believe you."

After he leaves, I digest the new information that Leslie used to work in design. Wandering out to Cara's desk, I ask her about it.

She makes a face. "Leslie sat over there." Pointing to a station now occupied by a talented guy named Carlos, whose only been in the department a couple weeks longer than me. "Honestly, she wasn't great at design and took a lateral move to accounts. I always thought she had the hots for Andy.

"My predecessor," I say, having seen his name often enough.

"Nice guy. Left rather abruptly, but he did some great work. I'd miss him except you're just as pleasant to work with and, I have to say, more talented."

With my ego fluffed, I thank her and go back to my office. I wonder what would've happened if I hadn't shown up at that meeting. Would I suddenly find myself called into Chris's office, or even into Adam's and blindsided with accusations?

Under those circumstances, I wouldn't be too happy. But in almost any other situation, I would welcome seeing the bossman again. It has been too long since I've laid eyes on him. And it's the main reason I don't go home when work stops early for the company Christmas party.

These things are usually awkward. Most people who work together are only tepid friends. Being forced to hang out can lead to a tedious, cringeworthy party. My jaw drops when I enter the lobby, which is where the party is being held.

While we were all upstairs, caterers and party planners have remade the space. There was already a tree, put up right after Thanksgiving. It's been joined by an explosion of tinsel garlands, fake snow underfoot, red-clothed tables groaning with party platters, a DJ in one corner, and two fountains—champagne and chocolate.

It's only four o'clock, but it's getting dark out and people look like they're going to party as if it's midnight on New Year's Eve. Even the three paintings have been festooned with garlands of tinsel. I smile as I take a glass and fill it at the champagne fountain.

"Glad you didn't duck out," comes the voice that makes me shiver. I turn to face Adam Bonvier.

I eye him over the rim of my glass as I take a sip. "Why would I?" I ask. "Just because I barely know anyone, because I have to take the subway home when it's seriously frigid outside, and because some people are undoubtedly going to get drunk and embarrass themselves?"

His eyes crinkle at the corners as he smiles. "And you don't want to see them?"

"Nope. I would hate that, in fact. You look good in silver and gold, by the way," I add.

"Do I?" Then he looks past me to his portrait where a piece of tinsel has fallen, appearing as though it's purposefully draped down the side of his head and onto his shoulder. "I do!"

I laugh at his expression. He's adorable in a sexy AF way.

"Plans for Christmas?" he asks.

I dread this question as well as any follow-ups, but I answer truthfully. "Heading home to New York."

"Are your parents there?"

"Yup." Still telling the truth.

"Siblings?"

What is this? *The Spanish Inquisition?*

"Nope," I tell my first lie of the conversation, and I hate doing so. But if I said I have a brother and a sister, he would ask their names. While Adam might not think much about a woman named Clover, if he learns my sibling's names, Basil and Lark, he will definitely know we are the Henley family. That is, if he's ever heard of us before. My parents were pretty good about keeping us low-key, especially the younger ones, until we turned eighteen.

Anyway, it wasn't a risk I was willing to take. If I'd said yes, then I would have had to make up names, and that seemed a tad psycho. So I lied in order not to lie. And I feel crappy about it. All I want to do, in fact, is spill my guts over who I am, what I'm all about, and how much he turns me on. In a perfect world, with a different scenario, that's what I would do.

Before he can ask me more, I turn the spotlight on him.

"What about you? Any Bonvier brothers and sisters?"

He pretends mock shock. "I'm hurt and dismayed you haven't read every magazine article about my fascinating family?"

I grin. "I may have seen you in a tabloid or two. But you definitely weren't with siblings." I think of every photo I've seen with him and some gorgeous woman.

Apparently, he finds this funny. His smile is just crooked enough to be sexy, and he has a dimple. Of course he does!

"I have a younger brother, Captain Philip Bonvier," he says. "Air Force pilot. No interest whatsoever in the family business and a bit of a wild child."

"A wild Air Force captain," I muse.

"I think the call of duty will have tamed him a little. I can't wait to see his ugly face at Christmas. It's been too long. We all gather at my parents' house in Weston."

"Tell the captain thank you for his service," I say, and I mean it.

"I will. I'll say Clover Mitchell, my fabulous art director, says thanks."

Is he flirting, or just teasing me? Either way, I feel hot in places that pulse, and I take a drink of champagne to cool me down.

"How are the shoes?" Adam asks.

It takes me a second. "Oh, the Marion Parkes."

He frowns. *Still looks sexy AF!*

"My shoes," I explain. "That's the brand. They were ruined."

"Sorry about that." Sweetly, he looks genuinely apologetic.

"Me, too," I mutter, thinking of the price tag.

I can't believe I'm having this conversation with my boss. Also, we're blocking the fountain. He probably has a lot of people to chat with, so I fill up my glass under the stream, smile at him to let him know he can move on, and I walk away. But when I stop beside the festive tree that nearly touches the ceiling, Adam is still with me.

"I feel responsible," he says. "About your shoes."

He is closer than he has ever been since shaking my hand the first day we met. I catch a whiff of his cologne. Other men at work wear aftershave and cologne, and women are allowed to wear perfume, unlike at some companies.

But Adam's fragrance is in a class of its own. It has to be custom-made for him. It probably cost hundreds an ounce, and I would say it's worth all that and more. Uniquely subtle yet intense, utterly sexy and luxurious, and all those words I've read when designing a label for a cologne company while still at Parsons. *Woodsy, spicey, fuckable!*

Probably that last word isn't in any cologne description, but this fragrance definitely makes me want to put my face against his bare skin and breathe deeply. In fact, I desperately want to bury my face in his crotch and inhale this scent, not to mention lick it off his skin. *Definitely fuckable!*

Maybe I'm drinking champagne too quickly, but I wave my hand to indicate I'm dismissing his culpability.

"Not your fault. You don't control the weather, do you?"

He grins, and my stomach flutters. Thank God he doesn't know my filthy thoughts.

"Not yet. My secret weather balloon won't be launched until next year. Seriously, though, if I hadn't slowed you down by—"

"By kindly offering me a ride, which, had I accepted, would have probably saved my shoes?"

"Something like that," he says.

"Next time, I'll accept and climb in," I say, then freeze. It sounds way too chummy, not to mention implying there'll be a next time. "I didn't mean . . . ," I trail off, not sure what I intend. Then I drain the glass in a big gulp.

He is watching my mouth on the glass rim and then his slate-gray eyes lock on mine, and I swear, I can feel a sizzle. I've heard the saying that something passes between two people, but I have never felt it until now.

It's a little scary, especially given who he is. When I break eye contact to trail my gaze across his impressive cheekbones and strong jaw before finally settling upon his attractive mouth, I am struck with longing. I want to feel those lips first with my fingertips and then with my own lips.

I'm dead certain kissing him would be the bomb. And if we weren't in a crowded lobby, I can almost imagine we'd give it a try since he hasn't moved a muscle while I study him, and I haven't taken a breath in too long.

"Clover," he says, making me look him in the eyes again while I lick my suddenly desert-dry lower lip.

"There you are!" exclaims a loud, unwelcome female voice. And I take a guilty step backward.

Adam grimaces just as Chelsea Sweeney barrels into him, forcing me farther away while he has to grab hold of her to keep them both on their feet.

"Hi, handsome," she says. Then she turns to me, projecting territorial vibes. "Merry Christmas."

"Merry Christmas," I manage, and I nod to Adam, not bothering to say any more since he literally has his hands full.

I wander over to Cara and meet her significant other, Jenny. They're clearly a devoted couple. After a few minutes of chitchat, I'm done. Definitely not venturing over to Leslie who's wearing a Santa hat and getting increasingly sloshed, nor to Chris, standing with a group of guys I vaguely recognize from other departments.

It has quickly devolved into the type of office party I loathe. I gather my things, bundle up, and head outside past the tinsel-covered portrait of the man with whom I need to stop teasing myself.

But it's super difficult. And that night, alone in my bed, I give in to a wicked fantasy of Adam touching me everywhere, making myself climax in record time.

9

Clover

It isn't my place to give a damn who is photographed hanging on Adam Bonvier's arm. But I nearly lose my Sunday breakfast when I see him with Chelsea Sweeney on the cover of the gossip magazine at the supermarket checkout.

Fascinated, though, I can't help but pick it up and start flipping through the glossy pages. I drag in a sharp breath when I come to the color spread about the billionaire playboy and the inane socialite. Obviously, it doesn't use that word exactly, but she oozes superficiality from every vacuumed and Botox-injected pore. *Ugh!*

And she isn't only "on his arm." In each shot, whether they are entering a landmark Boston eatery on the Common or passing the crowded line to enter a jazz club near Harvard Square, she's leaning her half-exposed breasts against whatever part of him she can. Her fur coat is always open, despite the temperature, and her cleavage is on view. And instead of holding his hand, she has both of hers strangely clasping his forearm or even up around his neck.

I make a sound of disgust. How could he walk straight with Chelsea draped around him like an albatross? A slutty one at that.

"Lucky bitch," says the lady behind me.

I startle before I realize she doesn't mean me but Chelsea Sweeney.

"I wouldn't mind being in her shoes for a night," the woman adds, leaning closer and drinking in a good long look. Then she sighs. "She must have felt like Cinderella."

My own sex-starved brain fantasizes about Adam taking off more than my shoes. I'd imagined him so many times stripping me of my panties and getting to business that the vision now dances before my eyes.

Groaning with frustration, I take another look at Chelsea freakin' Sweeney. I doubt she's wearing any. Panties, that is. At least not by the end of the night. I note the date of the images to see they are from before the Christmas party.

Before Adam and I shared approximately five transcendental minutes.

Another wave of longing, conjuring a vision of our joined bodies—Adam on top, his expression intense as he rides me to a scorching climax—leaves me damp. Envy is a weird thing that I haven't experienced much of in my life. I certainly didn't envy Laura when I saw her with Jason. But at this moment, I envy Chelsea.

Swallowing, I put the magazine back in the rack and square my shoulders.

"None of my business," I mutter.

"None of any of our business," the lady says, before she pushes my things along the conveyer belt with one hand and plops a giant bag of cat litter into the space she's created. "But that doesn't stop us from looking and longing, does it?"

"No," I say softly. "I guess it doesn't."

I've been featured in a few magazine spreads myself. I was touted as the teenage heiress to the Henley fortune, as if somehow simply being born into the right family made me worthy of an article. I'd had invisible braces on my teeth and green contacts in my eyes, thinking they made me look exotic. It wasn't even a gossip rag. It was a confectionery industry magazine.

My younger brother and sister were also in the article, with the reporter wondering which, if any of us, would follow in our father's footsteps to run the candy company.

The answer, as it turned out, is both of my younger siblings. They don't run the company yet, but they work for it, and they do it in Australia, of all places, where my dad's parents are from and still live.

Later, when I was Jason's girlfriend, we'd been caught by paparazzi, much like Adam and Chelsea. Jason was the draw as one of New York's eligibles, and photos of him could make bank for a photographer. My parents successfully kept all three of their children out of the limelight, for which I've always been grateful. To the paparazzi, I was a nobody.

"Pretty mystery woman has captured this business tycoon's attention." Or some such equally demoralizing caption had made me nothing more than female bait and eye candy.

I have never thought of someone standing in the same checkout line, envying me when I was in the photo. Worse even is the emerald green streak of actual jealousy snaking through my body. Unnerving and entirely inappropriate. Unlike a very reasonable reaction to Jason's betrayal, it's utterly sketch for me to feel the least bit proprietary over Adam.

As I drive home to the Hudson Valley for Christmas, munching on the snacks I just bought, I decide that he didn't look all that happy in those magazine images. Maybe he took Chelsea out for business reasons.

I roll my eyes. Sure, he was only interested in her assets!

Not my concern, I keep reminding myself, and then I try not to think of him—*much!*—while I enjoy a quiet Christmas with Mom and Dad. Our home is grand in a way, but more hunting lodge than palace. With the family business, the one thing I know is we'll have plenty of sweets. Chocolate Santas, chocolate-covered pretzels, chocolate truffles. Even chocolate martinis. Absolute bliss for a frustrated working girl with a crush on her boss.

The real bummer is that my sister, Lark, and my brother, Basil, aren't coming home this year. The former is happily married and very pregnant, and the latter hates flying so much he's using our grandparents as an excuse to stay in Australia.

On the phone a month earlier when I mentioned hoping to see him, Basil said, "Got to keep an eye on Gran and Granddad, since you're covering home base."

And yes, their names make me feel downright happy about my own relatively normal one.

After big hugs from both my parents, I settle into a cozy chair by one of our massive stone hearths, the fire warming my toes. A bowl of chocolate balls at my left, along with a cup of hot chocolate, my dad's two dogs snoring on the rug, it's heaven. Only missing one thing, one attractive, intriguing man who has gotten under my skin.

$♥$♥$♥$

It's the new year and I'm happy to be back at work. I wonder how many of my co-workers feel the same way. At Bonvier, probably a higher percentage than anywhere else I've ever worked because . . . hello, half-price lattes!

But for me, there's another obvious reason. Only at work do I have the chance to see those gorgeous gray eyes I've been dreaming about. Not that I know when or if it will happen on any given day, but it's a mental game that keeps things interesting.

Like today, a larger-than-usual group of us are in the account department's conference room, late in the day. Due to everyone's schedules, this was the only time all the principals could gather for a strategy meeting about one of Bonvier's oldest clients. And today, my "wondering if I'll see Adam game" scores a win when he enters.

No jacket, wearing a navy-blue sweater with a high collar and buttons at the throat, he looks like he's ready to sit by a roaring fire in a ski lodge. Man, would I love to swish down the slopes with the bossman.

Seeing him after nearly three weeks is a shock to my system. How is he even more handsome? He looks around the room, his gaze resting on a few people as he nods to them in greeting.

And then Adam looks directly at me. My heartbeat speeds up and a quiver shimmies along my thighs, making my legs tremble as he saunters down one side of the long table and takes the empty chair beside me. To be clear, there are other empty chairs.

He leans toward me, and his cologne tickles my nose. It tickles other parts of me, too, and I cross my legs. No man should smell so irresistible! *Not unless he gifts me some of his cologne to spray on my pillow.*

"Nice to see you, Ms. Mitchell," he says into my ear. When he says such a banal pleasantry and my last name, I swear it sounds like dirty talk. I can't turn my head or we would be touching noses. His next words are even softer, meant for me only.

"Let's hope the presentation doesn't last all night."

I nod although I wouldn't mind staying in that seat for the rest of my life with him beside me, smelling like ultra male. I realize he isn't serious anyway. He's the boss and can hold us here for hours or dismiss us whenever he wants. Perhaps he's thinking of getting out to be with Chelsea, but then why would he bother coming in the first place?

Chris is leaning on a stool by the large screen that fills one wall. He clicks a button and the lights dim, making me even more aware of Adam close beside me.

Another click and the display shows an old magazine ad designed by Bonvier, followed by a sharp image of just the product, a beautiful glass bottle of perfume, its signature white-and-gold packaging.

"From my father's time at the helm," Adam says, loudly enough for everyone to hear. "It still holds up."

"Right you are," Chris agrees. "Made Bonvier a ton of money, didn't it? As did these others over the years." He clicks through a dozen more ads, showing various bottles with only a few updates to packaging.

"Mrs. Lovell wants a complete overhaul," Chris says. "Product label, packaging, and of course, ad campaign."

My mind starts whirling, thinking of what's classic, what's fresh, what will sell.

"I can hear your wheels turning," Adam says.

"What was that?" Chris asks.

"I'm sure our new art director is already thinking up some great ideas," Adam tells him.

"I'd like to have a few of their products in my hands," I say, assuming the budget allows for buying a few bottles of perfume.

Leslie, sitting opposite me and idly doodling on a pad of paper, stops. "You've never worn Lovell brand?" she asks, her tone mocking.

What was her deal?

"Not a problem. We have samples," Chris says. "Plenty of Lovell perfume on the premises."

Adam shakes his head. "I can't believe no one has shown Clover the supply closet yet." I can't tell if he's annoyed or just in disbelief, but I'm about to ask what supply closet when Leslie speaks again.

"I had lunch last week with one of their execs. He indicated they were looking for a retro, vintage vibe."

That doesn't seem right for this client, whose customers are upward of fifty and wealthy, but I hold my tongue. I'm still the newbie, after all, and my job is to create what the client wants. Besides, till the end of my career, I'll never forget the apple fiasco, which has taught me to wait until I see the specs.

Chris nods. "That could be."

"Could be?" Adam interjects. "Anything in writing?" he asks Leslie.

"Not yet," she says.

"How many meetings have *you* had with Lovell reps?" he asks Chris.

The VP visibly bristles. "The person Leslie and I need to see, high enough up the food chain to be reliable, isn't free until tomorrow."

"No offense," Adam says, "but why wasn't today's meeting held *after* that one? We have a lot of man—and *woman*—power at this table for working on sheer speculation."

Chris folds his arms and takes a seat. "Today's meeting was set because I was supposed to meet with the Lovell executive yesterday, but she bailed last minute. I thought it best to carry on anyway. There's still a lot we can discuss."

Adam nods, backing down and apparently agreeing. "We can talk numbers and not design."

A man I don't know speaks up. "What's the total budget, and how much will you need for print versus television versus Meta versus—"

"You don't need to list them all, Carl," Leslie says.

I guess Carl is from accounting. Not usually the most popular department as they tend to throw a damper on spending.

Chris sends a page full of numbers skittering down the table toward Carl. "The budget requests are all on the spreadsheets I emailed everyone."

A woman from the media department suggests getting a well-known sponsor for a commercial and discusses how tongue-in-cheek is selling better than a product taking itself too seriously.

Since she has brought up the most expensive aspect of the ad campaign, a lengthy discussion ensues over how much each department would like to get to make this all happen, and Carl writes notes all over the pages Chris just gave him.

The aforementioned spreadsheet will be obsolete in five minutes. Next, a few people toss around ideas for male and female actors who could sell the perfume if the ad campaign goes in the direction of a celebrity sponsor.

Adam stays silent, as do I. He's watching and listening while I'm scrolling through the previous magazine layouts on my tablet from the files Chris sent earlier. Bonvier has done a great job overall for decades. It will be tough to keep on trend and to do even better.

Finally, Chris says we've gone as far as we can go until he and Leslie have their meeting at Lovell in the morning.

For my part, I can literally do nothing unless I want to take a stab in the dark, which I do. With my stylus, I'm already scrawling a few ideas based on nothing more than gut instinct while the room starts to clear.

"I'll get you notes and specs by tomorrow afternoon," Chris tells me. Leslie, as usual, doesn't give me any friendly vibes, as she walks out.

"Thanks," I say, watching Carl still scribbling on the sheet in front of him.

"I think Clover should accompany you," Adam says before standing and stretching. Even that is sexy, and my mouth goes dry watching him. But then the import of his words filters though my sex-starved, lonely brain.

Wait, what?

"Leslie is coming," Chris says. "She manages the account and has done the footwork, as she mentioned. I don't think a designer has a place at the client's table, not when we're going to their office. We've never done it that way."

JANE MCBAY

Adam brushes all those legit reasons aside. "Humor me," he says, leaving no room for disagreement. "Clover can hear it directly for herself. Then the three of you can talk afterward to make sure you're all on the same page. This is an important client. They all are, but Mrs. Lovell has been a part of this firm longer than I have."

It sounds as though he doesn't trust his head of accounts to get the correct info. At least, that's how I take it. Apparently, Chris does, too.

"If that's what you want, Adam, then that's what we'll do." His flat, sulky tone is unmistakable. He'll do what the CEO wants, but he doesn't have to like it.

Then turning to me, Chris's eyes narrow. I have a notion he thinks it's my idea to go with them.

"Meet us in the lobby at eight forty-five sharp."

"I'll see you then." I so wish I wasn't being dragged into the middle of whatever power struggle is going on. But like the accounts director, I have no choice.

Carl suddenly says, "The time!" He grabs up everything in front of him and rushes through the open door. I can't help smiling, as he reminds me of the white rabbit from *Alice's Adventures in Wonderland,* a favorite childhood read.

Until I realize his hasty departure has left only the two of us. The bossman and me, just like in one of my dreams.

10

Adam

As soon as it's only Clover and I in the conference room, she starts to move quickly. She scrambles to shut down her tablet and grabs for her ubiquitous travel mug. She fumbles and knocks it over, but nothing spills out.

"Anything I can help you with?" I offer, and I admit I like how cute she is when she's flustered. We haven't seen each other since the Christmas party when Chelsea spectacularly ruined the mood.

"No," her voice cracks. "Thanks."

"That was painless," I add, referring to the meeting. "And not too long."

She rounds the table in front of me so I get one of my new favorite views, her ass in a form fitting wool skirt.

"It didn't seem long at all," she says.

Of course, I like to think she enjoyed every minute because we were sitting together.

"I wasn't bored for a moment," she adds. "I've got so much to think about and plan for this new campaign. What my design team does will be integral to literally everything."

I love her enthusiasm. "I guess I've been to too many of these meetings. To me, they're more fun when the client's in the room. At least there's the exhilaration of the pitch and wondering if the client will like it or not. This was just mental masturbation."

We're walking side-by-side in the hallway, and her steps falter. I don't think it's due to her sexy three-inch heels, which she gets around in gracefully from what I've noticed.

In fact, she sends me a questioning look. Did I mention how adorable she is? Her brain has immediately gone somewhere sexual. I'd have to be an arrogant prick to believe she might think of me when she gives herself an orgasm.

But I do, especially when her cheeks tinge pink.

The thought of her spending one lonely night with nothing but me in her imagination makes me hard in seconds.

Too quickly, she slides her gaze away from mine to what's in front of us. Up ahead, the hallway is clear, except for Chris and Leslie, speaking quietly in front of the elevators. I wish I could lip-read. That would be a handy CEO talent, especially when employees often go silent at my approach, exactly as these two do.

"They're probably wondering how to ditch me in the morning," Clover whispers from the side of her mouth.

It's my turn to falter, but I don't. Inside, though, I'm laughing at her frank and outrageous words. As if we're in high school.

When the doors open, Leslie gets on the elevator, but Chris lets it go. Turning, he waits for us.

"I can show you the supply closet now if you want," he says to Clover, and oddly, all traces of his earlier inappropriate annoyance have vanished. He's downright friendly sounding, and I'm instantly on guard.

"The supply closet?" she asks.

Chris shrugs and sends me a rueful smile. "Sorry. It's what we call the samples room. The Lovell perfume is in there."

Given the hour, I think my VP should be ready to leave, not trying to seclude himself with my art director. Besides, as I said in the meeting, she ought to have been shown the samples room by HR when she was first hired. Makes me wonder if she knows we have a gym and an in-house lunchroom with soup and sandwiches offered daily.

"If you have time," Clover says, so innocently I nearly groan. "I'll take you up on that offer. Holding something in my hand, touching it, hefting its weight or lack thereof, that's always better than a mere visual, no matter how big the screen or how intense the subject."

Chris and I exchange a look, both of us thinking the same thing—that it sounds as though she's talking about having sex versus watching porn. I know men's minds go to this topic about every five seconds, but I'm especially horny around this honeyed-brunette hottie, and I cannot imagine Chris doesn't feel the same.

Especially when, a moment later, those perfect cheeks of hers turn ruddy, right over her cheekbones.

He coughs to hide a grin, I think.

"I'll show you." The words come out of my mouth before I even think them through.

My accounts director hasn't been behaving as rock solidly as usual. The last thing I need is for him to compromise our art director.

If she wants to be compromised, that would be one thing, although ultimately, she'd have to be fired.

If she doesn't want Chris's attentions, I'll be hit with a sexual harassment suit, which I would lose. And that's publicity Bonvier definitely doesn't need. In any case, it would still be an automatic out for both of them.

In the space of a few seconds, I convince myself that I'll be the safest choice to take her to the sample room. *What could go wrong?*

"Good night, Chris," I say to hurry him on his way.

His expression matches Clover's, something akin to astonishment. I ignore them both and punch the elevator button to call it back to us. What can my VP do? He gets on the elevator and says, "See you tomorrow."

After the doors close, I hit the button again.

"What was that about?" she asks, immediately pressing her lips tightly closed on the last word.

If I have to guess, it's because she reconsiders questioning me, the CEO, not the man.

"Sorry," she says quickly. "None of my business."

I don't know what to tell her. I'm not going to confess I feel the need to keep Chris away from her. It could weird her out.

"Stairs or elevator?" I ask instead.

"How many stairs are we talking?" She tilts her head as she gazes up at me.

Does she know she tilts when she questions? Does she know how sexy I think that is?

"I think you can handle it, but I'll let you decide. Eighth floor."

"Three floors mean six flights. It's the end of a long day, but I've spent most of it sitting. I can handle it. Let's take the stairs."

We abandon the elevator just as it opens, heading instead for the nearby stairwell door.

As we climb, I tell her about some company stories that made it to my ears by way of Janet when we got back from the holidays. By the time we reach our destination, however, I'm speaking less, and she's gone silent.

"We're too young to be puffing and wheezing," Clover says when I hold open the stairwell door to the eighth floor.

"Speak for yourself," I tell her. "I'm older than you by five years. And for the record, I'm not puffing or wheezing."

I take a long, deep breath, realizing she'll know I looked at her birth date. Like a damn stalker. "But I may be gasping a little," I add to deflect her attention.

"Well, I'm definitely puffing, and for the record, I'm six years younger. But who's counting?"

I can't help a short bark of laughter because she let me know she's researched my age, too. Or at the very least, she saw it in a magazine.

As we walk along the hallway, the lights turn on when we approach and go off behind us afterward.

"After all these weeks, I still think that's cool," she says. "Like I'm on a spaceship or something."

Granted, Clover's a bit nerdy, which I find attractive. I can't imagine someone like Chelsea ever letting me know she's excited by energy-saving lighting. But I'll never know because Chelsea, as they say, is history. The Christmas party was made longer and less enjoyable by her presence, which is the opposite to what you want when in the company of a female. I won't be calling her again.

"The supply closet," I announce. You can't see into the large space because the privacy curtains are drawn across the glass walls inside.

When the lights come on, Clover gives an expected gasp. I don't care how old you are or what gender, when you suddenly see shelves of "stuff," it makes you feel like a kid in a toy store.

With me following behind—for the view—she walks down a row of shelving, picking up a cell phone, then a shampoo bottle, a chocolate bar wrapper with no chocolate, and car pamphlets."

"What? No car?" she asks.

"Wouldn't fit in here," I tease. "We keep those on the roof."

Her mouth opens slightly, then she realizes I'm kidding and shakes her head.

"Hardly a *closet* though," she says, reaching the end and turning up the next row.

"And hardly the place you should come after hours with Chris," I say, wondering why I've become her protector and sound like I'm her father.

"After hours?" she repeats. "You make it sound like a strip club."

I wait for her at the end of the row, keeping my arms crossed, staying relaxed, wishing Clover hadn't said "strip club." My brain conjures up a vision of her, naked except for the black boots I saw her wearing when I first saw her, and, of course, she's sliding around a pole.

"Just ill-advised," I say.

She comes to a halt in front of me.

"Then it's not the place I should come with anyone," she says pointedly, "*after* hours." Sounding defensive, she adds, "And for the record, I have zero interest in Chris Arruda."

That's good to hear. I should apologize and tell her I didn't mean to imply that she did. But I am so turned on being near her, I have to distract myself. The company rule is being tested, and I'm determined it will stand.

I've stopped in front of the Lovell perfume collection, waiting for her to find it. But she's looking straight at me, not at the surrounding products. Leaning past her to grab a bottle, I brush her shoulder, which is clad in a soft black, mock turtleneck sweater. It suddenly seems as enticing as a bikini.

A small sound comes from her throat, and she closes her eyes, tilts her head back—again, super sexy. She thinks I'm closing in to kiss her, and the invitation is clear. Well, fuck!

"Here you go," I say, holding up the glass bottle I've just picked up.

Her eyes pop open. She frowns, coming back to reality, stares at my mouth a moment longer, which really stretches my control.

Then, still without speaking, she takes the perfume and studies it. Suddenly, Clover is all-professional designer again.

"It's the first one Bonvier helped bring to market, in the eighties," she says.

I'm impressed, and for so many reasons, but I only say, "You did your homework."

She nods, her attention on the shelf housing the collection.

"It's striking to see them all together, some that aren't even made any longer."

Picking up a few in turn, she runs her hand over the various shapes of the bottles, and then examines the packaging behind each. She snaps a photo on her phone, then finally looks at me again.

"Surely none of these are for taking since there's only one of each," she says.

"Follow me," I tell her and turn away, glad to stop looking at her for a few seconds as I walk toward the freebies room. With no cold showers handy, I think of my last great round of golf. Opening another door, I step back and let her go in ahead of me.

"In here, you can take whatever you like," I explain, "within reason. It wouldn't be cool to have the entire stock wiped out and find you've opened an eBay store."

That makes her laugh, and my desire is ramped up again. Keep talking, I remind myself.

"From what I understand, my employees find this to be one of the best perks of the job. And I'm sorry no one showed it to you before. Do you know we have a gym?"

"I do. And half-price lattes."

Then she hasn't been kept completely in the dark. "The only rule is that you have to leave two of something for the archives."

"And Lovell's products?" she asks, as single-minded as I am when chasing par on a favorite golf course.

"Not sure where those are, actually."

She smiles. "Not grabbing freebies too often?" Clover asks.

I shrug, and we wander the smaller room with fewer shelves until she finds the perfume. I notice they're from recent years. Boxes of them, next to boxes of other similar bottles of cologne and lipsticks we've created ads for.

"See anything you like?" I ask. And just like that, she's facing me, giving me that golden-eyed look that I find totally mesmerizing.

I see someone I like. But I don't say that out loud. In fact, I'm congratulating myself on how this is nearly over. Nothing law-suit worthy has occurred, nor have I broken any cardinal rules. And then the lights go out.

Clover shrieks and jumps toward me, slamming her body against mine. As soon as she moved, of course, the sensor-driven lights come back on. Except now she's holding onto my sweater with both hands, her knuckles pressing into my chest.

"Sorry," she mumbles, looking up at me, as blood rushes from my brain to parts south. Then her gaze looks on mine, and she doesn't step back. My body screams, *Hell, yes!*

Sliding my arms around her, I say, "I'm not sorry. Not at all."

Her eyes widen and her lips part. Then I do what I've wanted to do for months. I kiss her.

11

Clover

When Adam crushes his lips against mine, I swear—dramatic as this sounds—it is life-changing. A stupid cliché, except in this moment, it isn't stupid. I have never been kissed in such a way that I'm both dancing along the edge of the most intense desire I have ever experienced while also feeling the most comfortable familiarity.

My mouth knows his, as if we've done this before.

I relax against him, thrilled I didn't misread the situation as I did a few minutes earlier. The kiss is hard and fast, our tongues touch and tangle. My body is hot and desperate, and I'm throbbing between my legs, wishing I wasn't still standing.

I want to pull Adam down onto the floor and open for him, everything pulsing and aching and, yes, wet. In these few heady moments, I don't have an ounce of inhibition. I cannot think of anything beyond the fact that he is mine and

I am his. Just as though we've been a couple for a billion years.

My hands start to roam his chest up to his shoulders, flittering everywhere while wishing I could touch his skin. His hands make their way down my back to cup my backside, tilting me against him. His arousal is evident. I'm about to grind against it, but I'm not given the chance.

Adam is the first to pull back.

Shit! I hate that moment-after feeling. A little chill races up my spine and a big balloon of emptiness bursts over me, enveloping my body in wasted adrenaline and frustrated yearning.

"Now I'm the one who's sorry," he says, his tone annoyed. Or maybe that's how Adam's frustration sounds.

I wince. Not the words I want to hear but absolutely necessary if we are to put this behind us.

"Me, too," I say. "The thing with the lights." As if my momentary fear explained our making out like a couple about to enjoy a conjugal visit in the penitentiary.

"No," he says. "Entirely my fault. I just . . . reacted," he explains. "To your closeness and . . . We should get out of here."

Because it might happen again, I think.

He was affected by my closeness. I take that little nugget and store it away to consider later when I'm alone. Along with how much I enjoyed his hands on my butt.

So that our trip isn't a total waste—besides having the single most sensational kiss of my life—I snag three different packages of the client's perfume.

"Not going to keep them," I explain. "Just until the task is complete."

He shrugs, obviously not caring if I take every freebie in sight. Back in the hall, we fall silent on the way to the elevator. He punches the down button a little harshly.

I cannot help myself. I start to talk into the quietness. "It's awful when you get on an elevator and two people are already on it having a conversation. You become an unwitting eavesdropper," I say. "Sometimes they stop talking altogether. Not sure if that's worse. Then you wonder if they were speaking about you, or if it was simply something so juicy and private they had to shut up."

I jabber to cover the uncomfortable awkwardness that increases the further away we get from the moment our lips were fused and our tongues were stroking. But talking about juicy gossip is stupid since we just did something of the extreme juiciness.

"It's like the age-old question," Adam says, staring at the light display above the closed doors, which indicates the elevator is now being hauled up to us with the speed of tiny, exhausted mice. "Is it worse to overhear someone having sex, hoping they don't know that you hear them, or is it worse to be overheard and realize someone's listening?"

My brain empties. I've never contemplated that conundrum either way, and having him discuss sex after what occurred a minute ago seems incredibly poor timing. Stupid conversation, number two.

Before I can begin to argue for one side or the other, hearing sex or being heard having it, the elevator doors open. I step inside thinking this is going to be the longest ride of my life. But Adam doesn't get in.

I have a feeling I know why, although I might be stretching my own irresistibility a wee bit.

"I'm going back to my office," he explains. "Good night, Ms. Mitchell."

And then we stand here. The formality of my last name sounds more sensual than if he'd said my first name or no name at all.

"Good night," I reply. Still, nothing happens.

"It works better if you press a button," Adam says before reaching in and doing so. His arm clears the closing doors, and he disappears from view.

I hope I can make my way home with my brain still fogged by unfulfilled lust and that irritating riddle he posed. Quite a while later, when I'm in my own little, shared bathroom, brushing my teeth, I suddenly blurt out, "Chelsea Sweeney," spraying the mirror with toothpaste.

Why had he kissed me when he is dating her so publicly? I stare at my own horrified expression. I hope I'm not the other woman.

$♥$♥$♥$

I don't see Adam the following day or the next or the one after that. Not long in the scheme of life, but it feels like an eternity. I stop keeping track of how many days. I'm on edge from the sheer unknown of if or when I'll run into him. Plus, it snows big time, turning Boston into a commuter mess. My first storm since moving here. Before it hits, Chris, Leslie, and I had our fieldtrip to Lovell HQ on the North Shore, which is the seacoast north of Boston up to the New Hampshire border.

We end up in a city I've never been to with Chris driving, Leslie riding shotgun, and me in the back like their unhappy, unwanted child. The meeting was uneventful, and we were all glad to see the backside of one another after returning to the office.

Even during the car ride and in every quiet moment after that, I think of Adam, and I wish the kiss hadn't happened. Knowing how great it was makes me want him more than when I merely imagined how it might be.

I have no idea where he is. Each day at work, however, is another tormenting possibility that I'll see him. Half of me wants to run into him—truly, like around a corner with our bodies smashing full force against one another. I daydream that scenario whenever I leave my desk and stroll the hallways of Bonvier, Inc.

The other part of me, the sensible side, is glad our paths have no reason to cross.

Get a grip, Clover!

I stay late all week because currently, work is my life, and I have nothing to rush home to. I finish the art for an ad that will expand a client's saddle soap market to leather shoes. Right up my alley, bringing sex appeal to dirty shoes.

Last one on the design floor, I swing my bag over my shoulder and I'm humming an Adele tune when the elevator doors open. Abruptly the sound dies in my throat.

Adam! As luck—or really unfortunate coincidence—would have it, here *he* is.

Seeing him again unexpectedly because this is not his private elevator, I become a statue before remembering to breathe.

He flashes his lopsided grin, and I feel it in my chest, as well as between my legs.

Looking around, I see no one to ride down with us, and then the doors nearly close in my face.

That's when he sticks his arm between them and asks, "Are you coming?"

No, but I'd like to be. *Ba-da-dum-dum!*

With my mouth feeling like it's filled with cotton balls, unable to say something politely *normal* a scant week since his tongue was in my mouth, I nod.

Stepping into the suddenly too-small space, I turn to face the closing doors as one is supposed to do in a civil society. Although our madly passionate kiss and groping had been anything but civilized!

As we descend from the design floor to the lobby, I'm unable to think of anything except how his mouth devoured mine during those few minutes of madness. Intense, hot, sexy minutes that had left me wet and wanting, with my pulse pounding like a nightclub sound system.

My body is doing exactly the same thing right now with nothing but the memory. A powerful memory of a powerful man's perfect kiss.

Stay calm, breathe—at least shallowly. But breathing makes me savor his musky, woodsy scent, taking me right back to our astounding kiss. I'm so aroused I could climax with a single caress in the right spot.

Adam remains silent, just behind my right shoulder.

When he touches me, trailing a finger softly down my back, I gasp and jump at the same time. Whipping my head around, however, I find Adam isn't even looking at me, simply thumbing across his cell phone. Perhaps he's on the billionaire's equivalent of a dating app, swiping right or left for princesses, celebs, and socialites.

I could have been a socialite, I remind myself.

Despite being fascinated by this man, I'm eager to escape the descending metal cage, no matter how smooth and high-tech it is. And it is, like everything else at Bonvier, Inc. The lighting isn't harsh, classical music plays for the short ride between floors, and under my feet, it looks like Italian marble.

Far too romantic for a goddamn elevator. We're nearly at the lobby when Adam does precisely what I've been fantasizing about for the last thirty seconds. He presses the big red stop button.

No. He. Did. Not!

Yes. He. Did. *Shit!*

The next part of my fantasy has him pressing me against the back wall and somehow removing the winter layers between us—his worsted wool slacks, my knitted sweater dress and cashmere tights.

"What are you doing?" I ask, speaking without turning this time because I don't want to look into those steely-gray irises.

"In less than a minute, we'll go our separate ways for the evening," he points out. "I wanted to offer a better apology than I gave before."

My first thought is, *for what?* Followed really quickly by oh, the kiss! Yet to me, another round of *sorry, sorry, sorry* seems like picking at a wound. But I could humor him, especially if our rule-breaking kiss is bothering him this much. Frankly, it makes me a little sad.

Finally, I face him, instantly uncomfortable having the elevator doors at my back. Also immediately captured by his eyes, oh so intriguingly locked on my own.

"I didn't want to make matters worse by coming down to the design floor," he confesses when I say nothing.

In truth, my brain has switched off again because of his masculine awesomeness, which he exudes as easily as some men waft B.O. Definitely a problem if I am to communicate with any degree of sense. Luckily, he's still doing the talking.

"Short of trapping you in this elevator, there wasn't any way to speak to you face-to-face without a big deal, like calling you up to my office."

His words finally spur my tongue. "You almost make it sound like you knew when I would be waiting for an elevator." I try to chuckle.

Adam's nostrils flare slightly, and he sighs.

Wow! He had known. I would make it a point to scan for security cameras tomorrow.

Meanwhile, I need to let him off the hook because we had both been equally culpable.

"Apology duly noted, but unnecessary," I tell him. "You didn't pounce on me, and I didn't shrink away and grasp for smelling salts like some Victorian heroine."

This earns me his smile again. "Victorian heroine?"

"I read historical romance occasionally." When I'm in bed before sleep. That is, if I'm not busy fantasizing about him!

"And in those books, does a lot of pouncing and shrinking happen?" he asks.

I smile a little. He's teasing me. "The men often mistakenly think the women are fragile and prone to fainting and, yes, shrinking away from any kind of passion. But in the stories I read, the ladies surprise the men. As it turns out, they are . . . ," I trail off.

"Up for it?" he asks.

I roll my eyes at the term.

"Is there a problem, Mr. Bonvier?"

I nearly jump out of my winter boots at the disembodied voice coming from the elevator's control panel.

I've forgotten where we are for a moment, and I realize I don't need to worry about cameras on the design floor. I need to think about the one trained on us now.

"Is that Jake?" Adam asks, keeping his glance on me and not gazing up at the camera.

"Yes, sir."

"I just wanted to have a private conversation with my art director. Not the smartest place to conduct our discussion, is it?"

"No, sir. I mean, yes, sir. I mean, I don't listen to the elevators, sir, unless the intercom button is pushed."

"Or the stop button," Adam surmises.

"No, sir. At least, not when I saw it was you in there."

"Thank you, Jake."

Adam punches the green button, and we start our descent again. My eyes are probably like dinner plates when I think about him apologizing to me. Jake may or may not have been listening. I think about what we said. Adam hadn't mentioned what he was apologizing for, but I'd talked about pouncing.

"I accept your apology for the harsh reprimand you gave me in front of my team," I insist loudly, hoping that satisfies Jake if he is, in fact, enjoying our elevator ride like a reality TV show.

Adam narrows his eyes, but gives a wry smile. He knows what I'm doing, and I hope he appreciates it. At last, the doors open.

"Good bye," I say before darting out of the elevator. I can't help glancing at the security desk and the aforementioned Jake. Naturally, I've seen him before because I'm often one of the last to leave.

He nods. I nod. I can't tell what he's heard or what he thinks about what he's heard.

And then I'm out, darting past Adam Bonvier's car and driver. Fortunately, not a drop of rain anywhere.

12

Adam

I don't rush after Clover. I never intended to. I'm doing everything I can to stay away from her and not risk repeating the idiotic stunt I pulled in the supply closet.

Except I just trapped her in an elevator with me.

The pretense of apologizing again was a ruse to get close and talk after I've been solid as a boy scout where she's concerned. I've managed to keep my distance for eight days. Sure, I had to put an ocean between us to do it, but I did it. I flew across the Atlantic to France last week to put Clover out of range. It was a convenient distraction since over Christmas, my father was on my case to get to Paris and make sure everything is fluid in the new office. In addition to still sitting on the board, he has my utmost respect, more than any other man I know, so if he says go, I go.

And after kissing my art director, I deemed it the ideal time. Almost pointless on all counts. At Bonvier Paris, I simply made everyone nervous that I was going to hire or fire. I never stopped thinking about Clover, and I've been back barely twenty-four hours, and already checking one particular camera feed on my laptop.

When she packed up her things to leave for the night, I got on the employee elevator that I was holding on the ninth floor. Totally premeditated move. But I figure if I encounter her only at work in benign places, like the elevator or the lobby, what will be the harm?

Of course, I shouldn't have touched her. It accomplished nothing.

As she disappears into the frigid Boston night, I make myself get into my limo and drive past Clover without even waving, when more than anything, I want to invite her to spend the evening with me.

After ending up with my hands nearly under her clothes a week ago, I've been doing some hard thinking. This obsession has thrown me for a loop. I'm good with telling Clover there can be no dating within the company. Maybe I should be more specific and explain no kissing or touching or fucking fellow employees, either. Even if the employee is me, and I'm behaving like an asshole who doesn't know any better.

I swear, at the moment when I looked into her startled eyes after the lights came back on in the sample room, she'd been one hundred percent irresistible. I conveniently forgot the company rule, or more precisely, I broke it like it was made of balsa instead of iron. I *had* to kiss her, even when my intentions had been to keep her safe from Chris because I'd suddenly felt protective . . . or more honestly, possessive.

For some reason, where she's concerned, I haven't been able to stay cool and aloof. Tonight was another misstep. Who knows what might've happened if Jake hadn't reminded me we were on candid camera?

It doesn't help that I can tell she's into me, too. If she wasn't interested, I wouldn't find her so attractive. Or at least, not as much. But not only did she let me kiss me a week ago, Clover was as hot for me as I was for her. It's not vanity that tells me Chris would be sporting a black eye, courtesy of our art director, if he'd tried anything in the sample room. It's gut instinct.

As my limo traverses the streets toward home, I conjure the long-deceased Rachel in my mind, letting the weight of guilt from her shocking car accident sit firmly on my shoulders. The thought of her sliding off the I-93 expressway, wrapping her car around a tree, manages to dampen any remaining ardor. If only Rachel had chosen to sue me and Bonvier, Inc., instead of getting wasted and going for a drive.

Even if the company had been brought to its knees, it would have been worth every penny for her to still be alive.

In order to make her death not be as senseless as it otherwise felt, my father and I put in place the no-dating rule, and in truth, it seems to make the workplace happier, less dramatic overall.

As soon as I finish wrestling with my conscience, chastising myself again, and banishing Rachel's memory, I admit I still want Clover. Now that I've tasted those bowed lips that I've been obsessing over, felt her shapely ass, and inhaled that sexy floral fragrance she wears, I want her more than ever.

Strangely, I'm also more determined than before to keep to my own blasted rule. Other than hijacking an elevator, I don't intend to spook Clover or make her uncomfortable. I plan to stop making myself crazy over her, too. I'll get out my little virtual violin and play myself a song of pity, but this isn't easy. I'm used to having what I want. The exact make and model car for when David isn't driving me, the insanely decadent vacation spot no matter how impossible to reach, the absolute most succulent food at the best restaurant paired with the rarest fine wine.

Whatever it is, if I desire it, I get it.

Self-imposed deprivation bites. It really does.

There's one alternative—ask Clover Mitchell if she would rather have a relationship with me than a job at my company. We would have a great time for however long it lasts. After that kiss and the way she responded—not to make light of how her ass felt in my hands, but I'm sure sex between us would be out of this world. And I know she's into me like I want her.

And if I'm reading her right, she would be a fun person to spoil with whatever her heart desires, be it jewelry or cars or more of her sexy shoes. It's the easiest thing in the world to picture her on my yacht this summer in a tiny bikini with a glass of champagne in her hand, reaching for my cock with her other one.

What a blast to show her a level of luxury she probably can't conceive of, a far cry from her taking the T to some shitbox in Allston.

Regardless, I think I know what her response to my offer would be, and my pride isn't prepared for that answer. She's driven to succeed and has a sparkle when she's talking about design projects. I want to see her sparkle outside of work.

Hell! Paris did nothing to assuage my infatuation, a good word for why I'm still imagining stripping bare a woman I've already written off as untouchable.

I woke up this morning, wishing I could see her golden-brown eyes first thing, maybe her sexy smile to start my day. I was thinking which color sheets would suit her best! Her caramel-brown hair splayed across my sapphire blue pillowcase while she drifts off to sleep after I've done my level best to give her the most intense climax of her life.

If I go home now, it'll be more of the same lewd fantasies.

I lean forward and tell David to take me to the indoor driving range on Washington Street. I proceed to whack the hell out of golf balls with my favorite Honma BERES driver until my rib cage is sore from twisting.

I have a feeling Clover's ribcage is a beautiful sight, and I want to trail kisses over every perfect rib. *Damn!* I have the hots for her bad.

"Another bucket of balls," I tell the attendant.

13

Clover

I don't know what to do, and it's not a state I'm comfortable being in. After that first disastrous presentation last year, which I remind myself was *not* my fault, I've never produced anything that the client didn't love. Even Leslie's ice-pop blow job had been comic relief to the client rather than a game-over mistake. Also, not my fault, although no one ever figured it out.

In any case, I've led my team to a string of great designs for Bonvier, Inc. But at this moment, it is not happening. I'm playing with the cap on one of Lovell brand's previous perfume bottles, twirling it in my fingers, staring at the bottle and its label, and the little cream-colored box it came in, but not *seeing* it. Not even really thinking about it.

And for the first time in my brief but stellar career, I can't come up with anything. Nada. Zilch.

Despite going with an uptight Chris and a hostile Leslie to the meeting the day after the kiss—and all things in my life are now thought of as *before* or *after* that kiss—still, I don't have a clear vision. We didn't meet with Mrs. Lovell, but rather with one of her top executives. She explained the new perfume was aimed at a younger demographic.

"With money or struggling?" I asked, having keenly felt the difference between buying whatever fragrance I wanted versus bargain hunting for something that didn't smell cheap but was light on the purse.

Leslie immediately added, "Not that we think any of your customers are poor. We know you're aiming at a better clientele."

Yikes! The Lovell exec and I exchanged a glance at her tactless words.

Then the woman said, "Mrs. Lovell, our founder's daughter, believes her company's scents appeal to people of all creeds, colors, and classes."

Well said. Even though to be honest, most of the fragrances were in the upper stratosphere of cost.

"To be clear," I said, because Leslie most certainly didn't speak for me, "I asked my question for a few reasons, none of which are because I think middle- or lower-income people should be marketed fragrance of lesser quality. I asked because the packaging could be made more cheaply and even the bottle design could be less expensive if the demographics warrant that. Apart from that, I'll give the label and package a different vibe if the perfume is meant to be on the fun, everyday end of the spectrum versus the special event end."

Leslie stared at me as if she had no idea who I was or how I got there. Chris remained silent, apparently wanting to hear the answer. The Lovell executive nodded.

"Are you sure you're the art head and not in marketing? Because you've really zeroed in on something crucial."

I couldn't even look at my co-workers, knowing they wouldn't be happy. I listened and took notes as the exec explained about the clientele they were hoping to reach with their new perfume, "Yes, Please!" It's youthful, sexy, middle income, everyday wear.

"We think our customers will wear this to their job but also add an extra spritz for clubbing that night. We don't want a fussy vibe. No diamond-dripping exotic beauty with bare shoulders in the print ad. A relatable model. Same for a live spokesperson, if we get that far. But always a trusted friend telling our buyer that this is *the one* to wear. Maybe the model has ear gauges or a nose piercing—not both. We don't want to go over the top and alienate the average young working woman or college student."

"Great," Chris said. "That's what we needed to hear. Our creative department will have multiple campaigns worked out for Mrs. Lovell when she comes in. And our art department will knock it out of the park as usual."

He'd gone all team-Bonvier on us, which I thought was a good idea given how Mrs. Lovell's exec had nearly given me his job.

So if I'm such hot stuff who understood the plan while in that meeting, why am I struggling? Basically, I *am* the demographic, yet I can't come up with something that isn't tired or cliché. Grabbing the desk phone, I tap Cara's extension before rolling my eyes at my own laziness. I could have stood up and gone out of my office to talk to her.

Instead, I watch through the glass wall as she picks up her phone about fifteen yards away. When she sees who it is, she turns to look at me while she speaks. "What's up, boss lady?"

I jump. That's not how I think of myself. I am just a designer trying to come up with something that will blow the client's socks off.

Maybe that's the problem.

"Get everyone together and meet me at the table."

"Yes, ma'am!"

I sigh. I don't like being *ma'am*ed, either. Although I know she's joking, some of the designers say it without irony. Others call me Ms. Mitchell or, as she just did, *boss* *lady.* So in five minutes, when I've given the team time to assemble, bringing their drinks and snacks with them because we are all like children who draw pictures for a living, I join them.

"First of all, I've never said this before, but from now on, everyone calls me Clover."

Eyes widening. Cara raises an eyebrow.

"I know," I continue, "it's not the most inspiring name for your team leader, but it's all I've got." That makes them laugh. "Seriously, though, I think I've been selfish, trying to make my mark here by doing all the big designing myself. Frankly, it's stupid, and I need help."

I have their attention. I set the three different bottles of perfume I've held onto since the kiss, as well as their packaging onto the table, facing me. Lovell might be visible on the side of the boxes, but otherwise, no brand is obvious.

"What do you think?" I ask.

The client's name comes springing from everyone's lips. Because despite not seeing the name, they've used the same pale Tiffany blue and gold packaging and clear bottles with pale blue labels since before most of us were born.

"Precisely," I say. "And when you think of Lovell, what next? What's your perception?"

A round of answers came flying at me with words such as *elegant, chic, sophisticated, expensive.*

I nod. "How do we come up with a new design—bottle shape, label, packaging—for a favorite brand, one that still makes everyone think of Lovell at first sight but not in exactly the same way? With all the good, high-qual thoughts but for a younger demographic?"

I give them my notes from the Lovell exec of what absolutely has to be included in the rebranding—the colors, the emotions, the shapes and textures. "Let the great ideas flow, people."

To my delight, they do. At the end of a mere half hour, I pull aside three designers who really seem to "get" it and who are engaged and interested. I put them solely on this assignment. I even tell them I will back off until they have a chance to make magic. Because our department has other demands and tasks, and I need to oversee them all, not just dive deeply into this one the way I've been doing.

"Please give me some fabulous, comprehensive ideas by the end of the week. Maybe three mockups, but I'll take two standouts. As soon as I get the scintillating campaign copy, I'll give it to you to make sure we match."

Off go my happy designers. Those who don't get to be in that glamour group are quickly delegated to other tasks I've been hoarding. Until I see everyone humming along with purpose and the tension seeps out of me, I honestly don't realize what a dreadful boss I've been.

From the first apple logo onward, I made the decision on every feature of each design and simply asked someone to make it the way I wanted it. Mostly, they get it right. If not, I redo it.

At that moment, I'm thrilled to climb out of the rabbit hole I've made for myself and excited to see what my team comes up with. For the first time in four months, I feel like a department head and not like the cocky girl who's been promoted prematurely.

And then I think of Adam Bonvier.

OK, it isn't like I don't think about him as soon as I open my eyes. Or enter the building, taking a long look at his painting as I pass it. Or every time the elevator doors open whether I'm inside peering out hoping to see him, or outside peering in. Or when I go down to the lobby at night, wondering if David will be waiting for him.

But I haven't seen him in weeks. The lack of Adam Bonvier should make things easier, but it hasn't. I am increasingly desperate to smell his cologne. *How pathetic!* And the only thing that keeps me from punching his floor number on the elevator's panel, just on the chance I might see him while the doors open and close, is the upcoming Lovell meeting.

Mrs. Lovell is his father's long-standing client, an important one. She helped put Bonvier on the map with her account decades ago. When she comes next week to see what we've been working on—the copywriters, live and print media, and my art department's designs—Adam will be there.

And for me, that day can't come soon enough. My thought process is messed up considering we didn't have our design yet, and all I want is to wish the time away until I lay eyes on the bossman.

Finally, it's the day. With high school mentality, I pray Adam will sit next to me like he did the last time we were in a meeting together. With an apprehensive shiver, I also hope he won't. It'll throw me off during the most important presentation I've yet been a part of.

I needn't have worried. At the time the meeting is supposed to begin, he hasn't shown at all.

I'm not the only one surprised and disappointed. The client seems downright miffed. Mrs. Lovell is in her seventies, dressed as elegantly as the brand she's known for, in a navy blue, large-collared, fitted jacket over a dove-gray turtleneck and matching slacks. Of course, I notice her low-heeled, navy leather, lace-up boots and envy them. We could definitely bond over those babies.

Currently, Mrs. Lovell's tapping her gold pen on the notebook she brought with her. She has already been served coffee, the chit-chat began and has now ended. Still, Chris doesn't lower the lights. He glances at his phone, either to see the time or to check for a text.

"Where is Adam?" Mrs. Lovell asks abruptly. She's old enough to be his grandmother, and her question sounds as though she's asking after a wayward child.

"Unavoidably delayed," Chris says.

I know he's lying. He has no idea. None of us do. After all, as CEO, Adam could be anywhere, even out of the country. Maybe he has forgotten and zipped back to Paris. Although I've heard his assistant, Janet, whom I hadn't yet met, is more efficient than God when it comes to getting our boss where he is supposed to be.

Chris texts a message and smiles at their important client. I think he looks sickly rather than reassuring.

"Shall we begin?" he asks after another minute of awkward silence. "Mr. Bonvier is not directly involved in this campaign anyway."

"Whatever do you mean?" Mrs. Lovell asks, tucking a lock of stylishly short, silvery white hair behind her ear, exposing a chunky gold earring that matches the buttons on her jacket. "He has always come to discuss my products."

"Not always," Chris says, and the client scowls at being contradicted. I think Chris has blundered.

"His father always had a hand in my company's account," Mrs. Lovell adds, reminding everyone in the room that she's been doing this longer than any of us. "Bonvier senior has a good eye."

I startle at the term, thinking of the man whose portrait hangs in the lobby. Does he share my passion for design?

"And Adam *always* comes to my meetings," Mrs. Lovell insists.

A battle is brewing, which I don't think Chris can or should win, when his phone buzzes. After he glances at it, his relief is palpable.

"Adam is in the building and on his way!"

The entire room perks up. Our CEO is suddenly our Duke of Wellington at the Battle of Waterloo. In truth, Mrs. Lovell's jacket reminds me a little of Napoleon's uniform.

Then the room falls silent. The final few moments of waiting are excruciating. The client doesn't want to begin, and Adam's tardiness seems like an insult that's being delivered over and over.

Mrs. Lovell keeps tapping the table with her pen.

Chris tries to say a few words about the campaign without saying anything important since the client is staring into the distance. Her eyes are narrowed with disappointment.

I fully expect Adam to get an earful when he arrives. However, as soon as he strolls in calmly a minute later, looking impeccable in a dark blue suit, she relaxes and actually smiles at him.

"Adam, you are late! You kept me waiting," Mrs. Lovell teases, almost coquettish.

What the actual? Does he have that effect on women of all ages?

"Indeed, I am, Maisie."

Maisie! I can practically hear the name repeated silently in every mind around the table.

"And my sincere apologies," he adds. Then he nods to those assembled, his gaze holding mine for a moment, making my body heat to a boil in under three seconds.

"Leslie, would you mind moving so I can sit beside Mrs. Lovell?" he asks.

Leslie does as requested. Unfortunately, this puts her next to me, and we are not besties by any stretch of the imagination. I can practically feel her resentment, the source of which remains a mystery to me.

"I apologize to everyone for not getting here on time," Adam says, "but I decided to stop off at our prototype group. I asked them to create something special for our client, and at the last moment when I was on my way here, they told me it was ready."

Like a courting lover, he places the package he's been holding in his big hand on the table before her. "For you, Maisie."

"Oh my," she says, and I could swear she flutters her eyelashes.

We all lean forward as she puts down her pen and opens the crisp, bright-white paper sack. Looking in, she exclaims. While the rest of us wait with bated breath, she pulls out . . . my team's design for the latest perfume bottle.

I am stunned, to put it mildly. I thought we were showing only graphics today. Seeing it in 3D is rather amazing.

"It's perfect!" Mrs. Lovell declares.

"Then the meeting is over," our boss says, "and I can take you to dinner now."

Everyone laughs. Adam probably could have got away with stealing the client from the meeting, but Chris chooses that moment to dim the lights with the press of a button.

Mrs. Lovell settles in with her eyes on the screen as she's presented with a storyboard for a commercial, a dummy magazine spread, my team's design for the bottle and its box, and finally, the new label. How much better for our success that she is holding the prototype in her ring-adorned hand.

"I am not sure I am sold on the music for the commercial," she says, proving she's involved and interested in all aspects of her company's product. Immediately, Chris presses another button and shuts off the soundtrack.

"On the whole," she says, "quite satisfactory. Who came up with this smashing innovation?"

She holds up the glass bottle in classic Lovell-blue. Other than the color, however, it doesn't look anything like its predecessors. Straight and angular on one side, the other side curves inward like a crescent moon. I like it even more in person. The cap is a risk, though. Instead of the usual gold color, it's imitation brushed nickel.

A few people look at me, but I think of those who are upstairs on the design floor. I mentally compose a list to give credit where it's due. Yes, I tweaked, but my designers designed to perfection.

"Ms. Mitchell is our art director." It's Adam's voice, not Chris's.

Leslie tenses beside me.

"Thank you," I say, feeling a little heat rise in my cheeks, "but I have a team of astonishingly talented designers, and in this case, Cara Richards, Mariel Burton, and Trevor McDonald were assigned to your account."

"A modest young lady," Mrs. Lovell says. "Since it was under your direction, you had better take praise when you can. Another day, you might as easily have to take the blame."

Been there, done that, I think.

Mrs. Lovell looks at Adam. "I'm ready for dinner in Boston's finest. And I hope you bring Ms. Mitchell along so I can tell her of some ideas I have to spruce up my perfume line. Even the classics could use a makeover."

I nearly gasp. Adam shoots his glance my way, then he smiles. "Of course. If you don't have any plans, Clover."

"I don't," I say, still not believing I'm going out with a client and the CEO to dinner.

I wait for Adam to mention Chris, who'd previously said to Mrs. Lovell how much he was looking forward to dining with her during the chit-chat before Adam arrived. Or there's Leslie, who is the nominal manager of the Lovell account, even if the Bonviers, father and son, have more connection to Mrs. Lovell than anyone.

Yet Adam says nothing more, rising to his feet. Apparently, he's unconcerned over how the others fight it out for a seat at the table.

Not to be left behind or have his plans rearranged, Chris says, "I've made reservations at Mistral's for four, including Leslie. I'll see if they can squeeze in another chair."

"I don't care for an odd number," Mrs. Lovell says. "Perhaps it's how I was taught to throw a dinner party. In any case, I've eaten with you before, Mr. Arruda. If they can't fit four chairs at our table, then I'm sure you won't mind staying behind so I can get to know your talented designer."

I bite back a smile at Chris's expression—utterly sour. However, in the end, he pulls rank and Leslie is left behind, positively fuming.

I'm going to enjoy myself tonight.

14

Clover

Of course the table fits four people, but I'm a little taken back to be one of the chosen. Fortunately, I dressed well for the all-department meeting, and my burgundy dress with black accents and patent-leather black Gucci pumps to match won't be out of place at one of the priciest restaurants in Boston.

Mrs. Lovell came to Bonvier by taxi from her hotel. Even though her company is on the North Shore, she lives far enough away from the city that she's spending the night in Boston. Adam's assistant ordered a stretch limo for the short trip to Mistral's on Columbus Avenue, so we all climb in.

There's a bar on board. When Mrs. Lovell says, "Champagne, if you please, Adam," it's as though I've fallen through a glamorous trapdoor. One minute, I'm in the conference room, ready for a night of foraging in my fridge for a meal alone in front of the TV. And now, I'm being whisked toward fine dining with interesting people, while my billionaire boss makes like a bartender.

Adam pops the cork and pours without spilling a drop. I'm impressed. Chris hands out the glasses, and we let Mrs. Lovell toast to the successful new campaign.

By the time we're seated at a quiet table, treated to the mouth-watering aromas of Mistral's French-Mediterranean cuisine, the champagne has taken away any nerves I have. I'm already enjoying myself, especially watching Adam out of work, speaking animatedly to Maisie Lovell, who clearly adores him.

Who wouldn't? There is literally nothing about this man not to adore! Adam talks briefly about his recent trip to Paris, mentioning Bonvier, Inc.'s expansion, occupying offices overlooking the Seine. I know the area well. Mrs. Lovell chimes in that she has a pied-à-terre in the same quarter, which upon further questioning sounds more like a townhouse than a small apartment.

When she turns her attention to me, I answer Mrs. Lovell's questions about where I learned my craft, happy to add to all the talk of France by mentioning that I went to 1984, an oddly named French design school.

"I audited some classes there, after graduating from Parsons School of Design."

Far more interesting to me, she tells me how she went to college and got a business degree, the first female in her family to do so.

Then, when asked, and only because she seems truly interested, I wander into the zone that usually makes people's eyes glaze over, explaining the principles of design—contrast, emphasis, pattern, repetition, movement, space, and balance.

Probably afraid I'll start drawing examples on a cocktail napkin, Mrs. Lovell slips in an unexpected question. "Where is your family from? Are they Bostonians?"

I hesitate, not wanting to delve into my personal life. Not one little bit.

"No." I glance at Adam to see him looking attentively in my direction. "My family is in New York." Not *from* it, exactly, just currently in it, but I don't elaborate. If I were to go into specifics of our Australian roots and our Rocky Mountain, Colorado, branch of the family where the first US Henley candies were made before the company moved to NYC, someone would put two and two together.

Chris appears bored, tapping his fingers on the tablecloth and looking for the waiter. He's already heard my incomplete, edited story at my job interview with him and the media VP.

"Anyone I would know?" Mrs. Lovell asks. "When my father was alive, our corporate HQ was in New York City. That's where I spent my youth."

I am momentarily tongue-tied. Yes, she would certainly know my parents, or at least, know *of* them. I'm about to shrug it off and lie like a rug, when she laughs.

"Don't worry, Clover. I'm not a snob really. I don't care if your father digs ditches or is a diamond king. I deal with people as they are and for who they are."

I nod. "That's refreshing." And then I don't say anything more about my background or my family. Instead, as smoothly as possible, I ask her about her company and where she wants to take it next. She is, as my father would say, a dynamo.

Nearly two hours later, Mrs. Lovell is yawning into her second glass of brandy, while still pushing her fork around the remnants of a small piece of tiramisu. Personally, I could doze off right where I sit.

Adam is leaning back, arms folded across his chest, relaxed and handsome as ever. I imagine it's how he looks in his own home, seated on an expensive super-comfortable couch, perfectly at ease. If I was on the receiving end of his heavy-lidded look, I wouldn't feel like snoozing any longer.

"Shall I signal for the check?" Chris asks. Of the four of us, he has clearly been the least interested in the entire evening, no doubt here for the sake of his VP status.

The waiter comes to the table before Chris has even finished the question. Naturally, Adam is the one to proffer a credit card, an uber-exclusive American Express Black card. He catches me looking at it and probably thinks I've never seen one before. My father has one, although my mother prefers her equally rare JP Morgan card.

Adam shrugs a little sheepishly, which I find charming.

Soon, we're walking through the nearly empty restaurant, Chris and I following behind our boss and our client

"Don't get used to this," he says quietly.

"What do you mean? Eating or walking?"

"Funny girl! I'm just letting you know that designers, even art directors, do *not* usually dine with clients. This is a one-off."

A little shiver runs down my spine at his tone. "I wasn't expecting tonight," I remind him.

He hesitates. "Of course not. I simply don't want your feelings hurt when you're not included next time."

Chris is only speaking from a place of kindness to save my sensitive state. Sure he is!

At the curb, Mistral's unusually generous complimentary car service awaits. Before she climbs in, Mrs. Lovell asks, "Who's going my way? I have a suite at The Four Seasons."

"Right by my place," Chris says, which I know is a bit of a stretch. He doesn't live near the Common but farther out, in the Back Bay. He boasted of it once when he looked over my résumé and saw my address. Nevertheless, he climbs in after her.

Naively, I ask the valet, "Will the driver go as far as Allston?"

The man's expression makes it clear that he won't. I step back as Adam leans down toward the open car door. But he doesn't climb in.

"Have a good evening, Mrs. Lovell." And then he closes it, and the car pulls away.

I find myself standing alone with Adam again. I'm buzzed from the hours of champagne, wine, and brandy, feeling warm and entirely at ease.

"Where the limo?" I ask.

"It was only hired to drop us off," he says, then shrugs.

Well, that's a bit of a downer, I think. But that's what Ubers are for. At least for the likes of me, but not for a wealthy man like Adam. I wonder if David is coming to pick him up.

"Are you planning on taking the T?" I ask, hugging my coat around me. Even as I say it jokingly, it strikes me funny. "My billionaire boss on the subway," I add, and I can't help chuckling.

He grins, crooked and sexy, at my words, and then he laughs. Really laughs, which makes me start up again. Finally, he turns to the valet. "A taxi, please."

There are many circling the busy area at this hour, and with the valet's signal, one pulls up instantly.

I stare at Adam. "Only one?" Does he think I'm actually going to take the T at that hour?

"We can share," he says. "It's safer."

Is it?

As soon as I slide into the back, I know the answer. It most certainly is not.

15

Adam

"I'm so impressed with you," I tell Clover as soon as I've given the taxi driver her address, which is far out of my way. I don't mind a bit.

Inadvertently, she sways closer before settling back against the hard, worn seat.

I know she's had a little too much to drink. Meeting with clients can do that to you. But the alcohol has made her drowsy rather than loud and obnoxious. That's confirmed when I feel her temple brush against my shoulder.

What can I do? I raise my arm and drape it around her. It feels natural and comfortable. And harmless. Not that I don't want to slide my hand around and over her full breast, but I won't. Another rule I live by is not to grope tipsy ladies.

"Are you really?" she asks, looking up at me, all soft-eyed and kissable. For a split second I forget what I've said.

116

I clench my teeth to stop from claiming her mouth under mine. Not going to happen.

All at once Clover realizes what she's doing. With a small gasp, she puts her hands on my side and pushes herself away.

I keep my face forward, not wanting to embarrass her, but I wish she'd stayed leaning against me. Then I understand her question.

"I am. Really impressed," I repeat. "The presentation was off-the-charts good, thanks to you."

"Your surprise prototype was the winner," she says softly.

"It was *your* innovative bottle after all," I remind her. "And the new package and label. All superbly designed to work together."

"My *team's* design," she says, even more quietly.

I think she might go to sleep. Luckily, there's little traffic at that hour, and we'll be pulling up in front of her home in less than twenty minutes. Or maybe that's the unlucky part about the evening.

"Maisie Lovell adored you," I tell her.

"She did, didn't she?" Once again, Clover is leaning over in my direction as she speaks.

It's the slippery, old vinyl seat that's doing it. I smile because she has a happy lilt to her sleepy voice.

We fall silent, until she says my name in the darkness in a breathy tone that makes my cock instantly hard.

"Adam."

I make the mistake of turning my head toward her. Clover's heart-shaped face is inches away, her lips parted slightly, and I can see her tawny eyes sparkling from the light of oncoming headlights.

I groan. I'm only fucking human. But somehow, I resist. That is, until she places her hand gently on my thigh. *Jesus!* She's tapping my leg like she's testing a melon.

"Adam," she whispers again.

117

And then I cave. I fail like a snowman on a hot day. What else can I do? Leaning down, I kiss her.

The next thing I know, my arms go around her, gathering her against me while I ravage her mouth as fiercely as in the supply closet. She smells and tastes so damn good. The only rational thought I have while this warm and luscious woman presses herself closer is a fervent wish that we were in my private limo, not this blasted taxi.

Somewhere, in a garage nearby, my Maybach Landaulet is parked for the night until David claims it in the morning. The seats don't exactly become a bed, but they recline enough to do the job. We could make good use of them, along with the dark dividing glass for privacy. At the very least, I would have slid my hand under her skirt and made her happy.

Instead, for a few minutes, we wrestle around on this aged seat, with various indeterminate odors and stains.

As her tongue meets mine stroke-for-stroke, my cock becomes chiseled, so hard it hurts. Encouraged by the way her fingers grasp my sleeves, I breach the gap of her open coat and palm her breast. Even through her dress, I'm rewarded when her nipple stiffens at my touch. With her breathy moan, I feel a little sweat trickle between my shoulder blades.

Has the cabbie turned the blasted heater up to scorching?

Clover traces a path up my thigh with her palm, working her way toward my crotch but not fast enough. *Christ!* I take hold of her warm hand and place it over my twitching cock, nearly seeing stars when she gives me a tentative squeeze.

After many mindless, irresponsible, frantic minutes of exploring one another, frustrated by clothing but mapping the shape of her until I could pick her out in pitch blackness merely by skimming my hands over her upper body, the taxi lurches to a stop

Fuck!

We can't exactly step away like we did in the supply closet. Instead, I rest my forehead on hers while we both gulp in a few long breaths.

"I promise I was intending only to get you home."

Feeling her nod, I finally pull back, unable to see her face clearly.

"Clover," I begin, not sure exactly what I intend to say. Perhaps an insincere apology because at this instant, I don't feel sorry for the quarter hour of sheer pleasure we just exchanged.

As she grasps the handle and starts to open the door, the harsh interior light snaps on.

"I'm exhausted," she says, sounding stone-cold sober and barely glancing back. Although for a second I see her face is pale except for where her lips have taken their share of hungry kisses and look puffy. And her eyes—they catch mine before she turns away. Her wounded expression is like a sucker punch.

I start to follow, only intending to walk her to her door as I would any woman.

"No!" she insists, a little too loudly, before glancing toward the driver.

She's worried I'll try to go up to her apartment. Or maybe she's scared she'll let me. Either way, her woeful face is the last thing I see before she goes up her front step without saying good night.

I wait for her to safely enter the brick building before I tell the cabbie my address. As we drive down Clover's street and back toward Commonwealth Avenue, I'm not entirely certain my designer will even show up for work tomorrow.

She's been in my employ not yet four months, and I've kissed her on two separate occasions.

What a dickhead I am!

$♥$♥$♥$

Maybe I thought about her too much last night, but suddenly, not being with Clover seems asinine. I went back and forth between my conscience and my libido and didn't sleep well. I nearly called her at some obscene hour to discuss the predicament. because it's clear we're in it together. Two flickering flames that combust as soon as we're alone and close.

The whole notion of *not* asking her to spend time with me, of *not* getting to listen to her thoughts the way I had at Mistral's, of *not* hearing her laughter, of *not* touching that amazing body of hers—it's all sheer torture.

And perhaps unnecessary.

Sometime between watching her dash up her front steps and when I enter my office this morning, I decide to break the insufferable rule into a thousand pieces and sweep it under the rug. Because after a single kiss in the sample room followed by an erotic taxi ride, I'm out-of-my-mind desperate for this woman.

I spend the first hour wondering if we can figure something out. As long as we're discreet and don't tell anyone, even if or when we break up, nothing has to change. If we go into an arrangement with our eyes open, plan for the ugly, awkward day in advance, then we could circumvent such an occurrence altogether. If we keep it totally a secret, then we can end it like adults and go back to "normal" with no one the wiser.

At least, that's all I got for a plan as I punch the fourth-floor button in my private elevator. Staring at myself in the shiny steel doors, I ask myself, "What the hell are you doing?"

But I want Clover more than I want to hang onto my decade-long good intentions. It is insane how much I want to get naked with her. And it wouldn't be a lie to say I've never felt this intense need for any other woman. Ever.

Don't think too long, I counsel myself. If I do, or worse, if I hesitate, I might give in to my better nature. And my baser one needs to come out and play.

Maybe I'm just going to make sure she has come to work and that I didn't scare her off. That's an honorable excuse for the very dishonorable mission I'm on.

Ignoring the worried-looking fool staring back at me, I go for it. Excited by the prospect of seeing her again, I don't waver once the doors open. My heart thumps harder than it should after a single shot of espresso this morning, but until I see her through the glass wall, I don't will myself to calm down.

I was more worried than I'd realized. From her eyes in the cab's light, I imagined her going into her apartment and packing. At the very least, she might have called in sick.

But there she is. And she has come in fierce and hot as hell. Wearing the sleekest charcoal-gray skirt that hugs her ass and hips and a dark pink blouse that my fingers itch to unbutton, she stands in the center of her office, talking to another designer.

I admit I don't know the other woman's name, although she looks familiar.

The moment Clover spots me, her face pales, but she tilts her chin. By the time I reach her door, I figure she's going to stand her ground. *Thank God!*

I rap my knuckles across the door and open it, just as she says, "I think your idea is great. I can't wait to see it.".

The other designer with hair as dark as mine but light blue eyes turns and flashes me a smile that could melt an iceberg. "Good morning, Adam."

I feel even worse for not knowing her name, but it isn't really fair. After all, everyone who works for me knows who I am from day one.

"Good morning. May I see what you've created?"

She holds up her tablet. A black orb seems to be coming out of some type of melon. I have no idea what it's meant to be.

At my expression, she laughs. "Don't worry, bossman. It'll all make sense when I'm done."

Clover chuckles, which further loosens the taut bands that have tightened around my chest in the night. She seems in good humor. Not about to quit or have me brought up on sexual harassment charges.

When the designer leaves, Clover folds her arms. I try—and fail—to keep my gaze level with her eyes. Just a quick dip to her breasts, now that I know how they feel and how touching them makes her moan.

Just like that, I'm hard.

"What can I do for you?" she asks, all business. Only the color rushing back into her cheeks indicates she's flustered.

I have no idea what she can do for me, not in a glass-walled office, and absolutely no valid excuse for coming to see her.

"I wanted to make sure you hadn't been poached by Mrs. Lovell. She seemed to be interviewing you."

Clover doesn't fall for my BS. She actually turns her back on me, giving me a gorgeous view, and goes behind her desk, putting it between us before facing me again.

"That would never happen," she says.

I don't bother apologizing as I did for our first kiss. Lying about being sorry isn't only pointless, given where I'm standing, it's also disingenuous. And she's no idiot.

"Fine," I say, apparently having lost my wit in the elevator.

Her eyebrows raise. "Fine," she repeats softly.

I don't want to leave, with no idea when I'll see her again. If I don't think of something quick, I'll be back at indoor golf tonight, working out my frustrations on a bucket of balls while my own turn blue. Better than getting wasted while imagining her in my bed.

I did that already, too.

I don't even bother trying to think of Rachel. It didn't work last night or this morning, waiting for the usual specter of guilt and foreboding to envelop me. Instead, all I can think of is Clover and wanting her.

The rule. The rule. The rule. Despite being ready to chuck it, I find myself chanting it in my head, and with the will of a super hero, I nod and retreat. Like the decent human being I am. But I only get as far as the door.

Fuck the rule.

"Clover," I begin, hoping I have something smart to say next. And then I hear myself ask, "Will you meet me after work today, somewhere private?"

Resting her hands on her hips, she shakes her head at my audacity. But *dammit*, we need to talk.

16

Clover

Adam is a billionaire playboy after all! And I'm incensed. "Are you really asking me out despite knowing what will happen? Despite having the same opinion about intraoffice dating as I do? Knowing I will be the one to lose in the end! That seems pretty callous. Not to mention careless . . . with *my* career!"

His GQ-level face becomes grim.

"Dammit!" he says. And without another word, Adam turns and walks out of my office.

I don't expect that. As soon as he made his request, I imagined some back and forth either until he persuades me to live dangerously or until I make him see reason.

But he's gone faster than Jimmy Choos on sale at Neiman Marcus.

That's what I want, isn't it? For him to leave me alone? No pressure from the bossman to start something that, when it's over, will derail me. Again!

Yet watching Adam stalk away, I feel the keen edge of disappointment. After all, he is the only male who currently inhabits my mental space on a daily basis. Plus, he has buns and thighs like a tennis player.

As Mrs. Lovell's perfume says, "Yes, please!"

My feet nearly follow him of their own accord because our make-out session still replays in my head during every quiet moment.

Instead, I slump into my chair, if only to anchor myself at my desk so I don't give in to my craving for a big helping of Adam between the sheets. The day crawls by until it's was time to go home. No more signs of my nemesis—the sexiest man alive.

The T drops me a couple blocks from home. A regular Wednesday night. I feel jittery after the day, and not merely because of the gallons of lattes.

Pam, my roommate, is out. By the time I change into comfy sweatpants, pour myself a glass of wine, and consider pasta, chicken, or both—I am patting myself on the back for how maturely I've handled everything.

Even last night. I drank too much, made out with the boss, but made sure to end it at the taxi door. It would've been so easy to invite him up and pretend it was the brandy speaking. But I resisted.

And again, today, while I didn't exactly say no outright, I turned the tables on him and made him think about what he was asking. I'm proud of myself, even though taking it further with Adam is all I can think about.

With a bowl of linguini in front of me on the coffee table—no red sauce, just olive oil, parmesan, and oregano—I lean back against Pam's tweed sofa cushion. After clicking on the TV, I access my inbox on my phone. Thumbing through a few from NYC friends and my mom and my sister, I delete the spam, and then I see it.

An email from *a_bonvier*.

Shit! My heart instantly speeds up while my insides are dancing. The sight of his name can now do that to me. And why not, when I know how fabulous his mouth is, not to mention his hands? He kneads my breasts with the skill of an old-fashioned taffy puller at one of the Henley candy factories.

Right now, my breasts feel heavy merely looking at his name. And between my legs, I'm pulsing to match my quickening heartbeat.

I am an idiot! This can't lead to anything good. I take a breath and click it open.

You're absolutely right. That was stupid of me.

I read and reread Adam's brief email. He doesn't say sorry or that he'll never ask me again. But there's nothing obscure I can read something into. Just those eight words. Not even a "fondly" or "yours truly" at the end.

My pasta is congealing so I wolf it down while watching a mindless show, trying to fend off the feelings of wanting and loneliness.

I used to have Jason both at work and at home. I also had good peeps in New York City. Some disappeared as soon as Jason did, but tonight, there's an email from Julia. And Sam texts me about something funny at Decker Financial. I have friends from my time in Paris and from Parsons, the latter I still hung out with before my move to Boston.

My social life is now all online, and it's a drag.

I have no idea where Pam is on this Wednesday, but I would have gone out with her if she'd asked. I switch to late-night local news to remind myself how fortunate I am.

After another glass of wine, I'm probably the only person wishing it was morning and time for work. I would prefer to be at Bonvier, Inc., feeling useful.

And always with the chance of at least laying eyes on my new impossible crush.

As it turns out, I don't need to wait until tomorrow. About to turn off the TV and go to bed, the anchorwoman suddenly shows me Adam's handsome face.

I drop onto the sofa again, my attention fixed to the screen.

"We're growing," Adam says. "Boston is our base, but I'm excited by the opportunities afforded Bonvier's latest expansion in France. It'll be easier to work with our European clients."

My ears perk up. I've only just started at Bonvier Boston . . . but France! I wouldn't be any lonelier if I lived overseas. Perhaps I could request a transfer. I wouldn't run the risk of starting something with the man I now know has the hots for me in return.

The interview ends. The last shot is of Adam offering the same confident look as in his painting in our lobby, one that seems to *see* me.

I shiver. No dating the boss! Lesson learned last time. How easily I could lose everything by making such a stupid, lust-filled mistake. I don't have to run to Paris to stop myself from making the same one again. I'm strong enough to handle it right here in Boston.

$♥$♥$$♥$

Over the next few weeks as winter turns to spring, Adam and I have no more dangerous encounters, neither at work nor away from it. By which I mean, no more drinking enough to loosen my brain cells and open-mouth kiss him, while letting my hands learn his body. I have to hand it to him. He did a pretty bang-up job of feeling every available inch of mine, too.

Recalling his big hands on my breasts, his firm lips fused to mine, and how his tongue explored my mouth—that was all it took to have me pulsing with need and reaching for my bedside toy. I'm wearing out batteries at home, thinking of him every night.

While I still spend too much time using him as my ultra-male fantasy, I also start to carve out a life for myself in

Boston. I go out with Cara and her girlfriend when invited. And Pam, my brunette roommate with a good sense of humor, who works at Mass General, begins to include me in her evening plans. I have genuine, light-hearted fun for the first time in ages. Where Cara and Jenny are already a couple, happy to go to the movies, try some trendy new restaurant, or find a good band, with Pam it's always bars and clubs. And men!

"I'm beyond ready for mating and marriage," she says, as we sip wine and survey the room. Pam nods toward a man ordering a drink at the bar. "There's an *E*." She uses a lazy letter for any *eligible* guy, meaning he meets her height requirement. That's basically the only requirement she has at this point.

For me, finding an *E* takes a little more than his being over six feet. And while she sometimes ditches me to enjoy a few hours either at our place or her prospect's, I'm stuck comparing each guy to Adam.

Men buy me drinks. I dance with some of them. Occasionally, I do a test kiss. I always go home alone.

They are like sipping water when you're expecting a thick, chocolate milkshake. Why is everyone else's kiss bland and weak where Adam's had been rich and satisfying?

After one guy buys me dinner and expects to get laid in return for an overcooked piece of chicken, I stop him at my apartment building's front door.

"It was a lovely evening," I lie, knowing I will never see him again. "Thank you."

"That's it, babe? I thought we had a connection. Or could make one." His smile isn't sexy, just leering.

"Sorry," I say, not bothering to mention a next time or even an excuse.

He rolls his eyes. "Don't tell me you're one of those who won't have a little fun unless there's a promise for the future."

"Nope," I assure him. "Not at all."

"Because sometimes, hooking up is enough," he insists. "If both people are satisfied, why make it about anything else?"

His words penetrate my sex-starved brain. I know a kernel of wisdom lies in what he said, but I need to be alone to consider.

"You may be right," I say.

"Damn straight." He sounds enthused as he reaches behind me to put his hand on the door handle.

"Good night," I say, slipping inside and yanking the entry hall door closed with a satisfying click.

"Hey," he yells.

"Thank you," I add through the glass before dashing up the stairs. In my room, I think about no-strings sex, which has never been my thing. Not because I'm a prude, but simply because it never came up as an opportunity. I've always dated guys who were into me for the foreseeable future, never one-night stands or friends with benefits.

In college, I even got engaged to a guy who turned out to be a golddigger. How I wish he'd only wanted sex.

Could I enjoy a satisfying and secret relationship with Adam while keeping my heart separate? Would the no-strings clause protect me from being fired when we stopped wanting sex? I had tried to suggest a polite break-up with Jason, but he hadn't given it a chance.

The alternative was continuing this seemingly endless ache and yearning for Adam. Maybe mutual satisfaction in bed would be the answer without rocking the Bonvier boat.

17

Clover

I'm not going to jump on the plan right away. I need to consider it from a few angles. The savings in batteries alone puts the idea in the *pros* column. But if I can't keep my feelings out of it and become jealous like I'd felt over Chelsea Sweeney, that would put the idea in the *cons* column. And maybe I should think about the other person involved. Adam might not want this type of arrangement. It might shock or disgust him.

I'm not sure how I would approach him anyway.

"Clover," Chris's voice breaks through my wild and wet musings. The rocky start has smoothed out over the months, apart from my being told the wrong time for a meeting last week. Leslie shrugged it off as a scheduling snafu, but I missed getting first-hand feedback on a prototype design.

"Yes," I answer, realizing he's looking at me, along with the client. I catch up to the issue in a few seconds, and it's not good. The entire design file has mysteriously vanished from the shared file folder, leaving Chris with nothing to show apart from his annoyed face as he stares at me in frustration.

"Didn't you just prepare this file?" he asks, ten minutes into the presentation.

If the client wasn't in the room, I might make a quip how at least we aren't being treated to a video of Leslie going down on something.

Luckily, we don't live in the age of fax machines and dial up. I simply run hell-bent for my office, upload another copy, as well as download one onto a thumb drive just in case there's a gremlin in the works. Then I take the stairs two at a time, throw open the stairwell door and . . . slam into Adam.

Except in this instance, we don't immediately start making out, hot and heavy like in my imaginary run-ins. Nor do I somehow magically have my legs around his waist as he backs me up against the wall.

"Whoa!" he says, while my body is tingling all over from the brief contact with his tall, muscular form, not to mention the delicious cologne that teases my senses.

That sharp, woodsy scent takes me right back to us putting our mouths and hands to good use, and I am instantly aroused.

"In a hurry?" he asks.

"Yes, I am." My voice is ridiculously breathless, but I blame it on sprinting from my office and not *only* from having just momentarily plastered myself against him.

I hold up the drive. "Emergency file," I say. "Gotta get it to Chris."

"Then I won't keep you," he says, but he also doesn't move aside immediately. "Although I'm glad to see you."

He is? *Why?* After I all but tossed him out of my office. Before I can say anything, however, he asks, "What's the emergency?"

"Somehow my designs weren't on the shared drive," I explain, lost in his stone-gray eyes, which are fixed on me as if I'm the only person in the world.

With something that feels like desperation, I lick my suddenly parched lips and know the only remedy is another of his kisses.

"Somehow?" he asks, staring at my mouth.

I lose the thread of our conversation. Or my pea-brain buries it under a blanket of desire.

I shrug, no longer recalling why it's urgent that I stop talking to Adam. "So, have you been away? Back to Paris."

One of his dark eyebrows raises, and his crazy-sexy, lopsided grin appears.

Before I can grow embarrassed over being caught keeping tabs on him, he adds, "No, just keeping my head in the game. Focusing on what I need to get done. I'm definitely not doing anything careless."

The word echoes in the air between us. I'd accused him of being careless with my career, and he remembers.

"I appreciate that," I say. But I now want to swing the direction of our conversation away from what I said before when I chastised him for daring to ask me to meet him.

"I've been wondering," I begin.

"Have you? About what?" he asks, folding his arms and leaning against the door jamb.

I thoroughly enjoy the view of his biceps and his chest, glad he's left his coat somewhere.

"Mostly, I've been wondering what you wanted to meet with me about in private."

His eyes narrow, he uncrosses his arms, and stands up straight. For a moment, he just studies me.

"Just being selfish," he says at last, and all traces of levity vanish. "I certainly wasn't thinking clearly. Not after our taxi ride. *Careless* was the word you used. And you were right."

Shit! Am I too late? "Perhaps we ought to . . . have that meeting," I say, hoping I don't sound lame. Or desperate.

Adam blinks, then cocks his head. "Clover, I—" He cuts himself off, jaw clenching.

My pulse races. He *what?*

"I think you better attend to your emergency."

"My emergency?" Does he mean the expense of double A batteries? Or the emergency of how much I crave him?

Adam gestures to the thumb drive in my hand.

"Oh, shit!" I exclaim. He must think me an utter airhead. At the very least, he knows I have the hots for him. I'm too far beyond being embarrassed at this point. "Gotta run."

"Yes, you do," he agrees, giving me a wry smile before stepping aside. "Before my company is smoking rubble."

As I pass him, though, I have the strangest feeling he might smack my ass. I look back to see Adam staring at it, which gives me an insane amount of satisfaction. It even lessens the humiliation of his witnessing how easily I can forget what I'm doing when I'm near him.

The client's coffee is cold by the time I get back to the presentation. Chris glares daggers at me, and I mumble an apology. However, my team's designs are fabulous and all is forgiven.

I spend the day replaying the encounter with Adam like I'm the nerdy girl in high school who runs into the team's quarterback in the library. He thinks asking me out was being selfish. That means he cannot possibly know how much I want him.

That's about to change.

$♥$♥$♥$

The following Friday, I'm jumpy all day long. I wait until the end of the week because if this blows up in my face, I won't have to look anyone in the eye the following day. I dress for success, meaning my sleekest, pale-gray professional skirt of the softest, finest wool and silkiest pale-pink blouse with a gray cardigan to stave off the March chill. My hair is down and my heels are high.

"Hot date?" Cara asks me at nine in the morning.

I jump. "No. Not really. Maybe. I don't know."

This sets her off on a laughing jag.

"You are too funny," she says. "I hope it works out."

"Me, too," I mutter under my breath, still not sure I can go through with it. But Adam isn't Jason, and I am not the same wide-eyed idiot. I have no intention of letting my heart get involved. And my body is very clear it isn't his heart I'm after, but something a little further south.

Timing is tricky. I know Adam is in the building because Chris mentions having lunch with him later. But whether the bossman will still be around at quitting time, that's anyone's guess.

As soon as it is safely after five, I leave my cardigan at my desk and head for the stairwell. I don't want anyone to see which way the elevator is heading, so two floors up, which is all I want to climb in my skinny pumps, I get on alone.

"Up, up, and away," I say softly, pressing the button for Adam's floor three times for good luck.

When the doors open, I hear his voice and my heart lurches into my throat. Is this a good idea? *Hell, no!* But it's become a necessity.

I go through the smoked-glass double doors and freeze. With his suitcoat off and his sleeves rolled up, Adam leans over to look at something on his assistant's monitor. I've never exchanged more than a passing greeting with Janet in the lobby, and Sean was the one who told me she was his assistant. Even so, from the way she walks with a long, confident stride, to the way employees constantly stop her for a quick word, Janet strikes me as a larger-than-life type woman who oozes capability and attitude. My father would call her "a pistol." And her enviable, rich red hair fits her perfectly.

"You're right," he agrees with something she's said. "I double-booked myself."

His assistant laughs. "I knew it wasn't my fault," she says, then notices me.

Adam sees me next, and his jaw tightens. When our gazes lock, he knows what I'm here for. I can tell.

"Ms. Mitchell, isn't it?" Janet asks, offering me a genuine smile. "Can I help you?"

For a moment, I can't get my tongue to work. Finally, I say, "Please call me Clover." After that, my brain dries up, and I can't think of a plausible reason for showing up out of the blue. I simply didn't expect to see anyone but the bossman.

"I asked her to come see me," Adam lies. "Problems with one of our designers."

"Naughty, naughty," his assistant says, rising to her feet, looking from me to her boss.

I take a step back. How does she know? Adam appears momentarily staggered as well.

"You didn't put it in the schedule," Janet says. "I'm sorry, but I have to get going. My daughter is in the school play tonight."

I let out an inaudible relieved breath, and Adam's expression relaxes.

"My fault," he says. "It slipped my mind, but I won't need you for anything."

"No documents?" she asks, reaching for her jacket. "No contracts?"

"Nothing, I assure you. Enjoy your son's recital," Adam says, practically ushering the woman past me, so close that I catch a whiff of his cologne and my body starts to hum.

"My *daughter's* play." Janet laughs.

"Just teasing," Adam says, pressing the down button. "Don't be late."

She stares at him, and he probably knows he's overdoing it.

Turning to me, he says, "This way, Clover."

I try to walk casually beside him toward his office, feeling Janet's gaze on my back.

And then I'm inside the unfamiliar territory.

"Freeze," he says, cocking his head.

He's listening for the elevator. Ten seconds later, it makes a familiar dinging sound. Casually, he glances behind him. Seeing his assistant is gone, he shuts his office door.

Before I can take in the sumptuous surroundings, Adam reaches for me. In a heartbeat, he presses me against the cool door he has just swung shut, and I melt in his arms.

More like I combust. My body is a flickering, pulsing flame, and he is the fiery kindling stoking it higher. Pressing my wrists over my head, Adam holds them both with one of his hands, while he uses his other hand to undo my blouse buttons.

I'm grateful he doesn't tear it open the way I want him to because that would leave me in a tough situation on the subway later.

We aren't speaking, barely looking each other in the eye, but we have the same goal—to satisfy the hunger from previous months of constant wanting.

His frustrated attempts to press his thigh between mine, foiled by my narrow skirt, match my own desperation to touch his bare skin for the first time. I swear he growls when he parts my shirt and tugs my bra down on one side, exposing my breast.

Immediately, his mouth latches onto my nipple, and I utter some wild guttural noise of pleasure. But as my desire floods my thong, I squirm, needing so much more.

"Please," I say, struggling against his hold.

He releases my wrists, and I sink my fingers into his hair, thick and soft, closing my eyes as all my awareness goes to my pearling nipples, both the one he sucks and the one that wants the same attention.

Barely breathing, I gasp when he captures the bud in his teeth while his finger rolls the other. Soon, it becomes torture. The rest of me is throbbing with need.

"Now," I say, quickly realizing the detriment of a tight skirt when he tries to draw mine upward.

"This has got to go," he says. With a practiced zip and a tug, he sends it dropping to my ankles, before hooking one of my thighs over his arm.

Quivering, light-headed, this is my every evening's fantasy before I make myself come thinking of him. I cling to his shirt, too late to start undressing him as I feel his hard arousal against my soaked thong.

"Pill?" he asks, barely halting.

"Yes," I say, wondering if he would have produced a condom out of thin air if I'd said no.

Still, he doesn't thrust inside as I expect. His fingers spread me, swirl and caress my lady bits, and drive me to begging.

"Adam!" I whisper.

"Not sexy," he says, "but I have to ask." His fingers are going to make me come without him. And I try to hold on.

"So ask," I say, gritting my teeth. Finally, we're looking at one another in the eyes.

"Clean?" he asks.

For a second, I don't know what he means. Then I think of Jason. He made me take some tests before we ever had sex, which I thought was insulting. Now I'm grateful because I know how careful he was.

"Yes," I say. "I assume you are, too."

Adam nods and buries his face in the crook of my neck, nibbling at the skin of my throat. His skilled fingers are still stroking me. When literally the lightest breath will have me cresting into that euphoric state usually reserved for a well-handled vibrator, he buries his shaft in me, balls deep.

"Yes!" I hiss. After he pulls out and thrusts inside me again, I climax.

I go off like a firework, way too quickly. Like some men have done in my life. Luckily, my early finish doesn't end the good time, nor ruin it for Adam.

18

Adam

When Clover comes, her pussy clenches around my cock like a vice. I follow her orgasm, slamming into her as all the pent-up desire of the last few months finally gets released. I haven't climaxed so fast since college.

Pulling out, I let her leg down gently, hoping she doesn't have bruises on her thigh by morning from my grip. I assume she's not hurt because she's laughing, not like a huge belly laugh, just softly.

Never having had a woman do that before, I hope it's a good thing.

"Something funny?" I ask.

"No," she says, catching her breath. "I think I always laugh afterward. Not intentionally, just . . . an all-over relaxation."

Infinitely better than crying. I would like to make her laugh again, too.

Always a gentleman, I snatch her skirt from the floor and shake it out. The gray fabric looks rumpled and stepped on, but she shimmies into it and is as beautiful as ever.

"How did you know?" she asks, buttoning her blouse.

I think she's referring to my knowing she came to my office for sex. Before I can respond, she switches to the more pressing topic, "Do you have a tissue?"

I point to my private bathroom. She enters and closes the door.

"Nice," I hear her say.

"Can I talk?" I ask. Some people don't like when you speak through the closed door, especially if they're in the bathroom.

"Go ahead."

"I knew because you came up here dressed like sex on a stick."

I hear her laugh. "I didn't dress for sex," she protests.

"Fair enough. You always look sexy. But even after you gave me a well-deserved reprimand, you came to my office where we would be alone. And we have a short but intense history of what happens when we're alone. When I saw you step off the elevator, I didn't think you could be here for any other reason."

Silence.

"Was I right?" Bit late if I was wrong, anyway.

She doesn't answer. Instead, she turns the faucet on. I move away and give her some space while I second-guess myself. What if I ravished her and all she wanted to do was discuss design?

The door opens, and Clover came out with her hair and skirt smoothed like magic. Her blouse is tucked in and she looks professional, but still sexier than any woman I've ever seen in business clothing.

"Yes," she admits, staring me right in the eyes. "You were right."

I can't help smiling. "It was great." I sound like a virginal teenager just having had my first kiss with tongue. But it had been exceptional, despite being rushed and accomplished it while standing. "Have I told you how delicious you smell?"

Clover blushes. This incredible woman who let me screw her against my office door actually blushes over a compliment.

"You haven't," she says. "And so do you, by the way."

For the price I pay for my custom cologne, it had better be the best fragrance she's ever smelled.

"Thank you," I say. "Do you want a drink?"

Her expression morphs from friendly to cautious. Not unfriendly, but in the blink of an eye, no longer a free-spirited sex partner.

"We need to talk," she says.

I nearly laugh. That's my line, and usually spoken after a couple weeks of dating when I realize the relationship is going nowhere. Definitely not words I say after a single outstanding fuck.

"Hence the drink," I say. Unlike those executives of yesteryear, I don't have a liquor cabinet in my office. Just a half-empty bottle of Scotch whisky that my father gave me a few years back. I pull it off a shelf in the corner that also holds some ad awards, a few books, and large cut geodes that serve as bookends.

"What would you like? Scotch or Scotch?" I ask, thinking I'm being witty as I hold up the bottle of amber Lagavulin.

"I thought you were asking me out for a drink," Clover says. Instead of sounding disappointed, her tone is distinctly relieved. "Which I definitely don't want to do."

Undeniably, she's an unusual female.

Then she asks, "Do you have beer or wine instead?"

I nearly repeat "Scotch or Scotch" when I remember Janet's supplies for clients.

"Yup. Hold on." I leave Clover in my office and pass through Janet's domain to the small room beyond. She even has a mini-fridge and a microwave. Everything is here for when she lays out a basic spread for a client who has decided they simply must meet me. Only the CEO will do.

Snagging a bottle of cabernet and two bottles of Belgian beer so all my bases are covered, I return with my score. In a minute, we're side-by-side on the leather sofa facing the large windows with a view of Boston's wharves.

After a quick clinking of the bottles as Clover opted for cold beer despite it dropping into the thirties outside, we each take a long swallow. Is she nervous? It seems a bit late for that.

"OK, talk," I say.

That makes her smile. She takes another sip, and I'm mesmerized by her lips on the bottle neck. *Down, boy!*

"I don't want to go out in public with you," Clover says. "I don't want to go anywhere with you. I simply wanted this." She gestures in the space between us with her beer.

"You wanted beer from Janet's fridge?" I tease, but I'm getting the picture loud and clear. And what she's saying has captured my interest.

"That," she says, pointing to the closed door, "was insanely good. I had a feeling it would be. I wanted that." Her gorgeous caramel-colored eyes meet mine. "I wanted you."

My cock is at full attention so I rest the chilled bottle in my lap to tame it.

"I wanted you, too," I say, thinking this has swiftly devolved into a mutual admiration meeting.

"I know," she says smugly. And the smugness is adorable on her, even as she blushes again.

Ready to ramp it up from talking to fucking, I confess, "I want you again, right now."

"Oh!" She bites her bottom lip, and I hope she gives me a chance to suck on it and bite it.

"If we only do *that*," she points to the door again, "here, I mean, then I'm in."

"You're in? Like a poker game?"

Clover takes a deep breath, which does spectacular things to her breasts.

"I'm in," she says, "like I wouldn't mind doing this again for as long as we both want to . . . do this. But nothing else. Nothing that would be construed as dating or a relationship or an entanglement. Nothing that could get messy or cause embarrassment or the need for me to leave or be fired," she finishes.

Ah! Now I understand.

"Pure sex," I muse.

She nods.

"Does it have to be up against the wall?" I ask, half-joking, but since she said "only that" I'm not entirely sure.

Clover isn't ready to laugh at my teasing. "No," she says distractedly. "Other positions are fine. But the main thing," she adds, sounding serious, "is when we decide to stop, we stop. Everything else remains the same. No break up, no awkwardness around the office. No need to change anything regarding my employment."

I smile. Her thinking is perfectly reasonable, a preventative measure so no one has to lose their job. Or their life. My smile dies, and damn me if Rachel hasn't crept back into my thoughts. For a heartbeat, I'm ready to say no. But what Clover suggested is the polar opposite situation to the tragedy of Rachel, and I'm intrigued.

"I understand what you're saying. You need to protect yourself."

"Exactly."

"What you've suggested makes a lot of sense," I agree. "It's the natural extension of not staying the night after sex. Or feeling obligated to call the next day. We simply don't do anything before or after sex."

Clover smiles, and it's gorgeous. "What do you think? Will it work? Does it bend the Bonvier rule too far?"

The damn rule. I've already made peace with snapping it in half. "After what we just did, I'm willing to give your plan a try. I'm in, too." We tap our beer bottles again.

"Can I have it in writing?"

Her words surprise me, but in her place, I would do the same thing. She has everything to lose, and I have nothing.

"I don't suppose a gentleman's handshake will suffice?" I ask.

"Nope."

Getting to my feet, I once again head for Janet's area, where I grab a blank sheet of letterhead from the printer. At my own desk, I scrawl across it a few lines about not firing Clover Mitchell if she no longer wants to have sex with me or vice versa. Then I sign it.

"It might not be worth the paper it's written on," I tell her, handing it over.

She reads it and smiles. "I trust you're a man of your word."

"Trust but make sure it's in writing?"

She shrugs at my words. "Yup."

When our beers are empty, I take her bottle and set it with mine on the hewn maple coffee table, littered with industry magazines. Then I reach over and touch her lips, tracing a path from the full lower that's been tempting me over her chin, down her neck to the sexy V of her cleavage.

Our gazes lock, and I raise an eyebrow, asking her silently. She nods and lets me unbutton her blouse again, making me wonder why she ever did it up in the first place. In seconds, we are horizontal on the couch. I'm glad I eschewed a designer's ultra-modern, stylish but stiff settee for this big sofa that allows me to crash when necessary. Like when jetlag gets the best of me in the middle of a workday.

I certainly couldn't have anticipated having this sexy dime-piece lying atop it, and I'm grateful we have some comfort and enough room.

"Ready?" I ask, sounding dispassionate despite wanting her just as much as I did half an hour ago. Then again, with Clover, I don't have to be romantic. I just need to get the job done.

In response, she pulls my head down for a kiss, making me realize I took her so fast against the door, we didn't even meld mouths. I was too busy nibbling on other parts of her. Now, I suck on her lower lip. It's as full and soft as I remember from the taxi. When I nip at that same sweet lip, she moans. My cock throbs in response, wanting to get down to business for a second go-round.

Her lacy bra covers only the lower half of her breasts. I tug down each cup to expose her tits and her dusty pink nipples. My mouth, tongue, and teeth go to work on them until she's writhing.

We try to go more slowly, taking our time. I even remove her skirt more carefully, but we barely last longer. When I pull her thong to the side and glide into her, she arches back, and I feel like the luckiest man in the world. Also the horniest.

Resting on my elbows, I rock into her, back and forth. Her eyes close, but I keep watching as she strains for another climax. Just before I slide my hand between our bodies to help her, she tenses, makes a sound of pure pleasure— *"mmmmmmaaahh"*—and has an orgasm that makes her body tremble beneath mine.

I'm a few strokes behind, finally closing my eyes as I surge into her and finish. It's as mind-blowing as the first encounter.

This time, her skirt is on the coffee table, not in a crumpled ball. Again with the laughter, she snatches it and retreats to the bathroom, letting me watch her perfect ass.

God, I love a thong!

Slipping on my coat and grabbing my phone, I recall for the first time since laying eyes on Clover that David is waiting downstairs. I send him a quick text.

When she comes out again wearing a satisfied smile, I match it.

Then comes the difficult part. I already know what she will say, but I ask anyway.

"May I give you a ride home?"

"Absolutely not." Her smile grows as she shakes her head.

I expected her answer, but I don't like it. "It's getting late."

"The T is crowded at this hour. I'll be perfectly safe amongst all the other riders."

She picks up the piece of letterhead, and I have to admit, it feels a little weird—like a business transaction.

"Let David drive you," I offer. It seems too callous to have screwed twice and then let her walk out into the night air. "I'll call an Uber for myself. Or I could call one for you." I'm starting to sound like a nag and immediately shut my mouth.

"Not going to happen, bossman. Next thing you know, we'll be stopping off for Indian food."

"Indian?"

"My favorite," she says, which reminds me that I don't know anything about her.

Immediately, I think of Shalimar. "I do, in fact, know a really good—"

"No, thank you." Clover strides to the door before I can get there to open it. "I'm going back to my office to collect my things and cover this wreck of an outfit with my sweater and coat. Then I'm going home to frozen pizza."

"Frozen pizza on a Friday night?" It sounds a little sad. I have a quick thought of sharing a pizza with her, but definitely not a frozen one.

She laughs and continues through Janet's reception area. "I don't actually eat it frozen, you know?" Then she presses the button and over her shoulder, she adds, "It's got a cauliflower crust, and honestly, it's not that bad."

Cauliflower crust? "Not that bad doesn't mean good," I say, and I'm closing the distance while she presses the button a few times as if that makes the elevator come more quickly. "Hold up. We'll catch the elevator together."

"Nope. You get in *your* elevator." With that, the doors open and she gets in, turning to face me, looking as though she's daring me to contradict or disobey.

Of course I could catch her, but I let the doors close.

Clover came up with a good plan, and I want to let it play out. Stepping into the lobby together and running into any late-working employees would upset her, perhaps swiftly ending this perfectly simple arrangement.

Nothing but the hottest sex of my life.

So why do I have a feeling that this could easily get complicated?

19

Clover

Can someone get injured from smiling too much? I smile all the way home on the train, reliving the best sex of my life. I smile while eating pizza, which isn't easy to do. And Adam was right. Frozen pizza is *meh*.

Pam left me a note to meet her at our local tavern around the corner from our apartment. I don't want to go. Despite it being Friday night, it's not the least bit tempting. I don't want to be around people. I prefer the company of my erotic memories.

Better yet, I no longer need memories to sustain me. After all, we agreed to do it again. For the first time in a while, I don't open my side drawer for my toy. I'd enjoyed the promised land, so to speak, of physical, sexual nirvana! So great and not even on a comfortable bed, either.

As I drift off to sleep, I wonder how much better it might be if we could both be completely naked and have room to move. For that, we would need a bedroom. I wonder if we would risk a hotel or if he would invite me to his home. No way will I bring the billionaire bossman back to my apartment.

"Stop!" I order myself, but soon I'm smiling again. I did it. I came up with a way to eat my boss's cake and have it, too. Adam and I had sex! Spectacular sex!

Holy shit! I can hardly believe it.

If we stay mature about this and don't waver from the arrangement, this could work. I genuinely like the man, what I know of him. He seems to be a fair boss, generous, in fact. I've witnessed him being polite to everyone in service industries, including his driver and the waitstaff at Mistral's. He threw an expensive Christmas party.

And he smells so damn good.

Despite all that, I intend to keep my emotions tightly in check. I might already admire Adam, but I'm not going to let my heart become involved. I'll be smarter this time around, so all he gets from me is admiration . . . and my body.

That makes me smile again. I hug my pillow, feeling on top of the world. But I'm suddenly not sleepy. Clicking on my e-reader, I dive into an historical romance.

$♥$♥$♥$

"You look happy," Cara says, entering my office on Monday morning, holding her tablet for our first scheduling meeting of the week. "In fact, you seem almost blissful."

"Why not?" I ask. Nothing can quell my happiness. I'm relaxed, satisfied, and the promise of tonight is still ahead of me.

"Because the weekend is behind us," she points out.

Yippee and thank God! I simply shrug.

"I take it your date worked out," she says.

I freeze. "What date?"

"Friday," she reminds me. "You were dressed kinda sexy for work. I thought you were going out after. Isn't this your post-date glow?"

"*Ohhh, riiiight.* Actually, I ended up at home eating pizza."

Her expression changes, growing solemn. "And you're OK? No bad scene with a creep or anything?"

"Couldn't be better," I assure her.

I hate to acknowledge to myself how great one single fact is making me feel—I have access to Adam's body for the next five evenings. And just as I hoped, by waiting until half past five to venture up to his office, he is alone. Janet has left.

His mouth covers mine a bare ten seconds after I enter his office where there are no cameras. When we come up for air, I realize something is different. He has dimmed the lights. Two glasses of wine are on the table in front of the now-infamous couch, which itself has a small blanket on it.

What other surprises does he have in store for me?

His big hands and his firm mouth and his hard body seduce me for the next half hour. I can't believe we manage to make it last that long before I fly over the edge into orgasm-land.

We end up in a sweaty tangle on the soft throw, which is much better than the cool leather surface. A couple minutes later, I come out of his executive bathroom to find not only my wine glass refilled but now a charcuterie tray on the table.

Grateful, I don't even wonder how he managed it, but I pounce.

"I'm famished," I admit, layering cheese onto a cracker before folding a piece of thin prosciutto atop it. Simple but delicious. "Thank you."

Adam, with his shirt still untucked and mostly unbuttoned, picks up a cracker and his glass before leaning back and watching me.

"Just because we're not going out to dinner, that doesn't mean we have to starve. How was your day as my head designer?"

"My day was fabulous." Mostly because I'd been thinking of him for the past eight hours. "Yours?"

He nods and grins. "The last thirty minutes of it were pretty damn great."

I laugh at his enthusiasm, mirroring my own.

"Anticipating it throughout the day wasn't too shabby, either," he adds, popping the cracker between his lips.

"What if I hadn't shown up?"

He cocks his head. "It never occurred to me you wouldn't."

My happiness falters. Either he thinks me incredibly slutty or . . . "I'm predictable?" I ask.

He shrugs. "I don't know you well enough to say that, but we had a great time on Friday, and only an idiot wouldn't want to do it again first chance. You're not an idiot, so you're here."

"And it was equally great today," I agree, knowing my smile is back in place. We ate and talked and drank wine, until I sighed.

"Shit!" he says suddenly. "I almost forgot."

With that, he goes to his desk, leans down and pulls out a package, which he presents to me, looking super pleased with himself.

I examine the box on my lap from an overnight delivery company. Butterflies take flight in my stomach. Having sex with Adam is perfect and mutual and entirely give-give. But a present from him makes me feel weird.

"Open it," he urges.

"OK, but I wasn't expecting anything. I hope it's not cash," I joke because, of course, we'd have to end this right now. Obviously, the box is too big to hold payment for services rendered, so I pull the tab that opens one end and shake out the contents.

"Oh my God!!" I exclaim. "My shoes!"

On my lap is a shoebox from Marion Parkes. I see the size is mine and the little picture at one end shows the same ones I ruined. I tear the lid off and gaze at my beloved suede shoes, blue and unstained. "They're perfect."

I look up at him, and I swear he looks even happier than I feel.

"How did you know my size?"

He grins, single dimple and all, and my chest tightens in a good way. What a prince!

"When you were up here last time, I looked at your shoe size while you were in the bathroom."

"Well, color me shocked, bossman," I mutter, looking at the shoes again. Then I put them aside, stand up, and kiss him. I am tickled on so many levels, but his thoughtfulness and the effort he put into this gift floors me the most.

When I pull back, he says, "I can't have my art director down a pair of her favorite footwear. And I found out how expensive they are. Do you need a raise?"

He's joking, but I feel a twinge of guilt. The old me didn't blink at the price. If he knew that, I'm sure he wouldn't be so pleased. But independent Clover knows what a luxury these are.

"No raise needed, thank you. I am very good at saving my pennies," I tell him. "I wouldn't have replaced these anytime soon. As you said, they're really expensive. I'll take better care of them." I would, too, because they were from Adam.

I have to admit, it makes me want to drop to my knees and give him a gift in return. But that would be a little too close to whoring, so I step away.

"I don't want to be out too late on a worknight. My boss might be annoyed if I don't come in on time tomorrow."

"I promise he won't."

"Maybe Chris would," I say. "I answer to too many men." I'm joking, but he sets his glass down, looking suddenly serious.

"About that," he says. "Actually, not about that precisely, but about us."

"Us?" I echo. That word has never sounded so alarming.

"I am not into bed-hopping. I want to be your only sex partner while we're in this arrangement."

I consider his words. To be honest, that's what I'd intended, but hearing him say it aloud makes this whole thing more real. Exclusivity sounds a lot like commitment, which is rather close to being in a relationship. Speaking of which . . .

"Chelsea Sweeney?" I ask before I can stop myself.

He raises an eyebrow, then shakes his head. "Haven't seen her since Christmas, and I don't intend to see her again."

I'm happy to hear that. "What if *you* want to sleep with someone else?"

"Not going to happen. Why risk superb sex for the unknown?"

I try again. "What if you meet someone with whom you want to start a real relationship? Someone you can take out to dinner?"

Both dark eyebrows go up at my continued hypotheticals. Then his expression grows serious. "I would be honest enough to break it off with you because I'm not a jerk. But I don't foresee that happening any time soon. It's more likely you'll be out at a club and some prick will want to hook up with you."

"I suppose that could happen." It already has, a few times since I started going out in Boston. "But I don't have to say yes." I never have, not once in all the months I've lived here.

"I would prefer you didn't," he says flatly. "If you feel the urge, however, then I ask that you tell me. Give me the choice to rethink this arrangement."

"So, you want exclusivity?" I ask.

He smiles slowly, and my stomach flutters at the gorgeousness of his face. "That's safer all around. It also bespeaks of a certain level of classiness. Don't you think?"

I nod. I guess it's as classy as being someone's fuck buddy can ever be.

"But if I meet your doppelganger at the local tavern, and he sweeps me off my feet, and I can date him without fear of gaining a reputation as the office slut, not to mention not having to worry about being fired for loving him, then—"

"Loving?" Adam interrupts.

I hope he doesn't infer that I'm falling in love with *him*. I tilt my chin.

"I hope to fall in love one day," I say.

"With *my* doppelganger?"

Damn! I did say that, didn't I?

"Probably," I say, tucking my hair behind my ear and looking away from him. This is not supposed to get personal. "Your looks are my type. That's all I meant."

"I see. No blond beach boy for you?"

"Nope."

"Back to exclusivity," he presses the point and this time, allows for no waffling. "That's what I want. And what I expect."

"I agree," I say. "Until either one of us finds someone we want to actually date."

"Agreed," he says before claiming my mouth a little more roughly than he had before.

He needn't worry. I know I won't stumble across anyone remotely like him. It's not like I haven't been out in the world. No one has ever made my body feel like its melting with a mere kiss. And then, even though I fully intended to leave, I let him ease me back down to the couch, still kissing me. He lifts my skirt, pushes aside my thong, and caresses my slit.

"You're already wet," he says, his finger delving between the folds.

"All this talk of our great sex," I whisper.

With one of his hands supporting the small of my back, I arch, giving his hungry mouth access to my neck. While he devours my throat with nips and licks, his practiced fingers stroke me to shaking with anticipation.

Before I know it, my hands are clutching his shirt and moving it aside so I can feel his bare chest, run my thumbs across his flat nipples, and . . . and . . .

I climax like a barrel going over a waterfall. Hard, fast, twisting slightly in his arms to grind against his hand.

When it's over and I'm adjusting my clothing, I ask, "What about you?"

"I'm fine," he says. "Just a parting gift to keep you from looking at anyone else on the T."

He is not seriously jealous, is he? His lopsided smile suggests he isn't.

"What if I drop to my knees and give you a gift in return?" Even more than before, I really want to take his cock between my lips.

His jaw clenches, his nostrils flare, and his glance goes to my mouth. I know he's imagining what I can do. But Adam finally shakes his head.

"I'll keep that image burning in my brain until next time. It's getting later all the time, Ms. Mitchell, and I want you home safe."

A gentleman! On slightly wobbly legs, with more inclination to lie down and snooze than to go out into the night air and brave the Boston T, I gather up my new shoes and leave.

$♥$♥$♥$

Adam

I hate to think of myself as insatiable, but damn me if I'm not clock-watching by three p.m. the next day. I don't usually go to work every day or always stay in Boston for the entire week. But here I am, ordering increasingly more elaborate meals each evening for us to share after intense, teeth-rattling sex.

I can't wine and dine the lady, nor do I need to, but I want to. I order from the best restaurants. And I do it personally because I don't want Janet involved. The food is brought in chafing dishes and sent up by nighttime security, staying piping hot until the even-hotter Clover claims her climax.

When we regain our ability to move and breathe and speak—and her pretty, telltale laughter is over—then we eat. While the food is good, the sex beforehand and the company afterward are better. All week I've been gorging on rich food and on sexy Clover.

Always trying and lately succeeding in not thinking of Rachel, I acknowledge it's a relief how "normal" Clover is. A well-adjusted, modern woman with a healthy enjoyment of sex. I even believe we could stop without ramifications—although denying ourselves this level of satisfying sex would be idiotic.

By Friday the following week, I wonder how long I can continue to crave her as if I haven't hooked up in a year. We've just tidied up from a particularly rambunctious romp on the sofa and are starting to eat coq au vin.

It seems a good time to tell her what I'm thinking. "I want you to come to my home tonight and stay the weekend."

Clover freezes mid-bite, surprise on her face.

Have I gone against some part of our arrangement? She can't want office sex forever, any more than I do. It's great, but we can explore so much more with a bed.

Then she chews and swallows, looking thoughtful. "I would arrive separately and leave the same way," she says.

I'm relieved I didn't freak her out, and she's not calling the whole thing off.

"No dog or cat to feed?" I tease, trying to ease the tension I'd created by throwing in a change to the status quo.

"Nope," she says. "Do you?"

"Not ready for that type of commitment," I tell her.

She smiles again. "It would hamper your ability to jet off on a whim."

I laugh. "Have you seen me jetting off?"

"Not lately," she says.

"Besides, a pet wouldn't hamper anything. I have staff who would take care of an animal when I go away."

"Of course you do," she says. "No one would expect Adam Bonvier to scoop poop, neither off grass nor from a litter box."

Clover is patronizing me, but I don't care.

We kiss to seal the deal—a messy wine-and-onion-and-mushroom kiss. Delicious! She's the reason I've remained in Boston and come into the office on time every day like a junior executive for the past two weeks.

"In the comfort of my home," I promise, "we can indulge in whatever you like, maybe explore some fantasies."

Her interest perks up. And then I see the moment she changes her mind.

"Some weekend, but not this one," she says.

"Hot date?" I shoot back immediately. But I don't really think for a moment that she's testing the waters and looking for that guy who can offer more than sex. I trust when she finds him, she'll tell me.

Rolling her eyes, she says only, "Nope."

And nothing more. No excuse, no reason. She simply isn't coming to my home this weekend. And I have no right to ask why. Maybe I'm being a little overbearing when I think I'm being chill.

"Fine. I'll see you on Monday then."

"Are you dismissing me?" she asks. "Because I have nowhere I have to be right now, and I was looking forward to the key lime tarts."

I smile. "Sorry. We can stay here as long as you like, although if it gets too late, I'll muscle you into my car and drive you home."

"Then I won't stay too late." She rubs her bare foot up my ankle. "Just late enough."

We end up having sex against the wall, just because why not? Then we enjoy dessert. But I really wish I could drive her home—or better yet, bring her to my house for the weekend.

It's still only about sex, but when you find someone who rocks your world, it's hard to wait through a weekend and another long workday to do it again.

20

Clover

Three days seem like an eternity. And then I make it even longer because suddenly I feel . . . sleazy going up to Adam's office as soon my phone alarm beeps at half past five. Today, I don't wait for the alarm. I decide to show some restraint and, hopefully, a little class. Instead of riding the elevator up, I go with Cara to have a Monday-blues drink.

It turns out to be an excruciatingly bad choice. Made worse when I get a text from Adam at quarter to six.

Red or white with pasta and mussels? Your choice. Food arriving soon.

I can't ghost him. I already feel terrible thinking about Adam in his office with hot food and a hard cock, waiting for me. I nearly make an excuse to Cara and leave. I could be back in the office in fifteen minutes if I hurry.

"Best margarita in town," she says, catching my eye.

I take a long sip. "It is. Where's your girlfriend tonight?"

"Even if Jenny were home, that doesn't mean I have to go directly after work."

"But you would want to," I say.

She smiles and shrugs. "She's taking a class at Salem State. Going for an occupational therapy degree."

"Good for her."

Cara nods. "It is. She's following a dream. What about you?"

I consider. "I've landed my dream job. That's for sure."

"There's more to life than a job. What about a partner? I think you like guys, yes?"

"Yup." I take another sip. It is a damn good margarita. "I got out of a bad relationship before I moved here. But now, I'm . . ."

What was I going to say? *Fucking the boss. Having the best sex I can imagine. Being treated to secret dinners and even some blissful all-over body massages from the company owner.*

"I'm content," I finish. Although Adam's invitation to go to his home last weekend spooked me. Small changes, like luck, can be good or bad. Hence my ditching him for time with Cara.

She raises her glass. "To contentment."

"To contentment," I agree.

"Although I think we could find you a man pretty quick."

"No, thanks," I say.

Her dark eyebrows raise. Then she gestures with her chin. "A handsome guy over there has been undressing you with his eyes since we sat down."

Naturally, I turn to see. Sure enough, a sandy-haired guy in chic Euro glasses is giving me *the look*. His eyes are the only part of him that will ever undress me.

"Not interested," I say firmly.

"*Hm.* Well, let me know your type, and I'll keep an eye out."

"Don't bother."

"Clover, don't tell me a bad relationship has caused you to withdraw and take a vow of celibacy."

Not even close.

"Hardly," I say, recalling one exciting session, I think it was last Thursday, when Adam pressed me face-down over the back of the sofa, which isn't against a wall, but in the middle of the room, strategically facing the windows.

With a shove of his thigh, he had moved the narrow table that usually stands behind it, making room for me.

My ass in the air, he took me from behind. One of the single best fucks I've ever had.

With my margarita hand trembling slightly, I squirm on the bar stool, knowing I could be in that position at that very moment if I hadn't pulled back a little to make sure I keep a life apart from work and sex.

"You OK?" Cara asks, calling over the server and ordering another round.

"Why?" I grab an ice cube from my near-empty drink, lift my hair, and run it over the back of my neck.

"Your cheeks got all flushed. Can't hold your tequila?"

"I'm fine." My phone croaks again. "I need to use the ladies' room. You alright alone out here?"

"I'll hold down the fort and fight for our table if challenged." The bar is getting increasingly crowded so she might have to do exactly that.

Out of her sight, I lean against the wall outside the bathroom and look at Adam's next text.

Everything good?

I type quickly. *Yes. But not coming tonight. Good evening.*

I hit send and then wish I hadn't written such a lame message. *Good evening?* Who am I, some pearl-wearing Victorian?

Thanks anyway, I add, hoping that sounds friendlier and softens the blow. I probably should add that I'm sorry, and my fingers hover over the phone pad for a second.

In the end, I don't because it's not like I broke a dinner date. Then I use the ladies' room to give myself a good talking to—I have nothing to feel guilty about, either way—before returning to our table.

Cara is no longer alone. The sandy-haired guy has moved in. At least he hadn't cornered me coming out of the restroom. I detest that creepy move.

With the unwelcome guy is another man who is ogling Cara openly. She appears fed up already and has probably been trying to get them to leave. I don't feel like playing nice or even trying to soothe their feelings with a gentle refusal. They really have no business barging into our girls' night out.

"There she is," I say. "My gorgeous fiancée." I lean in and kiss her, not just a quick drop of a kiss, but a passionate, leave-no-doubt one. "What's up?" I ask the men as I drape my arm around her. "You buying my girl and me the next round before we head home?"

"Nope," the sandy-haired guy says, rising to his feet. "Not wasting my time or money."

"Sorry," mutters the other, whether for barging over or for his friend's rudeness, I can't tell.

Cara's eyes widen. "Well played," she says when they're out of hearing. "But don't tell Jenny. She's the jealous type."

"No worries," I say, and we order nachos. My phone croaks, sounding louder than ever.

"A persistent suitor?" she teases.

"What? No!" I glance down to see only one word: *OK*.

My stomach twinges uncomfortably. I hope I haven't ruined our arrangement. What will happen tomorrow if I show up and he isn't there? It would be no less than I deserve.

I curse my impulsive nature. I don't want to appear addicted and obsessed. But Adam probably thinks me ungrateful, flighty, and childish instead. Even the notion of the wasted food gnaws at me. And I wonder how I'll make it up to him.

$♥$♥$♥$

The next day is absolutely endless. At quitting time, I think the elevator is going exceptionally slowly. And when I get off on Adam's floor, he isn't alone. Janet is still at her desk, and Adam leans against the wall, arms folded, chatting with her.

Both their heads turn toward me. His gaze is disarmingly neutral, almost aloof, but Janet offers me a welcoming smile and speaks first.

"I know what you're here for."

I stop in my tracks, feeling the heat rise in my face. Adam lets his arms drop slowly to his sides, but he says nothing.

"You do?" I ask, my voice choking.

"Yes, but I would have sent it down to you tomorrow. You needn't have come up. I'm sure you'd rather be heading home."

She grabs a large manila envelope from her desk and rises. "We can ride down together."

I don't know what's happening. Yet Janet seems confidently in charge as she grabs her jacket and her purse before crossing the room and handing me the envelope.

Glancing down, I see it's from Mrs. Lovell's company. Instantly, the tension leaves me. The day of the meeting and dinner, she'd promised to send her perfumer's written description, the top, middle, and base notes, etc. for the new fragrance. I'd expected them by email, something pithy about woody, fresh, or floral.

Then, with Adam filling my head, not to mention other parts of me, I'd forgotten all about it.

"She mailed them to Adam," Janet says, tapping the address with a long tomato-red fingernail. "She likes to deal with the CEO. That's her way."

I nod. "Thank you."

"Good night," Janet says to him and starts toward the elevators.

Not knowing what else to do, I send him a longing glance before turning and following Janet as if this stupid envelope had been my goal all along.

We'd nearly reached the elevator when Adam finally speaks.

"Clover, just a minute," he calls after us. "I wouldn't mind seeing that."

I let out a sigh of relief.

"For heaven's sakes," Janet says, pressing the button, "let the girl go home. It's just perfume descriptors. You wouldn't be interested."

"It's fine," I say. "It'll only take a minute." Then in case she decides to wait for me, I add, "I don't have anyone waiting for me like you do."

The elevator opens. After giving me a sympathetic look, she leaves. I nearly sag against the wall.

"First you don't show up, and then tonight you come a bit early," he says, not having come a foot closer. "I might have to punish you."

Punish me? My body reacts with a flood of warmth and dampness. *Yes, please*, I think, wondering if that's the true intent behind Mrs. Lovell's new perfume name. But all I do is shrug.

"I suppose we need a schedule," I suggest, walking toward him on wobbling legs. I attribute the feeling to the adrenaline of Janet saying she knew, followed quickly by relief. "I wasn't aware we were locked in for *every* week night."

To my surprise, he laughs. "We aren't locked into anything. But you missed out on a great meal, although after your text, I took it home."

We step into his office, and he closes the door. The next thing I know I'm in his arms, on the receiving end of a hungry kiss.

When he lets me up for air, I say, "I think I missed out on a lot more than food."

"We can make up for it tonight, but first, lean over the couch, face down, ass in the air."

His tone has become strangely authoritarian despite his expression remaining placid.

"Excuse me?"

"The punishment," Adam reminds me, taking the envelope and setting it on the edge of the table.

I hesitate. What if this isn't what I think it is? "Are you . . . ? That is," I swallow and clear my throat. "Do you want me to be . . . submissive?"

If that's what this is, then I want it. I've always fantasized about a man dominating me, just for fun, of course, and only in the sexual realm. But I'm embarrassed for Adam to know.

"I want you to play along if you think it would be pleasurable." His voice is normal again. Sexy but friendly. "Your eyes danced when I said the word before, so why fight exploring something new? If you don't like it, we'll stop."

I nod. Already, I'm super excited for whatever comes next.

"You ought to have a safe word," he says, "if we're going to do this right."

"That makes it sound serious."

"Doesn't have to be. It's only to make you feel comfortable."

"OK, then." I think a moment. "Marzipan."

His face says it all, so I explain, "I never liked the stuff."

"*Hm*," he says. "Other than it being some kind of candy, I can't say I even really know what it is." Then Adam shrugs, and I can see his expression to dead-pan stern again. It sends a shiver down my spine.

"Ass in the air," he orders once more.

With slightly shaky legs, I walk to the couch. The high table that's usually behind it has been moved to a new location against the far wall.

Facing the bank of floor-to-ceiling windows, I lean over the back of the sofa, bracing myself with my arms reaching down to the leather seat cushions. My knees are trembling, but in a good way.

I don't hear him approach, but suddenly, his hands lift my skirt, drawing it up my taut thighs and over my butt. That alone makes my heartbeat race.

"I do love your thongs," he says, taking each of my cheeks in hand.

I'm more than ready for him to drop his pants and slide into me. If a good strong screw is my punishment, bring it on. Eyes closed, I wait.

Slap. I jump from the shock of his palm across one cheek, not from any pain. But when he slaps my other butt cheek a little harder, it briefly stings.

"We might only have a sexual arrangement," he says, slapping my ass in a rhythmic motion, warming it while other parts of me heat up as well. "But common courtesy would dictate you not break our standing engagement without letting," *slap*, "me," *slap*, "know." *Thwack!*

Ouch.

He stops.

"How are you?" His voice is sexy low.

"Fine." More than fine!

"Good," he says. "Look up."

I raise my head and our glances catch in the window's reflection. He looks so bangable, so freaking attractive, I can scarcely breathe.

"More?" he asks.

My pussy is tingling. Damn right I want more.

"Yes," I say, and lower my face to the sofa again.

21

Adam

Unexpected and amazing! I've always been into the power dynamic of sex, and it's a welcome surprise to discover Clover is, too. Good thing we both don't want the same role.

I give her a spanking that does little more than bring a blush to her perfect ass, but she's making this cool, sexy humming noise, and I can see her fingers are curling into the couch. She's definitely enjoying it.

When it's me who can't take it another second, I unzip and pull her thong to the side. She comes as I enter her with a muffled cry that sounds like my name on her tongue. Her pleasure is heady stuff!

With a few strokes, I follow her over the edge into a roaring climax.

I haven't ordered any food ahead of time, because I wasn't going to be a fool twice. But we end up sharing a hot, delivered pizza because a hard-fucking couple needs to eat.

Refueled and recharged, I decide to test the boundaries of our arrangement.

She always tidies up and dresses after sex. This time, she hadn't even made it to the undressing part. No buttons tonight, I pull her silky top up and then drag her bra cups down to rest under the gorgeous swell of her breasts.

Her eyes light up as she knows I'm up for another round. When I slide my hand into the front of her thong, she closes her eyes and tilts her head back. After tugging on a pert nipple with my teeth, I release it.

"Look at me," I say. Slowly, like she's drugged, Clover raises her head and focuses on me.

"Come to my home and spend the night so we can have more time and be comfortable. Then I won't have to worry about you on the T afterward."

I'm also stroking her clit, so she doesn't speak at first. When the silence lasts a few moments, I stop touching her.

"Adam," she moans. "Please."

"Answer me. Agree to come over," I order before caressing her swollen bud with my thumb.

"OK," she says quickly, "but not on a week night or even a Friday night. Saturday morning looks nice and casual and not at all lascivious compared to arriving on a Friday."

"Looks nice and casual," I repeat. "Who's watching?"

She lifts her hips, begging for my touch, but we're still negotiating the deal. And I'm curious. I wait.

"I don't know," Clover says with exasperation. "The world in general. My roommate, especially."

"So only one night?" I ask, not pleased because I already know I'll want more.

"But two whole days," she points out.

"Deal." I stroke her to another orgasm before sinking between her legs and filling her. A few piston thrusts, and I'm off, still amazed at how quickly I climax with her. It could be a bad thing if I don't take care of her first each time.

The following day and the rest of the week drags, brightened only by the promise of her company on the weekend. We agreed she won't come up to my office for the remainder of the work week. I don't know why I agreed to such a stupid arrangement because I'm like a caged tiger by Friday afternoon—a horny, caged tiger!

I admit I'm looking forward to more than sex. We can eat at a real table, not on my office coffee table or in my conference room where we've had some of our more elaborate meals, but in my dining room. Or in my bed. We can watch a movie, and I'm interested to find out what she's like in the real world.

Best of all, I can reach for her all night, and I wonder if we'll get any sleep.

To make it to Saturday, when I'm not reading reports or dealing with issues before they become problems, I lunch with clients. I golf. A lot. Bucket after bucket into the driving net. I even take a day out on my yacht in Boston harbor, although it's still a little cool on the water. During all of it, I think of Clover. Naked Clover. Panting Clover. Clover under the shower spray. Clover in my bed.

I text her that night, wondering how she's fared during the week. I don't ask though.

See you tomorrow, as early as you can.

I delete the second part. *Come as early as you like.* That's less desperate and sounds welcoming, too.

After an excruciatingly long night, it's finally Saturday morning. I am disgustingly like an eager dog waiting by the door, except I'm killing time by working out in my home gym and listening for texts. Nothing new since her reply from last night: *Will do.*

Which told me very little, although I know she'll come. I can feel the overwhelming draw to be together and I believe she's equally affected.

Ping! The sound has me launching myself off the rowing machine to grab my phone.

I'm here. How do I get in?

I smile. *Stand by for buzz sound. Then push door open. Make sure it clicks behind you. Meet you in front hall.*

I hustle over to the closest security panel and buzz her into the front hall before dashing down two flights of the architectural wonder of my oval-configured staircase. Clover is waiting politely in the antechamber between my front door and what I think of as my other front door, which I wrench open.

When she sees me, she laughs. A delightful Clover laugh. The sound makes me instantly hard. But then, everything about her makes me hard. And happy.

I don't know what comes over me, but I grab her arm and tug her into the foyer before enveloping her in a hug. I don't kiss her or let my hands roam her body. We just embrace for a long moment.

"I only came on the T," she says finally when we step apart. "It wasn't a trek through the Amazon jungle."

"Don't mention that word in this house," I say. "My father had a similar idea for an online store in the nineties and didn't run with it."

She laughs again, and I take her stylish leather backpack from her, setting it down on my dark, polished, century-old entrance hall floor. I can't believe she's here.

"You lied to me," she says, sounding strangely delighted.

"Did I?" I'm still grinning, ear-to-ear.

"You once said giving me a lift from work would be on your way. More like out of your way. You'd have had to drive past your home to get to mine."

"That's what I employ David for. It wouldn't have been a problem."

"Still, I'm shocked at your fib, trying to get me in the back of your fancy Maybach."

When she puts it that way, I sound like a creep. "I don't usually lie about anything," I tell her, sounding as solemn as I feel about it. "Not a fan of prevarication—on the giving or receiving end."

Her smile dies. "I'm teasing you," she says unnecessarily. "You were trying to save me a crowded train journey home, and I appreciate that. Sometimes, people . . . bend the truth for good reasons."

Personally, I don't think there are a lot of good reasons to lie to someone. And I decide right then never to lie to her again. She deserves better.

"How about a tour?" I offer, genuinely hoping she likes my place. I'm not one for owning a bunch of residences all over the world that I don't care about. I have a few and I want them all to feel like home. To suit me. This one does perfectly.

"I knew it would look like this," she says, proving my office décor is an extension of that same aesthetic. "It's very minimalist but welcoming. I love the espresso-colored floors contrasting with the white and gray above walls and trim. And so much light is surprising for a Beacon Hill townhouse."

She's talking with a designer's eye.

"But do *you* like it?"

Her smile is back. "So far, I do."

My Boston home is more than a standard tall, narrow brick townhouse. For one thing, it's ten thousand square feet of living space, and I'm about to show it all to Clover.

The first room at the front of the house is a formal dining room. I open the French door, and we stick our heads in, looking at a room I rarely used except for parties. A dark wooden table matches the floors with ten upholstered gray chairs, two dark buffet cupboards, gray rug, marble fireplace.

I can't think of the last time I've used it. Through the front windows, you can see the view of narrow, tree-lined Louisburg Square.

"Lovely," Clover said. "But this isn't where you dine, tête-à-tête, with a lady-friend."

Is she fishing to find out whether I bring a lot of girlfriends over? I won't lie and say I never have, but probably fewer than she would imagine.

I play along. "The tête-à-tête room is at the back of the house overlooking the terrace and yard."

Heading to the back of the house, we pass the massive staircase, which no one can miss because it's a work of art, designed in a more gracious time. Stark white risers and balusters met black treads and railings with a gray runner all the way up for four flights. You can look up and think ornate seashell, but I like the dizzying view from the top to the bottom even better.

Clover eyes it appreciatively and gives a quiet "wow."

I ignore a closed door, the first of my eight bathrooms, and we head to the open, modern end of the first floor. My chef's kitchen has my actual chef standing in it. Amarra, in her forties, likes working weekends for me because she wants to cook every weekday night for her teenagers. She's amazingly creative, using her unusual ancestry of black, Greek, and Creole ethnicities to cook singularly original dishes.

And she can also make a mean meatloaf. What's not to love?

"Amarra, this is Ms. Mitchell."

"Please, call me Clover."

When we enter the living room where I spend most of my time, she says in a whisper, "I thought we were going to be alone."

"We are," I whisper back.

"Amarra," she says.

"Staff doesn't count. I can't handle this place by myself. Amarra cooks on weekends when I'm in town because there's only so much gourmet restaurant food a man can handle."

Clover still looks freaked out at being together in front of someone.

"It's not as though I invited friends and family over to get to meet you."

Her eyes widen.

"Don't worry about it," I say. "Is it too early to ply you with liquor and make you relax. Is there anything you want?"

"Water," she says. "Please. And for you to tell me how many staff are here."

"I have a housekeeper, but she doesn't come on weekends."

"Good." Clover still sounds nervous. "What, no valet or butler?"

"Ha! I keep both at my country estate," I tease, then I add "I'm joking," just in case she was serious and thinks I am, too. "A cleaning crew comes once a week, but that's on Tuesday."

I take a sparkling water and a plain one out of the small fridge set discreetly behind a wall panel in the living room.

"Which?" I ask, holding up both bottles.

"Plain, please. Sparkling always leaves me thirsty."

"Huh!" is my brilliant comeback. I hand her the plain water and open the sparkling for myself.

"So this is the room where we can watch a movie or . . . whatever?" she asks, seeing the flatscreen above the fireplace, which I will definitely light that evening to set the mood.

"Whatever *you* want," I tell her. "In fact, whatever the lady wishes to do for the next thirty-six or so hours, that's what we'll do."

"No private movie theater?" Clover teases.

I won't lie. "I have one. Right under our feet in the cellar."

"Of course you do. What self-respecting billionaire wouldn't?"

"True," I agree. "But it's better used with a group. For two, this room or the other sitting room upstairs is preferable."

"I make really good popcorn," she says, giving me the sweetest smile.

What an adorable talent. "I can't wait to taste it," I say.

She continues her scrutiny of my home. Looking at the dove-gray, soft leather sofa, she nods in approval. "Looks comfy."

Wandering around, Clover scans my books, glances at the sparse framed photos of my family, and even examines my plants.

"They're real," she says, her tone surprised.

"Why wouldn't they be?" *Do I seem like a plastic plant person to her?*

"I don't know." She pauses in front of my 1923 Gibson guitar in its stand.

"I'm not great, so don't ask me to play," I say quickly before admitting, "I just goof around on it sometimes. It deserves a real guitarist."

"I'll get you to play for me," she vows, and I have no doubt I'll comply even though I am mediocre at best.

Then she reaches the French doors to a sunroom, also my breakfast and lunch area most weekends.

"The tête-à-tête room," she guesses, making me chuckle because I rarely hang out down here with the women I date. We go out to fancy restaurants, concerts, sporting events, and the like. And then to the bedroom, theirs or mine.

Beyond the sunroom is a classic Beacon Hill south slope garden, not huge but landscaped with flowers, some mature trees, a spacious terrace with a huge grill and smoker, and outdoor furniture for those perfect New England summer evenings.

I imagine Clover in a strappy sundress when the temps are warm enough, sipping one of Amarra's original punch concoctions, smiling at me with her lush mouth, her glorious eyes shining.

"Would you like to go upstairs?" I blurt, wanting her in my bed. "I mean, do you want to go *see* the upstairs."

"Thank God no elevator," she quips, and then sees my expression. "You have one, don't you?"

I almost feel indecent. "Yup. Do you want to try it?"

"Nope. Let's walk."

Another small, turn-of-the-century servants' staircase is hidden in the wall, but we stroll back to the foyer.

"Almost feels like I'm being naughty and climbing on a museum piece," Clover refers to the artistry of the staircase.

At that moment, however, my eyes are solely on Clover, keeping her in front of me as we climb.

"What are you doing?" she asks. But she knows.

"Watching your ass sway," I confess. "And I do feel like being naughty."

She laughs, gives an exaggerated wiggle, and keeps climbing. On the second floor, we enter another sitting room. For some reason, Clover turns and stares at me.

"It looks identical," she says.

"It doesn't," I protest. "This one faces the square, and that gray sofa isn't leather, it's more upright and . . . some kind of fabric. Not leather."

"Riiiight," she humors me.

Hey, when I find something I like, even a style, I don't see a point in reinventing the wheel.

This floor also holds a casual table and a mini kitchen or large butler's pantry—either way, it has a sink, a coffee maker, a shit-ton of glassware, a bunch of discreet cupboards that I've never opened, and a wine fridge. It isn't obscenely large, but holds enough if I spontaneously throw a party for sixty or seventy.

She glances at the second-floor deck but doesn't make a move to step outside, but she does poke her head into a vintage style bathroom, with black-and-white tile and a claw-foot tub. "Nice touch."

"What's in there?" she gestures to the closed door beside it.

I show her my home office, complete with a conference table, and then we're climbing the stairs to the next level. I scoot past my bedroom door and show her one of the guest rooms that I've turned into a gym.

"You were in here when I arrived," she says, examining the training equipment, grasping hold of one of the elliptical handles.

I'm in the doorway, still amazed that Clover is in my house. "How can you tell?"

"You're dressed for it," she points out, since I'm wearing basketball shorts and a T-shirt. "Besides, I can smell you in here."

I resist the urge to sniff under my own arms, and she continues, "I don't mean that in a bad way. It's not stinky body odor assaulting my nose. You have a nice 'man' scent beyond your fabulous cologne."

Waving her hand around, she adds, "It's in the air. I like it."

She likes my sweat smell! Why does that please me so much?

"Upstairs is another guest room and bathroom, along with a basketball court."

"You're joking?" she says.

"Just a quarter court so I can dribble and shoot."

"Naturally," Clover says. "Let me see."

She doesn't remark on missing my bedroom, but she has to know if we go inside, we won't come out for a while.

We complete the tour on the next floor and even take a quick jaunt up the only modern staircase in my home, leading to the roof deck. Peaceful, private, perfect for rolling Clover under me on one of the cushioned sun-loungers.

I take hold of her hand and pull her toward me, enjoying when her fingers rest behind my neck. As she threads them into my hair, I lean down and kiss her. Everything that seemed a little weird about being with her outside work falls away. It's just her rocking body against mine and her fragrance filling my senses.

When she parts her lips, I delve inside, my tongue fencing with hers. Without even realizing it, my hands drop to her round bottom. I can't help myself. She's a bombshell, and her rear end is sublime.

I guess I'm an ass man, too.

We don't end up on a deck chair. When we break apart for air, we stand side-by-side in silence for a moment, and it isn't awkward. It's nice. We take in the view of the park and the neighborhood around us. Then she turns her golden-brown eyes to me.

"I have to admit, I'm surprised you don't have a penthouse at Millennium Tower or at the very least, the penthouse on top of the Four Seasons."

I chuckle. I have a real estate friend, Marcus Parisi, who advised me to buy a place at the Tower, which I rent out at a profit.

"Millennium Tower reminds me too much of an office building," I explain. "And the Four Seasons had nothing available when I was looking to buy."

Nodding, she looks again at the historic homes on both sides.

"Why?" I ask. "Would you prefer one of those?"

She shakes her head. "I simply wondered about your choice. To me, this is preferable. It's insanely gorgeous, but it's not . . ."

"Not what?" I ask when she pauses.

"Not what I expected for a billionaire playboy."

I wince. "Is anyone called a *playboy* anymore? If they are, please count me out."

That brings out her sunshine smile. "This is obviously a rich man's place." She gestures with the now-empty water bottle. "But it could be a family man's home, too."

With that, she turns and goes back inside.

I nearly say, *I could be a family man.* But I don't. As long as she works for me, we're sex buddies and nothing more, except maybe friends.

I follow her down two flights of stairs. To my extreme happiness, she goes directly to my bedroom door.

I've been ready to jump her bones since she arrived, but I wasn't sure she wanted me to pounce. Now, I'm getting a good vibe.

Clover takes in the large room that runs the entire front to back of my house, from the reading chairs in the bay window overlooking the square, past my bed, to the French doors leading to another deck overlooking the back.

To stop myself from saying anything sappy or stupid, I toss my bottle over my shoulder and tackle her. My momentum carries us both straight onto my bed, with her shrieking, but with glee.

When we came to a stop, we're finally lying together in my bedroom. I roll off her onto my back, and we stare at the high Victorian-era ceiling. Instead of this being a sensual and sexy moment as I've imagined, we are both laughing.

At least we were for a little while, then gradually, we face one another. I stroke her shoulder and down her arm.

"I like seeing you outside work," I say, nearly blowing it immediately, as Clover tenses.

I have to read the greens better or I won't be sinking this putt. In a heartbeat, I settle over her and kiss her. The sensation is like hitting the gas pedal in my favorite Porsche. The 718 Cayman GT4 goes from zero to sixty in four seconds. I don't think it takes us that long to be open-mouthed, tongues fencing, hands roaming.

Better to shut up and have sex before I scare her off. To that end, our clothing goes flying in a way it can't at work. At least some of it goes, all we have time for. Basically, she yanks at my shorts and joyfully tosses them, before I tug her dark jeans down her slim legs and hurl them to the floor.

"Nothing fancy," she says, spreading for me.

I take this to mean she's as ready as I am. Still, there's always time to knead her breasts and roll her nipples, having learned Clover is very sensitive to both. Since we didn't bother to remove our shirts, I reach under her top and shove her bra up to give me access.

"That goes straight to my lady bits," she says, her eyes already closing as she starts to arch her neck. "Now!" she adds.

I thrust inside her, wondering how we'd spent this many minutes alone without having sex already.

Her fingernails dig through the fabric on my shoulders, and her lips part as I repeatedly sheath myself deep inside her and then withdraw, a rocking motion that quickly brings us both to panting.

Holding off my release, I lean on one arm and slide my other hand between our damp bodies. More than any woman I've ever known, Clover has a magic button.

I barely graze it, continuing to pump my hips, when she moans and tenses up. Her pussy milks my cock as I follow her climax.

"Yes," she hisses, and I bury my face in the soft space between her neck and shoulder. A favorite place to kiss her, too.

"Mm," is all I manage against her skin.

When we're lying next to one another again, Clover says, "Funny, but I thought we'd be entirely naked the first time here and exploring those fantasies you mentioned."

"Me, too. Also, less hurried. Sorry about that."

"Don't be. It was perfect." Then she sits up. "Bathroom?"

Clover is in for another surprise. She probably assumes it's merely an elegant room with a shower and a commode. It's a little more than that.

Wearing only her T-shirt and holding a pillow against the front of her, she heads across the room. Her ass is a work of art, and I'm sad to see it disappear behind the bathroom door.

22

Clover

I gasp. Truly, I do! And loudly! Adam Bonvier's bathroom causes me to gasp. Basically, it's a private spa—complete with a hot rock sauna at one end enclosed in some type of good-smelling wood, a hot tub in the corner, a granite shower with six heads, a soaking tub in the other corner, and a massage area. The man has a freaking proper massage table.

I set the pillow I'm holding on top of it.

Has he forgotten a toilet? I find it in a separate little room. I pee because the bottled water has gone through me. Then grabbing the pillow again for a modicum of modesty, I open the door to the bedroom.

"Adam," I call.

He appears in only snug boxer briefs, stealing my breath for a moment, although I've seen them a few times. Cotton, extraordinarily soft, and fitting him like a glove, they are officially my favorite article of clothing in his wardrobe.

"A massage table?" I ask.

He grins. "Of all the wondrous things in here, that's what you ask about?"

I wait. He shrugs.

"I like my own comfortable table when my masseuse comes, which is twice a week."

"Male or female?" I shoot back.

He raises a dark eyebrow, probably at my hint of jealousy although I'm only teasing. Then he says, "I never noticed."

This cracks me up. I know he's just saying that. When I stop laughing, I confess, "This is the most macked out bathroom I've ever seen."

"Me, too," he says. Then quickly adds, "I have a similar one in all my residences."

"Makes sense. Shame you forgot the toilet."

"Through there," he says, pointing to the closed door.

"I'm joking. I found it after first getting lost in the walk-in closet." I discovered Adam has a ton of towels and sheets for his massage.

Then we stare at one another.

"So," I ask, deciding I'm ready to play. "Shower?"

"Is that your choice?" he asks, "We could start in the hot tub."

My stomach chooses that moment to grumble. Earlier, before I came, I was too nervous to do more than drink a cup of coffee.

"Maybe after lunch," I say hopefully. "For now, a quick shower would be good. Gotta see where all those heads hit."

"They can target wherever the lady likes. They're all adjustable except the rain heads coming out of the ceiling."

"And obviously, there's room for two." My voice goes a little quiet because this will be the first time we're both stark naked.

Adam goes to the closet and pulls out a thick white towel, which he hands to me like the sexiest pool boy I can imagine.

"What about you?" I ask.

180

"I don't want you to think you can't take a shower without me being all over you. I can go tell Amarra were nearly ready for lunch."

Instantly, I imagine his private chef downstairs waiting for us, knowing what we're up to. *Ugh!* I think I finally know the answer to Adam's question: To me at least, it's better to overhear someone else and be a little embarrassed if discovered, than to find out someone has overheard you having sex.

In this case, I know Amarra can't possibly have heard us in Adam's bedroom, but I wonder if she thinks I came here for a booty call!

I have to push it all out of my mind. We're grown-ups, and this is our arrangement, and it's not hurting anyone. So I ask him for what I really want.

"How about you jump in with me?"

I don't need to invite Adam a second time. He starts turning on taps and dials on the shower. I won't be surprised if the whole stone and glass enclosure lifts off and shoots into outer space.

We enjoy not only long minutes in the hot water that pulses and sprays and massages and dances across our bodies, but—because we can't help ourselves—we also have a quick fuck against the craggy granite shower wall.

I hold on to two small outcroppings, letting one of the shower heads pummel the throbbing area between my legs from the front while Adam enters me from behind. I try to hold off longer than him this time. But can't. With his cock stroking my insides and his hands—one on my breast, one on my clit, caressing my outsides, I couldn't stop the orgasm from rolling through me even if I had a gun to my head.

It's spectacular, and I swear I float away into the realm of pure sensation. I lean my head back against his shoulder as I return to myself, catching the tail end of his climax. He surges into me, his hands having moved to my hips to hold me steady while his rasping groans fill the steamy air.

Finally, we step apart, rinse off, and grab our towels.

"What's for lunch?" I ask, making him smile.

$♥$♥$♥$

Hours later, during which somehow we've managed to keep our hands off one another, we've eaten a tasty lunch outside and are now simply talking under an aged elm in his yard. It's comfortable, interesting, and fun, but I skirt most family questions except those I can answer generically. I leave out our own international vacations in exotic places, my parents' yacht, my parents' collections of expensive things, like cars and paintings.

At this stage, I'd hate for him to suddenly see me as a candy heiress who might quit her job at any time. I don't ever want to seem frivolous or entitled when what I am is dedicated and driven. Thus, I ask him as many questions as I can, utterly content watching Adam's attractive mouth move while he tells me a story from one of his sailing adventures.

His gray eyes aren't forbidding or stern or gloomy. They're the brightest, happiest gray I've ever seen.

And then, as often happens this time of year, a thunderstorm blows in from the hotter south, and we make it indoors just in time before the dark clouds open above us.

I shiver.

"You scared?" he asks.

"Nope." And then I jump as thunder booms close overhead.

"Wait for it," he says, coming up behind me and sliding his strong arms around my waist. I lean against him and a few seconds later, lightning splits the early evening sky. I jump again.

"You sure you're not scared?" he teases.

"I'm not. Just edgy because I'm here, I guess." I turn in his arms, slide my hands up behind his neck, and pull him down for a kiss. His hands grab my butt and squeeze before tilting me against him.

"Mm," I murmur.

"Mm," he answers.

When he lifts his head, I look up at him, my mound tingling with desire again. "What do you want to do next?"

I fully expect him to take me to bed, but he says, "We haven't finished the tour. To the basement!" Adam declares, grabbing my hand and leading the way. The staircase is narrower than the main one and hidden behind a door, but it isn't a dark or dingy stairwell. Not only is it well lit, when we reach the bottom, the basement has none of the dankness I expect. It's probably the cleanest, freshest cellar I've ever seen.

"My housekeeper has her own room through there." He points to a closed door. "Although she rarely spends the night."

In the opposite direction, we pass through a brick area, basically a wide passage between steel racks filled with wine bottles. More bottles are behind refrigerated glass. It's the kind of cellar in which you don't worry about cobwebs or spiders.

Beyond it is an extra-wide wooden door. Adam holds it open for me, and a light comes on as we enter, reminding me of work. Three spacious rows, each with four plush leather chairs, slant away from me toward a large screen.

"I suppose it has the best surround sound, too," I muse.

"Otherwise," he says, walking to the front of the room, "what's the point?" He drops into one of the chairs and pats the one beside him.

"It's too comfy," I say, pushing it back to a reclining position. "I would be asleep in five minutes and miss the movie."

"I'll have them all removed and install ladder back chairs, maybe with nails instead of cushions."

Shaking my head, I close my eyes. The chairs really are heavenly, but when his hand touches my inner arm, caressing right above my wrist, a jolt of excitement courses through me. I'm not even halfway through my visit, and it feels like we have all the time in the world.

"We could watch a movie here, after all," he offers. "Who needs a group of friends?"

It's a strange thing, having an adult sleepover. A part of me wants to cram every activity I can into the two days, but the rest of me just wants to chill.

"I'm OK not doing anything," I say finally. "Honestly, I'm just happy to be here." *With you*, I want to add but don't. It's too gushing, too relationship sounding, when we aren't going down that route.

If we did, we'd start leaving work together for a drink or a meal, text each other at all hours of the day and night, and slip up in front of someone who might raise a stink about the Bonvier dating rule being obscenely broken.

"I'm happy you're here, too," he says, and switches to holding my hand.

I sigh.

"What is it?" he asks.

"Nothing. Everything is perfect."

"We can make it more perfect," he says.

"How?"

"Let's try out a fantasy or two later."

And just like that, I have something to look forward to—a sexual treat that keeps me humming with anticipation. Till then, we play cards, which I love and always have, and then watch a movie in the living room while eating dinner. I've changed into a clingy black dress that I'd rolled up in my backpack.

At first, I feel silly since we are staying in, but the appreciative look on his face buoyed my confidence, and he quickly changes into slacks and a lightweight, crewneck sweater.

Our dressy clothing adds to the sexual atmosphere all through the movie, which isn't even a rom-com. When the adventure film credits are scrolling, by mutual yet silent consent, we go up to his bedroom, each carrying a glass of crisp dessert wine. Adam uses a remote to turn on the gas fireplace and put on sexy music that comes through speakers in the walls. My insides do a frisky little dance.

It is fantasy time.

"So how does *this* work?"

"You've never done *this* before?" He makes a lewd gesture with his thumb poking through a circle of his fingers. Silly man!

I laugh, which breaks the tension I've been feeling. Taking a sip of wine, I try unraveling the game.

"We said we could . . . *would* try some fantasies if we were ever at your home. Do I just say one out loud and hope you don't cringe?"

He comes closer and takes the wine glass from me, setting it on the mantel above the flickering flames, along with his own glass. I nearly object because of the possible damage to the wood. But when he takes my hands in his and gives me *that* look, right in the eyes, deep as can be, I forget about everything except him.

"First of all, Clover Mitchell, I'm certain no sexual fantasy of yours could make me cringe. Secondly, I have an idea to put you at ease."

"What about you?" I ask.

He releases my hands so he can cup my breasts through my gown's slinky fabric, making me catch my breath.

"I have to say," Adam remark, "I'm pretty at ease with you."

His thumbs brush my nipples, and I relish the zing that goes straight to the apex between my legs.

He doesn't stop his small movements as he continues. "Why don't we write what we want? We'll both jot down a few ideas."

I can hardly think with my nipples stiff under his touch and my core throbbing. Finally, I push his hands away.

"We can put them in separate piles," I say, getting into the nuts and bolts.

"Even into hats," he teases.

I ignore him. "I can read one of your notes, and if I don't like it, I can put it back and it won't hurt your feelings."

"Sounds good," Adam agrees. His hands go to my ass this time, drawing me close.

"Who goes first?" I ask, as his swollen cock presses against me.

"Ladies first," he says. "Always."

Ten minutes later, after much laughter, drinking wine, and scribbling of notes, with him sneaking a peek and me trying and failing to snatch one of his to look at, I find myself about to enjoy something I've only ever dreamt about.

I could never ask aloud to be tied up and teased until I'm desperate. I've written that I want him to bind my hands. As fantasies go, it's probably a little tame, but I'm beyond thrilled when, after he read one of my pieces of paper, he doesn't hesitate.

"Maybe when we get used to these games," he says, already coming out of his closet with a silk tie in hand. My mouth goes dry as I know what it's for, guessing which fantasy he's chosen. "Maybe then we can add to them. Will you give me the freedom to embellish if it's in the same realm?"

Speechless, I nod, staring at the blue and silver silk in his hands. Thinking of it will precipitate, it fascinates me.

"You can do that," I agree.

"Stand up," he says, and I swear his tone has changed. Something sensually commanding, something that says he won't tolerate my disobedience. It sends shivers along my spine.

Rising to my feet as he looks me up and down, recalling how he's "punished" me before, I half-wish I'd written "spanking" on all three pieces of paper.

"Just considering what I need to take off you now because it will be hard to remove later, unless I tear it off."

"I see." My voice is barely more than a whisper.

He drops a kiss on my lips. "Delicious! I can't wait to see what the rest of you tastes like tonight."

Whoa! I nearly sit down again, knees quivering with anticipation.

A moment later, his hands are spinning me away from him and he unzips my little black dress. I'm glad it isn't going to be torn off. Sliding it down my shoulders, he tosses it over one of the chairs sitting primly in front of the bay window.

I know he's staring at my ass, almost fully exposed because I'm wearing a black satin thong. A girl has to be prepared.

"Turn," he orders.

I like this new, unfamiliar tone, and I obey. His gaze drops to my demi-cup, black satin bra that pushes the tops of my full breasts up and nearly over.

"Very sexy!" he says. "If I'd known, we probably would have skipped dinner *and* the movie."

I manage to chuckle although my throat feels tight.

"And your bra undoes in the front," he says. "That's a bonus. Onto the bed."

I sit and then scramble backward. Not exactly graceful, but every nerve ending in my body is on high alert, waiting, wanting, and I'm nervous AF.

Luckily, he doesn't laugh at me. In fact, not a hint of a smile appears when I lay back. Following me onto the mattress, Adam straddles me.

All I can do is watch and grow wet as he takes hold of one of my hands and knots the end of the silk around it. He threads his tie around the headboard and soon, my other wrist is similarly bound.

"Try to pull free," he says.

I do, and a wave of alarm crashes through me. I'm truly captive and helpless.

"I think we can add to this, like frosting on a cake," he says before drawing two more ties out of his pocket.

"What are those for?" I don't want one stuffed in my mouth, and I'm about to tell him so when he backs off of me.

"Let's tie you up properly and do this right."

"Properly?" I echo.

Soon, both of my ankles have also been restrained, each silk tie disappearing over the end of the bed where it's fastened out of sight, presumably around the leg of the frame.

So excited, I can barely draw in a full breath. My heart pounds in my chest until I can hear it. I bet he can, too.

"That's pretty good," Adam says. "Not precisely *your* fantasy, but I hope you don't mind. You comfortable?"

I nod. I don't think I can speak. My legs are spread in a gentle V, but I don't feel crude since I have on the prettiest undergarments I own.

"You look petrified," he says.

I shake my head. I wanted to look alluring.

"No?" he asks. "Good, don't be. Remember marzipan. Just enjoy this." He draws his cashmere sweater over his head and off with one hand.

Nothing underneath, I note, appreciating the span of his chest and his broad shoulders. He has the shape every female admires in her man, with flat nipples and a six-pack torso sloping inward to his trim waist.

My man. I swallow.

Adam undoes his belt buckle before the lowering of his zipper sounds loud in the room despite the soft music still playing. When he sends his pants to the floor, I make a weird, strangled noise.

Luckily, he doesn't hear me or choses to ignore it. I hope when it's his turn for a fantasy, he'll be equally coiled with anticipation. My skin is prickling, desperate for him to begin.

Unlike his sweater, he does have something on under his pants. Charcoal gray boxer briefs donned after our shower. Form-fitting—and what freaking form! An erection like a thick python is scarcely contained under the cotton fabric, which is stretched to the point of tearing.

I sink my teeth into my lower lip. Not a habit of mine, but necessary to keep from humming with eagerness.

Instead of stripping further, he crawls between my spread legs, up and over me.

"Hello, gorgeous!" he says. "So far, I am loving your fantasy."

My cheeks warm. "Me, too," I whisper.

This time, he's the one to chuckle. "And we haven't really begun yet. Isn't that right?"

"True," I say, all breathy and hopeful. I start to squirm.

He claims my lips in a long, slow kiss. As I tilt my head and settle into it, he leaves my mouth and nibbles a path down my neck. Naturally, I arch to give him access.

He teases my nipples through the fabric of the bra, which at this moment is frustrating as hell. I want his lips and teeth directly on my skin.

In complete agreement, he deftly opens the front clasp with his thumb and finger. I'm impressed. And then, well, I can think nothing coherent at all.

His mouth is on one breast, his capable fingers knead the other, rolling my rosy nipple before pinching it with just the right pressure.

I gasp. After a minute or so, in which I can feel the moisture pooling between my legs, he switches and gives the opposite breast the same treatment.

"Adam," I say on a sigh. And nothing more.

"Clover," he replies, before putting his mouth to better use than speaking. Licking a hot, wet trail down my rib cage to the single ruby stud in my belly button, he pauses and says, "I should get you a diamond one."

"Mmph," is all I can manage while straining against the knots at my wrist. I don't know what I would have done if one had come loose. Probably floated away. But I would like to sink my fingers into his hair at the very least.

His tongue swirls around my belly button, making me clench my tickled stomach muscles, and then . . . *thank God!* . . . he goes lower.

Looking down my body, I watch him hook his fingers under my thong—grazing my throbbing clit, before he drags the triangle of satin sideways. Then my head falls back. I close my eyes when I feel a puff of air against my closely trimmed curls. And when his fingers gently part my pussy lips, I lift my hips helplessly toward him.

"Easy, lady," he says, his tone husky, and I try to settle down, to relax.

But it is so fucking hot! Also not having to ask for his mouth on me is incredibly freeing. With all four limbs restrained, I can't make Adam do anything he doesn't want to do, nor can I stop him. My brain says he must be into it, and that's an exciting notion.

His tongue sweeps up one side of my clit, then the other. *Oh, baby!*

He does this until my fingers are clenched into fists and my hips are shaking uncontrollably.

And then, he flicks my nub with the tip of his tongue.

"Ahhh," I half groan, half sigh.

He does it again and again. Perfect. God, yes! Up and down. Then side to side. Just how I like it. I'm not into being sucked down there or chomped on like I'm a piece of fruit. I like his Little. Fast. Flicks.

So much that before I know what's happening, I climax. It sneaks up on me and doesn't let go. Spasms, muscles clenching and rippling, heat zinging through me, and while I still can't catch my breath, an orgasm the size of Texas— the whole shebang!

She-bang!

I dissolve into post-coital laughter, my entire body light as a feather.

Thank you, silk ties.

23

Adam

I have to admit I feel stupidly proud of myself for what I've done. Clover has one of those out-of-mind, out-of-body climaxes that leaves a person drained. And in her case, laughing.

As her eyes flutter open, looking dazed, she says, "Wow!"

I can't help smiling. It's rewarding to give a partner that type of experience. Also a massive turn-on.

I don't hesitate. In record time, I shuck my briefs and settle between her thighs, looking down at those caramel-colored eyes which appear drugged. Her pupils are dilated and dark, indicating she is entirely into this. I drag her sexy thong to the side again and fit my cock to her opening.

Easing in, feeling her pussy grip me, I wish I'd taken a moment to untie her ankles so she could wrap her legs around me. But it's too late to stop. Seeing her restrained on my bed and watching her pulling at the ties while coming, I almost climaxed when she had. There's no going back now. Her hands bound over her head, lifting her breasts, is wildly sexy. I didn't know it would be so hot.

We are watching each other, her mouth making these sweet shapes and small moans. I think I lose control a little, burying myself deep inside her. My body is so revved up, and she feels so good, it's impossible to slow down.

Unless she asks me. Thankfully, she doesn't.

After only a few powerful thrusts, I come. She doesn't climax a second time, which is my fault for rushing and slamming into her. At this moment, though, I am all animal—no brain, no finesse, and absolutely no gentleman.

As soon as I draw out, again I wish I'd untied her already. It isn't as much fun working the knots loose when wanting nothing more than to lie down beside her and stroke her smooth skin.

But she's patient and relaxed. Soon, I'm on my side, spooning her for the first time. It is a little unusual for me. It's not like I want to cuddle. Even the word sounds sort of childishly repulsive. But I do want to hold Clover close for a few minutes and just be peaceful in the aftermath of that intense round of sex.

"I'm glad you didn't jump up," she says, as if reading my mind. "I need a minute to get my bearings."

"We'll get up when we're ready. When our legs don't wobble."

I haven't heard her giggle before, and I like it.

"Would you like to soak in the hot tub?"

She eyes me sideways. "Yes."

This is the best damn Saturday of my life.

After five more minutes, I get up. "Come along." I tug her by the hand when she doesn't immediately follow.

She groans. I wonder if I was too rough at the end.

"Are you OK?"

"Oh, yes," she says. "More than OK. Just a little tired."

I gesture for her to precede me. "The hot tub will either knock you out completely or revive you. Who knows?"

The hot water knocks us both out, and we go to bed satiated and exhausted. Fortunately, around two in the morning, we're ready again. I know we can't realistically sustain this level of hunger for one another, but we're determined to take full advantage while it lasts.

$♥$♥$♥$

Waking up this morning beside Clover, watching her sleep for a few moments before she stirs, it's . . . nice. Better than nice. She has a few freckles across her nose I never noticed before. Maybe she hides them with makeup. And her burnished-brown hair has dried while we slept, curling slightly.

"Do you straighten your hair?" is my first question when her eyes flutter open. She punches me in the shoulder and rolls over for another few minutes of snoozing.

Eventually, we have breakfast wearing only robes, the way people do in movies or magazine ads, some of them created by Bonvier in fact. Luckily, I have one for her, too.

"Billionaire playboys are expected to eat in their dressing gown," she states and squirts grapefruit across the table as she plunges her spoon into a ruby-red half.

Even without trying, she is endlessly amusing.

Eventually, we dress, and I convince her it's safe to take a Sunday stroll. Beacon Hill is a great neighborhood for walking, with mature shade trees and quaint cobblestone alleys. After much coercion, and kissing, Clover agrees but only if she can wear an oversized hat and sunglasses.

"There's no bright sunshine," I point out, looking at her ridiculous disguise. In fact, though it's not raining, the air is cool.

"I feel safer this way," she says.

As if anyone would know who I am or care whether she's *with* me. We traipse around for an hour, then another, ending up walking around Louisburg Square. Now that she's comfortable out in the wicked world, I offer to take her to brunch.

She nearly agrees when a neighbor walking his dog says, "Hey, Adam," and gives me the friendly thumbs up.

OK! I acknowledge that people do recognize me around here.

Clover turns heel and hurries toward home. We end up switching on a couple heat lamps and eating on my terrace in front of the waterfall feature. To me, the sound of the water cascading down the stone wall gives the back yard a little something extra.

"Nice touch!" Clover says.

"I always get the pump working as soon as the weather's warm enough. I know it doesn't replace an ocean view or a pristine lake," I half apologize.

"I'm sure you have both of those at one of your other residences," she guesses before shoveling a forkful of fluffy omelet into her gorgeous, kissable mouth.

"I do, in fact." Clover has nailed it.

We stay outside to read the news on our tablets despite the weak sunshine. It's quiet, apart from some spring birds, and I'm not bored for a second. When Clover gets up to stretch, I set down what I'm reading.

"Want to shoot some baskets?"

"Is that your favorite sport?" she asks as we mount the stairs.

"Golf is my favorite. What about you?"

"Tennis, I guess," she says, "but my favorite activity just for fun is swimming. Not serious swimming, not doing a zillion laps or anything."

I wish I could surprise her with a pool on the roof or in the basement. For no other reason than to make her happy, although seeing Clover in a bathing suit would be a bonus.

When shooting baskets, she was naturally graceful even if a tad short. Barefoot, since she didn't have appropriate footwear, we played for a half hour. She spent more time peering down through the plexiglass floor to the four-story stairwell or looking above to the skylight overhead.

"This is really an ingenious way to get the light down through the entire house, right to the first-floor foyer," she says.

Since I made the alteration to the house—not personally, but I paid for it—I took credit. "Thanks. I'm glad you're not a purist. Some might say it was sacrilegious to put this in a Victorian home."

"If you had put this in," she gestures with the basketball she's holding, "without the skylight and the clear floor, it would have been a shame," she said. "But you've enhanced the beauty, not detracted from it."

Surging forward, I pick her up from behind and hold her as high as I can.

"Shoot," I say, and despite laughing and sending the ball ricocheting off the backboard, she makes a basket.

The day goes by like the Shanghai maglev bullet train. But it isn't over yet.

"Fantasy time," she says out of the blue at four o'clock.

"Yes!" I exclaim with a pump of my fist, not at all sophisticated. I think about what I wrote on my bits of paper, and my mouth goes dry.

And just like that, we're back in my bedroom, and Clover has made her choice. Her smile makes my cock jump to attention.

"Sit there," she orders, pointing to one of the winged reading chairs.

"Yes, ma'am," I quip and do as I'm told.

"That's all you have to do." She disappears into the bathroom and comes out in some insanely spiked pumps I haven't seen before along with her black dress from the night before. I don't give a damn that it's a repeat. I know what fantasy is coming.

Breathing shallowly, I wait for the show.

Without music, without a hint of atmosphere, she strips slowly for me—easing her dress down over her curves, turning to show me her ass, unclipping her bra and tossing it aside, and finally, shimmying out of her thong and sending it in my direction.

I catch it and hold it to my face to breathe in her scent before resting my hand on my thigh. And all the time she keeps her gaze on mine, her lips in a small smile, until Clover wears nothing but a confident expression and her sexy shoes.

Fantasy going extremely well. Check.

Again, she turns and shows me her perfect rear as she snags a pillow from the bed and drops it at my feet. My focus is riveted as she kneels on it and reaches for my fly.

"Someone is very horny," she says, releasing my cock and holding the length in her hand. Then I get my fantasy— a gorgeous woman, naked except for those fuck-me heels, going down on me while I'm fully clothed and don't have to do a thing to pleasure her in return.

Gripping the base of my erection with one hand, her other fondles my balls, tugging a little, and even pressing her fingers back behind them in that spot which feels so damn good.

How does she know that?

Her mouth is very busy, too. Clover licks me, base to tip, while every few moments looking up at me from under her lashes. Those tiger eyes, as I think of them, are like precious jewels. *Damn, she is good at this.* Is it natural talent or practiced skill?

As her full lips finally go around my cock, I stop any jealous thoughts. When she sucks, I make a few loud and somewhat embarrassing sounds, already mere moments away from coming.

I try not to touch her, letting her set the pace and depth of taking me in. She is a generous lover, letting the tip of my dick hit the back of her throat.

When I'm no longer thinking with the correct head, I can't help sinking my fingers into her silky hair, holding her momentarily still while I thrust into her mouth, once, twice. It's sheer heaven!

Ultimately, I put my head back, hands behind my neck, and let her finish me unimpeded.

Fantasy better than expected. Check and definitely A plus.

I don't even consider whether Clover will pull away at my climax. That's up to her. Turns out, she doesn't. She continues to suck me while I come. And come.

Eventually, she releases me, but it takes a few moments to stop seeing stars and return to my senses. I swear I'm a little lightheaded.

She has a smile of satisfaction, and I whistle. "You are amazing."

Clover blushes, looking pleased. Remembering my manners, I tuck myself back in, zip up, and give her my hand to draw her to her feet.

"Your turn," I say.

"Nope," she says. "You don't get to do a thing." With that, she grabs her clothing and sashays her hips as she retreats to the bathroom.

When she comes out, she has on her regular casual clothing.

"I fell asleep in the hot tub," she says. "What did I miss?"

Her little joke strikes me funny, but it maintains the illusion. I can almost imagine the "fantasy Clover" is hiding in my room somewhere, wearing that black dress and only ever performing her show for me.

24

Clover

Adam looks so happy I hate to be a downer, but it's growing late. When he asks me what I want for dinner, my reply erases his easy manner.

"Thanks, but I should be going."

His smile falters. "OK. Or you can stay longer."

"OK," I repeat. "Or I can go home."

I manage not to apologize and say "Sorry, I need to go." After all, I've set the rules. Saturday morning through Sunday evening.

"You got a cat or a dog after all?" he asks.

That makes me smile. "Nope. Not ready for the commitment."

"Don't you want to have my favorite dessert?"

I'm curious, so I ask. "Which is?"

"Don't laugh," he says. "A banana split."

I wrinkle my nose because the traditional strawberry, vanilla, and chocolate trio of ice cream have nothing on my fav raspberry-chocolate-chip.

"Not you, too," he says.

"Not me, too, what?"

"No one appreciates the perfection of a banana split. They're barely offered on any menu. It's all cheesecake, tiramisu, and flourless chocolate cake."

I'm nodding because he's clearly crazy.

"I have all the ingredients right here."

I glance at his crotch.

"No," he says. "I'm serious. Downstairs in the kitchen, bananas are at the peak of ripeness, but not a day too long. Three flavors of ice cream—you know the ones. And hot fudge, caramel, whipped cream. Even nuts if you like."

"I do like," I tell him. "What about cherries?"

"Of course, cherries. And strawberries, too."

"That all seems like sex food," I say.

"Are you making fun of my favorite dessert?"

"Of course not, but come on. Bananas? *Duh!* And whipped cream and strawberries. Don't forget dripping hot fudge onto my breasts. It's all erotic."

He smiles, showing his dimple. "Lady, I like your style. Let's go."

"Sometime, I would love to try your banana at its peak." I touch the outline of his cock beneath his pants. "But not now."

Adam can see he isn't going to win. "Get your stuff, then. I'll give you a—"

I hold up my hand. "No, you won't. I can call for an Uber, but I'll probably take the T."

Luckily, living on the same line as a bunch of colleges, the T continues until midnight, even on a Sunday. But I intend to be indoors long before the Cinderella hour.

His eyes get that steely look. The bossman doesn't like to be thwarted.

"Don't start," I say. "It's only five. I'll be perfectly safe. Still light out."

"That's my point. Amarra can whip us up—"

I give him my most determined look.

He sighs. "You win."

After stuffing everything into my buttery-soft but amazingly strong leather backpack, a gift from my mom when I went to Paris, I'm ready. It feels good to be this independent and to conduct myself in the polar opposite manner to how I was with Jason Decker. I moved stuff into his penthouse too quickly, let him have his way when he wanted me in his apartment most every night.

After we broke up, I had to wonder what went on the nights I didn't stay with him. So far, with Adam, I feel more trust. I know one thing for certain—he isn't banging anyone else.

As we go down the gorgeous staircase, uplifting my spirit with its magnificent elongated oval design, I realize I can once again afford to splurge. A little. After nearly half a year at Bonvier, my bank account is becoming healthy again. I could take an Uber home.

I choose not to. After I leave with just a friendly wave—neither of us attempting to kiss goodbye as that is too much like a relationship move—I begin the five-minute walk to the Park Street station. Although I can afford an Uber, having one pick me up would leave a trail that I've been there. One time won't be an issue, but if we make a habit of this, and why not since it has been better than my dreams, then multiple pick-ups at Louisburg Square might end up making someone nosy.

For all I know, paparazzi watch me leave Adam's home. He is Boston's best-known billionaire bachelor, and if gossips get word that he has a female visitor, someone will start digging to discover my identity.

I shudder at the thought, glancing nervously around me as I cross the Boston Common toward the station. No one seems to notice or care. Without any commuters, I'm back in Allston fast.

Pam is home, and we make the usual chit-chat. She assumes I spent the previous night at a guy's house. No lie, but I don't dish out the details.

"Just a guy I know," I say.

"From work?"

"Yup." Otherwise, she'll wonder if it's one of the men we've met when out together, and she'll ask a bunch more questions.

"Good for you," she says, reaching out her knuckles for a fist bump.

Good for me, I agree. I feel fucking great! No longer frustrated, no need for my vibrator. And more than merely the sexual satisfaction—*merely!*—I had a good time with Adam doing ordinary things. Well, as ordinary as a billionaire ever does anything when he has a private chef and his own basketball court.

Everything I learned about Adam Bonvier during the past two days, I liked including the type of shampoo he uses, the softest, most luxurious sheets he has on his bed, and how much he enjoys a blow job.

That isn't surprising, I guess. It's not like you often meet a guy who says, "No, thanks." If ever. But the entire fantasy he'd wanted made it special for me, too.

So yes, I wanted to rinse and repeat.

Which we do.

$♥$♥$♥$

After two exquisite months of truly idyllic weekends at Adam's, I screw up. I get careless. We're strolling around his neighborhood as we often do on a Sunday morning, this time venturing onto Beacon Street because he has shown me a spectacular bakery with donuts made from croissant dough, which have become my weakness.

We should stay off the main drag. Worse, I remove my sunglasses when we go into the bakery and don't replace them when we leave.

"Clover!" comes a familiar voice.

"Uncle Samuel?" My tone rises an octave in shock. Out of the corner of my eye, I see Adam glance at me. It's the first time anything personal regarding my life outside of Bonvier, Inc. has entered our insular world, apart from small tidbits I've shared.

Uncle Samuel leans in to kiss my cheek. "I just saw your parents last month on their yacht. We were all in Valencia before it becomes too hot and touristy. They said you'd moved to Boston this past fall. You look well."

"Thank you." My brain freezes, and that's literally all I can say.

Uncle Samuel takes another look at Adam, and his weathered face breaks into a smile of recognition. He sticks out his hand.

"Samuel Longacre."

Adam shakes it, but because he knows my paranoia, he doesn't offer his own name.

Unfazed, Samuel looks at me again. "They didn't say anything about you dating Adam Bonvier."

I flinch. He knows Adam on sight. Of course he does.

"That's because . . . ," I start. I simply stop talking, not knowing what my reason could be. It's a Sunday morning. We're wearing casual clothing, not holding hands but definitely walking close. I can hardly claim we were meeting on a business matter.

And whatever I say next might let Adam know too much about the real Clover.

"Because we're keeping our private lives private," Adam fills in the lengthy pause, with a bit of an edge to his voice. "You understand, sir, how intrusive and brutal the media can be."

Uncle Samuel nods. "Of course."

Should I ask him not to mention anything to my parents? I open my mouth, but Adam speaks first.

"Her parents didn't tell you because they don't know about me."

"Not true," Uncle Samuel counters, and I jump, exchanging a look with Adam.

"They told me Clover got a *job* at Bonvier." Uncle Samuel raises an eyebrow and winks at me. "That you are *working* there."

"I did, and I do," I say, straightening a little, not realizing I've started to shrink inside myself, wanting to disappear. He has construed I'm not really working for Bonvier, Inc., just warming the boss's bed. *Ugh!*

"I'm the art director."

"I see," he says. I'm trying to figure out if Uncle Samuel is being patronizing when Adam speaks again.

"Look, Mr. Longacre, Clover is a top-notch designer, and my company is lucky to have her. Right now, we're just taking a Sunday walk and talking shop. We'd appreciate it if you don't mention to anyone that you saw us together."

Uncle Samuel nods, seeming to understand. "I won't mention it. Tell your parents I said hello when next you see them." He kisses my cheek again and strolls away, having left immeasurable damage in his wake.

We stare at one another.

"So?" Adam says. "Uncle Samuel?"

"Yup." What can I say? "He's not really my uncle. Just a family friend."

He narrows his eyes. Obviously, that's the least important of all the things I should explain.

"When were you going to tell me who the hell I'm sleeping with?"

25

Clover

I am still congratulating myself on escaping the encounter without Adam hearing my real last name when he fires off his question.

"What do you mean?" I ask, my heart practically stopping. Perhaps he knows that successful businessman Samuel Longacre is best friends with my father, Russell Henley. This isn't how I want him to learn I'm the eldest heir to a fortune. I'm close to telling him, but I want to do it on my own terms. For now, I really want to be nothing more than the art director for Bonvier, Inc.

"Your parents have a yacht, and they float around the coast of Sicily. You never gave me any indication you came from money. You live in Allston—"

"Hey, rent is not cheap there," I remind him.

"You take the T everywhere. Do you own a car?"

"I do, but I'm not paying Boston parking prices so I leave it in the lot behind my apartment."

"Is it a Ferrari?" he asks. "A Lamborghini, perhaps?"

I roll my eyes, thinking of my current little runaround, although my parents could easily buy me one of those luxury cars, and they would if I ask. Adam can't possibly infer such wealth from what he heard today. After all, regular people save up and buy boats.

"Definitely not." No need to mention my previous car was an Audi A5, a gift from my dad after I returned from Paris. I sold it when I left New York as I needed the money, but I had loved that shiny red coupe, and I'm not averse to getting another one someday.

"When were you going to tell me you're only playing the part of a hand-to-mouth waif?" he asks.

I blow out my cheeks and sigh. This is why I changed my last name, in order to be taken seriously.

"Never," I say stubbornly.

"At least now you're being honest." He's actually mad, and I don't think it's because my parents have money. I think it's because I withheld the truth. Or maybe because he was enjoying showing me the *good life*.

People go around where we stand in the middle of the pavement, and causing even a minor scene is making me nervous. "Can we go back to your house?"

After we turn and retrace our steps, I start talking again.

"I'm not hand-to-mouth, thanks to Bonvier, Inc., but I moved to Boston without much savings and went through what I had until I got the job. That's why I keep my lifestyle lean and mean."

"Why?" he asks curtly.

"What do you mean, why?"

Adam shrugs. "Why don't you have any savings? You had a design job in New York."

"New York City is expensive," I protest.

But that isn't the whole reason I arrived nearly broke in Boston. I was careless when I thought my job and my rich boyfriend were secure. I used to spend everything I made on rent and clothing—particularly shoes. *How I love shoes!*

And the rest went to purely fun stuff, like treating my friends to drinks and food. Out of grad school, the moment I got my first real job, I stopped taking an allowance from my parents, but I still spent like a spoiled rich girl.

It got worse after I started to date Jason. I bought more expensive clothing to fit in with his social life. And since he paid for our fine dining, for Broadway shows, and for concerts, I became even more magnanimous when I was out with my friends. I wanted to treat them the way I was being treated.

A shallow, credit card-driven existence. I look down at my dope, high-qual footwear, however, and feel a surge of pleasure. *It sure had been a blast.*

"Anyway, I got the design job on my own merit," I say, thinking about the slightly underhanded way I wrangled references out of Jason's company and even from Jason, himself—if he only knew how well Sam had played the part of Decker Financial's CEO. "I would never go to an interview and start talking about my wealthy parents."

Adam doesn't argue the point, but he doesn't let me off the hook, either.

"It's been a long time since that interview. And we're not at work now. You could have said, 'Hey, you know how I seem really normal. My parents have a yacht, so I'm not.'"

"A yacht makes you abnormal?" I ask, feeling a fizz of humor now that the initial scare over Uncle Samuel revealing my identity has passed.

"Depends on the size," he shoots back.

"Size matters?" I ask, and a chuckle rises in my throat.

"With yachts," he says.

"You have one, I assume. Maybe more than one." It's a safe guess.

"I do. Small and sporty and an obscenely giant one. I also have multiple houses, multiple cars, a jet—"

"Not multiple jets?" I tease.

"No need," he says. "And lady, I am *not* normal by any stretch of the imagination. I live in the rarefied world of the superrich. I try to be thoughtful, fair, and kind to those who have less, which is pretty much everyone I know or meet. But I'm also a self-indulgent bastard who can have anything I want. Right now, I want you, but I like to know who I'm dealing with."

His speech surprises me. That's some healthy self-reflection, a trait I never noticed with Jason.

"I know you want me," I say. "We're on a level playing field when it comes to how much we both have the hots for each other."

That earns me his lopsided grin so I continue. "But my parents having a yacht has nothing to do with me. I'm still the same Clover." I tap my chest.

Suddenly, it occurs to me we are getting a bit too deep for two people casually hooking up. I need to remind us both of the ground rules because if we continue along this path, pretty soon, we'll be full-on dating, and I'll be out of a job.

Not gonna happen. At least, not yet.

"Let's not forget that this," I gesture between the two of us, "is a mutually agreed upon arrangement, right? For sex."

An older couple passes us, and both turn to look at me.

"Just sex?" he asks. Their heads swivel to Adam, but he doesn't notice.

Strangely, his smile vanishes, which isn't the usual reaction to that particular word or topic, especially when you're getting some. And he's gotten a lot lately.

But saying we were only having sex was another lie.

"Sex and more. Companionship, too," I add, although that seems like an old-fashioned word.

"Not friendship, apparently," Adam says, using his fingerprint to make his front door lock open. "Because friends don't lie about basic things like their background or their family."

That stings. Now I'm caught between confessing more or letting him get used to what he's already learned. I choose the latter.

"You know who I am," I say, feeling about four inches tall.

"I know your body as well as I know my own," he agrees, "but *Uncle* Samuel means big business if he's the owner of Longacre Development. If your parents hang with him, then they're jetsetters, which means you're not some Allston chick trying to make bank for your rent and groceries. You certainly don't have to take the T, causing me to worry about you at all hours."

He slams his way into his home and goes straight upstairs to the small basketball court. I follow in his wake, although he's a few steps ahead of me all the way, no longer interested in watching my ass climb four floors.

When I catch up, I'm breathing hard.

"That's the thing. I *am* an Allston chick. At least, for now. I haven't taken a dime from my parents since I graduated. I'm entirely self-sufficient. They've never helped me get a job, and they don't pay for me to live my life. And you can see how different your perception of me would have been if I'd stamped 'rich parents' across my forehead."

My words sink in and seem to soothe him. He reaches for one of the balls in the corner and sends it flying toward the hoop. Nothing but net, as usual.

He continues to snag the ball, dribble it, and shoot around for a silent minute. Then he tucks the ball under his arm and faces me.

"I understand you not wanting to be beholden to your family. I get that you're independent, and I admire the hell out of you for not taking the easy way."

With little warning, he sends the ball whirling my way. *Oof!* I catch it with my stomach as much as with my hands. I stand here, waiting for the "but."

"But I don't like feeling left in the dark or fooled," he finishes.

Adam Bonvier doesn't like to be lied to. I already know that and should have taken note of it more seriously. After all, having been cheated on, I understand the pain of humiliation all too well. Plus, his pride is wounded.

"I'm sorry you were blindsided," I say before sending the ball back to him without nearly as much emphasis. "I guess it proves I'm not with you because you're a Bonvier. After all, now you know I'm a child of yacht people!"

Adam makes a weird growling sound of frustration.

"I already knew you weren't into my money. You've never seemed like the clichéd golddigger. Far from it. Although I'm not sure what 'with me' means to you exactly. You really don't want anything but sex?" It's the second time he's sent me that question today.

Since I'm standing in his home, a place I'm starting to get too comfy being in *every* weekend, I guess pretending it's only for sex is silly.

"I like being with you, no matter what we're doing," I confess.

"Your face looked pained to admit that." Adam shakes his head. "Frankly, it sounded as though you were choking on rocks."

"I don't know what else to say. Everything is fine the way it is." I'm certainly not going to choose this testy moment to tell him the unexpected thoughts I've had lately—that I would rather have him in my life full-time than be the head of his creative department.

It's true, though. But it feels like giving in. It feels like failure.

Regardless, as long as we keep seeing one another, I can hang on for a few more months with our current arrangement. A solid year of stellar work will give me the references and experience I need to land the next job without faking references.

Meanwhile, I've definitely started to imagine a life in which Adam and I brave the press and become a real couple. My clothes in one of his closets, being together on a Monday night, bringing over my somewhat tacky frog collection. Him finding out I'm not really Clover Mitchell, and being OK with it.

Letting myself fantasize about such a change, let alone suggest it, makes my chest tighten. As he said, my throat closes up so I sound weird. Adam is *not* Jason. But Adam could hurt me far worse—at least, that's what my heart is telling me.

Jason's betrayal would be merely a bruise compared to what would happen if Adam messes me around. Panic gripping me at the direction of my thoughts, I turn and walk out of the mini-basketball court.

He follows me.

This is supposed to be about lust and desire and fun, not a potentially broken heart!

"I think I better go." I head for his bedroom where my overnight bag always is.

"You're leaving? It's not even noon."

I sit on the bed, not knowing what I want to do. "I think it would be best."

Adam sits beside me. "Is your not-real uncle going to blab?"

"I don't think so."

He takes my hand. "Would it crush you if he did?"

Tears prick my eyes. "Everything would change." More than he knows. It would be heiress and billionaire all over the news, spelling the end of my anonymous, merit-driven career as I know and love it. "And not on my terms."

He squeezes my hand.

"Not on *our* terms," I amend because maybe he wouldn't want to be one half of a power couple with a candy heiress. Maybe he'll freak when he finds out.

He lies back on the bed, pulling me down with him. I stare at the now-familiar ceiling, a high, white plaster with elegant crown molding.

"Would you like it if we . . . were . . . ?" *Ugh!* I choke on the words. Am I really going to date the bossman again? I groan.

To my surprise, Adam laughs. "If we were what? You can't even say it, can you? If you quit Bonvier, not that I want to lose your talent, then I would definitely ask you out on a date."

I want that. *But . . . my job!*

"I love my job," I whisper. "If Uncle Samuel tells anyone, then I will have to quit. Not only because of Bonvier's rule but also for my own sanity. Right now, I really don't want to quit."

"Perhaps eventually, you'll make a different choice," he says as if reading my mind. "Even if we got married—"

I jump, and he puts the flat of his palm on my stomach, like he's calming a skittish animal.

"Even if we were married for a decade," Adam revises his words, "and then we broke up, I would still keep the company because it's my family's business. And because of how godawful awkward it would be to work with my gorgeous and angry ex-wife looking daggers at me, Clover, sweetheart, you would still have to leave. I don't think there's any way around that."

He's right. And then, it hits me. I need to be my own boss. Bosswoman Clover Mitchell. No. I would reclaim my name. Bosswoman Clover Henley. I would never have to leave my own company.

All I need is more time. I'll keep saving until I can open my own little design firm. There's plenty of design business for everyone. Besides, I don't want to compete with Adam and own an advertising agency. If I just do design, my company can work for the big guys, not only Bonvier but other agencies.

I'm back to my original idea of waiting, maintaining the status quo. I might draw up a business plan so I can figure out how long it will take before I can quit. It means no splurging on shoes or other luxuries, which is a bummer. Just when I thought I could give in to my baser, consumer impulses again.

"You're too quiet," Adam says. "It's sort of unnerving."

"Sorry. My brain's going a mile a minute."

"Do you still want to go home early?"

In answer, I wrap my arms around him and pull him on top of me. Looking up into his intelligent gray eyes, I want to be as honest as I can.

"If we're good and if everything can stay the same, then I don't want to leave yet."

"How about a fantasy?" he suggests.

I smile, instantly aware of my body tingling in anticipation.

He pretends to be stern. "I think your poor-girl deception calls for punishment."

We have hours ahead of us, cocooned in this impossibly beautiful house. And me in the bed of this impossibly attractive, sexy man.

"Indeed, it does."

26

Adam

With her permission, I tie her to the bedposts, face down and ass up on my sheets, and put a pillow under her hips. She looks amazing. My cock is already granite as I strip down to my jeans and stand beside the bed.

"Ready?"

"Do it already," she says.

"Rather a commanding tone for someone who's not holding the paddle."

"Paddle?" She twists to see what's in my hand. I've borrowed a small flat wooden spatula from Ray and Amarra's kitchen gadget collection. Not exactly a paddle, but I know it will provide a little something extra.

"Stay still," I order. "And silent." She quiets. I caress her inner thigh from ankle to pussy with the tip of the spatula.

"Nice," she says.

I give her ass a resounding thwack for disobeying the silence command. Instantly, it flushes pink.

Then I caress up the other leg, letting the spatula come to rest against her slit once more.

"Umph," she makes a muffled sound against the bed clothes.

"Clover," I warn before letting the spatula land squarely across her shapely buttocks again. The blush color made my cock twitch in appreciation.

I have to admit I spank her a little harder than I have before. I've been on a rollercoaster all morning, and I don't appreciate it. It isn't merely being ambushed by her nosey so-called uncle. It's the scare Clover gave me when I thought she was about to bail, not only on the rest of this Sunday but on our arrangement and maybe even her job.

The domino effect of her lie causes me to turn her gorgeous, pert ass a cherry red before checking in.

"OK?"

She doesn't speak, merely nodding, which makes me smile. She knows any sound will bring another strike. Wickedly, I change the game.

"You didn't answer me and must be punished." Another firm thwack, and I hear her gasp. Her ass had to be really smarting now, and the rest of her is probably heated and pulsing.

I touch her inner thighs, back and forth from one to the other. "Spread them, as wide as you can."

She does, and I groan at the sight of her reddened cheeks above her glistening pussy.

"You're wet already." My voice sounds hoarse. I tap the end of the spatula against her lower lips.

"Mm," she says, lifting her ass off the pillow, giving me better access.

"You like?"

She stays silent, which means she wants to be punished for not answering.

Far more gently than on her ass, I spank her pussy with the spatula. She strains higher, and I continue with a steady rhythmic whack, occasionally alternating across her ass cheeks.

"I'm going to come," she whispers. "I can't wait."

I've never gone so far as to try withholding permission for her to climax. I can't since I love seeing her fulfilled.

As it rolls through her, she moans loudly. I wonder if I ought to put in better soundproofing so my Beacon Hill neighbors aren't privy to my sex life.

When Clover stills, I swiftly undo her ties, but put a hand on the small of her back.

"Stay," I order, yanking open the front of my button-fly jeans and freeing my cock through the boxer briefs. "You are perfectly positioned." Kneeling between her legs, I plunge into her tight wetness.

Riding her for a few heart-pounding strokes, I support myself on one arm while reaching under her to play with her neglected clit. As she writhes against my fingers, I continue thrusting.

"Good?" I ask. "Ready again?" Because I'm about to explode.

"Yes," she hisses.

Thank God! The tension has built low in my spine, and I can't stop my climax now.

In one of those rare, flawless moments, Clover cries out at the same time as I come. *Simultaneous orgasm achieved!*

And then I bundle her against me, spooning her as we fall into a deep sleep. It happens easily since sex often interrupts our sleep at all hours on a Saturday night. It's at least an hour before either one of us stirs.

"I have to go home," she says.

"No cat," I mutter against her shoulder, keeping my eyes closed and hoping she drifts back to sleep.

"I'm going home," she insists.

Sighing, I open my arms and let her escape. Clover gives me a sexy eyeful before she disappears into the bathroom.

She prefers to shower here rather than using the one in her apartment. Her dingy shared apartment that now I know she could leave any time she wants and live in luxury if only she asked her parents. Not that I've seen it, but I'm starting to imagine her living in wretched conditions in order to maintain her independence.

Maybe I will give her a raise tomorrow. Will that piss her off? I never know with Clover.

With my fingers laced under my head, I stare upward. If her Uncle Samuel ruins our cover, what will the fallout be? Some journalists will want to know who I'm seeing. Her parents will probably enter the picture. Mine, too.

Again, I have no idea how Clover would react, but I have a feeling it wouldn't be good.

Stop it, I order myself. Don't borrow trouble. That isn't my usual M.O. After battling with my desire to join her in the shower, instead I throw on my clothes, wishing she'll let me drive her home.

Home. This place, all 10,858 square feet if the realtor didn't lie, has felt more like home since Clover started coming over on weekends than it ever has before. Her weekly twenty-nine hours in residence give it a sheen of normalcy and warmth and comfort it never had before— and that it doesn't have during the rest of the hours I live here.

After months of fucking her lights out, I've only just discovered that in an emergency, she doesn't really need her Bonvier salary. She can always go home.

As I pull on my socks, I consider something radical. I could fire her. If I thought she wouldn't entirely freak out, which she would. No doubt. Instead of bringing us closer, she would probably vanish from my life entirely.

I couldn't stomach that. I'll keep playing this her way because I've never wanted a woman to stay in my life more than I want Clover.

"Ready," she says, grabbing my attention off my somewhat maniacal thoughts, swinging between giving her more money and cutting off her income altogether.

Clover looks amazing for someone with pink skin from a hot shower, no makeup, and only partially dried hair. Is she hurrying to escape? She finishes stuffing her leather backpack in five seconds, looks around, and appears satisfied she has everything.

"Back to the real world," she says.

She has never left a thing here, I realize. Not even a spare toothbrush. It pisses me off and makes our tenuous arrangement seem even more fragile.

"That doesn't have to be your reality," I say, jamming my hands into my jeans' pockets to keep from reaching for her. I'm about ready to declare something or ask her the wrong question or . . . I don't know what might come out of my mouth. But how cool would it be if we were planning Sunday dinner?

If she weren't about to take all the fun with her.

Her hard glance shuts me up. "Yes, it does. For now, it does."

Then she departs the room, ahead of me on the staircase, but she softens her message with words over her shoulder, "I may have a new plan for my future."

"Your future," I mutter. She's the least clingy woman I've ever met, and it's starting to drive me nuts.

She stops, and I nearly slam into her, which might have ended with a classic two-person tumble down a flight of antique stairs.

"Maybe *our* future," she revises softly, giving me the sweetest smile.

Whoa! Those three words shouldn't fill me with a happy lightness, but they do.

"In that case, I'll keep my fingers crossed for success with your plan."

A few days later, I discover crossing my fingers isn't going to solve anything.

27

Clover

I decide to mix it up a little with Adam. He has a client to see in Quebec. I've traveled there before with my parents but never as an adult. After living in Paris for design school, I know it'll be interesting to hear the different French dialect of the Quebecois inhabitants. But I'm far more interested in hearing Adam's sexy voice when he answers his hotel room door.

I've never surprised him with anything, not with a gift, not even with a cupcake. I'm consciously restraining my enthusiastic nature after being way too eager-to-please with Jason. At the time, I could wipe out my paycheck giving him a tie clip, leather gloves, or cashmere socks.

The thought of my former happy-puppy mentality sickens me.

But showing up to give Adam my body won't cost me anything more than a one-way plane ticket. The night ahead has me humming a little tune as I take a taxi from the airport to Le Château Frontenac hotel.

Having copied Adam's itinerary from his laptop—*don't ask!*—I know he will have finished dining with the client in the hotel's *bib gourmand* restaurant. The client is planning to catch a commuter flight back to Montreal in the early evening, so they won't have eaten late, and the coast should be all clear.

It's nearly eight-thirty when I enter the nineteenth-century hotel that looks like a massive red-brick and green-roofed castle or fortress, perched on a cliff overlooking the St. Lawrence River. With my excitement building, I cross the marble foyer that wouldn't be out of place in any European city. Inlaid ceiling, walnut paneling, chandeliers—it makes me wish I'd worn a more upscale outfit.

"Would you give me Mr. Bonvier's room number, please?" I ask the desk clerk in French. Naturally, he won't tell me, but he calls the suite. No answer.

Tamping down my initial disappointment, I decide to stroll around the hotel's public areas until I find him. A treasure hunt, with my boss being the best treasure I can imagine! If I'm unsuccessful, then I'll ruin my surprise and text him.

Traveling light as usual, I sling my bag over my shoulder. After all, it's only one night, just like going to Adam's townhouse. I plan on flying home to Boston with him in the morning, which means relaxing my paranoia long enough to be on his private jet and show up on the passenger manifest, but I don't think Janet or anyone at work is going to be checking it.

Thinking he's having a quiet drink, I soon discover I'll have to search a few eating and drinking places aside from the formal restaurant where Adam dined with Ms. Acton, the client. The first bar is a cozy circular room with hardwood floors, a lit fireplace and antique bookshelves filled with hardbacks. The pub chair area gives way to a more modern aesthetic of a gold-and-brown marble bar top and chic pendant lighting. I would love to stop here for a drink, but there's no bossman in sight.

I traverse the hotel's enormous central lounge. On the inside, the idea of a castle is less apparent except for the building's size. Chandeliers and floor-to-ceiling windows, comfy modern divans and ottomans fill the space that is empty at this hour of people checking in or waiting for airport transportation.

I keep going across a lot of square footage of marble floors, carpeting, wooden flooring, and up and down massive marble staircases. I'm getting quite a workout.

"Workout!" I exclaim, realizing he's probably doing precisely that. Giving my feet a break, I take an elevator to the sixth floor. I can't get into the hotel gym without a key card, but another guest comes out as I approach. Slipping through the doorway, I scan the room. No Adam amongst the machines and free weights.

I'm starting to get antsy. Maybe he was in the shower earlier. I use the workout room's phone to ask the desk clerk to try Adam's suite again. Still, no hunky billionaire bossman answers.

Stymied, I send a quick text: *Guess where I am?*

No reply. *Well, crap!*

Leaving the gym, I follow my nose and the scent of chlorine. Adam said he likes to swim, although I've never been to a pool with him. Unfortunately, it's another place I can't get into without a key card, and no steady stream of swimmers appear to let me in, either. I peer through the darkened glass, but it's meant only for guests to see out.

Eventually, when a couple get off the elevator, I open my backpack and scrabble around as if looking for my card.

"Where did it go?" I mutter loudly.

"Permettez-moi," says the man. *Allow me*, in his French-Canadian accent.

"Merci," I reply. *Thank you.*

He holds the door and lets his wife and me enter first. The pool contains only an older woman doing laps.

However, at the far end, in one of the two hot tubs, I spy a dark head of hair.

Adam! I should have known. He loves a good soak after a long day, and it explains why he's not using his phone.

Walking along the length of the Olympic-size pool, I bend down once to feel the water's temperature. Perfect. I wish I'd thought to bring a bathing suit. And then my attention is captured by Adam climbing out of the hot tub, his long, lean back to me. I'm about to call out when he reaches down and takes the hand of a beautiful woman.

My feet carry me forward another few feet before I stop. They're standing under the bilingual sign that states "Adults only (Over 16)! / Adultes seulement (plus de 16 ans)!"

A massive adrenaline rush kicks my heartbeat into high gear, but I'm frozen. This cannot be happening. I must be misunderstanding. He hands the woman a towel, and she dries her arms and thighs before putting her hand on Adam's arm. Bracing herself, she leans down to slide her feet into flat sandals, and then he puts his hand on the small of her back, smiling down at her. He's about to turn and see me.

I've been in this situation before with Jason and am beyond stunned to find myself in it again. I literally cannot breathe. If I could, I might gasp with the pain slicing through me. Or I might shriek at him like a jealous shrew.

I do neither. I'm still motionless, wishing I could disappear in a puff of smoke. At that instant, he spots me, and his astonished double-take frees me from my stonelike stupor. I turn and run, right past the sign that states, "No running in the pool area! / Pas de course à la piscine!"

Fuck the piscine!

He calls out my name as my hand touches the door handle. Without hesitation, I push it open and sprint for the stairs. No way am I going to be caught waiting for an elevator by Adam Bonvier in his goddamn form-fitting swim trunks. I don't want to hear any lies or excuses. At the same time, I don't want to believe the awful truth.

Even riskier would be letting myself be persuaded there's something in between.

Upon reaching the lobby, I slow down. Already an interloper who doesn't actually have a room, dashing around like a wild thing will only make me more conspicuous. With as much composure as I can muster considering I want to melt onto the cool marble floor and weep, I stride toward the exit. I need a taxi to the airport.

"Mademoiselle Mitchell," comes an unfamiliar voice behind me.

Turning, I see no one I know.

"Mademoiselle Mitchell!" It's the desk clerk from earlier, and he's holding a phone receiver.

"Yes?" I call back across the empty space. How did he know my name?

"Monsieur Bonvier requests that I take you up to his suite immediately. He said there has been a misunderstanding."

I gape. I nearly say, "Mr. Bonvier can go fuck himself." But I'm too much of a lady to shock this nice Quebecois clerk. Instead, I reply, "There has indeed been a misunderstanding. He's right about that. But I am going home."

I turn away.

"Please, Mademoiselle Mitchell!" the man calls after me again, sounding more than a little desperate. "Monsieur Bonvier says if I let you leave, he'll buy this hotel and fire me." He frowns as he clasps the receiver to his ear. Then he pales. "He's going to fire everyone currently working here if you don't let me show you to his room."

The two other people working at the lobby desk stare at me in silence.

I can't help rolling my eyes. "You don't really think he's serious."

But the clerk looks as though he might cry. He covers the mouthpiece. "Please," he says again. "I can assure you that he is most serious."

Sighing, I reconsider. I don't know a vindictive side to Adam. But he's powerful and used to getting what he wants. I suppose it's possible he could buy the hotel out of spite. Improbable but possible. I put the desk clerk out of his misery.

"Fine! Show me to his suite."

The man says something into the phone, then nods and replaces the receiver. He all but jumps over the desk in his hurry to get to me.

"This way," he says while giving me a formal little bow as if I'm royalty. He leads me to the bank of elevators, both of us pretending we haven't just had the oddest of exchanges. Neither of us speaks while the lift climbs. He keeps his gaze trained on the floor, and I stare up at the numbers lighting our path as we rise to the top floor. When the doors slide open, he gestures for me to go ahead.

"Just give me the number," I snap.

"Oh, no, Mademoiselle Mitchell. I am to escort you to Monsieur Bonvier's suite and let you in if he has not returned yet."

"Fine," I say again with less vehemence. "I suppose you're going to lock me inside until he arrives."

"No, miss. I'll wait in the hall."

But as we reach the door next to a plaque that proclaims "The Van Horne Suite," the other elevator's doors open with a ding. The hair on the back of my neck rises, knowing it's him. And then Adam gets off. Alone.

He's in black sweatpants, a crewneck shirt, and flipflops. And his gorgeous black hair is slicked back.

"If it isn't Aquaman," I say tartly, looking behind him. "Where's your mermaid?"

He ignores me, thanks the desk clerk, and dismisses him all at once. Then he holds his keycard to the door and pushes it open.

I don't move a muscle. "How dare you threaten that man?"

"It worked, didn't it? I'll give him a generous tip tomorrow." He shrugs slightly. "I wasn't thinking I'd need my wallet at the pool."

Mention of the pool has me fuming again. I still block the doorway, truth be told not intending to go into the room. But Adam has other ideas, and I yelp when he sweeps me inside with a strong arm around my waist as if I'm nothing more than a tabby cat.

"Hey!" I start to claw at his arm. Maybe I really am a cat.

"Stop it," he says, carrying me straight through the suite, bypassing a bedroom on the right and a dining room on the left, to the living room overlooking the river. "I know you're upset, but that was merely the client you saw. You knew I was coming here to meet with her."

"The client," I say in clipped tones, "had a ticket for Montreal ages ago."

"Which she decided to skip. That's her choice. She's wealthy enough to get a room here and go shopping or sightseeing or whatever the hell she wants to do tomorrow."

He releases me finally because it's ridiculous to carry on a heated conversation while I'm hanging off the side of him. I move away to the other end of the blue-and-white sitting room, stomping past silly traveler's trunks used as end tables. The curved wall with seven windows reminds me we're in one of the hotel's towers. Outside, the St. Lawrence River is a dark ribbon, dotted with shimmering light from the hotel's bright lampposts.

Taking a breath, I face him.

"What she wanted to do was to play with you in the hot tub. And you looked rather happy about it, too. You touched her." Hating that my voice wobbles, I stand as straight and tall as I can and cross my arms.

He fixes me with his piercing gaze, the one he usually uses when he's saying something complimentary, often while we're naked. "Clover, two adults can be in a hot tub without it meaning anything. Other people could have got in at any time."

But I'm not having it.

"If I hadn't shown up, you two would have dried off and been up here in your bed in a New York minute."

"That's insulting," he says, and manages to look the part, insulted and annoyed. "And you're entirely wrong, but there's no way I can prove that to you. She's married, by the way."

"That doesn't mean jack," I spit out.

"It should, at least where I'm concerned. Do you know me at all?"

I hold my tongue. Do I? Maybe I'm simply a really poor judge of character.

"As you may have noticed, I can have my pick of women."

I wince. *Not a great time to boast that,* I think.

"So why would I play around with a client of all people? To me, that falls under the same category as not dating an employee."

I purse my lips and toss my hands up. *Hello?* I am his employee, after all.

"That's different," he says, even though I don't state the obvious. "We're *not* dating."

A little devil in me has to ask. "And if we were?"

Adam drops onto the two-seater couch and puts his feet up on the coffee table. "Even though you and I have this modern sex-in-the-shadows arrangement, I wouldn't cheat on you. I'm happy with what we have."

"I see." I don't know what to say. We aren't a real couple. I should have remembered that ten minutes ago. Perhaps I could have reined in my anger and jealousy. He actually is free to have sex with whomever he wants with a caveat we once discussed. Tell the other person ahead of time. I grabbed onto that.

"If you want to have an affair with the client or with anyone else, you need to tell me ahead of time. I want the opportunity to say thanks but no thanks to sharing you."

For some reason, this makes him smile.

"I don't want an affair with the client or with anyone else," he quickly adds when I open my mouth. "You may not have realized, but I left Ms. Acton in the pool area while I sprinted for the locker room and the hotel phone to stop you. Not very gentlemanly of me."

I sniff, wanting to believe him, but I saw what I saw. "She didn't look like she was interested in the gentlemanly side of you."

"By the way, I'm elated you're here," he says. "It was really sweet of you to surprise me."

"Really sweet of you," I mimic, making a face, but the fire has gone out of me because he sounds so reasonable and normal.

"Come here," he says, patting the navy-colored sofa cushion beside him.

28

Adam

As slowly as she possibly can, literally dragging her feet with each step, Clover joins me on the couch. She plops down with little grace and folds her arms again.

Even pouting, she's lovely. I don't reach for her yet. I have a feeling we've only uncovered the tip of some iceberg that could sink us. And I hate that she came all this way only to get the wind knocked out of her and feel upset.

"You were really quick to pass judgment," I say. "We didn't even have a glass of wine with us at the hot tub."

"It's probably not allowed," she argues.

Clover needs it all explained, and I don't mind at all. "I went to the pool by myself, and she was already doing laps. When she finished, she joined me. We talked a little more business. She told me earlier she'd decided to stay the night, and that's her choice. As for touching her, I gave her a hand up out of the hot tub because I'm a—"

"A gentleman," she mutters. "I know."

I want to smile at how she says the word like it's a bad thing, but she still doesn't sound happy or certain of me, which makes me keep going. "You and I have been enjoying a great time for months. Have I given you any reason to doubt me or think I would betray you? Did you ever come up to my office unexpectedly and find me banging Janet?"

I laugh. Not because Janet isn't attractive. But she treats me like a naughty child half the time. There's zero sexual tension or attraction between us.

Yet Clover's face becomes a rigid mask of . . . hurt! Her nostrils flare, and I can see how hard she's gritting her teeth. In this moment, I know she's been cheated on. Big time!

I don't make her come to me. I scoot closer and drape my arm across her slender shoulders so I can hold her close.

"Oh, baby, I'm sorry."

She shakes her head. "Don't be all soft and sweet, or I'll cry."

No man wants to see a woman cry, but if she needs to let it out, I can handle whatever it is.

"I'm sorry I put you in a position of reliving something awful. But I'm not whoever you're thinking of. You know that."

She nods, and I give her shoulder a squeeze. "Talk if you want."

Clover draws in a long breath. "My last boyfriend did, in fact, cheat on me, and I walked in on them."

First, I'm really, really sorry, and I say so. "Shit! I'm sorry."

Second, I cannot imagine any guy would cheat on Clover. She is the complete package.

"I thought he was one of the good guys." She shoots me a look then drops her gaze to her lap. "I think you're one of the good ones. But I don't know."

"You do know," I insist. "I've never lied to you." I nearly asked his name but found I didn't care. "Were you dating or just . . . like us?"

She stiffens. "Not like us. I've never done anything *like us* before. I told you he was my boyfriend. We were a couple in every way. And I hate to sound dramatic, but he broke my trust."

I'm glad she doesn't say *heart*, although at the time, it probably felt like the asshole stomped on it. This isn't the time to feel jealous, but I do. Some idiot was in a real relationship with the skittish Ms. Mitchell and messed her around. What an asshole!

"I felt betrayed and humiliated and foolish," she says. "It was awful. And all for what? To have a quick fuck? If he wanted her so badly, all he had to do was tell me. Show me a little respect, so I could have maintained my dignity. And she was married, by the way."

Ouch! Her reticence to get involved with me in the first place becomes much more understandable, also why she freaked out when she saw me with Selina Acton.

All I can do now is take her mind off the past.

"I can't believe you came all this way for me." I give her shoulder another squeeze, but she isn't perking up as I'd hoped. Maybe a diversion will help. "Do you know who this room pays homage to?"

"No." Her voice still sounds thick with emotion, obviously with pain and maybe regret, too. I hope her thoughts don't stay in the past with her boyfriend.

"Sir Cornelius Van Horne," I tell her. "A superb businessman. He was president of the Canadian Pacific Railway. The railway pushed for the construction of Château Frontenac in 1893."

I lapse into silence. After a couple seconds, she says, "I don't understand. Is there a message in your stupid history lesson? Is it relevant to me? To us? Did his wife cheat on him or something?"

"No, I just thought it might snap you out of your funk."

She does her classic Clover punch. Since she can't reach my shoulder, she strikes her fist against my thigh. And just like that, I have her nearly back to normal.

"Since you are here, and it's only," I glance at the mantel clock, "nine-ish, what do you want to do? Are you hungry? Do you want to go for a stroll?"

Her gorgeous tiger eyes turn to mine, and I swear she steals my breath. I sink my hands into her silky, pale-brown hair, drag her close, and claim those sweet, full lips. She wants reassurance, and I want Clover.

Kissing leads to making out on the sofa before the stupidity of not using the king-sized bed in the next room strikes me at the same time as the arm of the couch jabs the middle of my back. Like in a movie, I carry her through the French doors, past the massive sketch of an old-time steam locomotive hanging over the fireplace, and set her gently on the bed next to the windows.

We strip bare in record time, tossing our clothes onto the floor. And I give her what she needs, letting her know in no uncertain terms I don't need anyone else in my bed. Gentle, take-our-time sex that ends in her having an intense orgasm.

When she opens her eyes, looking up into my soul while my cock is still buried deep inside her, just before I come, something changes. Not in the outside world, but in me. A shift of epic proportions. As I feel it, I climax, also in epic proportions!

If I didn't already know it, I know now. I can see my own reflection in her tawny eyes, and I look like a man in love.

Because I am.

We don't go anywhere. The bedroom hearth is prepared with wood and kindling, so I light a fire, and we stay in bed, turning on the TV at some point before I call the butler who comes with the suite. I try not to abuse the service, especially at odd hours, but my woman is hungry.

When her heart's desire shows up at the door—not the fancy morsels from The Champlain where I'd dined hours earlier with my client—but a hearty grilled chicken on sourdough with a side of authentic poutine, we move to the suite's dining room. Even though I've eaten, I order the same for me.

Again, while The Champlain is excellent, the food had been more decorative than nourishing.

"I wish everything wasn't closed," she says, polishing off her sandwich in record time and starting to dig her fork into the french fries smothered in cheese curds and brown gravy. "I haven't seen Quebec since I was a child."

"We can walk around and look at whatever you want tomorrow."

"Tomorrow is a work day. Assuming we have an early flight, I was going to go in after lunch. I can't just call in sick."

"If you're with the boss, you can definitely call in sick," I remind her.

She chews thoughtfully, and I can see she's battling with the side of her that wants to be treated like a regular employee without any perks from our arrangement.

Then she offers me a large grin that fills me with happiness.

"OK," she says.

That little word opens up a ton of fun. Early the following morning, we go hunting croissants and espresso outside the hotel. After walking around the old city before the tourists are out of bed, we sit on the stone wall overlooking the river, eating warm pastry and drinking hot coffee. With this particular woman beside me, it's the best morning of my life.

"What time is our flight?" she asks.

"Eleven," I tell her, having already given instructions to the butler to contact my pilot.

Clover looks surprised. "We should get moving then."

"No, eleven tomorrow. We're staying another night."

"I can't do that," she says immediately.

"Did you get a cat?"

I always ask her that when she wants to leave me. "Or maybe you have some goldfish."

231

"No, but . . . Can we do that?" She shakes her head and sips the traditional *allongé* coffee, basically a shot of espresso with more hot water for longer enjoyment.

I shrug, not sure I understand the question.

"Well, I know *you* can," she adds. "But what about my deadlines and my designers."

"Delegate," I say. And that's that. She calls in to tell one of her designers that she'll be gone all day and most of the next. Surprised that the world doesn't explode, Clover has a bemused expression.

"Cara didn't even question me except to ask if I was feeling all right? She's going to tell HR for me."

"Why?" I ask, mystified.

"Because they have to keep track of my sick days."

I feel my eyes widen before I rearrange my face. "I knew that."

"No, you didn't," she says. "You have no idea how worker bees have to behave and follow rules."

"Are you saying I'm the queen bee?" I grab her hand and place it high on my thigh. When she's around, I'm always half aroused.

She giggles, gives my cock a quick squeeze, and quickly pulls her hand away, before looking around guiltily. As if anyone cares about a couple groping in the cool morning air!

"A king bee, then," she muses.

We have the best day, doing nothing except being together and looking at stuff that is *not* Beacon Hill for a change. Doing "nothing" isn't entirely true. Historic Quebec City is full of old stone buildings housing shops, which we traipse in and out of. We both use our passing French lingual skills all day. I admit, Clover's accent is better.

"Why is your accent so good?" I ask.

"The design school in Paris," she reminds me.

Hand-in-hand, we tour the awe-inspiring Notre-Dame de Québec, and have a lively discussion comparing this cathedral to the one in Paris.

We eat lunch and dinner away from the hotel, and take note of other restaurants we'd like to try if we come again.

When she says "next time," I keep my cool. But I can't help thinking at some point, my sexy designer may decide we're better together as a couple than as a boss and employee.

I also get to wrap my arms around Clover for the antique toboggan slide that juts out from the Dufferin Terrace, between our hotel and the river. She screams and laughs the whole way down because I'm palming her breasts as we slide down at about forty miles per hour.

Occasionally, I have to tamp down a question about the asshole who hurt her. How long ago was it? Was she living with the guy? Does she want me to hunt him down and rearrange his face?

None of it really matters or has any impact on us, so I keep my curiosity reined in. That night, Clover dons the skimpy turquoise bikini I bought her, and we take a swim in the hotel pool.

Man! She is a fish in the water and can hold her breath longer than me.

While we sit in the hot tub afterward, though, and I recall how upset she was when telling me about being betrayed, I ask one question.

"Are you still hung up on the cheating asshole?"

29

Clover

It seems only minutes earlier we were eating a buffet breakfast in the hotel's Place Dufferin restaurant and then our romantic escape comes to an end.

One moment I'm admiring Adam's French as he speaks to the hotel staff—actually, I'm admiring his mouth, which looks even sexier when speaking French. I seriously want to climb him as if he were a tree. Then the next instant, I'm fastening my seatbelt in Adam's private jet at the Québec City Airport.

Not my first time in a jet like this, but definitely the most enjoyable. I wish I could tell him about my father's plane instead of lying again. Each time I'm less than truthful with Adam, it gnaws at me like a beaver on a tasty tree branch.

At least I never flew with Jason. I can honestly say I am not a member of the mile-high club, which makes Adam promise I will be. Very soon. That's all it takes to make me start throbbing between my legs with anticipation.

Sure enough, three and a half hours later, I am a member of those who have added to the excitement of flying with an orgasm in the sky. And proud of it, too. Grateful it wasn't a quickie in an airplane bathroom, I let Adam lead me into a posh little cabin. Still a quickie because of the short flight and the hovering steward behind the thin door, but we did it on an actual bed.

After landing at Hanscom Field, in Bedford, Massachusetts, I allow myself to be talked into the limo and allowing David to drive me the forty minutes home to Allston. Adam tries to get me to go back to Beacon Hill with him, but I put my foot down.

"My cat," I say with a shrug.

His crooked grin makes me shiver with happiness and lust. But because we're back in the real world, I don't kiss him goodbye. After all, I am not his girlfriend. I dash inside hoping no one noticed the gorgeous vehicle or the gorgeous man inside.

Hurrying to change into work clothing, determined to get to Bonvier and check in, I have an epiphany. Adam's place on Louisburg Square and even the hotel room in Quebec feel more like home than my apartment.

Common denominator: *Adam*.

Seeing him with Ms. Acton really shook me. I am in deep with the bossman for sure. Deeper than I have ever been with anyone before. I thought it hit me so hard because of Jason's betrayal. But I can't lie to myself any longer. I have strong feelings for Adam Bonvier. I hate to accept the truth, but I'm in love.

Love. *Love!* I try the word out a few times.

The evening before, in the hot tub, Adam asked me point-blank if I was still hung up on Jason. That was an easy answer. Nope! But I didn't tell him that I've never felt this way about anyone before.

It's exciting until I consider how much it would suck if and when we part ways. In comparison, losing Jason will seem like losing a favorite pair of shoes—not a pair of

Christian Louboutin's extravagant crepe-satin, red-soled eye candy, either. Maybe more like a moderately priced Andrea Carrano leather pump. Painful to part with, but not devastating in the scheme of things, at least not in retrospect.

In fact, my feelings for Adam puts anyone who came before him in perspective. There haven't been many. A school boyfriend, my college five-second fiancé, a Parisian fling, and Jason.

I come out of the T station and hurry down the street to Bonvier, and I feel vulnerable. I can't imagine anything I can do to protect myself. How will I gird my loins against future heartache involving Adam?

I can break it off now in anticipation of being hurt, a coward's solution that means terrible pain now rather than later.

Or I can let the future take care of itself and hope for the best. The idealist's path, which is fraught with danger and uncertainty, but also, possibly, blissful happiness.

Naturally, I opt for the latter, deciding to continue on the path of saving money to create my own freelance company. As soon as I think it's the right time to quit, with enough corporate designs in my portfolio that I will be taken seriously, then I'll ask Adam if he wants to begin a real relationship.

Nothing will make me happier than telling him the whole truth because lying causes a shadow over every minute we're together. I push it aside, even lie to myself that it's not that awful to keep secrets from him, but it is. Sometimes, I cannot look him squarely in the eye. But I continue because I'm sure it's for the best and because it's temporary.

I'm actually looking forward to the day I can face the paparazzi and the fifteen minutes of infamy. Then, hopefully, the world will leave us alone.

If that's the future he wants. If not, then I'll have my own business and not have to run into him at work. Win-win! But it would really be a massive lose.

$♥$♥$♥$

"Can you come to my office now?" Chris asks me on a regular Tuesday morning the following week.

I look at my planner and see I have time before a meeting with my team.

"Is it the Purdy account?" I ask. I've been unsure of the direction to take the logo given the scant information Leslie provided me. Not the first time, either.

"No." He hangs up without clarification.

Curious as that cat I don't own, I make my way to Chris's office one floor up. Leslie is already inside on one of the chairs, sipping from something purple. The curtains, I notice, have been drawn closed.

"Hey," I say and drop into a chair, by now thoroughly comfortable with no longer being the new employee. I have even hired a designer during my time here after one left.

"I hired you," Chris begins, shooting an unfathomable glance at Leslie, who rolls her eyes, "so I thought I better talk to you *before* I bring up your termination with HR."

This straightens my spine in a hurry. So much for being comfortable. "What are you talking about? What's wrong?"

"You're seeing someone in the company," Leslie says, her voice a little too gleeful.

My breath catches while my brain casts around trying to figure out how they know.

"Don't bother denying it," Leslie adds, with a nod of satisfaction.

I shoot her my best *mind your own business* look, which she catches and ignores.

"You broke the rules," she says triumphantly.

I don't confirm her accusation. "Why are *you* here?" I ask.

She smirks, but it's Chris who answers. "She came to me with the disturbing info, and I thought it only fair that you face your accuser."

Sweet mother! Face my accuser? As if I'm seriously on trial.

"In deference to your privacy," Chris continues, "Leslie hasn't told me who you're *seeing*. I won't ask. I don't care. If I find out, though, whoever he—or she—is will have to be fired, too."

Fired? Chris really doesn't know, or he would realize the absurdity of that statement. But if Leslie knows, then this ambush is puzzling as hell.

Her expression and manner exude the inexplicable maleficence I've seen before. Does she want Adam? I can't figure out her motive otherwise. Have I got in the way of her own dream to sleep with the bossman?

My departure isn't going to help her in that regard. I'm secure enough in my current relationship with Adam, utilitarian as it is, to know there isn't anyone else at the company he'd rather be sleeping with, nor anyone else with whom he'd risk this exact outcome. This ambush.

Termination.

But I still don't confirm Leslie's accusation. I can probably get Adam to make the problem go away, although short of him pulling rank on Chris and explaining exactly why he doesn't want me fired, I don't know how Adam can help.

I could tell Chris who my parents are. That usually results in my problems disappearing. I'm not sure in this case whether it would do the trick.

"Before you start thinking of ways to squirm out of this," Leslie says, "I have photos. But I won't do anything with them to harm the other individual, as long as you give your notice today."

Now I'm starting to think she's taking a wild stab in the dark. No way does she have photos of me and Adam. If she knew I was seeing *him*, he would be the last person she'd threaten.

I don't know whether to call her bluff or talk to Adam first. I'm not ready to leave Bonvier. I don't yet have enough savings to live off while starting my own design business. If I left now, I'd have to get another job, and switching positions again inside of a year won't look good on my résumé.

This could get ugly, but I have to stand my ground. I address Chris, not Leslie.

"Our clients will be disappointed," I say to him. "We have a lot of things going on at all stages of design."

Leslie runs a hand through her edgy, blonde hair. "We managed before you. Didn't we, Chris?"

He frowns, not looking pleased, then asks, "Can you recommend someone from your department for your position?"

That's a kick to the gut. "If there was someone else who could do what I do," I say, "then wouldn't you have hired him or her instead of me?"

He says nothing. Still, I should start thinking of that for when I do leave. Cara is an excellent designer. She'll totally be management material if she focuses on procedures a little. Nothing a good flow chart and schedule won't cure.

Leslie, I notice, is staring hard at Chris until he looks at her. Almost imperceptibly, he shakes his head, and she sinks back into her chair, sipping her drink like a sulky child.

Just like that, a possible reason for her all-out attack occurs to me. It's not Adam she wants. It's my job. It's the only reason I can come up with as to why she has disliked me from day one.

This time, I speak directly to Leslie. "You were in my department once. Do you have good graphic design skills or not?"

She startles, then she raises her chin and dares to look down her nose at me.

"I do, in fact."

I look at Chris. "Does she?"

He shrugs, noncommittally. I can see he's uncomfortable with the direction this conversation is going in.

"I do!" she repeats. "I'm an excellent artist."

I sigh. "If you think design is simply about drawing well, then you're mistaken. You can be as good an artist as Da Vinci or Holbein, but that doesn't mean you understand design."

She crosses her arms, looking mulish.

"Do you want my job?" I ask her. "Did you apply for it already? What happened with the art director before me?"

"Clover," Chris interrupts. "Let's get back to the rule violation that Leslie has brought to my attention."

But I smell a rat. I would bet my last black thong that Leslie had a hand in getting rid of my predecessor, too. And all the weird fuck-ups that have happened since I got here, even putting her own face in that gelato commercial so I wouldn't suspect her.

Chris should have given her the job in the first place, so she could succeed or fail on her own merit. I wonder why he didn't. Now, though, I know it would be a bad idea. I've worked with her long enough, and she's what Sam used to call a bad apple when Decker Financial hired a get-ahead-at-any-cost employee.

I hate like hell using my close relationship with Adam for business matters, but because these machinations could mean trouble for Bonvier, Inc., especially if Leslie ever wheedles her way into leading the design team, I'm going to have to tell the CEO.

"Wow!" I say, rising to my feet. "Talk about scheming your way into a career."

Leslie scowls, but Chris defends her. "No one is scheming."

I don't believe him, and I have to consider whether it will be intolerable to remain working with these two clowns.

Ultimately, I'm going to have to do so until I've saved enough.

"I am this close to tendering my resignation," I tell Chris, hoping he doesn't see through my bravado of a bluff. "So you had better call her off." I point at Leslie without even looking at her.

"How dare you!" Leslie says.

Chris narrows his eyes. "Do you deny you're seeing someone who works for Bonvier?"

"Absolutely," I say, deciding Leslie is blowing smoke—not to mention ice pops and maybe Chris, too.

With that, I nod to him. "I have a lot of work to do. I suggest Leslie finds herself a hobby, maybe bird watching. But she needs to leave me the hell alone."

I reach the door. "And I don't want any more of her brief as hell, cryptic notes sent to me as specs. Either I hear the client's wishes from you or from the client directly."

Then I walk out, keeping my ears pricked for Chris's voice calling me back to fire me. I hold my breath all the way to the stairs.

30

Adam

When I return from lunch with a client, Janet hands me an envelope. It has no markings on it except black ink scrawled across the front: "Private: For Mr. Adam Bonvier."

Not the first time I've received mysterious, anonymous mail. Probably not the last. I've had women send me nude photos with no information other than their phone number.

I open it while Janet pretends to take cover.

Inside, there is a bomb of sorts—glossy photos of Clover wrapped around some man.

Immediately, my blood boils. Who the hell is this? Why is she letting him put his hands all over her in a crowded place? She would throw an absolute fit if I ever did that in public.

Despite my heart pounding at seeing my woman—*and dammit, that's how I think of her*—hanging off the arm of some sleazeball, I calm down. This is clearly someone she was with *before* me. Someone she didn't have to hide.

I look at the next one. *Damn.* Her breasts are practically falling out of her dress, and the guy is loving it. They're entering a dance club in New York City, if I recognize the street correctly.

I want to see her in that dress, and I want to be the one going clubbing with her. If I still did that, which I don't. Frankly, I would rather sit in a tranquil bar, enjoying a decent drink and listening to one good band or solo artist than have my eardrums assaulted all night by a pulsating beat.

Although nothing outdoes mindless sweaty dancing with a hot woman, except mindless, sweaty sex with the same.

Scratch that. *Mindless* is out. Smart, deliberate, well-thought-out sex is in. And Clover is the one hot woman I want.

I look at the last photo, a different place. It's Central Park. The two of them are lip-locked and oblivious to the photographer.

Even knowing it's from the past, it doesn't sit well. I'm jealous, plain and simple. I have to be honest. If I'd seen Clover getting out of a hot tub with this guy, I would lose my shit, too.

As I've recently realized, I'm not in a sex-only relationship after all. I want all in. I want her to belong to me, and I want everyone to know it.

Then the significance of the photos gets past my jealousy-numbed brain and settles in. I'm so irritated at seeing her with another guy, the obvious didn't occur to me at first—someone knows Clover and I are meeting up. And they want me to know that they know. Why else would I be sent these if not to rattle me?

"You have the oddest look on your face, boss," Janet says.

I forgot she's here. Forgot where I am, too. When I shove them back in the envelope, one slides from my grasp and onto the floor, nearly at Janet's feet.

We both stare at it.

"Well," she says, and then reaches down to retrieve it. "That's Clover Mitchell, isn't it?"

"I believe so." I sound wooden, my weird tone probably matching my strange expression Janet just mentioned.

"This isn't current, is it?" she asks.

Clover's hair is shorter in the photo, cut in a sexy bob, but I like the longer length of how she wears it now.

I shrug, trying to appear disinterested.

"Because Clover would have to be racking up the frequent flyer miles," Janet adds.

"I don't understand."

She hands the photo to me. "Sorry, it's none of my business."

"Tell me what you know," I say. My assistant never holds back.

"That's Jason Decker. I've seen him in magazines and what-have-you. He's a New York City businessman, almost as famous and handsome as you." She winks at me, but I don't feel the least bit amused.

I frown down at the photo. *Jason Decker.* It's vaguely familiar. "Why would I know his name?"

"He's the CEO of Decker Financial. And you've probably heard of him because he's a smooth-talking, in-your-face, attention-grabbing type of guy. Although in some magazines, he's called *personable*. If I recall correctly, and I usually do, the Bonvier board looked into having his company handle some investments a few years back. But they decided to go with your current financial advisor."

I remember now. There was some disagreement among board members about four years ago, and that's where I'd heard Decker's name. I look at the other photos again before sliding them into the envelope.

"Is something wrong?" Janet asks. She's staring at me placidly, and I cannot believe how restrained she is. I expect she's got a spreadsheet's worth of questions chattering in her brain and is dying to ask me the main one—why did I receive these photos?

I don't answer even her simple question. But something is wrong, and I have a strange feeling in the pit of my stomach.

"Get me HR on the phone." I go into my office and close the door.

A few minutes later when I have some facts, I start to text Clover, but I stop myself. She'll be coming up tonight after work. Rather than jump to conclusions and get all weird, I can be patient. What's one interminably long day to wait, anyway?

It's exactly that. Half a dozen times, as the hours drag by, I nearly go down to her office or call her up to mine. Finally, Janet leaves, and I know the next person off the elevator will be Clover, hopefully with some answers.

Sure enough, not a minute late, she comes through my office door, eyes flashing, talking a mile a minute.

"I had a meeting with Chris early this morning. It was unnerving. And Leslie was in fine form!"

She tosses herself down on the leather couch, then asks, "Why are you still way over there?"

I'm trying to figure out if anything she just said has to do with what I want to talk to her about, but I don't believe so.

"I nearly asked you up here today," I say, before sitting beside her.

Clover relaxes and leans back, looking at the ceiling while she stretches. This pushes her breasts up and snags my attention. Any man would be lucky to have her. When she crosses her legs, it causes her skirt to ride up. She has the prettiest legs. Finally, she looks at me with golden-topaz eyes.

"You go first," she says. "What's up?"

So casual, I almost don't want to say anything to ruin the moment.

"Why did you come to Boston?"

"To land a great job, and I did."

"Did you come to Boston specifically for Bonvier?"

"You were top of my list." She touches my thigh.

I can't smile. "You mean my *company* was?"

She laughs. "Yes, but you have been an added perk, Mr. Bonvier."

Leaning close, she kisses me. Her scent alone heats my blood. The feel of her lips against mine makes me want to do crazy dirty things *to* her and *with* her. I'm not an idiot. I respond in kind until she's panting and I'm biting her lower lip, ready to forget everything apart from fucking her on the couch.

When our mouths are no longer fused, however, I tuck a strand of hair behind her ear and think of those goddamn photos. "I'm not your first boss lover, though, am I?"

Shit! That isn't exactly how I meant to start this conversation.

Clover shrinks back so no part of us is touching. "What are you talking about?"

I'm not sure what answer I expected. Maybe I thought she would deny it or laugh it off. She certainly isn't laughing. Her face drains of its usual healthy hue.

"I'm talking about Jason Decker. A former lover of yours, I believe. Previous boss, too, as it turns out."

She rises to her feet. "Why were you looking into my background?"

Whoa! Still no answers, only some defensive hostility.

"I wasn't. Some information was given to me indicating you had a relationship with him. HR confirmed his company was listed as your previous employer."

She purses her lips and goes to the window to look out at the city.

"I had a life before I came to Boston and to Bonvier, Inc. Didn't you?"

"Yes." But the issue isn't dating other people in general. I never went out with my art director. For one thing, the guy before her didn't have her legs!

Clover spins around to stare at me. "So what does it matter?"

"He's the CEO of Decker Financial," I point out as if she doesn't know.

She takes a deep breath and crosses her arms under her gorgeous breasts.

"And?" she asks, lifting her chin.

Is it simply a coincidence, or is it a pattern? I don't like to think I'm replaceable or interchangeable. Clover might simply have a thing for powerful, rich men. She might intend to hop ship in a few months and go after another CEO.

That's totally within her rights, but it would certainly change the way I'm letting myself grow attached to her.

Apparently, my silence irks her. "If you're putting two and two together, let me remind you that *you* pursued me first."

That was true. She hadn't thrown herself at me or even flirted. She'd kept her distance, and I had dogged her like a . . . well, like a dog.

But not a *cheating* dog! It dawns on me that Decker is the one. In Canada, she'd said her last boyfriend was the asshole who broke her heart. No, not her heart, her trust.

"Decker's the one who cheated on you." It took me a stupid amount of time to figure that out.

"With his executive assistant," she confirms, glancing toward the door, beyond which Janet usually sits. Clover has to know by now that there will never be anything between me and Janet.

Before I can state that unequivocally, she adds, "I didn't want to name names. I saw no need. Plus, I had a feeling you would jump to exactly the conclusion you did, that I like dating my boss when it's actually the opposite. After Jason, which turned out to be an all-around miserable affair, if you'll excuse the term, I vowed *No more bossmen*."

She shakes her head. "I guess you were simply too irresistible. And too persistent!"

Clover had put up some solid defenses, and I'd plowed right through them until she gave in. It's painfully obvious she's not a man-hunter."

"Come over here, please." I pat the sofa. "I'm sorry. It was just a shock seeing you with him."

"*Seeing* me?" She gets all riled up again. "What the hell are you talking about?"

She doesn't come back to the couch. Clover wants answers, and I wonder how this got turned around when I thought she'd be the one on the hot seat.

"Someone sent me photos."

"Leslie!" she exclaims.

"Leslie? From accounts?" That's a big leap. "Why do you think it was her?"

Finally, Clover sits beside me, not close, but at least she doesn't appear adversarial any longer.

"Because she told me she had photos of me in a relationship. I thought she meant with someone here at work. She tried to get Chris to fire me."

"What?" Irritation quickly flares to full-blown rage faster than my MTI catamaran speedboat makes it out of Boston harbor.

"You're shouting," she says, her own voice now even and calm.

People at my company were behaving like utter children, and my becoming hot and jumping into the fray wouldn't help matters. I calm the fuck down.

"When did this happen?" I ask.

She scrunches up her face, seeming both annoyed and a little defeated. I reach over and touch her hand, but she draws hers away.

Too soon for that, I guess.

"I tried to tell you before you started your interrogation," she says. "When I came in this morning, Chris asked me to go to his office. Leslie was there. Chris said he didn't care who I was seeing, but I would have to be terminated."

That seems high-handed and overstepping his authority to fire a department head without mentioning it to me. It's also crazy that I'm learning of it only now.

"Why didn't you tell me right after it happened?"

She waves a hand, dismissing my words. "We don't see each other until five thirty."

Well damn. "I think this was worth breaking our schedule, at least with a text. What if you'd been fired without my even knowing?" I was getting pissed off again. "Do you still work for me?"

"I planned on telling you as soon as I saw you," she says, "And I thought I handled it. I left Chris's office still having my job, and I assumed Leslie was bluffing. After all, she wouldn't threaten me if she knew I was seeing you."

"So why send me photos of you and Decker?" I ask.

Clover flinches slightly. I would love to punch that jackass in the nose for hurting her.

"I have no idea," she says. "Perhaps without knowing about you and me, she thought letting you know I was involved with . . . with *him* might make you question where my loyalties lie. Or maybe she merely wanted to imply I'm the type who dates within my workplace."

Clover's theory seems far-fetched, but it's as good a theory as any.

"Tomorrow, we'll go see Chris together."

She blanches. "Really? Why poke the bear? I think I convinced Chris to get over it."

"First, it's not his place to get over anything. He should have talked to me, and you shouldn't feel threatened at your job. Besides that, I don't want to receive any more surprise envelopes. Maybe the woman is unhinged."

I reach for her hand, and this time, she lets me hold it. A part of me wants to ask a bunch of questions about how she and Decker got together and how long they were a couple. But more of me doesn't want to know. I certainly don't want to think of them together. It's enough to have seen that photo of him kissing her and how happy she looked.

"May I kiss you?" I ask.

She hesitates, staring at me, then her lips part slightly, and she nods.

I'm not going to wait for more of an invitation. I sink my fingers into her hair and hold her steady while I claim her lips with mine. She is starting to taste like home, something I've never experienced with any other women. They always tasted like playtime, fun and games, sex and liquor.

But Clover—she is warmth and caring and dedication and truth. I am starting to think she is forever, too.

31

Clover

I was never one of those girls who tried to get the upper hand in school over anyone else. I didn't need to. My parents were wealthier than Midas, and I'd been blessed with manageable pre-teen and teenage years. I didn't go through the super awkward or ugly stages. I knew I was lucky on all counts and tried to be my best self. To that end, I was kind to everyone who came into my orbit.

But the following day, when I walk along the hall of the account department's floor with Adam by my side, I feel like kicking butt. Leslie's butt, to be honest. But it seems Adam wants to tackle Chris first.

I recall Leslie's smug face and the way she looks at Chris as if he's a tasty bird and she's a hungry cat. And then there's how she screwed me over on my first presentation all those months ago, and the strange minor annoyances that have happened since. She wants me out, and she wants my job. And I'm pretty sure Chris wants to give it to her if

251

appearances will allow him to do so without exposing nepotism.

As we approach, I can see Chris in his office. He isn't on the phone, nor meeting with a client. And what a surprise— *not!*—Leslie is leaning against the wall, arms crossed.

Without any warning other than his signature rapid knock, Adam pushes the door open. Leslie straightens up immediately, her expression going from astonished to worried. Chris rises to his feet slowly, obviously disconcerted at seeing me beside the boss.

"What's up?" he asks.

I watch Adam, who has immediately shrunk the room with his presence and his stance, legs slightly apart, one hand casually in his pocket, the other at his side. He sends Chris a curious look.

"You tell me."

Chris glances at me. "Are you referring to my meeting with Clover yesterday?"

"Is the account department attempting a coup of the art department?" Adam asks.

It was a humorous statement, but Adam's tone is deadly serious.

Both Leslie and Chris look at me, clearly surprised that I have gone to our boss.

After a moment, Leslie says, "I guess we should get this out in the open." She pulls her phone from her pocket before smirking in my direction. "You thought I didn't have a photo."

Adam sends me a querying look. I shrug. It still seems inconceivable that she's going to show him a photo either of us together or of me and Jason, which is entirely irrelevant.

"Didn't you send them to me already?" Adam asks.

Appearing confused, Leslie shakes her head. "No, not yet. After yesterday, I wasn't sure how to proceed. Instead of being contrite over breaking the rules, Clover seems to think it's my fault." Her tone is petulant. "Chris and I were just discussing—"

"You should have come to me." Adam addresses Chris. "Personnel issues are not up to you and Leslie. At the very least, you ought to have spoken to HR and had Clover called to Tina's office."

At that moment, Leslie says, "Take a look, Adam," before handing him her phone.

Seeming reluctant, he takes it. I can't see the screen so I watch his face as it changes from hesitant to downright perplexed. My insides churn.

What is he looking at?

Then he holds up the screen in my direction, and I get a glimpse. After a heart-stopping second as I make sense of what I'm seeing, I start to laugh at the image of me kissing Cara in our favorite bar.

Relieved not to see a photo of me with my hat and dark glasses on walking next to Adam on Beacon Hill, I keep laughing.

"It's not funny," Leslie says.

"Indeed, it's not," Chris agrees. "It doesn't matter that you're dating a woman. You're an executive, and she is under you!"

His cheeks turn ruddy. "Not that I'm saying—"

"I know what you meant." I put him out of his misery.

Adam is still wondering, with a dark eyebrow raised but an unconcerned expression. If anything, he's thinking of a sexy threesome and adding it to his fantasy notes.

Not going to happen, buddy!

"I was simply helping Cara get rid of two unwanted guys at our table. Nothing more. She's in a committed relationship with a live-in partner, and she'll laugh just as hard at this as I did." I turn to Leslie. "If you want my job, you'll have to do better than that."

Adam appears taken back. "You want Clover's job?"

"No," Leslie says in a knee-jerk response to his pointed question. "That is, yes," she adds. "If she were to get fired, then I would apply."

"Why didn't you apply six months ago?" Adam asks.

"I did," she says, sending Chris a glance.

"Why didn't you hire her?" Adam shoots this question to Chris, who has remained silent.

"I didn't want to play favorites." Somehow his saying it that way made it obvious something is going on between them, confirming what I'd suspected.

Adam looks from one to the other, letting the tension grow.

"If you gave it your best try and hired a great candidate who had to be fired," Adam surmises, "then you would feel justified hiring from within even if Leslie isn't the best applicant. Is she?"

"She's an excellent artist," Chris hedges, "and she could grow into the role. We work well together."

"Did you know she deliberately gave Clover the wrong specs on the first job?"

Chris's hesitation is telling, not to mention Leslie's widened eyes. Adam somehow had figured it out. Or has he? Because Leslie suddenly sticks up for herself.

"I did not handle the specs for that job. I was out sick."

"That's right," Adam says, and I wonder if he believes her. "Were there any other acts of sabotage?" he asks me.

I honestly feel bad for Leslie at this moment, but her conduct toward me has been shitty from the get-go. I nod. "A few. Some missing files or badly altered ones. I sorted them out. No harm done."

"I see." This time Adam's piercing stare is censoring me. "You should have brought this to my attention."

He's right, of course. I should have.

"You're fired," he says. I jump before I realize he's looking at Chris, whose olive-skinned, Portuguese complexion pales with surprise.

Leslie gasps into the stunned silence, but Adam doesn't take his gaze off his VP. And in classic alpha bossman style, he fires Chris first and now asks questions.

"You knew about these issues?"

"Yes." To Chris's credit, he doesn't deny it. Nor does he grovel. There's no point since he's already lost his job.

"And you let it go on," Adam says, "jeopardizing my company in the process."

Chris's jaw tightens. I can see the little, telltale muscle jumping.

"And I expect it was you who set Clover up at her first presentation," Adam continues, a claim I would never be bold enough to make. "You weren't expecting her to attend and certainly not me. It would have been easy to tell me afterward that she'd royally fucked up. I would have looked at the stupid apple and agreed you'd made a mistake in hiring her. You'd get a small reprimand for poor judgment, and she would've been terminated without the chance to fix it."

"That's not fair," Leslie says, although I would bet she's already considering whether, somehow, she can get Chris's job.

"You're fired, too," Adam tells her, making her blanche nearly as pale as her Marilyn Monroe hair color. I believe I hear her whimper. "I already knew you two were in a relationship," Adam continues and hands Leslie her phone, "and I let it pass, hoping you would be the exception who didn't let it affect your work."

He knew! More than anything, that surprises me, but I realize he's tougher on himself than on his employees. He let them get away with it.

"What about a reference?" Chris asks.

We all know they're worth their weight in gold, especially for a long-time employee. Finding the next position would be difficult without a solid reference. I know only too well the desperation when Jason refused to give me one, and I'd been forced to go around him.

"I'll provide a good one," Adam promises. "I have no gripe with the quality of your work."

"I appreciate that," Chris says. He's taking it well.

"What about me?" Leslie persists. Quite frankly, I'm impressed by her undaunted attitude. Adam, on the other hand, appears momentarily disgusted.

"Chris is free to give you a reference," he tells her. "I guess once you started sleeping with him, you really had him under your thumb."

She doesn't blush or look away. *Damn!* Leslie's a tough cookie. Maybe I should congratulate her on her Adobe Premiere Pro skills because I'm now sure she edited the gelato video. No one would suspect her of humiliating herself in order to make me look bad.

"Terms?" Chris asks.

"I'll talk to HR about a package. Clean out your desks and security will walk you both out in ten minutes."

Finished, Adam makes for the door. "Make sure you leave a list of passwords for all company accounts," he says over his shoulder, sounding pissed off.

I nearly forget to leave with him. I certainly don't want to stay and gloat. The whole thing is sad, in my opinion. Two careers derailed.

More than that, we now have a problem. I hurry to catch up with him. "You've just decimated the top tier of the account department. While I can play one on TV," I add, hoping to bring a little levity, "I'm not a real account exec."

"I know. I'll talk to Chris privately and see if he thinks anyone in the department should be promoted. Otherwise, we'll poach someone from Madison Avenue by Friday."

His tone expresses that he's still annoyed. His next words confirm it, and his annoyance is directed at me.

"You should have told me this was going on."

Yikes! "I should have," I agree. "One hundred percent. I thought I had it under control."

That earns me a long stare. Then he shakes his head and switches gears.

"You aren't dating a member of your design team, are you?" he asks, so quickly I nearly miss it.

"Nope. And you know it. So, why'd you ask?"

"Because that kiss was hot," he says. We're alone in his private elevator where I'd blindly followed him.

"I knew it," I said. "You want a threesome."

He bursts out laughing, all trappings of anger vanished as he presses me against the back of the elevator car and grinds against me.

"I don't," he objects. "OK, maybe in a fantasy. But not a real, let's-do-it fantasy. Just a keep-in-my-head one."

And then his mouth crushes mine and our tongues enjoy a quick dance. When I can breathe again, I peer past him toward the corner.

"Camera," I warn.

"Turned off," he says and puts his hand on my breast.

"Dangerous," I say.

"Yup," he agrees, and his other hand slides down my leg, slips under the hem of my skirt and draws it up. When he cups my mound, I catch my breath.

"Now?" I ask, hoping his finger is going to slide under my thong.

"God, I wish," he says, but barely strokes the thin fabric before he steps back. At the same time, the elevator sounds the floor, and the doors slide open. He blocks Janet's view as I make sure my clothing is in order, and then we step off.

"Wait," I whisper. "Why am I here?"

"Because I needed to kiss you in the elevator."

That doesn't give me a viable excuse. Janet stops typing as we approach. Looking up, she startles when she sees me. I can't help wondering if she's seen the photos Adam mentioned of me and Jason.

"I appreciate your help with . . . that matter," I say to Adam's back when he continues on toward his office as if nothing happened. "I'll return to work immediately. Always lots to do." I'm babbling because Janet is still staring at me.

Adam halts. "More work than you know until we get the new hires." Then he addresses Janet.

"Chris Arruda and Leslie Baker no longer work for Bonvier."

Janet takes that in stride with little more than the raising of a single eyebrow.

"Please send their schedules to me," Adam tells her. "Every upcoming meeting and deadline they have. And send them to Clover, too, as well as the heads of live and print media because these terminations directly impact their departments. And then get me HR on the phone. Again! I talk to them more than I talk to my father."

I start to edge away. I don't belong up here during work hours.

"Clover," he stops me in my tracks. "Go to all the client meetings until we get the new hire. I trust your judgment, even if you're not an account exec." He winks at me.

"Yes, sir," I say, then realize how odd that sounds when we're not enacting a fantasy. My cheeks heat as Adam offers a slow smile, and Janet sends me a curious look.

"Enjoy the day," I say to them both and scurry back to the elevator—the public one, this time.

While riding down, I consider the morning. I see Adam in a new light. Yes, he has always been kind to me, but he's also in charge of this huge organization. He fired those two fast enough to give me whiplash. No inquiry, no discussion, simply two heads lopped off and rolling in the space of a minute.

It gives me pause. I definitely need to stay on top of my game at work. Bonvier, Inc. is his first love, and I've seen how ruthlessly he defends it. Poor Chris! I never want to be on the other end of one of Adam's most piercingly pissed-off stares. Or the words, "You're fired."

32

Adam

Clover isn't supposed to come up to my office for dinner and sex tonight, but I want her. Fuck the fact that it's Wednesday.

Maybe I'm still stinging from how happy she looked in Jason Decker's arms. Maybe I want to make it up to her for how Chris and Leslie have treated her.

Maybe I'm just horny as hell. When she said "yes, sir" earlier, I knew what I wanted to do to her, something she really gets off on.

I send her a text, telling—*not asking*—her to present her sexy self in my office at five thirty. And then I wait for Janet to leave just after five.

I'm not standing at the elevator, but I'm listening for her. As soon as Clover appears, I know it would be easier on me if we did it fast and pounding, but tonight, I'm not giving in to what's easy.

"You wanted to see me, boss," she says, eyeing my raging boner pressing eagerly against the blue virgin wool of my Kiton slacks. A small smile curves her lips.

A little sassy and flippant. *Good!*

"This way," I order and let her trail me to my conference room. I draw out one of the armless chairs, purposefully purchased as being a little uncomfortable so no one dozes off or gets too relaxed during a meeting. I sit and turn to face her.

"Take off your skirt and blouse."

She hesitates, a little crinkle appearing between her eyebrows. When I say nothing more, she swallows before shimmying out of her skirt and unbuttoning her blouse, laying both over a chair. Stripped down to her bra and thong, looking like a freaking goddess, she waits.

"Come here." I pat my lap.

"You're angry," she says.

"I would never touch you in anger. I won't even spank you in anger. Don't forget *marzipan*." I remind her that she has the power, in one single safe word, hidden so we don't ruin the fantasy. "But I don't like repeating myself. Come here."

Swiftly, Clover approaches and lays herself over my thighs, presenting me with her perfect pale ass. It won't be pale for long.

"Bonvier is my company," I say and give her an initial swat with the flat of my hand.

"My employees answer to me." *Smack.*

"*You* answer to me." *Smack.*

"Even though you and I are more than boss and employee." *Smack.*

"That doesn't change the line of command." *Smack.*

"If you see something at my company that's wrong." *Smack.*

"Then you tell me." *Smack.*

"Immediately." *Smack.*

"Ow!" she says, but there's laughter in her voice. I start to caress her now-reddened flesh.

"I didn't want to bother you over something I could handle," Clover adds.

I sigh. She doesn't get what I'm saying. It isn't her place to *handle* my employees.

"Stand up." As she does, I adjust my cock which is starting to demand attention. When Clover sees the bulge, she smiles. But she's epically misreading the room. We're not done with her punishment

"Face down across the table," I say.

Her giddy, sexy expression falters. "Adam?"

"Now."

"Well, OK, but I don't know what I'm being punished for any longer."

"And that's why we're continuing," I tell her, removing my black leather belt. "Once I explain this to you, I don't want you to forget."

"Adam?" Her voice is high and breathless, but her glance at the belt in my hands is sheer excitement. She rests her breasts and stomach on the table.

I wrap the buckled end around my hand and give her a cursory zap with the other end.

"Ow!" she says with more emphasis than ever before.

"You don't decide," I tell her before sending the belt across her bottom with a swift flick.

"Ouch!"

"When it comes to Bonvier, it's not a question of what you can handle." *Flick.*

"Yow!"

"You tell me immediately if anything is going on." *Flick.* She hisses.

"Chris didn't tell me, and now he's gone." *Flick.*

"Seriously, *ouch*!"

"If anyone else withholds similar shit from me." *Flick.*

"Please, Adam!"

"They'll be fired, too." *Flick.*

"Owww!"

"Including you." *Flick.*

"Jesus!"

I place my hand on her red ass and caress it.

"All three of you kept information from me, but the one that bothers me the most is the one I didn't fire. Do you understand? You ought to have told me as soon as Leslie started messing with you. At the very least, you should have let me know the second Chris tried to fire you."

"My ass is on fire," she says, barely above a whisper.

"Am I clear?" I ask without striking.

She says nothing, just breathes hard.

"Do you understand?" I ask again, tracing the end of the belt across her ass and then dipping it between her legs. She parts them instantly.

"Yes, I do."

"I'm the boss. Say it." I pull her damp thong to the side and touch her clit. We're both ready, but if she says something sassy like, *"I'm* the boss," I swear I will give her ten more lashes.

"You're the boss."

Thank God! I'm bursting to come inside her. "Roll over."

She turns and faces upward, looking at me as I part her legs and step between them.

"The cool table helps take away the sting," Clover says, wryly. "Thanks for asking."

I smile. "Look me in the eye and say it again."

Her expression grows serious once more. "You are the boss, Mr. Bonvier."

Satisfied she's got the message and will never undermine my authority at work again, I unzip my fly. Clover wraps a hand around my cock and tugs me closer. Considering the heightened emotions, it's no surprise she wants it hard and fast, and I deliver.

Sinking into her wet pussy, I feel her body tremble. Drawing out, I watch her gorgeous mouth gasp and bury myself inside her again a second later. I piston in and out of her, and we're too far gone for the niceties of me kissing her mouth or nibbling on the skin along her sensitive collar bone. Instead, palming one of her breasts and pinching the pearled nipple, I caress her clit with my thumb until she moans with a long, shuddering climax.

A few strokes later and I roar out my own climax with a final deep thrust. I do not collapse atop her. In fact, quicker than usual, I grab her hand and pull her to her feet. We're both a little amazed we had such good sex on what is basically a hard, uncomfortable slab.

"I'm famished," she says, arranging her thong and snatching up her clothes. "I hope you ordered already."

Watching her wriggle into her skirt before, hopping around as she puts on her shoes, I want to tell her what she means to me. But I don't. Enough drama for one day, and this isn't the place I want to be when I tell her I want more than to be her sex buddy.

33

Clover

After Chris and Leslie are terminated, despite the initial turmoil, work becomes smoother. As Adam promised, he hires a new accounts director by week's end. I like her. She seems top notch. Not intentionally, he hires a male account exec to fill Leslie's wicked witch shoes.

"Let's hope they don't spark a liking for one another," Adam jokes.

Funny man. Our new VP of accounts is a seasoned professional with her first grandchild on the way. And the recent hire to take Leslie's place is a newlywed. Probably, it's a safe bet they won't begin a torrid affair.

However, knowing *we* are still flouting the rules makes Adam and I both start to feel crummy.

Not that we stop what we're doing, but sometimes, it preys on our consciences.

"What if there are people at Bonvier who are meant to be together?" I venture over coffee one Sunday morning.

He shrugs. "I used to think that, as long as they are on the same level, it would be fine with neither party having power over the other. But even if one can't coerce and fire the other, someone might be forced to quit if they get uncomfortable. And they might start out on the same level and then one gets a promotion." He shakes his head. "It's just a bad idea to piss in your own pool."

"You mean fish," I say.

"Why would you fish in a pool?" he asks.

"You wouldn't," I say. "Isn't that the point? Why wouldn't it be OK to pee in your own pool? Better than peeing in someone else's?"

We stare at one another. "I think you're right," he says. "It was the wrong analogy."

"But the right thought," I add. "Not dating within the company just makes sense. So what about us?"

I toss that out a bit recklessly because we've been at this for a while now. And while neither of us really believes it's solely about sex any longer, at least I don't, we've never called our hook-ups a *date*.

He swallows the last bite of eggs benedict before taking a sip of coffee.

"Being the CEO has to give me some perk other than my own elevator and a private bathroom," he says.

Not sure what answer I expect, but not that flippant one. I'm not the equivalent of having a spacious toilet, am I?

"And I'm just a perk?"

He gave himself permission to have a special arrangement with me because he is the boss. That's great for him, but not especially flattering for me.

"Stop it," he says. "I can see the wheels turning. I wouldn't be enjoying this particular perk with anyone but you. I've had plenty of opportunity over the years. And I didn't take them."

About that shadowy past, filled with numerous women, I've never asked . . . until now.

"Why not? Weren't you ever tempted?"

"Do we have to have this discussion?"

We don't, but now I think there must be something to discuss. I've picked at a scab apparently.

"You started working for your dad as a young, rich hotshot. You didn't enjoy a little corporate pussy?"

He shakes his head. "Listen to your mouth. You may need to be punished."

While that sends an instant zing of lust to the V between my legs, I won't let myself be distracted. Not while we're fully clothed and finishing brunch.

"Let me restate the question, Your Honor. Didn't the twenty-two-year-old Adam see some attractive females in his father's company and go for them?"

If ever the term "clouded over" applied, it's right then. Adam's face becomes grim.

"I did. It was wrong and stupid. People got hurt."

Shit! I reach over and touch his hand. "I'm sorry."

"Thanks. I probably should have told you. It's worse than you think."

"I think some pretty ladies hoped to become Mrs. Billionaire and got their panties in a twist when a lusty young man had no such intentions."

"You are a smart woman, Ms. Mitchell. And, yes, that's mostly what happened. They were too willing, and I was too horny to be selective."

"And someone at Bonvier had to fire a few of them?"

He nods.

"What aren't you telling me? Because I think I know you well enough to say that's not the expression of a man who has left a few ten-year-old flings in his past, knowing those women have all moved on by now. What's up?"

He puts his fork down. "My father had me spend time in every department. And I was screwing my way through them like a jerk."

He pauses, looking embarrassed.

"Go on." I urge, feeling like I'm listening to the tale of a train wreck, about to get to the part where screeching metal causes sparks on the track.

"There was one person, Rachel. She was in accounting. Pretty, super smart, quirky. I locked her in my sights as soon as I saw her. She was less willing than the others. Meaning, she didn't drag me into an empty office or try to get me to fuck her in the stairwell."

Yikes! I don't need to hear about every sexual antic he's had in the building. But I hold my tongue. After all, I asked.

"She finally agreed to a date and let me kiss her that night. Nothing more. We went out a second time. And a third. We had sex. By the fourth date in two weeks, I knew I was at the end of whatever we were doing. She thought it was the beginning."

He fidgets with the silver teaspoon on the table, twirling it absently between his fingers.

"Stupidly, I told her at work after she blindsided me about making plans to introduce me to her family. She ran out of the building and died in a car crash later that night."

I gasp, which is a bone-headed reaction, making him wince. Poor Adam! When I get my thoughts together, I ask, "Did she take her own life?"

"Not intentionally, I don't think. She went right out of the office and drank all afternoon. She already had some problems, not only drinking but some mental issues, which I didn't hear about until her sister started screaming at me right before the graveside service."

At first, I don't know what to say. Then I do.

"Her sister needed someone to blame other than Rachel, but people break up all the time and don't go on a bender and die. I didn't," I remind him.

"I know you're right," he says. "Still, I felt like a monster for a long time."

"You're a bit of a control freak, and something huge happened that was out of your power to fix."

He looks at me and blinks. "You're good. You should change professions." Then the sadness descends on him again, and all he can do is shrug and look like a beaten dog. I hope I can make him think a little differently because that's a hard cross to bear.

"Don't get me wrong, Adam. I feel dreadful for her family. But Rachel did a pretty shitty thing, drinking that much and driving, knowing full well if something happened it would make you feel guilty the rest of your life."

While he frowns and considers my words, I add, "So I guess she never really cared about you, not even as much as you've cared about her all these years."

He appears shocked. We stare at each other.

"I never thought of it that way."

"That's a big burden you're shouldering," I say, "and maybe you should give yourself a break. Just think about it."

He nods. We finish up and take our usual walk around the neighborhood. The weather is now truly warm, and it feels cleansing to be out in the sunshine with this man. Because I'm feeling bad about having asked him to relive such a painful event, I slide my hand into his, and we stroll around holding hands. Something we never, ever do.

Adam is a little quiet, but the rest of the weekend is like any other we've enjoyed, apart for the one when we ran into Uncle Samuel.

Luckily, he had complied with Adam's request and never told my parents. I know this because Mom would have called me immediately to ask about wedding preparations. She did that when she found out about Jason and, of course, Dan, the fortune-hunter from college. It isn't that she's desperate to marry me off, although I am her oldest, but she said she's always wanted to throw a wedding party.

She'd also told me she hoped I would marry *before* she had to have any "work" done.

"You can always tell, even with the best surgeons," Mom once mused a little despondently.

Considering my mother still turns heads, I figure I have a few years before she puts herself under the knife.

Having heard Rachel's story, I balk at telling my parents I'm dating anyone. Nothing spooks a man more than a woman's family wanting to meet him—and measure him for a tux.

"We're both quiet today," Adam says, as I pack up my bag to go to Allston. "I like being quiet with you."

I feel all warm and happy, like I've been dipped in melted chocolate.

"See that smile," he adds, although of course I couldn't. He traces it with the tip of his finger. "I love that smile. I love *you*, Clover. I think you should move in with me."

Adam

I surprise myself, and I surprise Clover even more. Not that she should be shocked about how I feel. We understand one another. We talk endlessly about everything, or say nothing at all for hours. Either way, being with her suits me perfectly.

But we've been limiting ourselves. I want to enjoy the outside world with her, stroll around a museum and listen to her thoughts on what we're seeing. I want to hear her speak French while we travel through the Riviera and see her in a bikini in a quaint little spot I fell in love with in Spain. I want to be out at a play or a concert, showing her off, and I want to hear her sexy laughter in public or find out why something makes her cry.

We could explore the world. Instead, we remain cocooned on the upper floor of Bonvier or at my Beacon Hill townhouse.

Not that such an insulated relationship is a bad thing. We fill every moment pretty well. Spectacularly well when having sex.

So, after my heartfelt, blurted assertion of love, why is she looking at me like I have two heads?

More importantly, why isn't she rushing to fill the silence with her own similar declaration?

Instead, her gorgeous caramel-colored eyes widen. Her lips part, but for a second, no words come out. Then she tilts her head.

"I was not expecting that, but it's really sweet to hear." She takes my hand, which makes my stomach drop. She ought to be throwing herself against me so I can wrap my arms around her. We ought to celebrate the change in status quo and the exciting new adventure.

Then she says basically the polar opposite.

"I'm not ready to toss paint on the canvas and see where it lands. Everything is so smooth for us right now. It seems risky to stir it up."

"I was *not* expecting that," I echo her words. My ego is bruised, but I'm Adam Bonvier, who can have anything I want. Usually. This is just a hiccup. If I want to make a life with Clover Mitchell, I'll have her in the end.

After I manage an awkward shrug and send her what I hope is a smile, not a grimace, I pull her into my arms anyway.

"That's fine. We'll move at your pace. No pressure."

I can't see her face with her head against my chest, right over my heart, which is thudding with disappointment, if I'm honest. It's not such a leap to think of Clover at my place during the week, whether sitting at the kitchen island as she likes to do while chatting with Amarra, now that she's over being embarrassed, or running the water for the soaking tub, or even watering my plants that she thought looked a little parched.

Clover fits so well into my life. On a Sunday night after she leaves, I always miss what I've never had, Clover living with me full time.

For fuck's sake, it's the first time I've said those words to anyone who wasn't family. How odd to choose a woman who doesn't glibly say them back. It's given me a hollow, lonely feeling, even though I'm holding her tightly.

And then I realize she's crying. *Well, shit!* I definitely didn't hit a hole in one by telling her how I feel and asking her to move in. More like I sent the golf ball flying onto another fairway entirely.

I rub her back. If there's a guy in the world who knows what to say or do in this situation, I wish he would clue me in.

"Is it something I said?" Those three stupid words, perhaps?

She nods against my shirt but says, "No. It's me."

That's clear as mud.

"Everything would change," she chokes out, amidst sniffling noises.

"Not everything," I say. Then I think about it. "You're right, it would."

"What if we have a fight and I have no apartment to go to?"

"We never have that type of fight. Besides, you can go into a guest bedroom if you need to get away from me."

She sniffs. "I'd have to quit, right when you need me the most to help get the account department back to normal. The new hires need me."

"You wouldn't have to quit right away," I remind her. I nearly said that she wouldn't have to quit at all, but she would. It was inevitable that Clover working for me during the day and sleeping beside me at night would clash. About that, we both feel the same way.

She makes a growling sound, not of passion but of frustration.

"What if you change your mind?"

Of all her reasons, that is the one that doesn't worry me. In fact, it makes me feel a little better. She's holding back because she's scared, but I can be patient.

"I won't change my mind."

"You might."

"Nope." I can only imagine she's gun-shy after Decker. "Hey, I'm not the asshole. Remember?"

"I know."

"Why are you crying?" I ask.

"Because."

"Thanks for the explanation."

If anyone should be worried, it's me. Having decided Clover is *the one*, it doesn't bode well that she's too uncertain even to move in with me. "We'll keep things as they are for now, but I don't consider you my sex buddy anymore."

As intended, the silly phrase makes her laugh a little, which is a whole lot better than crying.

"I like being your sex buddy," she says, leaning away so she can look up at me.

"We'll still have sex," I promise. "I meant to say *not only* that. If you weren't working for me and we'd been dating all these months, then you'd be ready to move in together."

"Maybe," she says

Maybe? She is definitely making me work for every inch. I don't mention that she might have fallen in love with me already if we'd handled this differently. It's too awkward to bring up again until I'm certain of a return in kind.

After that, we ignore the whole thing. Not only as I say goodbye to her, but the next week at work. Clover is at the meeting with the new staff, and I drop in occasionally. There's no weird tension between us. In fact, everyone seems happier.

Except me.

The longer we carry on, the more likely we'll be caught as hypocrites. It's a shitty feeling. But I trust she'll come around. Because every time I sink into Clover's warmth and wetness, with her desire for me obvious in the way she fully offers her body, I can tell this isn't just sex for her, either.

Something shines out of her eyes that looks an awful lot like what I'm feeling.

So why does she lie to me at the earliest opportunity?

34

Clover

I've become used to glass walls. Everyone does eventually. It's unusual to see the privacy curtains closed anywhere in the building. One time, I discussed it with Cara, bringing up the lack of walls.

"I think it's like men at their urinals," she says during lunch.

"Do you have to use that word while I'm eating?" I ask, putting down my turkey and mustard on rye.

Cara laughs. "I mean, I've heard they don't look at one another. They don't look right or left. Only straight ahead. That's how I am at Bonvier. I don't look into each office as I pass. Do you?"

"You're right. I don't."

Which means the first time I close my office curtains on all sides except out to the street, four stories below, I should have guessed it would draw attention. In my hand is a package addressed to me from Decker Financial. When it's brought up from the mail room, the first thing I do is shelter myself behind the gray drapes.

Seeing the logo that I updated for Jason's company takes me right back to that awful afternoon. To finding him and his assistant, Laura, going at it. To my utter devastation and feeling like an idiot.

It rattles me more than it should, which is why I closed the drapes, a clear indication I want to be left alone. And I open the small box.

Shit! It's actually from Jason. He has written a note on company paper. Stupidly, I bring it to my nose, wondering if it smells like him, a bold, musky scent that I used to inhale when I pressed my face into his shirt or his chest.

The paper doesn't smell like anything. I squint at the writing, not even sure it's his.

Thought you might want to see this, one of your best designs.

Digging through the packing peanuts, I uncover an expensive-looking, white leather box with a hinged-lid, as if I hold the largest, mother-of-all engagement rings. Stamped on it is Decker Financial's logo in gold. I open the lid. Nestled in cheerful royal purple silk is a crystal egg—like an extra-extra-large chicken egg—with an almost invisible seam for sliding a small photo inside. The goal was to create a gift for clients who opened up a sizable investment account for their baby, with a place for the child's photo.

I did a damn good job if I do say so myself. But my hand is shaking slightly because I've read the next line and am trying to pretend it doesn't mean what it says.

I'm coming to Boston soon and want to see you. Don't say no. You owe me at least a face-to-face.

That is rich! *Owe him?* He's the one who'd fired me. And the cocky asshole didn't even sign the note.

I don't have a trace of good feeling for him. Even if the note simply had "sorry" written a thousand times over in his blood, I wouldn't agree to see him. Why go over something that's ruined and finished? Like trying to fix a bad watercolor painting. Watercolor is unforgiving for mistakes, as am I.

No, that's not it. I simply don't care enough to ever see him again. The days and weeks and months—and Adam's talented fingers—have taken the edge off my anger and hurt. There is nothing I need to say to Jason, and nothing I want to hear.

I breathe out a long breath and put this unpleasant interruption behind me. Placing the crystal egg back in its container, I close the lid with a snap and drop it along with the note back into the box to take home. It has no place at Bonvier.

Jason is not only firmly in the past, he's a pale comparison to what I have with Adam, despite all our self-imposed limitations.

Not even close. So why have I been so scared lately?

Adam said he loves me. And I froze, panicked, and then cried. I still haven't apologized for that disastrous reaction. Nor have I told him how I feel. Why can't I spit out the words? Because I do love him.

You know why, I say to myself. And I did. It was right after I told Jason I loved him that he screwed Laura in his office.

He went off the deep end probably because he felt trapped. Anyway, that's how I finally excused Jason's atrocious betrayal. Now I know Adam ended his relationship with that unfortunate woman after she wanted to introduce him to her parents. Another case of being boxed in, feeling trapped. And he broke it off with Rachel right away.

What if he regrets asking me to move in with him when I'm underfoot every day? I simply am not prepared to go from a fun and flirty part-time sex goddess to a drudging full-time, in-his-space and in-his-face girlfriend.

Plopping down in my chair, I rest my head back, closing my eyes.

Not only am I making excuses for being cowardly over three little words, I'm also wasting valuable work time.

Pressing the button that opens my curtains, it strikes me what a good analogy they were for how I've been living my life.

Frankly, I don't know how Adam can believe he loves me when I have held back about so much. How I got this job, for instance. On top of that, he's never been to my apartment to see the real me when I'm not at work or playing house at Louisburg Square.

I decide to be the tiniest bit brave and invite him over. Pam is going away to visit her family in Wisconsin for an early summer vacation. I would have our place to myself from Tuesday to Sunday.

"Come to my place," I say when I go upstairs that afternoon.

"What do you mean?" he asks, his smooth forehead furrowing.

I can't help smiling. "I don't live downstairs on the design floor," I point out. "Remember how you thought your teacher lived at school when you were in kindergarten?"

Without missing a beat, he deadpans, "You mean Mrs. Woltzer didn't? I'm devastated."

Thinking of young Adam makes me smile. He was probably the cutest little boy in school.

"Yes!" Adam says.

"Yes, what?"

"I'll be there. When? What time?" He's grinning like a fiend.

"Don't look so thrilled. It's Allston, not Paris."

"I know, but it's *your* home. I'll get to finally see the real Clover in her natural habitat."

Oh, boy!

$♥$♥$♥$

"**I** love it," he declares as soon as he arrives on Friday night.

I laugh because we're standing in the doorway in front of the wall of aluminum mailboxes on the ground floor. The intercom works, but the entrance buzzer currently does not, so I had to dash down the stairs as soon as I heard his crackling voice.

Also amusing is the way he's dressed per my request. Here is my billionaire boss, in faded jeans, sneakers, and a hoodie with a baseball cap and glasses.

"You didn't let David drive, did you?" I try to peer past his ridiculously broad shoulders, thinking his fancy limo might be hovering at the curb.

"No," he says, leaning in to give me a toe-curling kiss.

In his current outfit, it's almost like making out with a stranger. Until I smell his cologne while his tongue does that special thing that makes me feel particularly hot.

When I stand aside to let him enter, he adds, "I drove my favorite car."

I freeze. "Not the bright-yellow Porsche?"

"Relax. I fit right in."

I bite my lip. Somehow, I doubt it. His gorgeous car will be sandwiched between the beaters and used rust buckets that are the neighborhood's norm.

"We'll have to move it around back if one of the visitor spots is available," I say. "That's all resident-only parking on the street."

"So?" He looks genuinely puzzled.

"You'll get a ticket," I inform him. Doesn't he know how the world works?

Adam still seems nonplussed. "I'll gladly pay the cost of a parking ticket," he says, "to leave my car right where it is"—he points to the curb—"and stay here with you."

Ah! How romantic. Although it would be more so if he would feel the pinch from a single ticket fine, or even a thousand.

"This way. Your choice," I say.

He follows me upstairs to my front door at the back of the late-nineteenth century, three-story walkup. No elevator. My thighs have become toned since living here.

"I like this place already," he says. "Excellent view."

I smile to myself. There's something irresistible about a man who always admires my ass.

Adam has been to my building only the one time in the taxi that fateful night after the Lovell meeting. I never let him bring me home on a Sunday because my rule is as ironclad as his. Although come to think of it, we've turned his rule into swiss cheese.

Anyway, this evening is another first for us. I push my door open and go in ahead of him. Adam walks past the closet that makes up the entirety of our entrance hall—I don't think he even notices it—and directly into our dining room.

It's small, and it's the central hub of our apartment. A rectangular table takes up most of the room, and it's pushed up against the right wall, which is the one we share with the adjoining apartment. If we ever need anything from the college boys next door, like a can of beer, we can pound on the wall.

He sets his Italian leather overnight bag under the table on which I always have fresh flowers now that I can afford them again. Scanning from one side to the other, he takes it all in, which is easy to do since he can see each room, or at least each door, from where he's standing.

His presence shrinks not merely the room but the entire apartment by a few feet.

"Kitchen is through there," I point beyond the dining room to the opening at twelve o'clock and then go counterclockwise. "The bathroom is behind the door next to it. My room is next to that." I point at nine o'clock to the only room without a door. "Obviously that's the living room, and my roommate's bedroom is back there." I jerk my thumb over my left shoulder.

Adam strolls across the worn hardwood floor into the living room, which I confess has a slightly shabby vibe to match the rest of the apartment. I brought very little with me, no furniture at all apart from my bed and dresser. Pam owns the tweed sofa and end tables, the dining table, and the rest.

"I bought it all from the Goodwill," she told me when I moved in. "Because some day, I'm going to marry a guy with good taste, and we'll pick out our forever furniture together."

Forever furniture made me laugh until I realized she was serious. I contributed a navy blue throw over the entire ugly sofa, and a pretty navy-and-gray area rug.

At least the ceilings are high, befitting the building's era. Often, the place is sunny, because no tall buildings block our windows, which all face the precious, coveted parking lot out back.

At this time of early evening, the sun hasn't set yet, but I've turned on a few lights to chase away the lengthening shadows, and I lit a sweet fig-and-orange scented candle, hoping to create a little ambiance. Trying not to cringe, however, when I look at my home compared to Adam's, I wish I'd put out a fruit bowl on the coffee table.

Adam looks out the living room back window to the fire escape and glances down at the cars parked below. It's worth the extra rent not to have to circle the cramped and crowded streets each evening.

"Mine's the silver Ford Focus by the back fence."

He looks for it and nods. "Definitely not a Ferrari." Then he adds, "No balcony?"

I can't tell if he's joking or serious. I imagine he already sees me differently in light of my modest accommodations. And yet, Pam and I each pay fifteen hundred dollars plus utilities.

"Actually, if you come this way, through the kitchen—don't blink or you'll miss it—we do have another fire escape on the side of the building, and it has room for two people to sit."

"This, I have to see."

Leading him into a kitchenette with a decent amount of storage and a working dishwasher, I shrug at the ugly Formica countertops. Nothing I can do to make it look more like granite. Most of the cabinets are builders' specials, but a section of old-style, etched-glass front cabinets from the previous century is where we keep our liquor.

"Would you like a drink?"

"I'm good. Show me your spacious balcony."

"Ha-ha." Funny man! I open an old, painted door with a curtained glass pane, and step onto our prized fire escape, which we call "the terrace." As promised, a small, round wrought iron table and two chairs, as well as Pam's plants, give it a bit of charm.

"Are you sure we should both be out here? At the same time?" Adam asks, looking down to the alleyway between my apartment and the back of the next street's nearly identical, late-Victorian era buildings with the same brick design, interspersed occasionally with wooden triple-deckers.

Our view is of the other people's fire escapes, balconies, and the deckers' decks. Those directly across the way are big enough to have a small party on, which happens whenever the weather allows. The students get very loud.

"I haven't been here for the summer yet, but it's been warm enough lately for people to hang out and play music. If you drink the right amount and if you let your eyes move quickly over the old wrought iron railings, this humble alleyway resembles New Orleans' French Quarter."

"Why, Ms. Mitchell, that's poetic," Adam jokes. "Except for needing to drink heavily to turn this into anything other than an alley."

I shrug. It doesn't look busy now because we've had a cool end of May. Also, it's a little early. Only a couple guys are drinking beers across the alley on the floor below mine looking up at us.

"If it were a little warmer, I would've set up some wine and cheese." But we turn and go back inside my cramped apartment, and I shake my head. "You could fit like ten of my home into yours." The only thing they have in common is the era when they were built—mine for the working and middle class, his for the Boston Brahmins.

I let Adam pour us each a glass of wine and then I continue the tour to show him my modest bedroom.

"Dear God," he exclaims. "What's with the frogs?"

My collection, which started in childhood, has grown to about forty in all shapes and sizes, and in all media, from wood to ceramic to little iron figures with curly tails. There's even a painting on the wall.

I barely notice them anymore. "Just a silly fondness. What's wrong with them?"

"Nothing," he says. "It's just . . . you're a designer. If you were going to collect something, an animal, I would expect something more elegant or stylish, like swans or horses."

"Frogs beat both. I know swans mate for life and horses are majestic, but frogs!" I shake my head.

His smile is an instant aphrodisiac, and I go up on tiptoe to kiss him.

"That doesn't tell me anything," he says.

Fine. I'll explain my nerdy admiration for frogs.

"Look at those glass ones." I point to my prized grouping of brightly colored frogs. "Those are their real colors. That stunning blue and green and yellow. Exactly how they look in real life. And look at the turquoise and brown one. That's an Amazon milk frog."

He's staring at me, not at my frogs.

"What?" I ask.

"You are so fucking sexy when you discuss amphibians."

Half an hour later, we're breathing hard, propped up on my pillows, and finally drinking the wine.

"Nice to know it doesn't matter where we are," I say. "That was still pretty good."

"Pretty good?" he scoffs, and we both laugh.

After another moment, Adam says, "Your parents have never visited you."

"How do you know that?"

"Because no way in hell would yacht owners let you live here."

"*Let* me?" I bristle. "I'm an adult."

"I know. But you're their only kid, a lovely daughter, and if I were to wager, I'd say you've never lived in a place like this before. Right? I would also predict they wouldn't like it, and you wouldn't invite them here because it might upset them."

I wince over having lied about being an only child, but it's not the right time to say, "Hey, by the way, let me tell you about Lark and Basil." I can't say anything now because then I would have to go into the whole enchilada of prevarication, and I've only just got up the nerve to have him over to my apartment.

"You're right. My parents have never been here." Truthfully, my mother would flip a tit if she saw this place. "I'm not ashamed, though. I invited you over, didn't I?"

"It only took seven months."

"Only five from the time we started . . . hanging out," I correct. "Not that I'm counting."

He draws out the stuffed frog that had been pushed between the pillows during our energetic exertions. "Now I know all your secrets."

Not quite. But soon, he might.

"Do I know all of yours?" I counter.

"I think between our Saturday sex-sessions and our Sunday long talks, you know more about me than anyone else on earth."

Happiness trickles through me like melted caramel, warm and sweet.

"Can you guess what I want now?" he asks, placing his hand on my breast.

Rolling my eyes, I nod. "More sex."

"Actually, I was thinking of chicken." He taps my thigh with his other hand. "Maybe fried."

I brush his hands off in mock outrage. "Tough luck. I'm in the mood for pepperoni pizza from a little place around the corner. They deliver."

"So that we don't have to go out," he guesses. "Because you think people around here will recognize me?"

I sigh. "Adam Bonvier, people worldwide will recognize you. Sometimes, I think you have no idea how high-profile you are."

He shrugs. "Fine, but I like sausage and onion better."

"No, you don't. Are you testing me?" I slide into my cotton robe and go hunting my phone, placing the order while opening another bottle of wine. Five minutes later, when I return to my bedroom, Adam is wearing only his boxer-briefs and standing by my stamp-sized desk. He's holding the crystal egg I designed for Jason's company.

I feel a wave of panic until I remember he knows about Jason.

"It's very clever," Adam says.

"Thanks." In his other hand is Jason's note.

"You didn't tell me," he says softly.

"Because there's nothing to tell. I ignored it," I explain, retrieving and crumpling the paper before I toss it into the tiny trash bin in the corner.

Adam places the egg back in its leather container and closes the lid with a snap.

"Will you see him when he comes to Boston?"

"Nope. Not interested." I send him a smile. "In case you haven't noticed, I have my hands full."

He nods, and puts the container back where he found it.

"Pizza ordered?" he asks.

"Yup." I know he's ruminating on the note when his next question isn't about delivery time of the hot, cheesy deliciousness.

"What do you *owe* him, Clover?"

I can look him in the eyes and answer honestly. "Nothing. Asshole wouldn't even give me a reference." I bite my tongue. I shouldn't have mentioned that, but Adam doesn't ask how I got a job at his company. He's still thinking of Jason's note.

"What do you think he means?"

"I don't know." I have a feeling Adam doesn't believe me, so I add, "I suppose he means for giving me a good job initially when I didn't have much corporate experience. Not that he hired me personally. It was my grad school portfolio that got me the job."

After another moment, Adam says, "I'm sorry I looked in the box. I shouldn't have. I saw Decker's logo on the side."

"That's OK," I say, although it isn't. He shouldn't have snooped. More than that, it has put an unnecessary pall over the evening, and I'm not sure how to make it dissipate. Silently, we get dressed.

Is he thinking of me and Jason doing the same thing? I nearly blurt out how much better *our* sex life is than what I've had before. Yet that's like bringing Jason into the bedroom with us and might make Adam think I spend time comparing them, which I haven't.

"More comfortable to eat in the living room anyway," I tell him, starting to chatter into the silence. "That's what I normally do. In front of the TV or surfing on my laptop."

"It's good to know you don't eat alone in bed surrounded by your frogs like a crazy frog person," Adam quips, and just like that, he has let it go.

35

Adam

I thought going to Clover's home would bring us closer. When she invited me over, it seemed like a breakthrough, considering I'd already told her I loved her.

In one way, being with her in that crap apartment opens my eyes to the fact that she is a real person. An obvious realization, but true, nonetheless. For me, there has always been something fantastical about this tawny-eyed beauty. As if I conjured the perfect woman in her black-and-white checkered skirt when I looked out the conference room window that day. I know I was experiencing a sense of dissatisfaction.

Then I saw her.

My life became exhilarating again, even while I was biding my time and resisting the trek downstairs to meet Clover for the first time. Even after meeting her, when I did nothing more than crash a few meetings to ruffle her feathers, it was fun.

But it seemed, in my self-centered brain, as though this woman exists only when she's with me. And if I turn that on its head and am brutally honest, I started to feel like I exist only with her. I look forward to every other night when she comes up to my office suite and didn't fight her when she deemed it better if we hooked up only twice during the week and one weekend night.

But I'm sick of our sneaking game and of breaking my own rule. Forget about it being a company rule. I know it's something I personally should live by. Not that Clover is anything like Rachel, but the lesson shouldn't be wasted.

It rankles my sense of decency. If I didn't think it would piss off every one of my single employees, and some of the married ones, too, I would send out a company-wide memo stating:

Ms. Mitchell and I are a couple. We're breaking the dating rule because I can do whatever the hell I want. But you can't. Deal with it.

Yeah, that would go over well. I'd be sued up the ass before the email landed in everyone's inbox.

Anyway, I'm still digesting her crappy car, which I can't imagine parked at a Beacon Hill address, her frog collection, which is welcome to my home any day, the ugly beer-can strewn alley, which I'd be content never to see again, and most of all, her receiving packages from Decker. Why doesn't the jerk leave her the hell alone? He had his chance and blew it.

But the note said he was coming to Boston. Will she tell me if he contacts her when he comes?

Thinking she might not let me know is a massive bummer, giving me a pinching sensation in my gut. I want to trust her as much as I want her to trust me. But she's holding back. Whenever I think that's only in my mind, something happens to shake things up—such as Uncle Samuel keying me in to the fact Clover didn't have to live hand-to-mouth before she got the job with my company, those fucking photos exposing who her ex-boyfriend is, and her nearly getting fired by Chris and neglecting to mention it for a whole day.

Nothing big, but all things she could have told me right off the bat. Perhaps Clover is keeping other things private that she could or should share with me—if I'm going to be in her future.

$♥$♥$♥$

Three weeks later, she arrives on a Saturday at one o'clock, grinning like a fiend. It's the first time in months she hasn't arrived early to squeeze out as many hours as we could from the weekend.

I pull her toward me for a kiss. "I was wondering what happened to you, lady?" In truth, I was worried and fretting like the proverbial old woman. "You didn't answer my texts."

She smiles. "Busy morning."

"Doing what?" Damn me if Decker's smirking face doesn't float before my eyes. Did the bastard turn up and take her to breakfast?

"You'll see tomorrow," she says.

"I will?"

"When you take me home. I promise."

"You're letting me take you home?"

"Yup!"

This is a new development, and it changes my weekend perspective. Usually, I make every minute with her last, with slow sex in my bed, hour-long shower sex, even going down on her in my cellar movie theater. We take turns watching the movie while one of us kneels in between the other's legs.

But she's so bubbly with her secret, my curiosity grows until I want it to be Sunday afternoon, and even a spectacular blowjob isn't distracting me enough not to wonder.

"Time to go," I say at four o'clock sharp, which is when she usually starts thinking of leaving and when I start trying to make her stay longer.

She laughs. "It's killing you, isn't it? Not knowing my surprise."

"No," I say, shrugging as I carry her bag through the door to my garage, which opens up to the next street. Previously a carriage house with housing for servants, it's now my garage, nestled in a narrow street of expensive little homes.

Holding the car door for her, I confess, "Maybe it's driving me a bit crazy."

"You'll see soon enough." She gives me a playfully familiar punch in the shoulder and then types an address into her phone.

"I thought I was taking you home."

"Just follow the directions, bossman."

To my surprise, instead of going west through the Back Bay to the suburb of Allston, I drive us south, through the South End and Roxbury to Dorchester.

On a Sunday evening, it's a fairly easy drive but on a weekday during rush hour, it is one of the worst commutes. I pity the people who drive it daily.

"That's it," Clover says, excitement in her voice like a child seeing the entrance to an amusement park.

I pull over and double-park in front of a modern, ridiculously ugly, white and gray, blocky blob of a building. Two banners beside the off-center door proudly proclaim "Now Leasing."

"I don't understand," I say.

"I'm home!" she announces. "Come in and see. Visitor parking is over there. And there's a covered parking garage," she adds. "Can you believe it?"

Feeling particularly dense, I follow her into a corner building through a set of security doors and past a bank of mailboxes.

For some reason the sterile lobby with industrial vinyl flooring reminds me of a hospital. It's probably supposed to look minimalist and yuppified, but it fails.

"Look," she says, sounding pleased. "An elevator! But I'm only on the third floor again, so it wouldn't have mattered if there wasn't one."

We wait only seconds for the fingerprint-covered, steel door to slide open.

"Well?" she says. "You haven't said anything."

"You moved," I finally guess, my brain as swift as cement. "To Dorchester?" Immediately, my brain thinks of how many times it's on the news for its crime problem. Not as dangerous as neighboring Roxbury or South Boston, but it has some pretty bad streets.

"Don't say it like that. It's up and coming."

Only because it can't go down much further. No one moves to Dorchester if they can help it. Frankly, she was better off in Allston with all the college kids. Naturally, I keep my mouth shut and squeeze her hand.

Her apartment door is in the middle of a long hallway. I know what it will look like before she even opens it. A long, rectangular space allowing natural light through windows only at one end and probably a bunch of doors to a tiny bedroom and a tiny bathroom.

I'm wrong. When Clover flicks on the lights and says, "Ta-da!" it's a modern space with fake wood flooring and no bedroom. I know this immediately because, just past a short hallway, I can see her bed situated in the single spacious room that makes up her entire apartment.

From where I stand, her non-descript bed frame, holding a bare mattress and box spring, is the only furniture.

"Come in," she says, sounding excited. "Come see."

We pass by an open bathroom door on the right with a sealed box on the floor and another one on the counter. On our left, I assume is a closet behind bifold doors. Then we're in the main living area of her apartment. The kitchen is a single line of countertops, steel appliances, and cupboards on the left wall. Functional, modern, entirely lacking personality and totally underwhelming.

"It's only a studio, and it's a little more than I was paying, but . . . no roommate!" She hugs her arms around her and does a little twirl with her backpack swinging off her shoulder.

"My bed should be up against the bathroom wall." She gestures to where her dresser from the Allston apartment is tucked around the corner.

"And where my bed is should be the living area," she adds. "But I don't have any other furniture yet, so I'll just sleep in it where it is. Actually, I'll have to eat in bed for a little while, too." She smiles like it's a grand adventure.

"Your surprise has definitely surprised me," I say. "When did you move here?"

"Yesterday morning. That's why I was late to your place. I had some neighborly help for cheap. A couple college guys from next door in Allston."

I imagine them and don't like knowing young studs came to her rescue.

She tosses her bag onto her bed. "After I saw my old place through your eyes, I got to thinking that I didn't need to live like a college student to make ends meet. I'm a professional."

That stops me wondering whether the guys made passes at her as they carried her stuff. "Wait! You moved because I finally saw where you lived?"

"No. Well, not exactly. I wanted to get out of that area. It's all BU students, and—"

"You didn't mention anything about moving," I point out.

"Didn't I?" She flips on some accent lights hidden under the upper kitchen cabinets, illuminating the white counters. "Pam has a work friend who needed a place. Now, they can commute together to Mass General. One of my designers told me about this place. Vickie said the people in the building are chill, and—*bonus!*—they're not a bunch of loud, beer-guzzling college students. It was a great opportunity."

"Was it?" I mutter, feeling inexplicably annoyed but not wanting to burst her happy bubble. Then I think of Clover's usual caution.

"Should I be here if a colleague lives here?"

"No worries. She and her husband moved out." Then she adds, "I really wish you could stay if it wasn't a work day tomorrow."

I nearly say, "I'm staying." But without an actual invitation, I would be pushing too hard. That she moved into a new place instead of moving in with me speaks volumes. Worse, she didn't even ask for my help.

"I wish you'd told me yesterday morning was moving day," I say, recalling her giddiness when she arrived at my home.

"Why?" she asks, leaning her ass against the countertop and crossing her legs at the ankles. Her legs look a mile long in snug jeans. "It's not like you were going to help me tape up boxes and move them."

"Why not? Because I'm rich—"

"Filthy rich," she interrupts me. "Indecently, filthy rich. And billionaires don't pack boxes. Go on, when was the last time you did that, if ever?"

Sassy hands on her hips, she's taunting me in a teasing way.

"Moving my stuff into my college dorm," I say, trying to recall if I actually packed anything or just carried a few things from a rolling cart through the doorway.

But that isn't the point. "You don't think I can move some furniture?" Like a bonehead, I lift both my arms and flex my muscles.

Clover giggles. "You didn't get those from lifting boxes of frogs or lugging mattresses."

She's right, but that doesn't mean I can't use my gym-earned strength to help her. We are as disconnected in the everyday aspects of life as if we still only get together for a quickie on the couch in my office.

"I don't like how you can just disappear and not tell me."

She cocks her head. "OK. I'll remember that."

Clover takes four steps, which carry her from her kitchen to the bed, and she sits down on the end. "But for the record, I didn't disappear. I didn't even dodge out of our weekend. I only moved across town."

Anything I say now will sound sulky or desperate. I don't think I'm either of those things, but it's probably time to go hit a bucket of balls.

"You look sweet," I tell her, "in the middle of your empty place." I want to join her on the bed. Instead, I shove my hands into my pockets and stay where I am. She doesn't make it any easier by tossing herself back onto the mattress.

"First night in my new home," she says, her excitement obvious.

Briefly, I wonder if she had the chance to get any food stowed away yet or if she even owns her own plates. But clearly, she doesn't want or need me to be her savior, so I won't pry.

"I'll get going and leave you to enjoy it." I'm not sure why I make this abrupt declaration, but it's out there.

Clover sits up quickly. Her smile looks so bright, it hurts. Why? Because her happiness is entirely separate from anything to do with me. I know that's a healthy thing, but at this moment, I feel shut out. She's happy, living alone in this stark apartment. With her sense of style, she'll turn it into a warm and comfortable home. I should be happy for her in return. Yet I want to pick her up, carry her to my car, and whisk her back to Beacon Hill.

I retreat a few steps while still facing her, and then head for the door.

"Next time, I'll have an apartment-warming gift," I say over my shoulder.

She hurries to catch up with me. Is she going to ask me to stay for dinner or change her mind about me spending the night?

"I'm glad you got to see it," she says. "And next time you come, I'll have some chairs on the balcony. It's a real one this time."

"With a view?" I ask, opening the door. But I turn to catch a shadow cross her face. "I'm joking. Whatever we see from your balcony, it's only you I'll be looking at."

"Thanks," she says, a little quietly. "I don't think there's much to see anyway."

Damn! I'm being such a buzzkill. For the first time I can recall, it feels awkward.

"Thanks for the ride," she says to fill my stupid silence.

"No problem." Then I give in and grab her to me. Almost involuntarily, my hands go to her ass and pull her up against my body as I claim her soft lips. Just as her hands reach up to clasp my shoulders, we hear another door open along the hall and then voices.

"Go," Clover says, like we're secret agents in a suspense movie.

Or fellow office workers carrying on a forbidden affair.

I leave without looking back.

36

Clover

Living alone in a new place is not all it's cracked up to be. Whatever the hell that phrase means. *Cracked up*. I imagine I might crack in half if I stare at the ceiling any longer. Right after Adam leaves without even a goodbye glance—as if he can't wait to get back to civilization—I return to my bed.

Right about now, I have a feeling I made a tactical error. Although standard height, the ceiling is a few feet lower than the century's old one I'm used to, and it seems to be descending.

When the sky outside has grown dark, I rouse myself from the bare mattress, close the drapes, and go in search of the box with my linens. It takes all of five minutes to have the bed ready for . . . nothing but sleep.

Another five to put everything where I want it in the bathroom. Then I wander around, wishing I had a big flatscreen to chase away the silence and sterility. The place even smells empty. I miss Pam and her ugly furniture. I miss hearing our neighbors singing loudly on the other side of our shared wall. I miss the neighborhood pizza place and the corner convenience store.

If I'd moved in last month, Vickie, one of my designers, would still be right upstairs. But it's a Sunday night, and she has a husband, so I wouldn't have gone barging up there anyway. Now, it's a moot point.

Besides, I can't possibly be lonely. I've only been by myself for an hour or so. Still, I wish I'd asked Adam to stay instead of practically throwing him out.

Tomorrow's a workday! What a jerk I am. As if that matters to the boss. I'd been nervous about him leaving, about how much I would miss him so I tossed him a big ball of bluff. He didn't catch it. What I really wanted was for him to join me on my bed. I tried to make it obvious at the end. Too little, too late!

I should have confessed to Adam the main reason I moved here was so I didn't have to worry about Pam discovering him. I wanted to be able to open up my home to him the way he's welcomed me into his. But saying that seemed so cringy, clingy, and needy.

I'm officially a fuckwit! If I hadn't chased him off, if I'd opened a bottle of wine, we would be christening my new home this minute.

Except I don't have any wine or glassware. *Shit!*

Another glance around the sparse room, and I open my laptop to make a list of things I should buy now that Massachusetts is really my home. I'd put off settling in by traveling light, by finding a roommate who had all the necessities, and by spending every weekend at Adam's.

But I do own furnishings. When I fled the wreckage of my New York City life, I put it all in storage on my parents' estate until I figured out my life.

"I guess this is as figured out as it gets," I say aloud.

And just like that, I'm already talking to myself. Then it hits me. I will, in fact, get that cat I'm always joking about.

Maybe two. They could keep me company all week and keep each other happy for the one night I'm away on the weekend. It adds only twenty-five dollars to the rent if I say I have only one.

My list now looks like this:

Retrieve TV, glasses, plates, furniture, etc. from Mom
Buy food, wine
"Borrow" plasticware as needed from work
Adopt two cats
Cat food
Cat litter
Cat beds?

Instead of going to Adam's next weekend, I ought to rent a truck and go visit my parents so I can pick up my belongings. I have a small cream-colored sofa, a blue-leather chair, a high-top bistro table with stools. All would go perfectly here.

Feeling better at the notion of soon having some familiar things around me, I dig into my box of non-perishables and bring out half a loaf of sourdough bread and a jar of peanut butter. I left all the cold things in Pam's fridge, with my blessing, but I have enough for a snack.

Settling on the bed again, I power up my laptop, start an old episode of something I'm not remotely interested in, and let my thoughts turn to Adam again. As usual, I focus on two things: He said he loved me. He asked me to move in with him.

If I was with him right now, we'd be in the first-floor living room. Maybe watching a movie and eating my homemade popcorn he's so fond of. It's a talent of mine to pop nearly every kernel without burning them. I usually add parmesan cheese. And if I'm really looking to impress, I make kettle corn, which is a tricky process with the risk of burned and blackened sugar.

Or perhaps we'd already be in bed. Not sleeping, of course.

I dig out a package of chocolate chip cookies to ease my mind. After eating a couple, I unpack my frog collection but have nowhere to put them except on my chest of drawers and on the window sill.

"Looks more like home," I say.

Now I'm talking to the frogs. *Sweet mother!*

What if I had made the leap, no pun intended, and moved into Adam's magnificent house on Louisburg Square? What if! I cram another cookie into my mouth. Plain and simple, I'm a coward without the necessary courage to offer everything and lose it all again. I've put my trust in another person twice and jumped off the deep end, in college and with Jason. The results got progressively worse. The third time might turn me into a bitter, man-hating bitch.

The thought of one day being forced to gather up my things and move out of Adam's house stops me being able to move in. I don't need a psychologist to understand why. I look around me at my new digs and let out a big sigh. This is the right decision.

The next morning, having slept soundly, dreaming of friends who have cat faces followed by my usual steamy dream about Adam, I find my new T stop and ride into work from south of the city for the first time.

Patting myself on the back for making it through my first night in my new place, I pick up a latte for me and for Cara.

"Ready for a new week?" I ask her, feeling cheerful to be back at work.

$♥$♥$♥$

Tension has eased by the time I go up to his office on Tuesday after work. He behaves as if nothing happened, and I think the weird tension was all in my mind. Sex is great. Food is good. Discussion is normal.

The only thing I wish is that he'd given me his special brand of punishment for not telling him I was moving. Maybe he was saving it for Saturday, not knowing I was going away. But for the first time in months, I am not going to Adam's home. I have no choice. Even while enjoying a comfy bed and a hot shower with good water pressure, I cannot continue in my new apartment without some "stuff."

It's a busy week with clients, including Mrs. Lovell again. She's a delight. I also enjoy a glass of wine with my next-door neighbor, Marissa, on Wednesday evening. We met by the mailboxes one day and are trying to make it a weekly thing. But when I see Adam on Thursday after work, I tell him that I'll be going away for the weekend.

And then, I know why I didn't tell him earlier. Because naturally, he wants to go with me as I suspected he would.

Fending off Adam's request to join me on my trek to the Hudson Valley makes me feel like slimy, lying snake. I tell him my parents downsized on account of their yacht purchase and don't have spare beds.

It's a really stupid lie. He knows it, too. I'm sure of it. He offers to get a hotel room for both of us.

"I want to spend time just being their daughter again," I say. "I'll sleep on their couch. They're kind of old-fashioned anyway. They wouldn't let us be together."

"OK," he says. "I understand. The last thing I want to do is annoy your parents."

All the way there, three and a half hours, I regret not having Adam with me. How much fun would it be to introduce him to my folks and show him around the estate?

But that's for another time, a later iteration of our relationship if we make it that far. The drive has given me time to think, change some decisions. No cats, for one thing. My home is too small. It seems cruel to confine a couple cats in such a small space. Plus, according to everyone I ask, my entire studio apartment will smell like a stinky litter box when I come home each evening.

Beyond that, during the hours spent driving, knowing how much I'll miss Adam this weekend, I consider whether I should quit my job next week or next month instead of next January as I'd begun to plan. On the one hand, a year and two months will look good on my résumé.

But I love him.

But I fear what loving him can do to me.

And then, I'm home.

First the hard work, then I can relax. With the help of Mr. Francis, my parents' estate manager, we put my boxes and my furniture in the back of the rental van. When we climb down securing the chairs, my mother is holding out a glass of lemonade for each of us.

"I put a tip for you on the kitchen counter and some refreshments," Mom tells Mr. Francis, who lives in a nice two bedroom with his wife, Christina, our housekeeper, on a pretty half acre of the property.

"You're not supposed to tip me, Bunny," he says, sounding amused. "I'm on salary."

Her mother smiles. "Oh, well. It's there anyway."

After Mr. Francis leaves us alone, Mom looks in the back of the truck and shakes her head. "I don't know why you didn't let us hire someone to bring this out to you, instead of doing all this strenuous lifting." Yet she watched me and Mr. Francis work, never lifting a finger. Bunny Henley doesn't move furniture and boxes.

"Then I wouldn't have had the chance to see you," I remind her. And it's really good to see her. My parents are not abrasive nor demanding. They've always been supportive of my choices, and those of my siblings, and I genuinely enjoy getting together with them. Occasionally. For short periods.

"That's true," she agrees. "But you only had to ask, and your dad would have sent your belongings, and we would've come to visit, too. You've been hiding in New England for long enough."

"I haven't been hiding," I protest. Although, happy as I am to see my mom in her natural habitat, Adam is one hundred percent correct about not inviting them to my Allston apartment. Mom wouldn't have even entered the building.

The Dorchester one, while modern and more befitting a department head, would be only marginally better in my parents' eyes.

"Well, what would you call it?" my mom demands, as we stroll along the path to the pool area. I need to take a break, and it's my favorite place to sit and chill. But Bunny isn't being very chill right now.

"You changed your name," she grouses, "left everything and everyone behind, and drove away without even giving us your address."

"You always had my phone number," I remind her. "And I took *your* maiden name. You always said you liked it. And now you have my new address, so it's all good."

"I don't think I like that saying very much," Mom says. She makes me laugh.

"What's so funny?" asks my father, approaching from the garage. He's been playing golf with his buddies and must've just returned. I hope one day soon, he will play with Adam. I also hope Adam lets my father win because Russell Henley is a competitive, proud man when it comes to that little white ball.

"Mom's funny. That's all."

"She's laughing at me, Russ," she says, but she's not really annoyed.

"I laugh at you, too, Bunny," my dad says. "You're a ridiculous person, and I wouldn't have you any other way."

I love their marriage.

37

Adam

This woman is driving me mad. And I must already be crazy in love with her. That's the only explanation for why I put up with Clover keeping me at arm's length and calling all the shots. She doesn't want me to meet her parents, I get that loud and clear. She hasn't met mine, either, so that's fair.

But she also won't let me unload her truck when she gets back. I have no idea how she got her things up to her apartment. Despite the fact that we still have sex twice a week at work and overnight on the weekend, I'm feeling practically emasculated and irrelevant. And I haven't been back to her place in Dorchester since I first saw it.

It's a regular Thursday evening, with July fourth being tomorrow. We haven't made any plans to break our routine and watch fireworks together, but I think about asking her tonight. She's right on time. I wonder if she knows that my security staff has figured out our torrid secret from her comings and goings in the elevator to my floor and from the food deliveries, not to mention the way we depart within a few minutes of each other every Tuesday and Thursday.

I don't bring it up because I think she'll cut down our time together to only Saturday night without blinking an eye. I have no leverage to stop her, and no say in the matter. Frankly, I'm in a crap position, and the reverse power dynamic doesn't make me happy.

"Take off your skirt and blouse," I demand like I do most every time.

She skirts my reaching hands, eager to help her undress, and rushes into my bathroom.

"Be right out," she says over her shoulder.

I make myself useful and press the button that locks my office door. Another button closes the privacy curtains on the interior walls, leaving the windows uncovered and the city spread out for us to see. Then I wait, but not for long.

Clover comes out of my bathroom wearing only a wide red, white, and blue ribbon tied across her breasts and a thong decorated with fireworks over her mound. *Hell, yeah!* Every patriotic cell in my body stands up and sings as my cock becomes a flagpole.

"Aw, and I didn't get you anything," I tease.

"I'm pretty sure you're going to give me something now," she says.

Truer words were never spoken. With a quick tug on the bow that holds the ribbon, her pert breasts are mine to play with. I never tire of feasting on Clover's tits. I discovered early on that sucking on her nipples causes a direct effect elsewhere, sending tingling sensations to her pussy.

The woman can come that way with no other stimulation. And she does, right then, about a minute after I start. It blows my mind how well we suit one another in the sexual realm.

She laughs as her whole body relaxes.

"Wow!" she says. "I think I need to sit down." She glances at the sofa, but I have other ideas.

"Not yet," I say.

She raises an eyebrow in question, and I offer her my hand, which she takes. When I draw her with me toward the floor-to-ceiling windows, she places her free arm over her breasts.

Slowly, I turn her to face outward and peel her arm away from her body, holding both her hands at her sides, exposing her.

"Adam?" she asks, her voice breathy.

Releasing her hands, I press her body gently to the window. The sun hasn't set, and we're high above street level with commuters surging out of buildings down below. The slight chance someone might look up and see us makes it even more interesting.

I unzip and pull out my cock that's been ramrod stiff since she emerged from the bathroom. Reaching around, I slide my fingers under the front of her thong, and she gasps.

Wet and ready. She places her palms on the window, along with her cheek as she turns her head.

Her profile is exquisite, eyes closed, lashes feathering her cheekbones, her pink lips parted, and her smooth hair draped between us. My woman is a goddess!

I enter her from behind. Her breasts are flattened against the cool glass. Thinking of how she must look from the outside, legs slightly spread, back arched to give me access, I wish I could see her from the other side.

I stroke her clit, and she moans.

With one of my arms around her slim waist, anchoring her in place, and my other hand resting on her mound, my fingers glide between her pussy lips, stroking her. My own legs tremble slightly as sensations build low in my back and behind my balls.

"You want this," I whisper against her ear.

"Mm-hmm."

"You need this," I add, caressing her clit faster.

"Yes," she says. "I need you."

I close my eyes, feeling exposed even though I'm not the one pressed naked to the glass.

I wish this could last longer, but she's dripping onto my fingers, and I'm having to hold back my own orgasm. Making sure Clover comes first—and it's loud as she moans my name, pressing against my hand—I climax after a few more deep thrusts.

Pulling out, I grab tissues for her from the table. The next time the window washers do their job, they might notice something, a sexy imprint or at least a smear of coral lipstick.

"Fast but not too fast," she says. "And it was a little kinky, but I liked it."

I'm glad to know we're still in sync, even though I hadn't asked her ahead of time. She needed the release, and I needed to take her up against the wall—or in this case, the window pane—with Clover entirely vulnerable, front and back.

Any man should be happy to continue with this uncomplicated relationship. Yet even after mind-blowing sex, I'm not. We've been in the *just-for-fun* stage for too long. If I was twenty-two, it would be fine for a while longer. But I'm closing in on thirty-two.

$♥$♥$♥$

My parents want to meet the woman I've been seeing. And they know there is someone because I haven't been interested in anybody they've tried to push my way, none of the daughters of friends or business acquaintances.

"You're smitten," my mother says over lunch on a regular Wednesday when I leave work behind, knowing I won't see Clover that night anyway.

"Smitten?" I repeat the word I've literally never used before. I don't think I've even heard it used. Certainly not directed at me. A silly, old-fashioned term. And strangely, it fits as well as my favorite pair of KJUS golf pants.

"I guess," I say, reverting to sounding like a teenager while I'm home in Weston, twenty-five miles west of my Beacon Hill home. My parents live in a Frank Lloyd Wright-inspired modern mansion on a twelve-acre patch of rolling green hills and woods.

I used to go often on weekends. Before Clover. Their house is far more modern than mine with a cheerful, bright aesthetic, built of limestone and copper with more windows than walls, different from the rest of the traditional homes in the area.

I think Clover would love the design, and she would thoroughly enjoy the infinity pool.

Mom and I are sitting in a century's old tavern, eating fish and chips. Dad's away on business, because although he's "retired," he hasn't really stopped working. It's not advertising business, but one of his other interests.

"I'd like you to meet the woman I'm . . . spending time with," I say, not wanting to lie to my own mother and call it *dating.* "I know she'd like it here."

I want to show Clover around Weston's small-town vibe, which recently had an eighteen-million-dollar makeover, although I thought it was fine beforehand. The pub I'm in now, along with other really old buildings that house eateries and shops, mark the long history of the area.

The way Clover examines the architecture of Beacon Hill, I know she'd find Weston interesting. And she wouldn't even need her disguise, since everyone here knows me and my family and treats us as the *normal* people we are.

"As long as you're happy," my mother says, "I'll like her. I don't suppose you're going to tell me her name."

"Sure." Then I think about my paranoid woman and say only, "It's Clover."

Not for the first time, I imagine ordering her to quit the company and start a serious relationship with me.

Also not for the first time, I picture how massive a wedge that would drive between us. As much as she loves having sex with me, she loves being a designer. And anyone who threatens her career will be immediately given the boot, a sexy, expensive boot.

Including me.

And while I know a lot about Clover Mitchell, I don't know if I am one of the things she loves. So the question I need answered is simple: Is *she* smitten with *me*?

38

Clover

When I get home on a Wednesday night in the middle of July, Jason Decker is lounging in my apartment. Not in the building's lobby, but *inside* my actual apartment.

"How the hell did you get in here?"

He rises to his feet slowly, giving me the long once-over. "Money opens doors, and hello to you, too."

"You've got to be kidding," I sputter. "I don't even know who you could have paid off to get in here. A building manager? Is there one?" I'm hopping mad as I set my groceries down on the counter.

"Apparently so. I rang up the management company, and they had him meet me at the door. I said I was your boyfriend, and then I gave him five hundred bucks."

Jeez! Five hundred dollars is the price of a woman's safety and privacy. I guess this place isn't as "modern" as I thought.

"Shoes!" I say it like a swear word when I realize Jason

has his on in my living room. And in my surprise, I walked all the way into my kitchen wearing mine. *Ugh!* "They come off at the door."

Belatedly, I return to the ottoman situated between the front door and the bathroom door for the very purpose of having a place to sit and undo any shoes that aren't slip on. "If you'd waited to be invited inside, you would have known that."

"I'll have the place cleaned," Jason says, not getting up off my couch.

"No! Really, take off your damn shoes." I plop myself down on the cushioned ottoman and unzip my ankle boots before putting them in the closet.

He sets down one of my porcelain frogs he was fiddling with and joins me at the front door.

"No need to remove them now," I say. "Just get out. If I wanted to see you, I would have answered your note."

"*Ouch*," Jason says. Ignoring my directive to leave, he removes his shoes before walking right past me and peering into the bags I'd brought in. "Whatcha got? I'm starving and your place is pretty empty."

"You looked through my things." What an ass! "You're way out of line. You know that, don't you?" I start putting groceries away. If it wasn't for the fact that we have a pretty intense history and that I have zero fear of him, I'd be on edge. Instead, I'm simply infuriated at the invasion of my home.

"What are we having? Or can I take you out to dinner?"

"Neither," I snap. "*We* are not having anything, and I have no intention of going anywhere with you. Seriously, what the hell is wrong with you?"

"What the hell is wrong with *you?*" he asks, but with a stupid smile. "I told you I was coming to Boston."

I never realized what a cheesy, ugly smile he has. Although he's a handsome man, his face creases into Kermit the frog when he thinks he's looking winsome. His grin is just too . . . *ick!*

"You used to be all sweet and soft and—"

"A fool," I interrupt. "You cheated on me, and I ended the relationship. What did you think would happen if you came to see me? That I'd welcome you?"

"Maybe."

Damn! Maybe he's a psychopath after all and I should be afraid. "Are you insane? I saw you balls deep in Laura. Believe me, it wasn't pretty."

He shrugs. "A one-off."

"Something got off all right."

"She's gone now. I couldn't contact you until she left. She threatened to sue me if I fired her and while I think she would've lost her extortion suit, it would've been a bad scene all around. I waited her out and then finally told her I would have to be straight with her husband."

The entire sordid mess sickens me. Then I ask the humbling question that has plagued me. "Why did you play around with her in the first place?"

Instantly, I wish I hadn't asked. I don't care. But I sort of still do. Hadn't I been worth a little loyalty?

"Honestly, Clover. It was a stupid moment of boredom. I'd been reading reports all day. She came in, wiggled her ass a certain way. Next thing, as you said, I was ball's deep and then you showed up. Bad timing."

"Bad timing," I echo, realizing I've never heard an apology from him. I'm not going to ask for one because it's meaningless. He's meaningless, and I honestly don't give a damn. He can't hurt me any longer because not even a tiny part of him is left in my heart. Nor do I wish we were still together, not even for a second.

"You do recall you fired me," I point out. By this time, I've poured myself a glass of wine without offering him any.

"Are you really going to be like that?" he asks.

"I really, really want you to leave now," I say. But he moves toward me so I step aside and let him help himself. He gives himself a big pour and holds the glass up like he's toasting something. What exactly? Our reunion? It sours my stomach.

I turned away as a frisson of disbelief skitters down my spine. If someone told me I'd be drinking cabernet with Jason Decker tonight, I would've laughed in their face.

"I had to fire you," he says, finally getting down to something serious. "You would've been angry and might've taken it out on my company. The last thing I could afford was a bitter employee."

"But it was *me*, your girlfriend." I can barely get the word out.

"Also my top designer," he says, his tone rueful. "Don't think it didn't hurt to get rid of you. At the time, I believed it was best for business."

He was more of a prick than I thought, and I'd thought him a humongous one. No wonder I haven't trusted myself to date again. Clearly, I have terrible judgment and am just damn lucky Adam picked me. I would never have seen him as anything other than a powerful man who would walk all over me.

My stomach rumbles. I am so over Jason, I don't care if he hears. I open the cupboard and am inspired by an easy dinner idea for this warm evening, something I will thoroughly enjoy after I get rid of him.

Grabbing a can of tuna from the shelf, I set it down before pulling out the mayonnaise from the fridge, along with carrots, celery, and an onion. I'll doctor it with a tablespoon of curry powder and be in heaven.

Some potato chips, salty and crunchy, and maybe a pickle will complete my meal. A meal for one, pleasing no one but myself.

"What do you want, besides a free glass of wine?" I ask, gesturing with my own as I take another sip. "Because I need you gone. I'm hungry, and when I'm hungry I get grouchy. Drink up and go."

"I want you back."

I choke. A graceless, inelegant cough and sputter! He watches me as I grab for a piece of paper towel and wipe my mouth, then dab at the burgundy drops that have trickled down my cream-colored silk blouse.

"Dammit!"

Jason's fault. I know the easiest remedy and want to apply it immediately because I have a fondness for my clothing. Not as high as my adoration of shoes, but still, I like nice clothes. Having to wait until after he leaves to strip off makes me want him gone even sooner.

"You've shocked me," I confess. "But I will never come back to you."

"Not even for a promotion?"

Wait a minute! Is he saying what I think he is?

"Are you asking me to come back to work for you?" Because I thought he was asking me to get back together with him.

"Of course. Nothing has looked good since you left. Well, good, yes, but not outstanding. That crystal egg is a gold mine. People are signing up their babies while still in the womb in order to get a Decker egg."

"I see." Do I? "Then you sent me the egg weeks ago and came here to offer me a job? No strings attached."

His slow smile says otherwise. "I got engaged. Did you hear?"

I wait a second but feel nothing. Not even a pinch of pain.

"Nope, but congratulations."

"Doesn't mean strings aren't still an option. We can play around a little or a lot. I mean, if you're back in New York and work in the same building, why wouldn't we? Sex was great, and you can't deny it."

What a colossal prick! He isn't even married yet and already planning to cheat. I nearly told him I'd discovered what great sex really is, but my personal life is no longer any of his business.

Maybe I should tell him my more important discovery—what it means to be respected and cherished. From what Jason just said, his marriage is already doomed.

But I'm in no position to give out relationship advice. Not while I'm still hiding from Adam's love in this apartment in Dorchester.

At that instant—with my past having reared its smug, entirely unappealing head—I would give anything if Adam were here instead, sipping this cheap cab and letting me spill my secrets.

My heart aches as my brain catches up to the truth. I'm wasting precious time. If I tell Adam how I feel about him and it comes crashing down around me in a week or a month or a year, so what? I'm strong enough to weather it. I know that now. More importantly, Adam is so worth the risk of pain and heartache.

After all, I picked myself up and started over once. I can do it again if I have to.

And what if the relationship with Adam never crashes? What if Adam and I last a lifetime? I am going to do my best to make that my future. You cannot beat a man who makes you laugh so hard wine comes out of your nose. And he's done that more than once.

"You're smiling," Jason says. "Does that mean you're thinking about some of the good times we had?"

"No. I'm not thinking about you at all."

He rolls his eyes. "I don't believe you." In a quick move, Jason leans down and kisses me.

I should be outraged or terrified, but ultimately, I know him. He's a womanizer, but not the type to force himself on me. With his status and good looks, he doesn't need to coerce anyone. He can walk out of my apartment and find a willing sex partner in about ten minutes.

He's just testing the waters. But it's demeaning and presumptuous. Turning my head, I break contact, even as the icy coldness trickles down my spine, turning me to steel.

I feel absolutely nothing. No sparks, not the barest hint of attraction. It's downright liberating.

But then Jason's hands start to roam, and I push him away.

"You cheated on me and fired me without an ounce of compassion! Why would I spend a second thinking of you?"

Why, indeed! I let this asshole take up far too much real estate in my mind for too long. I'm ready to release the doubt and the mistrust I've been carrying and applying to the wrong person.

He sighs. "You're mad because I got engaged?"

"What? No!" What an ego! I feel sorry for the poor woman.

"It doesn't matter," he says. "I promise we'll have plenty of opportunity. What do you say, Clover? I'll pay you whatever you're making and more. Bigger office, raise, and me!"

I laugh. A big belly laugh because he is so ridiculous. It feels great, especially seeing the surprise on Jason's face.

"Thanks but no thanks."

"I think you're being childish," he grumbles, not used to being denied.

"I'm going to get this stain out of my shirt," I say, grabbing the white vinegar from under the sink and hurrying toward the bathroom. Jason isn't worth letting this stain sit any longer. "And you're leaving."

"Don't you want me to start the sandwiches?" he asks.

His words freeze me in my tracks. I turn. "You don't know how to make a tuna fish sandwich."

"Watch me," he says.

In all the time I was with Jason, he never so much as put bread in a toaster. It is almost worth sharing a sandwich with him to see if he can make one. Almost.

"Nope," I mutter, as I reach the bathroom. "I'm not kidding. I want you to leave. I don't want the job, and I don't want you. Be gone by the time I open this door." And I go inside and close it.

After unbuttoning my silk blouse, I set it in the sink and pour the vinegar onto it. The way I love my clothes, I know how to repair or fix just about anything.

Since my bathroom is at the front of my apartment, I can hear the knock at my door. I frown. No one knocks. Food delivery buzzes for entrance downstairs, along with everyone else. *Shit!* It's Wednesday, so it has to be Marissa from next door. Upon seeing Jason, I'd completely spaced out about our hump-day glass of wine.

"I'll get it," he calls out.

"No!" I shriek. I do not want her seeing him in here, without his shoes and especially not answering my door for me. There'd be no end of assumptions and questions. And Jason's ego would get stroked if she so much as treats him cordially. Not on my watch!

I am closer, but I'm also in my bra. While I snatch my short cotton robe off its hook, Jason beats me to entry. I'm still tying the belt around my waist and coming out of the bathroom when he swings the door wide.

Adam!

39

Clover

This has to be the worst timing in the history of surprise visits. No, my catching Jason and Laura was the worst, but this is a close second, followed by my thinking Adam was about to have hot tub sex with his client.

Adam's face goes from *happy to see me* to *annoyed as shit* so fast I almost miss the happy part.

"Hi!" I say because my brain has blanked. I don't know what else to say or how to handle this. And then, because all I can think about is how a few minutes earlier, Jason kissed me, I touch my lips. I can't erase the kiss, but I can make sure I don't have any red wine stain around my mouth. "You're here," I add lamely.

Jason, of course, deals with my obvious discomfort in a neanderthal way. He put his arm around me, squeezes my shoulder, and sticks out his hand for Adam to shake.

"Hey, I'm Jason Decker. Aren't you Adam Bonvier, Clover's *boss?*"

Adam doesn't answer, nor does he shake Jason's hand, which drifts down toward his pocket. Adam stares at me as if I'm a stranger, taking in my robe and Jason's body touching mine at the hip. I shrug off his arm.

"I told you to leave," I remind Jason in no uncertain terms. This is not going to be one of those stupid misunderstandings like Adam and I experienced in Quebec.

"Let's finish our wine," Jason says cooly, "and our *plans*, and then I'll be on my way."

He is head of a financial empire, and he isn't going to meekly leave because the situation has grown a little hot. He even reaches over to wipe the side of my mouth with his thumb. I flinch. Maybe there was a telltale mark of red wine after all.

In a tone colder and more off-putting than I've ever heard, even when he was firing Chris and Leslie, Adam addresses Jason. "Ms. Mitchell asked you to leave."

Shit! I had totally forgotten that my family name could possibly come up.

I turn to Jason, seeing his eyes widen. Mine probably do, too. Then he walks back toward his wine glass on the counter while I cringe inside. Will he keep my secret?

In absolute agony, I trail him to the kitchen, knowing Adam is right behind me.

Jason leans against the counter and takes a sip while I send him silent, pleading looks to stay quiet about things that don't concern him.

"That's funny," he says finally. "Because I have no idea who Ms. Mitchell is, but Miss *Henley* and I were discussing our past and our future before you interrupted."

Asshole! White-hot hatred blazes through me before I remember I'm the one to blame. I should have told Adam ages ago.

"How did you get in here, anyway?" Jason continues, clearly enjoying himself. "Without being *invited* upstairs." Implying he hadn't bribed his way up to my apartment!

"Maybe he paid someone," I say, "the way you did."

317

"Someone came in at the same time." Adam's voice is a little subdued, and he's back to staring at me again, his eyes as dark and fathomless as in his oil painting. I can only guess what he's thinking: Clover Henley, a stranger!

"I'm starting to wonder why this building bothers with a locked lobby and a stupid buzzer. It's a damn free for all down there," I gripe, although it's clearly not the main problem I'm facing.

"I am so stupid," Adam says, still in that quiet voice that scares me.

"Probably," Jason quips, "but tell us why."

"Shut up," Adam and I both say to him at once.

This is going to be messy, and I have a lot of explaining to do.

"You need to go," I say to Jason.

"Do I?" he asks me. "After what we just . . . ," he trails off as if recalling he was speaking of something private. *The bastard!*

How had I never seen this nasty side of him? I mean, how did I miss it until the moment he fired me, two seconds after pretending he wanted to continue our relationship. All I had to do was overlook his cock inside Laura. I definitely noticed his mean side then! But there's no reason for him to screw up my current life.

That's the part I can't understand. Jason could have had me. He's the one who threw away our relationship. Why would he be so petty as to make trouble for me now? I answer my own question—because of the success of a stupid crystal egg. He wants me to be fired so I go back to work for him.

With the charged atmosphere between me and Adam, Jason must know where my interest lies. And it's hard to believe he's so damn arrogant he thinks I'll want to get back with him.

"Clover and I have a long history," Jason adds, rubbing it in.

"Not that long," I chime in, trying to diffuse a bomb that's already exploded.

Before I can say more, Adam asks, "How did you find her?"

That question has been on my mind, too, but I haven't asked. In a way, it's not important, at least not to me. Why is Adam wondering?

"Through her parents, naturally," Jason says. "A quick phone call. They remembered me from all the times I dined with them." Then he says to me, "To be fair, I asked whether you were seeing anyone. They said no."

He looks at Adam again pointedly. "They certainly had no idea about you, if that's what this is."

Adam takes a step in Jason's direction. "Nothing about me is any of your business," he bites out, disdain dripping from his words.

He has to know I don't care for Jason and don't want him anywhere close after all the pain he caused me. But when Adam's battleship-gray eyes turn to me, I can tell his thoughts are on the secrets I've kept. It's me he's angry with, and he speaks only to me.

"I'm leaving. Do you want me to get this loser out of here before I go?"

Jason does that thing men do when trying to seem tough, arching his chest forward while swinging his arms back. "You don't know me."

"I know what you did," Adam shoots back, "to her."

I can't believe this is happening. "I want *you* to stay," I say to Adam, "but *he* is definitely leaving." I gesture toward Jason.

Silence, as both men eye one another.

"You know what?" Jason says. "I'm going. The wine and *everything* were great, babe, but I'm not really up for a tuna sandwich anyway. Next time, we'll go out for Indian food." He brushes past Adam, intentionally knocking his shoulder.

Good thing he starts moving because Adam's hands curl into fists as he watches Jason leave. Two men, both used to

319

being in charge, both ready to show they are dominant—but a brawl is the last thing I want.

What I want, quite simply, is Adam. But he's walking out my door.

"Adam," I call after him.

He doesn't break his stride or turn his head, but I sprint after him as far as my doorway. He is standing with his arms crossed, looking down the hallway, making sure Jason gets on the elevator.

"Adam," I say again, "let me—"

"No," he says without looking at me. "Not now."

Silently, we watch Jason disappear. And then he uncrosses his arms and heads for the exit door to take the stairs. I don't go after him. I know he's not in the mood to listen, but he'll give me a fair hearing after he cools off.

Only when I'm alone in the hallway do I notice a medium-sized box tucked against the wall beside my front door. It has a big blue bow on it. Picking it up, hefting its weight, I carry it back inside and sit on my sofa.

I stare at it for a few moments, still processing what just happened—and knowing I'm in a state of shock. A small tag is attached to the bow.

The housewarming gift I promised you. Love, Adam

I start to cry as I open the box. A stainless popcorn pot, with a crank handle! Usually, I use a soup pot and have to continuously shake the kernels while they're cooking. My method is noisy and finicky.

I didn't know such a thing existed. With tears coursing down my cheeks, I turn the handle that sweeps a little metal arm across the bottom surface inside the pot. It will keep the kernels moving so they won't stick.

The most considerate gift any man has ever given me.

And he called himself stupid. Because of me!

$♥$♥$$♥$

Adam

What the hell was all that? As I speed back toward Beacon Hill, my thoughts are all over the place. What I just walked in on was a mind-fuck if ever there was one. I left her a popcorn pot. A dumb gift from a damn idiot. Clover absolutely fooled me. I'm only glad I hadn't given in to the impulse to bring her flowers or chocolates.

How ridiculous would I have been, holding a bouquet while Decker had his arm around her!

I hit the steering wheel with my palm. She was wearing a goddamn robe I've never even seen.

Clover and I need to stop surprising one another. Her showing up in Quebec was one thing, but this . . . whatever was going on in her apartment . . . it was a shocker. That asshole has hurt her, but they were looking so cozy when *he* opened her door. And he definitely was drinking her wine.

And fuck me if it didn't look like she was about to make tuna sandwiches.

I fucking hate tuna sandwiches.

Lucky for me, I'm more angry than sad. Or at least, that's what I'm telling myself.

Decker is a prick, just as I expected, but he clearly has a connection with her. And then there's her family. She and I haven't reached the stage of family introductions, too busy hiding under the covers. But now it seems ridiculous that I haven't met her parents, or she, mine, after so this much time has passed.

A precious lot of time wasted on her, whoever the hell she is!

Clover fucking Henley! Her parents have protected her from the limelight and done a perfect job of it. I've never seen a photo of her. She isn't a society bitch. So all she had to do was change her last name to be incognito.

Her being with Decker makes a whole lot more sense now. Of course she didn't simply stumble into him, meeting at a club. She also didn't walk into his business pretending to be someone else. Not in New York City, the Henley headquarters, one of the most popular candy companies in the world. She must have run in the same circle as Decker all her life—the uber wealthy.

I know it's actually *our* circle, but Boston and New York don't always mix or overlap. I've never met her parents, not at a charity dinner or a fundraiser. I wonder if my parents know them.

Clover! I keep seeing her shocked, pale face, getting caught in all her lies.

What kills me is the pointless duplicity. She knew I would find out eventually, so why hide her identity for so long?

I give the steering wheel another beating, pissed at how much this feels like betrayal. Almost as though I caught them in bed together. The sick part is I'm not sure they hadn't fucked five minutes before I got there. Not even sure she didn't invite him to her place, which is why I asked how he'd found her. One of the reasons, anyway.

It hurt like hell to learn her parents trust him enough to give him her address. Didn't she ever tell them what a cheating bastard he is? Maybe that's a lie too.

But I had to ask how, in case I had a leak in HR. The security of all my employees is of utmost importance to me.

Clover! *My woman!* I think about her working for Decker, sashaying around his New York office in her sexy shoes, and I am more jealous than I've ever been in my whole life. He knew who she was when she worked for him. Had they been lovers beforehand? I never asked.

Regardless, unlike me, he knew from the start whom he was sleeping with. Such a basic thing. Something I took for granted. Because who wouldn't?

A flash of gratitude slashes through the dark thoughts in my brain. At least her first name really is Clover. If I'd been calling her by the wrong name in bed and out of it all this time—well, *fuck!* It would have tainted everything even worse, and at this moment, it's already spectacularly tarnished.

The magnitude of her duplicity actually impresses me. Not only hadn't I the smallest inclination, but she fooled my HR department when she was hired. Someone needs a good kick in the ass at work. They mustn't have dug very deeply if they couldn't identify one of the wealthiest heiresses in the U.S.

Also the funniest, sweetest, prettiest, and sexiest woman I've ever had the pleasure to know.

As much as I can say I know her. Decker knew she likes Indian food, so I suppose the things she's told me weren't a lie. But it's like suddenly finding out I've been dating a spy. Too fucking weird! And all I keep wondering is, why didn't she tell me?

By the time I pull into my garage, the worst takeaway from my disastrous attempt to surprise her is learning how easily Clover can lie. Knowing she's this good means she could lie to me at any time. Living with her would be like living in a crystal palace knowing she wields a damn big sledgehammer.

I still feel stupid, incredibly so. Lust blinded me, and then I fell hard for a dream, and that may be all she is. For the first time in months, I'm doubtful about Clover being in my future. More than doubtful, I'm downright disinclined to carry on.

40

Adam

The following morning, I'm still walking on Planet Weirded Out. The arc of strong emotions hasn't stopped yet, swinging from angry to sad with a long stop at disbelief.

"Janet, get me someone from HR on the phone."

I have to be careful with my questions, so I get her entire file printed and sent up to me. The last thing I want is to get Clover in trouble for falsifying government documents, like her driver's license or social security card. Sure enough, she has a legit-looking driver's license with the last name of Mitchell, and her social security card matches. I assume her bank account accepts our direct deposits for her salary and must also be in the name of Mitchell.

Leaning back in my chair, I read the written references along with the notes that Chris took from speaking with the people listed—Scumbag Decker and a woman from their HR department. Then I remember Clover said something about her previous boss not giving her any references. Her file sure looked as though he had.

I start to think what I'm holding in my hands are simply more of her lies.

"Janet, get Clover Mitchell up here."

"Right way, boss."

It's Thursday. Usually, Clover would be coming up for one of our office dinners later anyway, but this is business. For the first time in months, I want to try to keep the two separate.

Five minutes later, she comes in looking like a million bucks. In a form-fitting, cream-colored, sleeveless dress that fastens with chunky buttons all the way down her front. The dress is open in a sexy inverted V from the last button to just below her knees. With copper-colored, high-heeled, linen shoes and her caramel-colored hair in a sexy, loose bun, she's as desirable as ever.

Although, if I'm not mistaken, knowing her eyes as well as I do from having stared into them so many times, she's been crying. A part of me I'm not super proud of is pleased. There's plenty of misery to go around.

"Janet said you wanted to see me." Her voice is a shadow of her usual enthusiastic tone.

"Shut the door, please." I stand and gesture for her to sit, not on the sofa but in one of the two chairs in front of my desk.

The atmosphere is charged, and not in a good way. Deception hangs like a shroud over our heads, and if I have to name how I feel about her at this instant, I'm unexpectedly dispassionate.

Having seen her attached at the hip to Decker, recalling how he'd casually touched his thumb to her mouth, Clover no longer seems like the same woman I'd been sharing sexual fantasies with. *My* woman.

This Clover is a stranger. I walk around my desk until I'm within feet of her and lean against it.

"How do you fake a driver's license and social security card?"

I've seen her without makeup and know her to be blessed with a uniformly clear complexion, practically flawless. She could be ready to go out in five minutes with eyelashes swooping out to here, a swish of peachy blush under her cheekbones, and some lip gloss that is a magnet for my lips.

But I've never seen her skin so pale. From what? *Fear? Guilt?*

"Are you asking me as my boss or my friend?" she says after a moment.

I sigh. "Not into playing games right now. But I suppose as your boss."

She raises a perfect eyebrow. "I think I'd prefer to speak to my sex buddy."

Clover can't get a smile out of me. When she shrugs, she draws my gaze to the square neckline of her dress where the upper curves of her breasts appear. Did she make that move on purpose?

I look away, back to her slightly reddened eyes, and I wait.

"I legally changed my name by petitioning the court in New York." She raised her chin. "I'm allowed to do that."

"I suppose you are," I agree. "And you did this specifically for applying to my company?"

"Not exactly," she hedges.

"Decker knew who you were. You were Clover Henley when you worked for him, weren't you?"

"Yes." Her breathy tone doesn't help me focus on questioning her because it interests other parts of me. I'm her sex buddy still whether I want to be or not.

"Why?" I ask. That single word covers a lot of things I want to know.

"I changed my name before I moved to Boston," she says. "New start with no one giving me a leg up because of who my parents are. Also, no one who knew I'd been

Jason's girlfriend could follow my progress or lack thereof, if I'd failed magnificently. I have some pride. But I confess as soon as I found out a dream position was open here, I focused on Bonvier, Inc. I didn't even apply anywhere else in Boston."

That made sense. She hadn't become *Clover Mitchell* just to fool me personally. I hope the next answer is as clear-cut.

"You said once that Decker fired you after you discovered him with some tramp—"

"I don't think I ever used the word *tramp*," she says.

"Yet a written reference is in your file, and Chris made a note that he spoke to Decker." I reach back and tap the file behind me. "And he also spoke to the HR manager named Julia Stowe."

"Riiiiight." She's squirming in her seat.

So much for clear-cut.

"Did Chris actually speak to Decker?" I ask.

"Not exactly," she says.

"Who *exactly* did he speak to? Who sent the written references?"

"I have friends there," she says. "Good ones. They thought I'd been given a raw ride, and they agreed to help me. They had access to the company letterhead, and it was easy to give their company phone extensions, too."

"That's really devious," I say, wavering between admiration and disapproval. Her scheme worked. However, if a less-qualified candidate had used the same tactics, I'd be pissed off.

"You could have got your friends into trouble, or even fired."

She lowers her head, looks at her lap where I see her hands are clasped. Something in her posture stirs me in a way that puts me back on the sex buddy side of things. I shake my head.

"It was reckless and dishonest." Maybe that's simply who she is.

"I wanted the job on my own merit," Clover insists. "And my friends who worked with me only told Chris about my work ethic, my job skills, and my dependability. Nothing that wasn't true. Besides, I wouldn't have asked them. They offered. As I said, they're good friends."

"Were you good friends with Decker when he hired you?" I ask, immediately wishing I hadn't. I'd gone from business to personal in a heartbeat. "Never mind. I don't really want to know."

Clover has a stain of color on each cheek, and she rises to her feet. "Too bad because I really want to tell you! The answer is *no*. I didn't sleep my way into that job or any job. Not ever!"

So much for the brief submissive pose that had started to make me hard.

"Sit down." I can't help the commanding tone, but I'm fed up with her antics. However, if our emotions escalate, and we start yelling at one another, then this won't end well. "And there's no need to raise your voice," I remind her, keeping my own controlled and even.

After the briefest hesitation, she plops back down. "Adam, am I fired or what? Because if I'm not, I can't change the past, not how I got hired, nor my relationship with Jason. And I have a shitload of work to do."

I don't appreciate her attitude. Defensive, rather than the least bit contrite.

"If one of your trusted designers was suddenly exposed as a fraud, what would you do?"

Her head tilts as she considers, and I stay silent, staring at her. Her heart-shaped face, pixie chin, and sweetly bowed lips have always attracted me. Now, I watch her mouth, wondering how many times she's used it to tell me lies.

"I hope I wouldn't give a knee-jerk response," she says carefully. "I know I wouldn't, not after my own situation."

"You've been here under false pretenses the entire time," I remind her, "lying to all your co-workers about who you are." I don't bring myself into it because that's another level of deceit. "Don't you feel ashamed?"

Oddly, she looks me right in the eyes and says, "No. Because I still think I did what I had to do. I'm not merely a last name, a legally changed one at that. I'm precisely the Clover everyone knows. That's who I am. I'm not living the life of an heiress secretly at home and then pretending to be thrilled with discount lattes. I support myself. That's all I ever wanted to do. That, and *not* draw attention to anything about me apart from my talent as a graphic designer."

Well-stated, except I'm not sure I can or should continue to let her deceive everyone.

"You got the job on your own merit, and you've made friends here. Why not come clean, after all these months?" At least, why hadn't she confessed the truth to me?

She shakes her head.

"Why not?" I demand. "Why won't you tell everyone who you are?"

"I'm afraid," she says, her voice dropping to a whisper. "Even though I am just me, Clover, people will be mad or jealous, or feel the way you do."

"How do you think I feel?" I ask, crossing my arms.

"Betrayed." Her voice is even softer.

She is dead right about that. And now I have to speak as her friend and sex buddy.

"Do you understand it was worse because I had to find out from that asshole, rather than from you?"

Clover winces, but she stares into my eyes. "I know, and I'm sorry. I didn't like keeping my identity from you."

I don't approve of her behavior, but she isn't asking for my approval. I believe she could have handled her circumstances differently. Maybe not at first, but certainly after we started having sex and when I invited her into my home.

We stare at one another in silence. I can't change what she did to me personally. As her boss, though, I can decide what happens from here on out. And I'm going to push her to tell the truth.

"Surely you know it's not a question of *if* you tell people but *when*. It's only going to get harder the longer you keep this up. Imagine if some client comes in who knows you through your family. Would you really want to be outed in a conference room in front of fellow employees?"

She frowns. "I was betting that wouldn't happen. My name is well-known, not my face."

"Sounds like you planned on leaving Bonvier without ever telling anyone the truth."

Clover startles, her eyes darting away from mine. All at once, I understand that she considers that a viable option.

"I see," I say. Has she also planned on ending our arrangement, without having the decency to tell me who I've been fucking—and falling for? "Is that something else you haven't told me? That you've made up your mind to leave."

She stands again. "I'm not ready to leave Bonvier. I don't want to. But I don't think it's necessary to tell everyone who I am." Clover falters. "Although I could begin to tell certain people who my parents are." She fists her hands at her sides. "But if you're going to make it public, with a company-wide memo, then give me fair warning, OK?"

I'm disappointed in her answer.

"I didn't take you for a coward," I reply, "but then I didn't really know who I was dealing with."

"Don't," she says. "I'm still me." She taps her chest, right above the breasts I adore so much. "The same Clover."

It will take me a little while to think of her as the same person.

I push away from the desk. "I won't blindside you," I promise her, although it wouldn't be any more than she deserves.

"Can I go now?" she asks solemnly.

It's weird to be within touching range and not pull her close and kiss her. It feels unnatural, in fact. I fist my hands at my sides to fight the urge to do exactly that.

"Yes," I tell her.

But then, the purely animal side of me, the one that craves her body twenty-four/seven, no matter how I feel about her actions, decides to add, "Are you coming up here after work?"

Her golden-brown eyes widen. I surprised her. Clover lets the question hang in the air, and I catch myself holding my breath, which is a pussy thing to do, especially considering she and Decker were sharing wine last night.

"If my sex buddy wants me to," she says with a hint of her usual spirit, "*not* my boss, then yes, I will. Definitely."

It takes me a moment, but I nod. Perhaps in seven hours' time, when we're off the clock, I'll ask some personal questions and believe her answers. Maybe we can put this aside and go on like before. Maybe not. But I have to admit—I'm eager to unbutton that cream-colored dress.

41

Clover

If I thought being called to Adam's office this morning was hard, it was nothing compared to going back there after hours.

That morning, I wasn't sure I would be going upstairs at five thirty. But just in case, I had chosen to wear a power outfit, sexy, stylish and classic. A little Jackie O and Marilyn Monroe mixed into one.

Still, my knees feel wobbly when I get off the elevator, very glad to see that Janet is gone for the day. I delayed my arrival just in case she worked even a few minutes late. When I was up here earlier, I swear she gave me the fish eye, and I didn't want to run into her again.

I stroll as confidently as I can past her desk and into Adam's office. He isn't behind his desk. The room is empty. My heart sinks momentarily, but then I realize he wouldn't have left everything wide open, nor has he ever stood me up.

I go out and along to the only other room on the floor besides the bathroom. The lights are dim in his private conference room, and at first, I don't see him.

I nearly turned away before he spoke. "You're late."

I jump. "I . . . I . . . wanted to make sure Janet was gone."

Adam's eyes narrow slightly. "That was for me to worry about."

His arms are folded, and he's leaning his hips against the end of the long, polished mahogany table. Legs crossed at the ankles, coat off, sleeves rolled up, he looks hot and sexy. Adam no longer looks like my disapproving boss.

He looks far more dangerous.

"I didn't know you could dim the conference room lights," I say into the gloom.

"There are a lot of things you don't know," he says. "Come here."

I go toward him as if drawn by a string, and it's attached low between my legs where I tingle already.

"So we should talk," I say, surprised at how even and steady my voice is, given the fact that I'm trembling like a leaf in the wind.

"Later." He holds out his hand and spreads his legs wide, making room so he can draw me between them.

I let him, until I'm nestled between his hard thighs. This feels right. This is where I belong.

Without warning, he kisses me, a long, open-mouthed, toe-curling kiss. I slide my hands up his chest, and he crushes me to him, never breaking the connection of our mouths.

Heat and relief spread through me. There were moments over the last twenty-four hours when I feared I would never be in Adam's arms again, never enjoy one of these heart-stopping kisses.

And then he begins to unbutton my dress, exactly as I hoped. While still kissing me, his deft fingers handle button after button. He stops at my waist before setting me away from him.

"You look so hot," he says, parting the dress to expose my lacy bra. "I've been wanting to unbutton it ever since I saw you this morning."

This is news to me. When I was in his office earlier, I was so on edge about so many things—was he going to fire me, tell my co-workers my identity, tell me he never wanted to have sex with me again?—I didn't think he noticed what I was wearing.

Gliding his hands into the opening he's created, he cups each of my breasts. I reach up to start unbuttoning his dove-gray shirt.

"Don't," he says.

I freeze, wishing I could see his eyes better. I thought he'd want to clear the air between us *before* we engaged in any sexual activity. I imagined him firing away with more questions about Jason or my family. But I'm not going to pass up whatever Adam has in mind.

"Finish unbuttoning your dress," he orders. "I want to watch you."

I grow damp between my legs. We both enjoy sex when one of us is still mostly clothed. It's astonishingly arousing, more than when we're both naked. I'm perfectly willing to be entirely bare while all he does is unzip his fly.

After I undo the last few buttons, he grabs my hand and places it on his zipper, letting me feel his stiff cock.

"You do this to me, whether I want it or not."

"I hope you want it," I say. "I want you," I add, giving his arousal a squeeze through the fine fabric of his trousers.

With that, he flicks my bra open from the front, letting my breasts spill out. When all he does is look at them, that's enough to make my nipples harden. But I'm hoping he'll have a taste or blow across them. Instead, he puts his hands on my shoulders and turns me around.

"Lay across the table," he urges. "Palms down."

I do as Adam commands while one of his hands presses between my shoulder blades until my breasts are against the cool conference table. His other hand is at the hem of my open dress, drawing it up and over my ass.

"You are perfection," he says, and I relax.

As usual, when I let him take control, I feel incredibly desirable and utterly turned on.

That morning I'd been exposed with all my lies out in the open. Now again, I'm exposed in a different, far more enjoyable way. When he runs his palm over each of my butt cheeks, I'm already drenched between my legs.

Leaning down, he puts his lips against my ear. "You've been naughty."

I stiffen.

"Probably the baddest woman I've ever known," he adds, tracing his fingers along the crease of my ass, going down and under, pulling my thong aside.

I suck in a breath.

"You need to be punished," he whispers, barely stroking the slit between my lips before removing his hand altogether.

A frisson of excitement dances through me.

"Yes," I agree.

"Are you ready?" he asks.

"Yes," I promise. My legs are trembling, and I tense, waiting for his hand or his belt. Anything. Whenever he spanks me, the blood flows hot all around my lady bits and my climax comes lightning fast. "Yes!" I repeat, wiggling my ass cheeks.

Nothing happens.

"Adam?"

Silence so complete if I didn't know he was behind me, I would think I was alone.

"Adam?" I say again, starting to lift my head.

"Stay still," he orders. "You look so fucking beautiful."

But I'm ready for the heat from the flat of his hand against my skin. I wait an eternity. When still he doesn't begin, I start to sweat a little. The anticipation is unbearable. I'm growing desperate, rising on tiptoe just a little.

"Please," I beg.

I feel a puff of warm air against my slit, and I know his mouth is right there. Groaning, I think if Adam does it again, I'm so ready I'll climax.

Still, no spanking, no unzipping of his pants. This game is far too slow for my liking. My pulse is beating in my ears as I start to grind my mound against the hard edge of the table. Anything for relief.

"Be still," he orders.

"Please," I say again.

Startling me, I feel a single caress up the seam of my pussy lips that draws a low moan from me while I spread my legs and arch to give him access, all the while aching for more.

Again, nothing.

I'm growing frantic with need, knowing he's watching me in the dim light, leaving me wanting. It's exquisite torment.

But it *is* torment, nonetheless.

"I prefer being spanked." If I think he'll laugh, I'm wrong.

When I start to rise, his hand on the small of my back holds me in place.

"Stay," he says.

"Then for the love of God, touch me," I plead. Even the sting of leather would be a relief. I switch tactics, trying the sub demeanor. "Please, sir." I give a wiggle of enticement. "Spank me. I deserve it."

"No."

Wait, what?

I choke on my disappointment. "Why not?"

"I'm angry with you," he says simply. "And I'll never strike you when I'm angry."

Oh! Some of my ardor vanishes, but not all of it. I'm still throbbing between my legs and know a good hard fuck would do me the world of good. As charged up as I am, I won't last half a minute.

"Will you . . . touch me, at least, or . . . are we going to have sex?" I am whining, but I can't help myself.

"Just be still," he says softly.

I sigh and fall silent. I wait. It seems an interminable amount of time. Torment turns to torture.

"Spread your legs wider," Adam orders.

Good. Now we're getting somewhere. The position heightens my arousal, knowing what an eyeful he's getting, and how easy it will be for him to slide inside me. I moan again at the thought.

"Can I touch myself?" I ask.

"Not now. When you're home alone, do whatever you want."

Hm! That doesn't sound generous or caring.

I wiggle my ass again, hoping to lure him into doing the deed.

"Please," I beg again, not liking how forlorn I feel and sound.

"At the end of your rope?" Adam asks, sounding a little desperate himself.

"Yes," I croak.

"If I so much as blow on you again, you'll come, right?"

"Yup." *Please, please, please.*

"Then we're done," he says. "I'll wait in my office while you button up."

By the time I realize what he said and push up on my hands, he has left. Only then does it dawn on me that I've just been punished.

Well, shit! And while I still felt the lingering flush of desire, I no longer want to touch myself to orgasm—alone in a conference room. Suddenly, I feel humiliated and embarrassed.

Doing up my dress as quickly as possible, vowing to put it in the back of my closet until I get over this, maybe for a decade, I traipse back to Adam's office. He's wearing his coat and has his back to me, looking out to the harbor.

"Ready?" he asks, then turns to take a look at me in the light.

I fidget, hoping my buttons are all in the right holes. Apparently, we aren't having dinner, either. Everything has changed since he found Jason in my apartment.

"I hope you're going to snap out of this," I say. "And return to normal."

"Normal?" he asks, as I precede him from the room.

"You know what I mean. Whatever that was, in there," I say, gesturing toward the conference room, "I didn't like it."

"It was punishment," he says, "for both of us."

"Both of us?" I hadn't considered he was having a difficult time restraining himself.

"Didn't you know that?" Adam asks, punching the button on his private elevator. We step in. "You think I don't want to take you against the wall right now."

"Why would you punish yourself?" I can't help asking.

"For being so blind all these months. I let myself be fooled. Some would say scammed. I don't intend to let it happen again."

Yikes! He's more hurt than I realized that morning. And hurting him fills me with anguish.

"I'm truly sorry. I certainly never intended to scam you."

"Didn't you?" he says, as we start to descend. Adam sounds weary. He leans against the back of the elevator car and crosses his arms, looking closed off. His face isn't stoney with anger though. It's sad, which makes my heart ache even more.

I reach out, needing to touch him, but he shakes his head, raising a hand as if to ward me off.

"I don't know why you didn't think you could trust me," he says, "but I do know we should stop what we're doing until you figure it out. And the next time we try to be together, we need to be open about it."

"Open?" I ask, feeling my throat tighten with emotion. He wants to stop our arrangement, which sounds like breaking up to me.

"That means you would have to tell the world you're Clover Henley."

"And quit Bonvier," I say quietly.

He nods. "But right now, your job and your secret mean more to you than whatever we're doing, so I'm out. When things change, let me know."

The lift doors open with perfect timing, as if we're in a movie and that was his exit line. Then he puts his arm out to hold one side, letting me go first. I only take a few steps before I stop.

In fact, it's an awful exit line because it isn't true. I'm ready to grovel and be honest, at least with him.

"*You* mean the world to me," I tell him, "and I don't want to put what we have on hold."

When Jason was in my apartment, I had an epiphany. I am ready for a life with this kind, generous man. And I was even ready to tell him the truth about who I am. But I waited too long to do it voluntarily. Now, my hand has been forced, and Adam doesn't even want to hear my revelation.

"I thought we were going to talk tonight," I remind him. "You said 'later.'"

"I changed my mind. You may be able to say the right words to convince yourself lying to me all this time was fine. Hell! You may even convince me." He glances away with a grimace, his dark eyes reflecting the lobby's chandelier lighting.

"Good night, Clover." He strides through the lobby, not even looking back.

I can't let him walk away, thinking he came second to my career. That wasn't the case, not any longer.

"Adam," I call after him, recklessly sounding like a rejected lover despite Jake standing a few feet away behind his desk.

When he halts by the exit, I hurry toward him. Grabbing his coat sleeve, I make him turn to me. Looking him straight in his steely gray eyes, I finally confess, "I love you."

To my shock and dismay, instead of being satisfied that I've spilled out my heart, he just stares at me, his jaw tightening. A shiver runs down my spine at Adam's exasperated, dismissive expression, the opposite to what I hoped to see after saying those words.

42

Adam

Clover shouldn't have come after me, but she did. She also shouldn't have chosen this moment to say those three words, when I'm really not primed to hear them. Or believe them. So, I ignore her.

Looking into her earnest, golden eyes, I ask something that sounds petty, like we're a couple of high-schoolers. But ever since I saw her and Decker together, it has nagged at me. If it isn't bad enough that she was belting up her fucking robe when I arrived, something about the way she touched her mouth when she saw me has made me suspicious.

And then that asshole touched her face, too, with his fucking, ugly thumb.

"Did anything happen between you and Decker the other night?"

The look on her face, guilty as hell, says *yes*. But she glances away and mutters, "No."

"I don't believe you," I shoot back, my instincts yelling at me not to trust her words. "You are lying to me. Again."

"OK," she confesses, and I wait with every muscle in my body tense.

Looking me directly in the eyes, she said, "We kissed. Or rather, *he* kissed *me*."

A whoosh of relief races through me, followed very quickly by doubt.

"You just said *no*, and yet there was a kiss. What else?"

"Nothing else. I said no because it was seriously not anything. He surprised me and I turned my head and pushed him away."

Fair enough. Maybe true, but how do I know? "Why were you wearing a robe? Did you have a bra on underneath?"

"I spilled wine on my blouse, and yes, I did."

"Spilled wine before or after he arrived?" I ask.

"I feel like I'm on trial," she says, frowning, but she answers, "After."

I draw in a steadying breath. "So you thought, what the hell, my ex-boyfriend is here, kissing me, I think I'll start undressing, too?"

"It wasn't like that," she protests.

"We agreed to tell one another if or when we want to screw someone else." I thought we were past this stage and way beyond it into total trust and fidelity. Since that's been shot to hell, the agreement bears repeating. For all I know, despite her sudden, poorly timed declaration of love, she still believes our relationship is about nothing more than enjoying each other's bodies. I just don't know.

"That's right," Clover agrees. "And I don't want to be with anyone else."

She glances over her shoulder to where Jake is getting an earful whether he wants it or not. I don't give a flying fuck.

Clover confessed to only a kiss, but the vivid image in my mind is of her on my conference table. Ready, open, ass in the air, begging. When she and Decker were together, did they do it in his office? In his conference room? Are we merely reliving her previous office affair?

I need to think about whether I can ever trust her again. And I have to do that away from her sad eyes and her luscious curves. I'm usually a gentleman, but I don't say another word before pushing the door open and letting it slam back in her face.

I only have to keep my dignity as far as the curb. David opens the door for me—he's wordless today because he sees the look on my face—and I climb into the back. I want to erase the past twenty-four hours. And I want to hit something—Decker's face, most of all, but I'll settle for a golf ball. This time of year, my clubs and a change of clothes are always in the trunk.

"Take me to Brookline," I say to David without looking back to see if Clover exits the building. He knows I mean the golf course, embarrassingly named The Country Club, like we all sit around drinking single-malt Scotch. It's actually historic, gorgeous, and twenty minutes away. Not merely a world-class course, but it has a pool that Clover would love.

After Clover and I became official, I had planned on getting her a membership. Now I know her membership card would have had the wrong fucking name on it. Legally correct, if we're splitting hairs, but a lie nonetheless.

My mouth goes dry as dust. I swallow, reaching for the morning's coffee that ought to have been cleaned out during the day, but sometimes David forgets. The stainless cup is still in the cupholder beside me, a third full. I despise cold coffee, even iced coffee. Foul stuff.

Just to be a martyr, I take a long swig, and the bitter taste helps quell whatever wretchedness is trying to break free from deep inside and swamp me.

Dammit. I put everything on hold for Clover for the better part of a year, believing I was taming a wild creature, too skittish from her previous painful break-up to commit.

So high-key painful, in fact, she let the asshole come back into her life and kiss her! What the hell?

She said nothing else happened. But it's hard to believe she didn't know he was going to show up. She didn't tell me about receiving that stupid note and crystal egg. She didn't tell me he was the one who cheated on her. She didn't tell me she was heir to a fortune.

It's been at least two months since I told the woman I love her. Basically, she let it hang between us, and I put up with that shit. After all, her precious career has to come before anything else.

What a crap time for her to say it back, when her words mean next to nothing. When all I can think of are her lies.

Except I still have a hard time thinking of her as the lying Clover Henley. She's *my* Ms. Mitchell, tempting, funny, smart, talented, and made for me in every possible way. Someone with whom I've been delighted to share my private fantasies and to learn hers.

My Clover Mitchell doesn't really exist.

I throw the steel cup across the limo. David is lucky the glass partition is up, but the stale coffee splashes back all over me. Even French roast doesn't sit well on an Yves Saint Laurent suit. Not to mention the white leather of my Maybach.

Fuck!

Acting out is not my style. Having a tantrum is definitely not. I need to get the hell away from her. Just like that, I switch plans. I press the intercom.

"Take me home, please," I instruct David, being as polite as possible, knowing I'll give him a generous bonus for the cleaning he'll have to do. Pulling out my phone, I call Hanscom Field and get my jet serviced.

"File a flight plan for Charles de Gaulle Airport. I'm going to Paris."

In answer to the rep's next question, I say, "No other passengers."

$♥$♥$♥$

Clover

Was I honestly supposed to tell Adam that Jason and I kissed? I can't imagine doing so the moment he walked into my apartment?

"My old boyfriend is here uninvited, and we happened to just lock lips. Good news, it did nothing for me."

When Adam asked me out of the blue, having just denied me a climax and teased me until my entire body was jangling with frustration, I should have lied. One more little lie among the many I've told. We might have gone back to my place together and driven out the wispy ghost of Jason's unwelcome visit with a good, long screw.

Then again, maybe not. Adam looked completely unyielding. I take the T home. Not because I still can't afford Boston parking, but because the commute to Dorchester is a bitch. The worst gridlock. If only I'd known.

After a glass of wine, I text Adam. No response. I tell myself I won't do that again. He knows how to reach me, and right now, he doesn't want to hear from Clover Henley.

The next day, I wait till after hours, not wanting to mix business with personal issues. I go up to his office at five-thirty, but no one's here. The lights come on as I step off the elevator, showing me Janet's empty desk. Adam's office door is closed but, as I discover, not locked. Maybe he's somewhere else on the floor.

Cringing slightly after my last time in the conference room, I scan it gingerly. No bossman waits in the darkness. Returning to his office, I push the door open and enter.

If I hadn't had sex on every surface of furniture and even the carpet and up against the window, I probably wouldn't be comfortable going in uninvited. I don't know why I do it, except in a weird way, it feels like home.

Obviously, he isn't hiding under his desk, for God's sake, but he's never stood me up so I persist. I even peek into his bathroom.

"What are you doing in here?" Janet's voice lacks its usual friendly demeanor. And why wouldn't it? I'm trespassing in the CEO's office.

"Sorry, I was looking for Adam."

"In the bathroom?" Definitely a pissed-off tone.

"*Ha!*" I blurt. "Silly, I know. On the other hand, it's pretty big in there, so you never know." I think a little joke might help. Nope. It doesn't.

"Well, *I* know," she snaps. "He's not here."

"I guess I missed him," I say, feeling uber awkward. "I would have asked you before I entered, but you'd gone already."

"Not quite gone," she says, gesturing with her hands.

"Right. I mean, here you are."

No smile, nothing. Just a deadpan look.

"I'll walk you out," she says.

"Has Mr. Bonvier left the building?" I ask, thinking he must still be around. If he appeared, then he'd send her away, and I wouldn't have to feel like a naughty child under her disapproving scrutiny.

"Clover, he's left the country."

I think I gasp. I hadn't expected that. Talk about not letting a girl have closure.

"You're surprised," Janet says. "Was he supposed to check in with you? Maybe apprise you of his schedule?"

Was she making her own little joke?

"Not at all," I say. *Use your brain.* "I have a design issue and hoped to run it by him. I can hardly do that if he's not here."

Janet cocks her head. "Well, he's not. He didn't mention a design meeting, either. Maybe you can run whatever it is by the new account head or one of the account execs. That seems more appropriate."

We eye one another. How could I ask where Adam is? If I'm just Clover Mitchell, it's none of my business where the billionaire boss is. I have a feeling she knows Adam and I have some sort of relationship, and for some reason, she doesn't like it. By her frowny face and cold attitude, Janet probably also knows we had a falling out.

"I guess I'll talk to him when he gets back." With his private jet, he could be—

"He won't be here tomorrow, either," Janet told me. "Just so you know." To be fair, she doesn't say it with glee, like she's lording it over me. She also doesn't say when he will return. "Let's head downstairs. I have to pick up my daughter."

Worse and worse. I've held Janet up from her family.

"Sorry," I mutter. In a minute, we're on the elevator together.

"I know this is none of my business," she says, breaking the strained silence, "but Adam is a wonderful boss and a good man."

"I don't disagree with either of those statements," I say.

"I consider him a friend, so I don't want to see him played by you."

That, I disagree with. "Look, Janet, I don't know what you're—"

"You have a thing for powerful men. I get that. A lot of the female employees have tried to catch themselves a top executive or even Adam, himself."

"It's not like that," I defend myself.

"I know Jason Decker came before Adam. Who will come after?" The elevator doors open. "Or are you hoping he'll be the last one, and you'll get a ring and a spectacular fortune?"

She steps off first, and I hurry to keep up with her.

"Janet, I'm glad you're looking out for him, but I promise you I'm not out for a ring, and I certainly don't need his fortune."

Adam's redheaded assistant, stops in her tracks, right under his painted portrait.

"He's a genuine gentleman, and I hope he's only going to fall for an honest woman."

I want to say "I am that woman," but I can't. All I do is nod, but as she starts to walk again, I add, "He's a great guy." My voice breaks slightly, which makes my cheeks instantly heat up.

"On that we can agree." Janet takes a deep breath. "Don't get me wrong, Clover. I have nothing against you. You're a superb designer and an asset to Bonvier. But I don't trust you. And just so we're clear on how loyal I am to him," Janet adds, "I'll tell you now that I'm the one who sent Adam the photos of you with your previous boss. He deserved to know *before* he got too involved with you."

Leaving me with my mouth open, she walks out of the building.

Huh! I hadn't guessed Janet, but it makes sense. On the other hand, it proves we were good at sneaking around if even his assistant didn't know how involved we already were.

I glance up at the painting. "Where are you?" I ask, not liking the taciturn look in his eyes. It's the same as the last one he gave me almost in that very spot the day before.

All at once, I know what I have to do.

43

Adam

I'm looking over the Seine from my apartment, while thinking of Clover. Even my view of the mesmerizing City of Light doesn't distract me enough to stop picturing her face when she said she loved me. For three days, in every quiet moment, my mind wanders over the past few months. Ruminating.

I surprised the Bonvier Paris office, but they took it in stride, keeping me occupied. I spend the days at work, impressed by the growing list of clients, and for the past couple of nights, I've gone out to clubs. Sometimes with one of the managers, sometimes alone.

In the glittering capital, lit up from one end to the other, I'm trying my best to be the man I was a year ago and attempt to think of anything besides a checkerboard skirt and the woman who wears it.

Except this morning, I'm back to staring at the sunlight on the silver ribbon of a river and feeling a stab of regret with Martine sleeping in my bed in the next room. An old flame, she never minds a spontaneous phone call, and we often hook up when I'm in France. She has no interest in anything more than great food, fun sex, and whatever bauble I buy her while we stroll the Champs-Élysées.

And that has always been totally fine with me. Uncomplicated sex—exactly what Clover and I set out to have before I stupidly became attached to her.

But sex with Martine was never like it is with Clover. Not mind-blowing. It never consumed me, only temporarily satisfied a regular yearning to get off with a pretty woman.

All of which is probably why I did the most jackass thing I've ever done last night—brought a beautiful woman to my apartment after a fine meal and two bottles of wine, and then *didn't* do the deed. Not even close.

Luckily, Martine is secure enough in her attractiveness that she feels more pity for me than annoyance. She didn't storm off, but I also didn't spill my guts. That's not the vibe we have. We watched TV, consumed some cognac, and she fell asleep.

Nothing in my life has ever compared to the intensity of being with Clover, how we rock each other, how we can get to the precipice of the best damn orgasm and then go over the edge together with a feather-light touch or a single breath of air. Just thinking about her mouth makes me hard again.

But it's also all the rest of her—the way her mind works, her gorgeous, sexy laugh—Clover has crept into my soul, twisting through me, and tightening like my mother's prized climbing roses on her trellises.

More like fucking weeds, choking me! A surge of anger blooms again.

And when it comes right down to it, even if she and I aren't in a normal relationship, I can't cheat on her the way Decker did. I would never be able to touch her again without feeling guilty, and what would be the point in that?

"Mon chéri," Martine calls out from the tangled sheets. Then switches to English. "I'm hungry. What about you? Petit-déjeuner, oui?"

I'm hungry all right. Unfortunately, the only thing that will satisfy me is a woman an ocean away and too caught up in her own past, her own unnecessary drama, to take hold of the future I offer.

"Sure. Let's go out," I say, thinking of all the times Clover and I couldn't do such a simple thing. I want bright sunshine, lots of people, and the best croissants my money can buy.

$♥$♥$♥$

Clover

The next morning, I go directly to HR and tender my resignation.

"Two weeks," I offer. "If you want, I'll find my replacement, too."

"We don't usually let the person who's quitting do that," Tina, the bewildered HR head, says, "but then, people rarely leave. I mean, it's a good place to work, don't you think?"

As I say, she's puzzled by my voluntary notice, especially a couple months shy of a year and with everything going so well.

"It *is* a good place," I agree. "I'm going to miss everyone here. But I have other plans."

"Well, that's fine, then," she says, with a shake of her head. "I've been here for ten years and still find my job to be rewarding. Although Adam himself recently told me we had to tighten up our hiring screenings. I guess there's always more to learn and more ways to please the higher-ups."

"Indeed," I say, greatly wanting to please one particular higher-up if only I could find him. Quitting is just the beginning.

"In any case, you can certainly give me your suggestions for someone in your department," Tina says.

I take my leave. Next, I talk to my team. I have projects to finish in the short time I have left.

It goes sort of like I expect. "Everyone, and I mean everyone. Meet me at the table."

In two minutes, they are crammed into the space, and I stand at one end with my heart in my throat.

"It's been nearly a year—"

"Oh, crap," Cara says. "You're leaving. Like Mary fucking Poppins! You've made your mark on the department, and now spit-spot."

"If you've been fired, we'll all quit, too," someone else says.

A few voices rise either in solidarity or in disagreement.

"No one was fired," I promise. "In fact, I quit."

Cue the noises of confusion and disbelief.

"You guys are the best," I say. "But I have to confess I haven't been honest with you."

The room goes silent. *Get on with it, Clover.*

"My family name is actually Henley. Before I changed it, I used to be Clover Henley. For those of you who don't know who I am—"

"Candy!" someone yells out.

"Choco-Charms," says another, referring to our signature chocolate-covered caramels that everyone knew us for and loved, a staple on most people's candy shelf and in every Halloween stash nationwide.

"*That* Henley?" Cara asks, and I can see in her face she's hurt. "Really?"

I hope to God she isn't also going to be super mad, but I'll talk to her more in private.

"Clover Henley, the candy heiress, lives in my old building in Dorchester?" Vickie muses, looked perplexed.

I send her an apologetic shrug.

"Our art director is Clover fucking Henley?" Cara's voice brightens. "That's some prestige, right there!"

Shit! I never imagined they'd think it a benefit. "Former head," I say. "I'm gone in two weeks."

A few groans.

"Why?" someone calls out. It's Trevor, who worked on Lovell's perfume with me.

I am not sure how to answer. I have no intention of talking about Adam.

"It's complicated," I say. "I'm going to start—"

"No," says Cara. "I think Trevor means why were you incognito?"

Oh. I want them to understand that I didn't do it to fool them. "For one thing, I wanted to get the job on my own merit. And Henley opens up doors to unfair advantage, which I wanted to prove to myself I did not need. Secondly," and I pause to smile wryly, "if any high-profile, rich bitch came in here and was given the lead position, admit it, you all wouldn't have given me an ounce of respect."

"Eventually," Cara says. "Eventually, we would have."

"I guess I didn't want to waste a bunch of time proving myself. So I lied." That is hard to confess. "And I'm sorry." That part is easy to say because I am.

"So why are you quitting?" Cara asks.

I still don't want to discuss my reasons. "That's harder to explain," I begin.

"No, it's not," she says, and beams a smile around to the rest of the team. "Is it?"

Another designer, Mariel, also from the Lovell team, chimes in, "You and our boss have the hots for each other, and you can't legit do anything about it until you leave."

My mouth drops open.

"Because of the stupid rule," someone else says.

They know! I am floored.

"Does everyone in this company know?"

Cara shakes her head. "We're an intuitive group. That's all. And you're gonna miss the hell out of us, Ms. *Henley*."

She's correct about that, and I tell her so. But Adam is more important to me than this job or any other. More important even than my independence. I still have two choices. Take another design job or swallow my pride and ask my parents for enough seed money to start my own business.

That night, I go with Cara to our favorite bar. "I am going to miss this," I confess. "Most of all, I'm going to miss working with you and the rest. You're all spectacular."

"Except for Graydon," she jokes. He's the designer I hired.

I smile. "He's just a little different, but he's brilliant.

"Maybe, but he sings when he's working, and he doesn't know he's doing it."

I feel a lump in my throat, and my expression must show it.

"Don't worry, Clover. I'll be happy to meet you here any time. Jenny, too.

I go home with the choice weighing heavily, deciding to spend the evening looking at the available positions in the city. I even fire off an email to a head hunter, explaining that I'm looking for a management-level job because I don't intend to go backward in status. I no longer need to prove myself, although explaining why I quit a great job will be difficult.

By the time I see Adam again, I have every intention of having a great alternative lined up.

As Janet mentioned, he didn't show up the following day, or the next, or the one after that.

I refuse to text him again. I know he got the previous one, read it and ignored it. But then, after a glass of wine for courage, I do something I'm not proud of because it smacks of desperation. But, *dammit*, this suffering is absolutely unnecessary.

If Adam is still under the impression I want Jason, then he might be getting all sorts of wrong thoughts in his head. I really want to tell him I'm ready to move forward with our relationship, and to let him know I quit Bonvier so we can do exactly that.

And mostly, I want to tell him how much I love him—*again*—and make him listen this time.

With my heart pounding, I dial his number.

44

Adam

I flew off on a whim to Paris, licking my wounds, hoping to put a little salve on them by way of Martine's willing, sexy body. Yet I end up working my ass off to sort out crucial problems. During the first few days, Bonvier's Paris office is thrown into turmoil due to a local regulation designed to thwart common sense.

It tests my patience and my diplomatic abilities. The French have a way they like to do things, and we Americans had set up something incorrectly. Eventually, my not-really-retired father joins me. We wine and dine a few bureaucrats who are obstructing our business. It turns out there's not much that expensive meals and hand-holding can't repair.

And then I do something I haven't done in years. I goof off on the Riviera with the other billionaire bachelors. At least, that's who I assume all the guys are. Clover would call them playboys, strutting around with dark tans and pretty women, each more scantily dressed than the last.

Great viewing, I think, as I stretch out on a beach towel. And viewing is all I'm doing. After Martine and I parted platonic company, I didn't hook up with any other women. Not while I was still in Paris, nor when I went to Nice, nor now that I'm in Villefranche-sur-Mer. I remain alone except for a little friendly chatting with people in bistros or bars at night.

Frankly, the whole head-clearing escape is a futile enterprise. If I'm honest, I think by staying away, I'm punishing Clover. Maybe I am. Maybe she's missing me every second, but I'm definitely suffering, too.

Because I miss her every fucking day. Even when I brought Martine to my apartment. Especially then! Trying to screw Martine had been a childish mistake.

I cringe with the memory of that night, and feel like a jerk. More for Clover than for Martine, who didn't have any emotional stake in it. How could I imagine I'd ever banish Clover from my blood when I can't get her golden-brown eyes out of my thoughts?

It was an awakening of sorts. I, Adam Bonvier, am officially beyond the fooling-around stage, and now that I know what I want, I can't go back. Nothing will satisfy me but a long-term relationship with the woman who attracts me in all ways, suits me physically and intellectually, and satisfies my needs.

Until Clover confessed she let Decker kiss her, I thought I fulfilled all that for her, too. Simpatico, and all that! But I have to keep reminding myself what a good liar she is.

Scores of tempting women are on the beaches. And yet I'm not actually tempted by a single one. Not even a little. I swim and walk the beach, but there's no point in doing anything more than appreciating the myriad of gorgeous females in skimpy bathing suits or tiny sundresses. I'm just looking. I'm a man, after all.

A few days later, my jet lands at Hanscom Field where David is waiting for me. He makes sure I notice how clean the back of my limo is, and I thank him again for rescuing the white leather from my coffee-throwing tantrum.

"It won't happen again," I say. It won't because if I don't get my shit together with Clover, then I don't intend to ever let myself get this tied in knots over another woman.

As we drive toward Beacon Hill, I'm surprised when I think how good it is to be home, despite the lack of gorgeous beaches and warm, blue seawater. Nearby, within driving distance, is Clover. She's the "home" I'm thinking of, and I can't find her anywhere else in the world.

Now that I'm back, I think about finally answering her text from two weeks earlier. But I don't. I waited this long to talk to her, and I intend to do it face-to-face. While I still don't entirely understand Clover's reasoning for her many lies, I'm now in the frame of mind to hear her out and to move forward. After all, I had plenty of time to go over everything while broiling in the sun. And if I have to take on Jason Decker for my woman, then I'm up for it. Ready to flex and fight!

The next day, I'm so eager to get into my office, I arrive while Sean is opening up the place.

"Morning, Mr. B."

"Morning, Sean. How are the Pats looking in the preseason?"

"We're going to the Super Bowl. On dead dogs, I swear."

I smile. He says that every year, but our chances haven't looked promising since we lost the GOAT of quarterbacks. Brady gave us an amazing run.

"If we do, I'll get you seats on the fifty-yard line."

"Shoot, boss! Why didn't you say so a couple years back when TB12 was still here?"

Shrugging, I head for my elevator. Of course, I mostly want to lay eyes—and hands and mouth—on Clover. But first, I have to deal with Janet and her lists and reports, learn my schedule of upcoming important meetings I can't miss, and take her scolding.

"Basically, you're forbidden from taking off like that ever again. Do you understand me?" my redheaded firebrand demands, hands on her generous hips.

I can't help grinning. It's good to be back.

"I do understand, but right now, I'm going to make the rounds."

Her eyes narrow, then she nods. "Have at it, boss."

What was that look for?

I take my private elevator directly down to the design floor. While I know I should check in with the VPs of accounts and operations first, I want to see only one person.

Having decided early on in our sex buddy arrangement that it was better not to get too close at work in case people around us notice our obvious attraction, I haven't visited the design floor in a while. Whenever I do, I easily recall how eager I'd been the first time I met Clover in person.

Around me, designers' heads lift as I weave my way through their stations.

"Good morning," I say.

Some of them offer overly friendly smiles, which I return with a nod. Others share a look. I'm starting to get a weird feeling by the time I reach the corner office. All the floor-to-ceiling curtains are drawn.

Good timing! Perhaps Clover and I can forgo clearing the air until later, and I can claim her sexy lips that have literally haunted me in my dreams. A makeup kiss with no one the wiser. Maybe even a makeup quickie if she wants to be really daring.

I tap, but I don't push the door open because of the closed curtains. A woman needs her privacy. But I hear, "Come in."

Not Clover's voice.

I enter and find another female, one I recognize with dark curls and café au lait-colored skin, sitting behind Clover's desk. In front of it, in the two chairs are another male and female designer, both holding tablets. An impromptu meeting, but why here? And why without their boss?

The familiar one behind the desk—*Tara, Dara, Cara?*—rises to her feet while the other two gawk. While I was away, I'd almost forgotten the effect I have on my employees.

"Hey there, Adam," says the familiar one behind the desk with pale-blue eyes. She sounds at ease, but she looks nervous.

"Hi." Since I have no way to alleviate her nerves except by leaving, I get right to the point. "Where's Ms. Mitchell?"

Three shocked faces are the only response. After another moment, the dark-haired designer responds.

"I thought for sure you knew. Clover *Henley* doesn't work here any longer."

I swear I can feel the blood drain from my head as I struggle to comprehend. I hate being caught wrong-footed.

"Since when?" is my dazzlingly, half-witted question. *Christ!* I've been away little more than two weeks, and the earth has shifted. Clover's gone, and they know her real identity. What else do they know? Is that why everyone is looking at me a little strangely, including Janet?

Janet! Why the hell didn't she tell me?

"Her final day was last week, on Friday, but she came in yesterday morning for a few hours to help me with something."

I missed her last appearance at Bonvier by a day!

"Tara, is it?" I ask.

"Cara." She smiles at me, not judging.

"Are you our new art department head?" I ask.

"For the time being, I am. Clover recommended me, but the account VP thought you should have final say."

"I say you're our art director," I agree since Clover wouldn't intentionally sabotage my company.

"Thanks, boss," she says. "I have big shoes to fill."

She does, indeed. Sexy, high-heeled ones, at that. But there is no way anyone can fill them.

"Do you know where Clover works now?" Instantly, I wish I hadn't asked her a personal question. It must be the shock.

Cara nods. "She decided to go into business for herself. I don't think she would've left us otherwise. She loved it here."

I feel like the biggest asshole. I'm the reason she jumped ship. I also know she doesn't have the money to do anything bigger than freelance at home. She can't possibly pay rent for office space in Boston to start her own brick-and-mortar business.

"Congratulations on your new position," I say, ignoring the other two designers who have observed our interaction like they have front row seats to a play. And a tragedy, at that.

As I head for my private elevator, ignoring the knowing glances, a shard of fear races through me. What if I've lost her? For the first time in two weeks, I text her.

Can I come over?

I wait. It feels like an hour but is actually three very long minutes. Three minutes in which she must have been deciding her answer. That doesn't bode well. Finally my phone pings.

No

Shit! I've been an idiot.

45

Clover

When I see Adam's text, I have two thoughts. *Thank God he has finally contacted me* and *Fuck him! How dare he contact me!*

The dichotomy of love and hate have been my constant companion ever since he took off for Paris, which I found out eventually—not from Janet, who wouldn't tell me squat, but from the new account VP.

Now, two weeks and a few days later, I'm no longer interested in hearing from him. Because, as it turns out, he is a shallow, billionaire playboy after all. I know this for a fact.

After texting and receiving no reply the day he disappeared, I waited as long as I could before calling him, hoping to have an adult, meaningful conversation. I wanted to offer my apology for lying, explain how little Jason matters to me, and again tell him I love him. A French woman answered Adam's cell phone.

"Allô."

I was struck silent momentarily. Then my brain kicked in. Obviously, he was at the Paris office and had put his phone down. Some employee had picked it up.

"Bonjour," I said. *"Je veux parler avec Monsieur Bonvier."* Asking to speak with him, I sounded perfectly calm.

"Je suis désolé mais Adam vient de quitter l'appartement pendant une minute. Il a oublié son téléphone. Attends. Laisse-moi m'habiller et trouver un stylo. Dis-moi ton nom."

This basically translates to her being sorry to tell me that Adam has gone out for a minute and that she is naked in his bed, so she doesn't have a pen handy. Then she asked for my name.

Those few words shattered my heart into a billion pieces.

I didn't leave my name. I couldn't even be polite. I didn't thank her. I think I said something about it not being necessary and hung up.

Hopefully, she forgot all about the call. I prayed he wouldn't look into his phone history and see my pathetic attempt to reach him while he was in Paris busy screwing another woman.

But I've replayed that sad conversation in my head about a hundred times until it's given me the strength to go on with my life. At least I didn't witness him fucking her. *Bonus!*

Now, he's back in Boston. Obviously, he knows I no longer work at Bonvier because, in his text, he asked to see me. But this man has no idea how quickly I can disappear. My car was already packed and ready when I went to Bonvier yesterday for two last painful hours with Cara, who desperately wanted my advice.

Ultimately, she nailed the design she was struggling with, at least in my humble opinion, and I did nothing but pat her on the back and told her, "You got this."

The whole time I was there, I feared he would return from his little French holiday. Running into him would have been messy, probably causing me to have to do major damage control to my mascara and eyeliner in the ladies' bathroom.

Leaving Boston after hugging Cara, I'd cruised along the three-hour drive and been welcomed home with a glass of wine and a poached salmon dinner at my parents' Hudson Valley estate. A green, wooded sanctuary, it has all the niceties except for city life, take-out food, and friends.

This morning, as Adam's nerve-rattling text makes my phone croak, I'm seated on the stone patio overlooking the Hudson far below our ten-acre estate. We have fifty precious yards of river access and a little sandy beach, but my favorite feature of our home is the large, deep pool. I took an after-dinner swim last night and then settled in for a surprisingly dreamless sleep.

Funny to think our house is smaller than Adam's Boston townhouse, but then, his is a one-of-a-kind residence where most homes on Beacon Hill are far smaller and even fewer have a garage.

Even with six thousand square feet in our main residence, I need to stay in the carriage house guest quarters for privacy and sanity, as well as to stop my mother from entering my old bedroom without knocking, just "for a chat."

With both of my father's yellow labs at my feet, I sip the last of the coffee I brewed in the guest kitchen and take a deep breath.

"What are you going to do?" I ask myself aloud.

The dogs, Pete and Lovey, in their middle-aged years, raise their heads. Pete yawns, but Lovey is a head-tilter, always trying to figure out words. Or maybe she's waiting for one she recognizes, like *walk* or *cookie*. When neither of those are forthcoming, she puts her head back down and issues a long sigh.

Since I still have Pete's attention, I say, "The problem is I have too many choices. I could stay in Dorchester or send for my things and never look back."

I brought any food that would spoil, most of my clothing because I'm a bit of a nut, and my frog collection. Again, because I'm nutty about some things. I left everything else behind until I make some decisions.

"If I stay there, I can run an online business or take that job." *That job* is a high-paying Boston design position. It was promised to me nearly as soon as the headhunter sent the company my résumé and samples the day after I gave my notice at Bonvier.

Pete doesn't have much of a doggy opinion and puts his head on his paws. I'm tempted to stretch out beside them. Maybe things are easier down on the stonework.

"On the other hand, I could come back here and run my online business." It would be easy to work out of the guest house, which is about the size of my Dorchester apartment, except with an entire second floor of equal square footage, and then an attic. "I could jump in the pool whenever I want." Lovey sighs again.

"Lastly, I can borrow money from Mom and Dad and set up a physical business in Boston."

That's the least desirable of the three choices. And why Boston? I have a suspicion I know why, and I need to tamp down any longing in that particular direction.

"You two want to swim with me?" I ask. Lovey lifts her head with interest as she knows the word *swim*. A morning dip is as good as a late-night one, and being joined by these two clowns will make it even better.

"Stay," I say, kind of unnecessarily since they don't look like they're going anywhere. I dash inside to put on my bathing suit and grab a towel. Then we cross the patio to the stone path leading to the pool.

My father likes an old-world ambiance, with wood and stone being his go-to materials in all architectural design. The bottom floor of our house is faced with stone—both a granite wall and boulder-like steps around the front and stone arches at the back where I am.

Indoors, granite floors and a massive, ski-lodge caliber stone fireplace leaves one in no doubt about the aesthetic. The house screams Rocky Mountains where my father was born and where he met and fell in love with my mother, although his Australian parents moved home years ago.

With mom's family being East Coast, he created this sanctuary of a home to raise us kids when we weren't skiing in Vale or on a yacht anywhere else in the world.

Dropping the towel onto a lounge chair, making me think of Adam's deck chairs on his roof, I kick off my flip-flops and dive in. The water temperature is always perfect, neither shockingly cool, nor smotheringly warm. I swim the length of the pool and come up smiling.

Lovey and Pete stand side-by-side with only their front paws submerged on the top step, watching me.

"Come in," I encourage them. Lovey walks in until the water is up to her eyes and then she starts paddling. Pete launches himself after her, making a huge splash. I go under again before coming up to float on my back, with the dogs swimming around me.

Until they both let out sharp barks and head back for the steps.

What has got into them?

Another pair of legs, definitely not furry or in the least canine come to a stop by the side of the pool. My gaze goes higher, past his sexy button-fly jeans to his hands in the pockets, then up to the black T-shirt, stretched over his magnificent torso, chest, and shoulders.

Adam. In. The. Flesh!

My mind short-circuits. That's the only explanation as to why I feel joyful, confused, stunned, furious, and relieved—all at once. Then I settle on irate when I think of him in Paris.

"What are you doing here?"

"That's a stupid question," he says.

Not a great start. Rather rude, really.

"OK. How did you find me?"

He rolls his eyes. Another pointless question, but he answers.

"I went to your apartment, and you'd clearly gone away because your frogs were gone."

"How'd you get in?" I demand, outraged all over again. Despite both Jason and Adam finding their way in the last time, it still shocks me. That apartment building might as well remove all the doors entirely.

He shrugs. Adam is resourceful and not used to taking no for an answer.

"Does it matter?" he asks.

I'm starting to think it doesn't. I'll just buy extra cans of mace and strap them to my body.

Meanwhile, Lovey and Pete have exited the pool to sniff around Adam's feet, dripping water all over his expensive leather sneakers. Serves him right! He reaches down and gives them each a pat on the head.

The dogs don't bother moving away before they each shake off as much water as caninely possible. Then they head over to a grassy area where they lay in a patch of sunshine to dry off.

My turn. As gracefully as possible, I climb the pool steps, feeling Adam's gaze take in my modest, bright-blue two-piece. Not a sexy bikini, like the one he bought for me in Quebec, which I tossed in the trash after hearing his Parisian lover's voice. This one makes me feel sporty.

Adam grabs my towel off the chair and holds it out to me, a perfect gentleman. A two-timing, disloyal, fickle . . . gentleman!

I give him my back, letting him drape the towel around my shoulders. Where his fingers graze my damp skin, I shiver.

The French lady who answered his phone, I remind myself. She enjoyed his fingers across her skin, too. He might sound the same and look the same, and even smell the same since at this proximity, I can detect his heavenly cologne. But the man I fell in love with betrayed me. I don't really know this Adam at all.

Clutching the towel closed over my breasts—yes, I appear like a prude—I lean over and shake out my hair. I probably look like one of the dogs. Finally, I face him.

"Well?"

$♥$♥$♥$

Adam

Clover is ready to battle despite being clad in the cutest swimsuit I've ever seen. Not the string bikinis I've been surrounded by on the Riviera, it still shows off her delectable curves, her toned legs, and plenty of cleavage. I love summer!

"Can we sit? Or I might as well get in the pool. My jeans are already drenched." I glance at the goofy dogs who are already snoring.

Clover doesn't say a word. She goes to the nearest lounge chair and perches stiffly on the end of it. I take the end of the one next to her, resting my elbows on my knees.

"Did you meet my parents?" she asks.

I shake my head. "I rang the doorbell, and a very nice lady answered, but she wasn't your mom."

Clover nods, not giving me any more info, so I continue. "She questioned me a little, but I passed inspection, and she directed me to the guest house. I heard you splashing about—or maybe I just heard those dogs."

She shrugs. "I think you should have texted or called."

"I did text you," I remind her.

"Too late," she murmurs. Then more loudly, she adds, "And I replied, which is more than you did for me two weeks ago. Or since."

She's right. "I know, and I'm sorry. I went to Paris, and business took over."

"Business, was it?"

"OK, you're right. I didn't respond to your text because I was pissed off. I couldn't imagine why you'd let that scumbag near you after how he treated you."

"How *he* treated me?"

I almost treated her just as badly, except I keep weaseling out of feeling guilty because Clover and I never established that we're a real couple. Secondly, I didn't actually have sex with Martine. *Almost* definitely doesn't count in this case. Thank God!

At this moment, back with the woman I love staring me down like I'm the enemy, I'm relieved I didn't let my other head do the thinking while in France. I would have had to confess to betraying her, and then this wouldn't go as well as I hope it will. In fact, there isn't any need to mention Martine at all. She was irrelevant, and now she's firmly in my past.

"What about how *you* have treated me?" Clover asks.

"I asked you to move in with me." I also told her I loved her, and it took many weeks and a bad scene for her to say it back. But I leave that aside for now.

She gives a mirthless laugh if ever I heard one, sounding nothing like her usual joyful happiness or post-orgasm, breathy laughter.

"I'm really glad I didn't fall for that trap."

Something isn't right. "What do you mean 'fall for that'?"

"Was it a revenge screw?" she asks, completely bewildering me. "Jason kissed me, and so you decided you had to jet off to France and have some Parisian pussy?"

"I . . ." *Huh!* My mouth is still open, but I don't have an answer. How the hell did she find out about something that didn't even happen? Until I got to Paris, I hadn't even known I was going to entertain the idea of a hookup.

But a revenge screw? No. I remember just feeling sad and mad, and wanting to feel better with mindless sex. No matter how I justify it, I would have been cheating *if* I'd gone through with it.

Clover gets to her feet. She looks how I felt—sad and mad.

"That's what I thought," she says, taking my hesitation for guilt. In a heartbeat, she is striding away from me toward the guest house where I'd first searched for her.

So far, I haven't handled our discussion smoothly at all. With a sigh that matches one of the dogs as they get up and follow her, I trail behind.

The whimsical, arch-shaped door is shut when I reach it. The yellow labs take up positions on the flagstones around the single granite step and watch me while I lean against the door jamb with one hand and knock with the other.

No answer. I should've jumped in the pool and joined her when I first saw her, looking so relaxed, splashing around with her furry friends. I would have held on tight to her slippery body and made her realize I'm craving only her.

"Clover," I call out, knocking again. Of course, I try the handle. Locked. I'm about ready to pound with my fist.

"Don't be childish. I drove all this way to see you." I need to bare my soul to convince her to give me a chance, so I add, "I know I jumped to conclusions about what happened in your apartment with Decker, but I'm ready to talk openly."

We have too much going for us to throw it away, especially on a moment's rash behavior. Even if, out of curiosity, she let Decker kiss her, I'm certain I can erase the jerk's tepid attempt to make out with my woman.

"Don't call me childish!" Clover's voice comes from the window to the right of the door. "And no one invited you to come. *No one*," she emphasizes, "wanted you to come. You're no longer my boss. You're no longer my anything!"

Shit!

"Let me in."

"Go away."

"I heard we have a visitor."

I turn to see an older version of Clover, her hair a little darker, but with the same striking eyes. Obviously, her mother, and I wonder how much she overheard.

"When our housekeeper gave me your name," she says, "I had to come see for myself."

I reach my hand out. "I'm Adam. You must be Mrs. Henley."

"Yes, I'm Beryl Henley," she says, shaking my hand. "But please, call me Bunny. Everyone does."

I nearly laugh. Is that why she named her daughter Clover?

"Christina, our housekeeper, said you were here to see my daughter? She works for you, doesn't she?"

I know Clover can hear every word. And apparently, she doesn't want me talking to her mother about anything personal or otherwise. The door swings open.

"I thought I heard voices," Clover says, blinking innocently. "Mr. Bonvier, how good to see you."

She must want to choke while using that sweet tone to address me.

"You mustn't keep handsome men waiting on your doorstep," her mother chastises. "Looks like you were swimming. Why don't you get dressed, and I'll take him up to the main house to meet your father." She turns to me. "We'll have something cold to drink. It's getting quite warm, don't you think?"

This is the hospitality Decker talked about. I might as well get in good with her parents if I'm going to swing Clover's favor back to me. Although, as I agree to go meet her father, I send a rueful glance over my shoulder.

Clover has ventured onto the step, looking irritated and uncertain.

Having shed the towel, she wears only her swimsuit, and I regret again not being able to take her in my arms and strip it off her slowly. With my teeth!

46

Adam

The dogs come with us, too, after Bunny calls out, "Come along, Pete. Come, Lovey."

A few minutes later, I'm sitting in a living room with a magnificent view of the Hudson Valley and the river below. Mr. Henley appeared quickly, and we're already talking golf scores.

The previously mentioned housekeeper, Christina, brings in a pitcher of lemonade, pouring into four glasses that are already on a massive oak sideboard. I've hardly had a chance to hear Russell Henley's wholehearted approval of my choice of driver and clubs when Clover rushes in.

With her hair still wet and slicked back, wearing capris, a T-shirt, and no makeup, she is fresh and simply stunning.

But her mother doesn't seem to think so. "You didn't have to hurry. We weren't going to scare Adam away."

"I know that," Clover says, sounding as if that was exactly what she was worried about.

It's strange to see her with her parents, rather than as an isolated New York City fish out of water in Boston.

"We never would have sent your old beau your way if we'd known you had a new one," her mother says with startling frankness.

But Clover isn't having any of it, nor dropping her guard. "Mr. Bonvier—"

"Please," I say, "call me Adam." As if I haven't licked and sucked every part of her body. "Remember, we're casual at my company."

"Adam," she amends through gritted teeth, "is my *boss*." Then she adds, "Former boss, as you know." She's addressing her mother, but sends me a withering look.

"Employed or jobless, I don't care why you came home," her father says. "Always glad to have Clover back under foot." He smiles broadly at his daughter.

"I suppose having only one child, especially a daughter," I say, "makes her even more precious."

Two people look surprised and one winces, her cheeks going pink.

"One child?" Russ, as he told me to call him, repeats my words. "I wonder how you got that impression."

Because your daughter is a world-class liar! Unaware of my thoughts, even as I fix Clover with a hard stare, her mother laughs.

"Because we've done such an excellent job of keeping our children out of the limelight."

"*You* have, especially," Clover's father says, looking adoringly at his wife.

Meanwhile, once again, I'm left with that feeling of not knowing who the hell Clover really is. Why would she lie about being an only child? And why hadn't I spent any time doing my homework after I found out she was a Henley?

I consider excusing myself to the bathroom and doing a quick internet search in case more surprises are in store. Maybe she's been married already or has six children and only one kidney!

"I have two younger siblings," she says, her voice sounding gruff. Clearing her throat, she adds, "My brother, Basil, and my sister, Lark."

I don't blink, but inside I'm vowing I will not let either of these maniacs name Clover's and my children.

"How fortunate for you," I say, crossing my arms and staring at her. "I cannot imagine how I was so misinformed. Do you all get together much?"

"In that regard, Clover *is* like an only child," her father says. "Her siblings both live in Australia where my parents are from and still live in Queensland. They have a sugarcane farm. Our kids come home sporadically."

"They would definitely come home for a wedding," Bunny Henley says without any shame, smiling at me.

"Mom!" Clover chastises her.

It's no big deal. My mother would have said something similar. And I don't mind Bunny's audacity because I've been leaning in that direction anyway. At least I was before a billion lies exploded all over me a couple weeks ago. I still think after living together for a little while, Clover and I will get engaged.

As long as there aren't any other skeletons, like—

"Her last engagement ended abruptly," Mrs. Henley reveals, "before I even got to plan the wedding."

Clover groans and grabs for a glass of lemonade, which she downs like she's dying of thirst. I bet she wishes she was enjoying something a little stronger—like Long Island iced tea or straight vodka.

"Her *last* engagement," I muse. "Was that with Jason Decker?"

"Jason?" her mother repeats. "It didn't get to that stage, did it?" she asks Clover. "I know you were practically living with him, but you never said anything about an engagement."

"No, Mom," Clover snaps, sounding like a fed-up teenager. "I wasn't engaged to Jason."

I wait to find out who else has won her heart or broken it. Maybe she has a whole string of guys in her past, like a strand of Christmas lights, some still burning, some shattered.

At first, she says nothing more. Finally, realizing all eyes are on her, Clover says, "Adam is not my boyfriend, so I'm sure he's not interested in my love life."

"But I am," I insist, both interested *and*, for all intents and purposes, her boyfriend. The only way to get the truth out of this lady is to have her on the hot-seat in front of her parents.

"She fell hard for a boy her first year in college," her mother says, snagging all my attention. "You thought she was too young, didn't you, Russ? But we'd been the same age, or thereabouts, when we met and married, so I didn't mind. I was never sure what happened?" Bunny looks at her daughter as if the answer might be forthcoming.

"Nothing happened," Clover grinds out. "We were, in fact, too young. That's all."

I would bet my last golf club there is more to the story.

"Are you staying the night?" Russ asks.

I try to let a mask of utter innocence rest over my face. "I hadn't intended to. I was just in the area, on my way to the city." They might believe I'd driven down the Hudson Valley on my way to New York City.

"A bit out of your way," Clover said, outing my lie. "From Boston."

"A nicer drive than going through New Haven, don't you think? And since I missed your last day at Bonvier, Inc., I thought I could ask you a few exit questions."

"If you hadn't been away on private, intimate, personal issues, rather than working," she says, "you wouldn't have missed my leaving."

"Mostly not so private," I say. "The Paris office is busy and some delicate matters kept me away longer than I intended."

"*Delicate* business," Clover says, ending on a long hiss. "I heard about that."

Mr. and Mrs. Henley are looking back and forth at our nuanced conversation as if watching a tennis match.

"Clover," her father interrupts, "why don't you show Adam around. Then you both can relax from what sounds like a lot of pressure at work. Take a swim or play tennis. If you stick around," he says to me, "I'll take you to my club tomorrow. I have a tee time at twenty after nine in the morning. We can play eighteen holes. The greens are like velvet."

"Then you will stay," Mrs. Henley says as if it's all settled. "Dinner is at seven. And you don't have to worry about accommodations. The guest house has two bedrooms."

Clover visibly startles. "Mom, I'm sure Adam would rather have a private suite at whatever hotel he's headed for." She shoots me a look that says I'd better be going. And soon.

"I would love to stay." I have my game face on, oozing friendly, cordial vibes like I'm at lunch with a new client. "And if Clover doesn't mind sharing the guest house, that will suit me fine."

I wonder if she'll continue to object. Those tawny eyes of hers narrow. But she relents.

"I'm sure we'll work out the accommodations if you insist on staying," she says without an ounce of graciousness in her tone. Her mother appears shocked. Perhaps to redeem herself, Clover rises to her feet.

"Are you ready for a tour? I only give the quick one. If you want to learn about every detail of how each room was carefully designed or where the materials were sourced—"

"Thank you," I say, quickly jumping up, knowing if she can, she'll palm me off on one of her parents. "The quick tour is fine. We can talk about . . . our business at the same time."

She purses her lips, then shrugs. "Very well."

"Your hair has dripped on that chair," her mother says, frowning at the dark patch. "That's what comes from being hasty."

"Sorry, Mom." Clover turns heel and walks through the alcove at the other end of the room.

Apparently, there isn't going to be a heartfelt invitation to join her. I know I better go quickly, but I can't simply rush off.

"Thank you, Russ. If I'm still here, I'd love a round of golf with you in the morning." I'm prepared to let the man win by a few strokes if it helps to get Clover's father in my camp.

"And thank you for the hospitality," I say to Bunny. "The lemonade was top notch."

She gives me a gorgeous smile, so like her daughter's. Then I hurry to catch up with Clover's sexy, capri-covered ass before she gives me the slip. I've no doubt she intends to do that as soon as she's out of sight and hearing of her parents. Basically, we're like children, and I'm the unwelcome neighbor's kid being foisted onto her.

Sure enough, by the time I reach the next room, she is disappearing through a door at the end of it. I trot through the hunting lodge-style dining room with the second stone fireplace I've seen, beams hold the light fixtures, and flagstones are under my feet.

The next room is a sunny sitting room overlooking a patio.

"Clover," I say, exasperated. "You can't shake me so why try?"

She comes to a skidding stop halfway into the room. Her hands clench into fists as she whirls to face me.

"Fine," she says, clearly spitting mad, and I don't know why. Hurt, I understand. After all, I ghosted her. But the fury coming off her in waves is out of proportion to not hearing from me for two weeks.

"Why did you come here?" she demands.

"Who'd you almost marry?" I counter.

"Not your business," she spits out. "*Nothing* to do with me is your business any more. It's really outrageous that you barged into my family's home."

Since I know the truth, why is she so pissed off?

"I guess the yacht didn't stop your parents from squeezing you into the guest house after all," I point out another lie. "What's outrageous is you quitting while I was away."

She fumes, arms crossed under her breasts, shaking her head of damp hair. My gorgeous girl. I can't wait another second to kiss her. In two steps, I take hold of her bare upper arms so she can't run away again and claim her lips.

They aren't soft or yielding like usual. They're firm and closed.

Women like to talk first. Make-up sex after. And they want to be heard and believed. Fine! I didn't give her a chance before I went away. I basically told her I didn't believe that all she and Decker did was kiss. I certainly didn't listen when she said she loves me. I'll start over with the question that threw me into a coffee-throwing mood, right now while I'm in a much better frame of mind to believe her. I give her arms a gentle squeeze and look into her achingly familiar tiger eyes.

"Did you and Decker do anything beyond kiss?" I'm probably insulting her because she drops her head. "Have sex with him by chance before the tuna sandwiches?" I know she didn't. Clover is not loose, and she wouldn't—

"Yes," comes her whispered reply, sounding anguished as she keeps her gaze somewhere in the vicinity of my chest.

Softly spoken yet the single word punches me in the gut harder than any training partner I've ever had. *What the fuck!*

Heat rises in my throat and stings my nose. When the initial shock releases me, I let go of her and walk away, going out the first door I find. Turns out to be French doors to a terrace, overlooking the pool. As I stride down the sloping path, I force myself not to break into an undignified run to get away from her.

378

I want to, though. I wish I'd come in my limo so I could climb into the back seat and drink myself into oblivion while David drives my wounded ass home.

I guess I've already forgiven a kiss but wasn't remotely prepared for a larger betrayal. There's no coming back from this.

Clicking on my seatbelt, not once looking back in case I catch a glimpse of the woman who has slayed me like a fierce fucking knight, I tear out of her parents' driveway.

Keeping my foot down, I speed away from the Henley estate. Fast, because if there's one thing a 718 Cayman GT4 is good for, it's speed. My imaginative brain effortlessly delivers a flash of Decker with his hands on Clover, his mouth covering hers, breathing the same breath. He would have palmed her breasts and nudged her legs apart

Something that feels very much like a sob rises in my throat, and I wipe the back of my hand over my face. What the actual hell am I doing? Crying for some disloyal bitch who isn't worth the effort?

Not some bitch. My thoughts battle themselves, and I begin to defend her to myself. I've waited for this exact woman to come into my life for longer than I knew. Ever since I started liking girls. Isn't that how everyone feels when they think they've finally found the right one?

It might've been simple scalding hot lust that raced through me when I saw Clover on the street. But when I met her for the first time, something about her reached out, like she was crooking her finger and beckoning me. Ever since that moment, I have wanted her—needed her—in my life.

Despite knowing it was wrong, and feeling like a hypocrite at work but a king on the weekends.

For Clover. For the sake of being with her, I lived a lie. And that's saying something because I've never been tempted, not once in a decade since Rachel's death. No matter how dishonest I've felt, Clover was worth it.

That's what I kept telling myself. For the past couple of months, I believed sometime soon, she would quit the company so we could date openly. She is so fucking talented she could walk out of Bonvier one day and get another job before the start of the opening bell on the Stock Exchange the next.

And she just tore it all to hell. For what? To see if a spark still existed with her former boyfriend? Why else would she give him another chance?

I zip past highway signs so fast I can't even see them, but my own thoughts are moving even faster.

Why even let him touch her? Probably because deep down, she still loves him. The one who got away. I grip the wheel so hard I think I could snap it off. That's the logical answer.

Well, they can damn well have each other. A liar and a cheat fit perfectly together.

She didn't even have the decency to look me in the eyes when she confessed. I take a long breath as that fact reverberates through me.

A second later, I downshift the Porsche and slam on the brakes.

47

Clover

I'm bawling by the time I hear Adam's car kick up gravel as he drives away. And my heart is pounding as if I just raced the Boston marathon despite walking slowly, like a zombie, down the same path he took.

Passing the pool, I enter the guest house, amazed how many tears can fall so fast. My cheeks are as wet as if I'm under water.

That one little word was the biggest lie in the past year. And for what?

Because this time, *dammit*, I refuse to be the only one who's been cheated on. I was so freaking careful to open my heart slowly, not to move so much as a toothbrush into Adam's home despite wanting him more than I've wanted anything or anyone else in my life. Ever.

I'd hoped I was somehow immunized against this wretched ache. *Wrong!* So let him feel some small modicum of it, if only because his male pride is pricked. Let him stew.

Let him think I allowed Decker to fuck me after the great and sexy Adam Bonvier has all but ruined me for anyone else. Well, *boo-hoo!*

Staring at my surroundings, an absolutely swank, Tuscany-inspired sitting room that is comfortable, soothing, and beautiful, I am lost. Utterly adrift and unsure what happens next.

Over the past week, I'd come to terms with Adam's unfaithful, disloyal behavior as well as with the certainty he won't be in my life any longer. I went from being excited to tell him I'd quit so we could be together to wishing I'd never worked at Bonvier in the first place.

At the very least, I should have not started up with the same type of man—rich and powerful. Spoiled and careless.

Slamming my palm against the wall until it stings, doing anything to shift the pain from my heart, I realize I am gasping. I can't catch my breath. Here I am, hyperventilating over some cheating asshole. Again!

Except this time, it's Adam. One of the good guys, full of promises and rules and seemingly trustworthy.

Looking around wildly for a paper bag, I settle for a plastic grocery bag from under the kitchen sink. Sinking onto the sandy-colored Italian tiles, I start to breathe into it, willing my pulse to slow down.

How dare he come here, expecting to charm me and my parents! It took Adam zero time to fly to Paris and stick his dick in some other woman. *After* I told him I loved him! Maybe sex with the woman who answered his phone had been meaningless. Then again, perhaps everything we did was just as meaningless.

That thought doesn't help my breathing. I remain in the middle of the kitchen floor ugly crying with snot coming out. No wonder I can't catch my breath.

What am I going to do now? Stay right here in this guest house and become a recluse. That's what. I won't go any farther than the pool. I'll set up a little office in the second guest bedroom. The closest I'll get to people will be Zoom meetings.

And if I ever start toying with the idea of going out with a man again, it'll be my head I hit against the wall, instead of my hand. I wipe my snotty nose with the plastic bag, which does very little, so I go back to breathing into it.

After a minute or two, I hear footsteps, recalling I left the hobbit door, as I think of the arched entrance, wide open. What a terrible time for one of my parents to see me, their super-independent eldest child!

I'm a hunched ball of misery, with the last of my body's moisture leaking from my eyes and nose.

"It's going to be OK," Adam's unmistakable voice promises me from behind. He gets on the floor with me, his rock-hard thighs slide around either side of mine, and his also-unmistakable arms envelop me in his scent, his strength, and his warmth.

Have I passed out? Am I hallucinating?

Motionless, I wait. If he's real, something else will happen. If he's not, I'll realize it in a moment and can have another bout of hysterics.

Adam reaches around me and takes the bag away from me while rubbing my back.

"Just breathe, deep breaths, slowly."

Inside, I'm saying, *What the fuck?* But I go along with his suggestion, and gradually, I calm down.

"When I saw you, I thought you were going to put that bag over your head." His tone is friendly and even teasing, which makes no sense. After all, I just confessed to screwing around on him. "Trust me," he adds, "I'm not worth it."

He's right about that. He's the one who screwed around on me! *Be strong, Clover,* I counsel myself, although being strong is hard to do from my current position of pathetic defeat. But I drove him away once, and I can do it again.

"You're right. You're not worth it," I say, wondering how he can behave so normally. I try to pull the hem of my

T-shirt up to wipe my nose, but his arms are restricting my movements. "Get your hands off me."

He doesn't. He rests his chin on the top of my head.

"Why are you so mad at me? Why did you lie about sleeping with Decker?"

I don't bother to be surprised that he figured it out so quickly. Instead, I struggle in his grasp, needing to put distance between us.

When it becomes an awkward wrestling match, he releases me from the craziness of both of us on the kitchen floor. If I wasn't so distraught, I might think it a victory to have brought the billionaire bachelor down so low. Then again, I'm right down here with him.

Before I can rise, Adam stands and offers me his hand. Ignoring it, I scramble to my feet and move away from him to the stainless-steel farmer's sink.

Taking a moment to splash cool water on my face, I hope to erase some of the blotchiness left after my epic crying jag. Besides, it's easier not to give in to his magnetic appeal if I don't look at him.

But I'm not going to the effort of lying again, and I answer his second question first. "I lied because you deserved it."

There's nothing but silence behind me. Drying off with the kitchen towel, I finally turn. He is solemn and seems older than half an hour ago when he was all charming with my parents. His face looks like he went through something, too, when he took his little joy ride around the neighborhood.

Or maybe my truthful answer has brought him low. Maybe he's sorry for what a cheating bastard he is.

"How'd you know?" I ask.

"That you were lying? Because you looked down. I know you can't look me in the eye and lie to me." He put a fist to his chest. "I know that with certainty, right in here."

Wow! I'm a better person than I thought because I can't spout lies while looking into his intense steely-gray eyes.

Adam is one hundred percent right. He is also one hundred percent as desirable as ever. Cheating bastard and all.

His hair is, frankly, a mess, which means he drove his Porsche with the windows down. And it makes him look sexier than ever. The perfect fitting, button-fly jeans, the T-shirt that's not too tight but tight enough, his tanned, muscular arms from golf, his eyes flickering over mine do the same to him.

Damn! I'm weak in a way I never was with Jason. I never once wanted to have sex with him after he cheated. Not for a second. But with Adam . . .

Leaning my hips against the creamy-white granite counter, I ponder his infidelity. If he says the woman in Paris looks nothing like me and that he did nothing with her he's ever done with me. If he promises never again to—

Before I can begin to consider forgiving him his French fling, he steps close, glides his fingers into my hair to cradle my head, and kisses me.

Twice ambushed within the space of an hour. Adam surprises me, or he never would have managed that sneaky maneuver. One second, there is plenty of breathing distance between us, and the next, his mouth covers mine. A lemonade-tasting lip-lock that causes my belly to flutter and my lady-bits to awaken. Traitorous body!

As his tongue demands entrance, I allow it. In the space of a heartbeat, I am sucking his tongue, stroking it, relishing the familiar heat dancing through me like flickering flames. Unfolding my arms so we can get closer, I slide my hands over his waist and lock my fingers behind his back.

He pulls me away from the counter. His hands move from my shoulders, skimming down my back to my butt. Tilting me against him, his arousal nestles against me.

This! I have missed this so much, I tremble while threading my fingers into his soft, dark hair.

"I want you," he whispers against my mouth. "I need you. Now."

My pulsing body wants to find the quickest way to get him naked, but my brain kicks back into thinking mode just in time. I push at him, and he releases me.

"Marzipan," I whisper. Because I am finished with this shit!

He looks shocked.

"I can't. I just can't do this," I begin. "If ever I needed a safe word, it's right now while I'm close to giving in to you again." At least I'm being honest finally.

"Then give in," he says, a small frown between his dark eyebrows. How dare he look so earnest and irresistible.

I don't give in. Instead, I clench my hands into fists. "Didn't you have enough sex in France?"

Unexpectedly, he grins then says, "Nope."

Man-oh-man, do I want to slap his handsome face and remove that smile. He looks too damn hot *and* arrogant.

"Because I didn't have any," he adds. "None at all."

"Liar!" I say, in a harsh tone that I never use. It doesn't even sound like my voice. "I called. I spoke with the woman. She was naked."

He frowned. "You could tell Martine was naked over the phone?"

Martine! A pretty name. She's probably drop-dead gorgeous and uninhibited. I see red. I swear it. Momentarily, an actual red haze clouds my vision. After I decided Adam was mine, he'd flown away and acted like a man-whore. I may start hyperventilating again.

"She told me she had to get dressed to find a pen!" I am not yelling, but I am not soft-spoken either.

"If they hear you, your parents are going to think you care about me."

"They'd be wrong," I spit back at him, realizing I'm lying again and looking at the floor. *Damn.* He is right. I make myself lock onto his gray gaze and hold it.

Adam appears unbothered. His nonchalance is begging for that face slap.

"Martine *was* naked, but I wasn't there, was I?" he points out. "What's more, I didn't get any message."

"I didn't leave my name with your lover!"

"We didn't have sex, so she wasn't my lover." He says it calmly, firmly, and I find myself believing him. As far as I know, Adam has never lied to me beyond saying Allston was on his way home.

"Why was she naked in a place where you'd left your phone?"

His reasonable expression falters. For the briefest moment, I think I see contrition, maybe guilt, and my stomach twinges with alarm. But his expression changes to one of resolve as he tightens his jaw, making those telling little muscles in front of his ears jump.

"She was in my apartment in Paris. And she was naked in my bed because I'd intended to screw her but changed my mind. Simple as that. No sex. Nada. Zilch."

The first part was the explanation I feared, but the second part wasn't as bad as I anticipated.

"Did you know her, from before, I mean?"

"Before?" he asks.

Was he being purposefully obtuse? "Before *us*."

He nods. "Yes, I did."

I'm relieved Adam hadn't picked up a rando and taken her back to his place, but I'm unnerved just the same. "What made you change your mind about having sex with her?"

He rolls his eyes. "That should be obvious. I'm here, aren't I?"

"What if you change your mind again?"

"About sleeping with Martine? Not going to happen."

I sigh. "With anyone. It seems you got pretty close to cheating."

"Close but no cigar," he says. "And I won't change my mind. It was an aberration. I thought you were playing with me, so I decided to play right back. But I couldn't."

"I see."

"Do you?" he asks.

Actually, I don't understand. Not really. "We were going along well, weren't we?"

"Yup."

"And then Jason kissed me, and I told you about it. I answered truthfully," I remind him. "And you decide to get on your private jet and go screw some former French girlfriend?"

"Not exactly a girlfriend," he says.

"Hardly the main point in what I just said."

"You're right," he agrees. "The main point is that I was tired of getting dicked around by you."

I take a step back at his sudden vehemence. "Dicked around?" Not a very mature thing to say.

Adam does something I've never seen him do before. He starts to pace. The casually upscale kitchen can't contain him. He strides past the rustic dining table to the small sitting room.

"From not telling me your real last name despite multiple opportunities," he says, reaching the multi-paned, antique windows on either side of the front door, before turning, "which indicates a pretty unhealthy level of distrust, especially with someone you're having sex with." By now, he's back in the kitchen. "To letting that asshole kiss you *after* he hurt you so badly you fled your home and gave up your family name."

He marches away once more. "And then you quit Bonvier the minute I turn my back."

"With good reason," I begin.

He puts his hands in his hair, still pacing.

"You moved without telling me. Twice! First to Dorchester, then back here." He releases his hair, and I'm glad to see tufts of it aren't caught between his fingers. "And you even lied about having siblings, for God's sake!"

He goes back and forth about four times across the carriage house's main level from the olive and cream-colored kitchen to the tasteful chintz-covered sofa and chairs. I follow him with my eyes, and I listen carefully. I have to admit my faults sound bad when he lists them like that.

"So yes," he says." I needed to get away from you. Because you are just so damn hard to . . ."

To love? Is he going to say I'm hard to love? That will destroy me. First Jason, then Adam. I hold my breath as he ceases pacing. His gray eyes lock on mine.

"You are so damn hard to *resist.*"

I nearly sag with relief, but he's not done.

"I've been honest with you and tried to get close to you for months. Over and over, I've found I can't trust you. And after everything about not wanting to date me because of Decker, not wanting to trust someone in power because his betrayal cost you your job *and* your lover, when you let him back into your life—"

"I did not," I protest. "He showed up, lying in wait when I got home. Not a good homecoming, let me tell you."

"You didn't throw him out. You let him stay. He was drinking wine with you."

I open my mouth, but he's right, so I shut it. I'm not going to lie, not even a little white one to spare his feelings.

"When I saw him there," Adam continues, "even before I knew he'd kissed you, it blew my mind. You, Clover, which is a rabbit or a donkey's name, for Christ's sake, you are a mind-fuck if ever I met one."

I wince, but I don't bother to defend my name or my ability to fuck with his mind.

Then, to my surprise, Adam walks away. But not outside. He goes upstairs. Naturally, I follow. My heart is singing a different tune—a light, happy one. He didn't have sex with anyone else. Martine has not enjoyed herself with my man!

And finally, we are talking. Now that anger and jealousy aren't clogging my ears and throat, I can listen and I can speak. I find him in the larger of the two guest rooms, sitting on my bed.

This is a good sign, I think, at least metaphorically.

"Where are your frogs?" he asks, sounding more like himself.

"I got here late yesterday. I'm still packed."

"And the furniture you left behind?" he asks.

I shrug. "I'm undecided."

"You mean you might be going back to Dot?"

I've heard the nickname for Dorchester, so it doesn't confuse me like some other Boston slang did when I first arrived: *blinkers, wicked pissah, woop,* or *tonic,* for instance.

"Looking less and less likely," I say. "For one thing, that building has a severe security issue."

He sends a wry smile my way. I return it.

"Also, I don't have to be in Dorchester if I'm going to have an online, freelance design business. I can be right here." *Or I can be on Beacon Hill. Or pretty much anywhere.*

"True. And is this," he gestures at our surroundings, "what you want?"

I sigh. That is the question of the hour, isn't it?

48

Adam

This is one of life's crucial moments. Clover might say she's done, that *this* between us is too hard. Especially if she is figuring out her future as a designer at the same time.

"I want you to know," she begins, "I didn't quit Bonvier because I thought you were getting your rocks off in Paris?"

"No?" I reach out and grab her hand, pulling Clover down to sit beside me. If I tether her here, we can get through this. I hope.

"I quit because I wanted to tell the world you were my guy. I wanted to get out from under the stupid rule."

"Not a stupid rule," I mutter, but I'm pleased with what she said up until then. "Do you want to start over?"

"You mean you still want the full-price tour of the Henley estate?" she asks without missing a beat.

"But I ducked out through the emergency exit. Is the tour guide annoyed?"

"Nope. Not any longer."

Although her eyes are red-rimmed, she looks more like her old self than at any time since I arrived. "Can we skip the rest of the house tour and let me explore every inch of your body instead?"

She sucks in a breath and releases it with a smile. "Nope."

Well, shit!

"First, more talk."

Double shit!

"I didn't open a bottle of wine to share with Jason," Clover explains. "He helped himself, and I told him to leave numerous times. When I went into my bathroom, I did it because I don't give a damn about him. I cared much more for my blouse, which was in need of immediate treatment. He was supposed to leave before I came out, but you arrived instead."

I nod. That all makes sense. I couldn't process it before because when I'm with her, we're always turned on and grabbing hold of one another. I'm glad she just wanted Decker gone.

She tucks her hair behind one ear, and I really want to nibble just behind it, her ticklish spot, but I wait. Her clearing the air is doing us both good, and I should stop wanting to jump ahead to the good stuff.

"I also want to explain how things snowballed for me," Clover says. "The lies, I mean. Once we started up as sex buddies, if I told you who I was, that would have mucked everything up. It would have practically forced us into a relationship, and you would have had to choose between lying along with me or telling my secret. Do you see?"

"I do see. But I think you should have told me sooner, at least after I said I wanted you to move in with me."

She hangs her head. It's adorable. I know if our kids do that, I'll never be able to say a harsh word to them.

"I handled it as best I could," she says. Her voice has dropped to a whisper.

"I know that now."

I move backward on the bed, hoping she'll join me. I can't help noticing the mattress is strangely squishy.

"I feel like I've been swallowed by a marshmallow."

Clover laughs and, with all traces of unease gone, she straddles me. "Mom and Dad have very different tastes. This is all her. The quaint, floral wallpaper, the glossy white, shiplap headboard, and the featherbed on top of a soft mattress."

"What about you?" I ask, drawing her top up and over her head.

"I'd say I'm somewhere in between the stone and wood castle-slash-hunting lodge style of my father and the Martha Stewart, chintz-filled décor of my mother. But I appreciate both."

"So, employment?" I ask, unhooking her bra but wanting to get the important questions out of the way.

"I received a job offer already." She looks rightly pleased with herself.

"I predicted you would. Where?"

She frowns. "I didn't even search any prospects outside Boston."

"I guess you weren't ready to see the last of Beantown."

"Guess not."

I reach up and roll each of her nipples between my fingers, enjoying the view as she arches toward me.

"The truth is," she begins and looks directly at me, "I wasn't ready to see the last of Adam Bonvier, even though I thought you were hooking up with some French lace."

I splay my hand across her flat stomach, so relieved I didn't do anything to destroy what we have.

"You've been very patient," she adds, looking down at me.

I nod, knowing I'm about to get my reward. Sliding my hand lower, under her stretchy capris, I touch her soft curls.

"I've been very patient," I agree.

She closes her eyes as I manage to insert a finger between her wet pussy lips.

"Mmph," she says.

"What was that?"

She says nothing while I'm stroking her. So I pause. She sighs.

"You remained within all the boundaries I set up. Despite my telling you flat out that I wasn't interested in anything but sex, you created a relationship out of office visits and weekends."

"I'm pretty damn perfect," I say, making her laugh until I caress her taut nub. I know she's throbbing with need by the way she leans into my hand.

"Anything else?" I ask, inserting two fingers into her soaked core while still teasing her clit with my thumb.

Clover gasps, leans her head back, and closes her eyes again while she reaches out and clasps my T-shirt to steady herself. She can't speak anymore, and I bring her to a swift climax while my cock rests stiffly behind her, saluting the crack of her ass.

She laughs for a few moments, as usual, before saying, "Thanks," her tone all sexy-gruff.

Drawing my hand out of her pants, I rest it on her hip and tuck her hair back behind her ear with my other hand.

"Any other questions?" she asks.

I consider as I gaze up at the woman I love, her face relaxed from the first of what would be many orgasms to come.

"I guess I'm good, unless you want to tell me anything else? Anything more about 'the man'?"

She rolls her eyes. "Why would you call him that?"

"Because Decker's the one who changed you. He was a pivotal relationship."

She shakes her head, talking while trying to tug my T-shirt off. "Jason cemented my mistrust in the male sex, but he wasn't the first. As my mother let slip, I was engaged in college—for about three minutes. I nearly married a guy who'd fallen for my last name and the fortune that came with it. I never told my parents why I quickly ended the engagement. But until Dan, I hadn't realized why they'd protected me and my siblings from the outside world so fiercely."

She shakes her head. "Jason's betrayal was entirely different. More painful. The worst, until I thought you did the same. That was a whole different level of hurt."

I wince and sit up, making her fall sideways off my hips. In a heartbeat, I strip her of every stitch of clothing and her thong. Then I press her back and settle over her, staring down into her golden-brown eyes, still a little puffy from crying.

Over me! What a waste of tears.

"Sorry to put you through that. You paid me back but good, though. I nearly trashed my Porsche. It would've been a shame as she's almost as sweet a ride as you."

I'm making light of the matter on purpose, and she punches me in the stomach.

"Oof." I grab both her hands and hold them over her head. In response, I receive a smile as bright as the sun outside the guest house window.

"So now what?" I ask. "Who do you want to be when you return to Boston?"

Clover

"That's easy," I tell him. "Clover Henley, out in the open. I know I've been super dishonest with you, but *you* have been my pivotal relationship, showing me what's possible. *You* are 'the man.' I'm ready to tell you anything about myself."

"That's leaving yourself rather vulnerable," he says, leaning down and licking my right nipple.

Yes! I squirm beneath him. It's such a turn on being naked while he's still clothed, especially when the fly of his jeans, buttons and all, rakes over my mound.

"I don't care how vulnerable I am," I tell him. "I trust you. I've lied to protect myself, but I'm ready to be utterly exposed."

Although, I can't get much more exposed than I am at this moment.

"You can trust me," he promises.

I recognize his cautiously hopeful expression because it matches the feeling in my heart. Then he licks my left nipple before giving it a tug with his teeth.

"Mm," I hum, ready for him.

"I'll be exposed, too," he reminds me. "Utterly, irrevocably soul-laid-bare. I have to tell you something."

I hold my breath.

"I like *unsalted*, chunky peanut butter."

Wait! What? I snicker. "That is a huge confession! And gross, too."

Adam smiles, his cheek lifting up on one side, and I swear I see his cocky spirit flow right back into this perfect body of his, until it shines out of the granite-gray eyes I adore. The Adam Bonvier from *before* the awful encounter at my apartment is back!

He stops asking questions. He simply believes me and firmly nudges my legs apart. Then, releasing my hands so I can touch him, with perfect timing, he licks his way down my body, halting right over my core. If he licks me again, I will come.

When he stops, I groan.

He sits up so he can reach over his own back to pull off his T-shirt.

With something akin to fascination, definitely admiration, I watch his fabulous, wide shoulders and strong arms move smoothly through the actions, making my stomach flip-flop. Watching his biceps flex is like porn for me. When he stands up to remove his jeans, I go up on my elbows to get the full show. Undo, push down, kick aside. *Yum!*

I am so ready to take the length of him inside me.

His thigh-hugging, cotton boxer briefs, the sexiest garment in the world and in my favorite color blue, need the same quick removal treatment. Although I admit, I'm enjoying the view. The outline of his rock-hard cock against the fabric makes my mouth go instantly dry while the rest of me grows even wetter.

Adam shucks them swiftly and sends them flying, but he doesn't immediately climb back on the bed.

"So, whatcha doing?" I ask.

"Relishing the moment and thinking about make-up sex," he says. "I've never had sex with a candy heiress before."

"Technically, you have,'" I point out. "You just didn't know it."

His eyes narrow. "I might have to give you a spanking first for all the lies, for kissing that jerk-off and putting me through hell."

A spanking! Am I being rewarded? I can't help grinning at the notion, while a flood of desire pools between my legs. I love being a woman!

"Are you smiling at my pain?" he asks.

"Absolutely not. You know, even if either one of us actually had cheated and had sex with someone else—"

He growls and holds out his hand. Instantly, I take it.

"It wouldn't really matter," I continue. "Sometimes, it's merely an act, an exercise. Meaning absolutely nothing except fun or stress relief."

"That's not what you said when you thought I screwed Martine."

I sober instantly and let him draw me to my feet. Apparently, make-up sex will have to wait.

"You're right," I say, while he pulls me closer. We're entirely naked, bare skin to bare skin.

"Is that what sex between us is to you?" he asks, with our gazes locked and serious. "Just fun and stress relief." His arms close around me, bringing me home.

"Nope."

That's all I have to say before he kisses me. The best, hottest, heartfelt kiss I've ever received, and I return it, hoping he recognizes my unconditional surrender to whatever life holds in store for us.

I think he does. All at once, his hands are on my ribcage, lifting me high until he can land a kiss on my stomach before letting me slide down the front of him.

"No more lies," he says softly.

"No," I agree, as he sits down. I am ready to stretch out on the bed again and let him ravish me in his stunningly talented fashion. Instead, I find myself tugged across his lap with my face against the comforter on one side of Adam's thighs, my legs on the other, and my ass in the air.

Seriously? God, I hope so!

Silently, he rubs my butt cheeks, and I take in a long breath, hold it, and wait.

He caresses my ass again, and then—*smack!*

It doesn't hurt so much as the speed surprises me. Immediately, he caresses the spot with his palm, and I release my breath.

Smack! This one stings a little.

Smack! This one, too. But it's warming me up nicely.

"Ow!" I exclaim for the hell of it, and a second later, his fingers move to my wet slit.

Sighing with relief, I lift my ass to give him better access. *Smack!*

I realize it isn't going to hurt any more than it already does, not with his palm. But I recall how it felt with his belt. And my brain can easily imagine a scenario with a little whip or a corded ribbon. And I want that, too. I want him behind me, flicking a whip across my lady bits.

Soon, I'll write that down on a slip of paper for our fantasy game.

For another few seconds, he goes between the two areas, slapping my butt and stroking my aroused core, until I am writhing against his stiff erection under me. This sensual punishment has to end soon, or we'll both lose out on something even hotter.

"Please," I beg on a ragged breath.

Adam stands, making sure I don't crash to the floor, although my knees are so wobbly, I would have if he hadn't sent me backward onto the bed. Climbing atop me, he crushes me with the hard planes of his body before settling between my legs, right where I want him. When he thrusts inside me, I lift my hips so he can go deeper.

We don't last long enough to work up a sweat. I climax in about a minute, and he follows me over the edge, pumping so hard and driving his cock into me so fast, his hips are a blur.

Breathing hard, he rolls to the side and gathers me against him, my back to his front. As his hand idly strokes my breasts, he says, "I missed you."

"I guess you did."

He gives the softest, sexiest laugh. "I craved you."

"Craved?" I struggle to turn in his arms, but he keeps me anchored. "That's intense. I don't think anyone has ever craved me before."

"I have. From the moment I saw you crossing the street in your black-and-white skirt."

"I will have to dig that out from the back of the closet," I tease.

"Better yet, why don't you move it into my closet, along with all the rest of your stuff. Frogs and all."

I freeze. "That's a serious suggestion."

"I'm a serious man."

"Hard for you to say that with nothing on but socks," I say lightly. More than merely dating and screwing my former boss, I would be giving up my independence. And for the first time, it doesn't faze me in the least.

"I have asked you once before, in case you've forgotten," he says. "But if you're not ready, we can wait until after the wedding."

"Whose wedding?" I'm not being coy. The fall, leaf-peeping season for marriage with a gorgeous backdrop is nearly upon us. I know of two people at Bonvier who are getting married within the next two months, and I've agreed to go to both of their weddings. I assume Adam has, too. "Haley's?" I ask.

He laughs. It's genuine, and I can feel it in his stomach muscles against my back.

Finally, he tightens his arms around me.

"Ours. If you'll have me."

"Ours," I echo. Then more loudly, "Ours? You're asking me to marry you? Although technically, you didn't ask. But not that long ago, we were still mad at each other."

I'm struggling to turn around again, flailing like a fish on deck. "That could happen again. I mean, even an hour ago, you didn't seem particularly pleased with me. And now you want me to be your . . . wi . . . your wi . . . ."

"Wife," he says helpfully, letting me turn to face him. "So we were angry, but look at where we are now, and how much fun it was getting here."

"Fun?" I am still repeating words like an imbecile. Plus, I question his sanity if he thinks the past few weeks have been a good old, knee-slapping time.

"OK," he amends. "We had some rocky moments, but here we are."

I nod. I may have imagined us moving in together—about a few hundred times. But marriage?

"What if . . . what if . . . ?"

He runs his palm across the skin of my hip, and I shiver. "What if what, sweetheart?"

"What if I screw up," I begin, then hear how pathetic I sound. "Or you do. What if you see some cute chick on the street in a better skirt?"

"Better than your checkerboard skirt? Impossible."

"Seriously," I say.

His sigh is long and thoughtful. "There are no guarantees, except that we will screw up, but not like that. Not in a huge way. I want you in all aspects of my life. Doing things or nothing at all. I think I've made that clear. As to letting my libido lead me, I've had enough women to know it's you I want in my bed. Why would I go to so much trouble to be with you only to throw it away on some random hot pussy?"

"If we screw up, we stay together and work it out," I reason cautiously, liking the sound of being with a man who matches my vision of a mature adult. "And I didn't mention pussy, by the way."

Adam laughs. "You didn't, but I figured that was what you were driving at." He cups my mound in his large hand like he owns it, making me close my eyes.

"I have all I need right here." He slides a finger between my folds, and just like that, he makes me ready again.

But after moments of delicious stroking, he halts. My eyes pop open, all of me frustrated but wondering what's up now.

"I love you."

His words catch me by surprise as much as him asking me to marry him. They aren't said in a squishy, soft romantic way. They're stated as a cold, hard fact I can believe in. I wasn't able to trust those words the first time he said them.

This time, I'm ready to hear them and to be entirely truthful.

"I love you, too. I have loved you for months."

His arms encircle me in an all-encompassing hug.

"I'm serious," he says after another moment. "Will you marry me?"

"Yes," I tell him. "I will."

Adam kisses the top of my head, which isn't a very sexy move, but it seals the deal. He has to push away and scooch down the bed a little in order to kiss me on the lips again, which he does, right before nibbling his way down my neck. It tickles, and it fuels my desire at the same time.

Feeling his arousal against my hip, I give in to the passion of the moment.

"I'll marry you *if* you touch me again, right now."

Immediately, his fingers delve between my folds. We don't break eye contact while he caresses me to utter madness. It's very hot, watching him watching me. Although my eyelids crash closed as I achieve a swift, scorching climax.

When I'm floating back to my perfect, charmed reality, Adam takes hold of my top thigh, raising it enough so he can nudge his cock into my slick channel.

"Yes," I hiss as he enters me. "I will."

EPILOGUE

Adam

Having a fiancée who is also the top freelance designer in Boston is . . . interesting. Clover's incredibly happy when running her own company of one. And a happy Clover is a frisky, sexy Clover. While she's not yet ready to have a physical office in the city and hire a team, she'll be financially able to do that in the next quarter. And she's done it all by herself.

I may have to ask her not to poach my designers.

Meanwhile, living under the same roof, *our* roof, is like my favorite dessert, a banana split. Playful, tasty, plenty of variety, creamy, hot, and never disappoints. We decided not to wait until we get married to live together. There's plenty of space on Louisburg Square, and Clover has her own bedroom if we ever have a fight.

She hasn't needed it yet. Minor disagreements are better handled with mind-blowing make-up sex. Followed by bowls of Clover's hot, buttered popcorn.

Best of all, with her working in a spacious home office, I can drop in on her morning, noon, and night. Office sex is still wicked fun, but now it's her office, not mine.

Her parents treat me like family already. Basically, the Henleys are normal rich people, people I can relate to. And they were a hundred percent behind their daughter changing her name back legally so I can marry the real Clover Henley.

Although I admit I still think of her as my uber-hot Ms. Mitchell.

Funny thing is she loves clothing so much, she still dresses for work as if she's going somewhere, right down to the sexy heels. Maybe it's for my benefit, but I think it's the sign of a true professional.

"It makes me feel more in control and creative," she says, "and I have online meetings. I can't be seen in a T-shirt. I have to dress right to land big accounts."

I may have been the cause of her taking a meeting wearing only her half-buttoned blouse and her thong this afternoon because I helpfully wandered in and pleasured her about two minutes before the client appeared on her monitor.

After that, she threatened to get a lock for her office door. As if that would stop me!

My parents love Clover as the daughter they never had. I couldn't be happier about it. They were frankly a little mental when I took her home to meet them. First female I've ever brought to their Weston estate.

Dad kept shifting between his French ancestry persona and his James Bond impression, and Mom was absolutely gushing over her as if Clover were a princess.

She is! *My* spicy princess. And I intend to treat her as such the rest of our lives—with flowers and love and really soft sheets.

Only my brother hasn't met her yet. Philip recently came back to town, stopping by the office in his Air Force blues, catching the eye of all available females. He didn't even notice their interest. For being a bit of a daredevil, he seemed nervous about meeting up with an old girlfriend he hasn't seen for five years. But he was "firewalled" and locked on target," his words, not mine. I wished him luck before making him promise to come to dinner soon. I'm eager for Philip and Clover to meet. Flaunting my incredibly smart and hot fiancée is just the kind of older brother move he expects from me.

Maybe just as importantly, Janet approves of us getting together. When I found out she was the one who sent the photos of Clover with the asshole, we had a tense few moments. She'd overstepped, in my opinion, going all mother-hen on me. It was Clover who reminded me how fortunate I am to have such a loyal assistant, one who really cares about my well-being.

After I saw reason, we went to dinner with Janet and her husband, Henry, to clear the air between the ladies. Henry was hilarious, giving me the heads-up on how to keep the peace at home with a feisty woman.

"Stay close but give her space. Always kiss her hello and goodbye. At the first sign of trouble, say, 'Yes, you're right,' because she usually is."

"Usually?" Janet quipped.

Henry laughed and covered his wife's hand where it rested on the tablecloth. "And for God's sake, don't let her get hangry."

Janet beamed. "I've taught him well. Being hungry puts me in a foul mood."

I intend to follow his advice and more.

Thank God no one knows the romantic thoughts in my head. That would definitely get me kicked out of the seventh-floor lounge where the dogs gossip. Yet I speak those crazy-in-love words to Clover every day.

She's the missing piece to the puzzle of why my life was empty despite having it all.

I'm not ashamed to say I really like being engaged. I like taking her out because I can. Showing her off because she's my woman. More than that, I adore having someone I trust implicitly right by my side, in my bed and in my heart.

Honestly, she's perfect! And sometimes, I cannot believe she's mine.

Clover

Adam Bonvier can certainly push my buttons, and in a very good way. In a *yes, right there! Do that again* way. And that's the best part about billionaire playboys . . . I mean fiancés. They are button-pushers because they can be. Because they have experience at it. Because we ladies let them, if and when we decide they are worth the risk.

Which means I'm going to marry Adam Bonvier. Imagine that! I think he wants me for my candy inheritance. *Not!*

My mother is busy planning the wedding, scouting the perfect venue, sending me dress suggestions, already asking us about food preferences. I'm happy to let her enjoy herself. After all, my father got a new golfing buddy out of the deal.

As for me, I get to live with my best friend, also the best lover on Planet Earth. Incredibly, my clothing and all my beloved shoes fit perfectly in the closet in our bedroom. Adam wasn't really using it anyway. Much.

And my frog collection looks great in our home, not only the vintage brass ones but also my stuffed toy frogs on the bed. I had to put my porcelain and glass frog figurines away because a week after I moved in, Adam surprised me with not one but two kitty siblings from the local MSPCA.

Shelby and Sabrina, our kitties with white-and-black markings, reminded Adam of my infamous checkered skirt so they came home with him. They're apt to knock things off shelves, the more breakable the better. Devilish, sweet creatures, they can race up all the stairs in under a minute, sounding like a herd of cattle while doing so.

My new company is thriving in my makeshift Beacon Hill home office. Maisie Lovell even asked me to work on a super-secret new project for her. Very hush-hush. Not perfume and not tied up with Bonvier, Inc. But we'll probably contract with them to do the print ads and the commercial.

In the not-too-distant future, I'll open a physical office and hire a few talented creatives so I can grow my business, Clover Design, Inc. No family last name, thank you. Neither the one I was born with, nor the one I'm about to take on.

Clover Bonvier! I guess I'm a little old-fashioned, but I think it has a nice sound!

The amazing thing is I will never lie to him again. I don't have to. What a relief! I'm not scared about losing him—or keeping him, for that matter. I'm strong enough either way and ditching the fear for my future.

After sex in my parents' guest house two months ago, while still trapped in that marshmallow mattress, we had a deep talk. It went like this . . .

"I will never lie to you," he vowed. "Can you promise you won't lie to me anymore?"

At the time, I hesitated. It felt like removing body armor when a shootout was imminent. Yet as I looked into his slate-gray eyes, I realized there was nothing I needed to protect myself from.

He ran a hand over the back of his neck. "When you don't answer right away, I want to put my fist through the wall. Since I'm not that kind of guy, it makes me want to pull back from you—if only I could."

"Don't do either. My mother would be pissed if you made a hole in the expensive, reproduction wallpaper. And I couldn't stand it if you walked out now. I only needed to think for a second about whether I'm ready to make that promise. I wouldn't want to lie about not lying."

"And?" he asked.

A huge smile spread over my face. I could feel my cheeks stretch.

"I am ready to promise you that I'll never lie again."

I watched the tension drain from him, as he accepted me at my word. After all we'd been through, he trusted me. What a gracious man. But he didn't mind being teased either.

"Except—" I began.

"Except?" he asked, tilting his head the way Lovey does.

"What about little white lies?" I wondered. "Like when you told my parents you were driving this way anyway."

He shrugged. "I should have told them the truth. White lies are a slippery slope."

"So, if I dislike your shirt or the way you pronounce *harassment* or if I cannot stand your haircut, I should blurt it right out."

"Wait. Do you mean the shirt I had on earlier?"

I rolled my eyes. "Not the point."

Then he ran a hand through his hair, looking vaguely worried. "I like this cut."

"Adam, focus please. Do you want the truth, no matter how brutal, every single day, every moment we're together? Because if I ask you whether I look great in a dress I've bought and saved for a special night, *after* cutting off the tags, I can tell you right now that I don't want you to say you prefer another color or that it makes my ass look like a pumpkin in a fishing net."

He snorted with laughter. "As if your ass could be anything other than perfect."

"Again, not the point. But thank you."

"I see what you're saying," he agreed. "First of all, unless you're cutting the tags off a yacht or a Lamborghini, don't worry about the money. Even then, don't worry about it. Secondly, I'm not saying we have to go out of our way to be painfully, brutally honest. We're not trying to hurt one another. But we shouldn't keep secrets."

"Unless it's a birthday or Christmas present."

"Naturally," Adam agreed. "But no lovers."

My mouth dropped open, and I snapped it shut. I couldn't believe we even had to say that was against the rules. "Of course not. Lovers are out!"

"Unless you tell me ahead of time so I can kick his ass and fight for you. That's the only decent, respectable thing to do," he said, making me feel all warm and cherished.

"Never happening," I echoed his sentiment.

"No hidden, emotional past shit that makes you do insane things," he added.

I frowned at the change of tone, but took a deep breath. He was right. "We'll try to open all the baggage and unfold the secrets as well as put the dirty laundry in the washing machine. I always like doing that when I come back from a trip, anyway. Or in this case, when I move in with a guy and take over his life."

His eyes widened, but he suddenly moved closer, which was hard to do as we were already stretched out side-by-side on the squishy bed.

"I can't hardly wait for you to take over my life," he said. "In fact, the first thing I want to do is end up in one of those stupid magazines, with a caption like 'Lucky Adam Bonvier nabs stunning candy heiress and designer, Clover Henley.'"

"Maybe it would be 'Fortunate Clover Henley nabs sexy billionaire businessman, Adam Bonvier.'"

"Either way," he said, starting to stroke the skin over my collarbone in tingly seductive swirls. "We're going public."

Two months and four days ago, to be exact. I moved in straightaway and got my first client as soon as I sent out feelers. In fact, the company that wanted to hire me was happy to save money on benefits by putting me to work as a freelancer.

I notice pretty quickly that Adam doesn't go into work every day. I found out he didn't used to, not until I started at Bonvier. That nugget still brings a smile to my face.

Today, he enters my office after a quick tap, just like he used to do at work. That also brings a smile. I set down my Lego frog that keeps my hands busy when I'm thinking, and I watch him stride in and stand before me, legs slightly apart, looking like the commander of a ship.

"What can I do for you?" Always a dangerous question, resulting in all sorts of fun.

"Well, Ms. Mitchell, I was hoping you'd ask." He sends me his killer lopsided grin.

The butterflies take flight in the pit of my stomach as usual. I love the exhilarating sensation that has never lessened. Anticipation courses through me. I rise to my feet and round my desk to be within the circle of his arms in record time.

My boss or not, Adam's got power over me. Strong, steady, loving power that lifts my spirit every day, fills my heart with contentment, and satisfies every desire my body can handle. And the remarkable thing is, it goes both ways. We're the closest to mated frogs that I could hope for.

I told him that once. About the frogs, I mean. A Peruvian frog—*Ranitomeya imitator*—has been observed to be monogamous. They're the first and maybe the only amphibians to stay together. True, they're poisonous, and one out of twelve doesn't stick with his or her mate. But those are pretty good odds. Besides, they're drop-dead gorgeous, little blue-green, black, and yellow jewels.

So, yeah, I found my froggy mate. And I'm imagining a future with a few froglets.

I lift my gaze to his, recalling the first time I looked into those steely-gray, gorgeous eyes, even then knowing I was going to fall in deep.

Just before his mouth claims mine, I tell him, "I love you."

And that's no lie!

The End (apart from *The Wedding of Clover and Adam* and *A Billion Second Chances,* Philip Bonvier's story)

ABOUT THE AUTHOR

Jane McBay is the pen name of *USA Today* bestselling author of historical romance, Sydney Jane Baily. She wanted to write about strong, sexy men who know how to treat a lady BUT who aren't wearing top hats and Hessian boots.

Trading carriages for limos, she's dreaming up mouthwatering billionaires with big . . . hearts. They're paired with clever, passionate females who have a hard time resisting these intriguing men. *So why bother?*

Give in, have fun, fall in love.♥ They do. And you will too! *NO* cliffhangers. *NO* frustration. *ALL THE FEELS*. You're welcome!

Contact her through her website, JaneMcBay.com.